PRAISE FOR THE
TRANSCENDENT SERIES

Transcendent 3

"In this spectacular anthology, Takács weaves together a beautiful
tapestry of worlds where trans people live, love, and thrive.
The characters collected within are varied in gender identity
and their relationships to their bodies."
— PUBLISHERS WEEKLY, STARRED REVIEW

"Some stories are light and pleasant, meditative; some are frightening
and wrenching; most of the pieces struck a resounding note regardless
of their approach, be that narrative or emotional in nature."
— QUEER SFF, TOR.COM

Transcendent 2

"Because so many of these stories are written by non-cisgender people,
the trans and nonbinary characters in them are not used as gimmicks or
tokens: by and large, they're complicated, diverse people whose genders
are not the most important or most striking thing about them.
To go from reading about almost no trans/enby characters straight to
full-fledged ones, without having to go through an intermediary
stage of diversity for diversity's sake, is a privilege."
— JAMES-BETH MERRITT, AUTHOR OF *BI-GENDER*

Transcendent 1

"...there are precious few entries in the science fiction genre by trans*
and nonbinary authors, so this anthology would be a commendable
addition to libraries with large science fiction collections."
— GLBT-ROUNDTABLE OF THE AMERICAN LIBRARY ASSOCIATION

TRANSCENDENT 4

The Year's Best Transgender Speculative Fiction

Edited by Bogi Takács

Lethe Press
Amherst, Massachusetts

TRANSCENDENT 4

Compilation copyright © 2019 Lethe Press, Inc.
Introduction copyright © 2019 Bogi Takács.

Published in 2019 by Lethe Press, Inc.
www.lethepressbooks.com • lethepress@aol.com
ISBN: 9781590216767

Credits for previous publication appear on page 268,
which constitutes an extension of this copyright page.

These stories are works of fiction.
Names, characters, places, and incidents are either products of the
author's imagination or are used fictitiously. Any resemblance to actual
persons, living or dead, organizations, events, or locales is entirely
coincidental.

Interior and cover design: Inkspiral Design.
Cover art: August-Lain Weickert

CONTENTS

INTRODUCTION

◄ Bogi Takács ►

2018 WAS A YEAR OF hope.

It was also a year that saw much upheaval around the globe, so I realize this statement needs some explanation. Trans and intersex speculative fiction is booming. For *Transcendent 4*, I had the honor to consider 198 stories from 2018; this is a large positive change, and it makes me very hopeful for the future. I opted to write a shorter introduction this year, because there are so many good developments this year that I wanted to list, and so many longer-form works that I wanted to highlight. But I do want to tell you about this year's stories I picked from those 198.

I feel 2018 represented not just a year of numerical expansion for trans literature, but also a year of deepening. The stories I chose engage with related experiences thoroughly and unapologetically. This also means that there is some heavy work in the bunch, examining topics such as domestic abuse, sexual violence, family conflict and medical trauma. (Please make sure to take a look at the author-provided content notices at the end of the book!) But there is also plenty of love, acceptance, and exuberance. The works in *Transcendent 4* often discuss complicated, difficult topics, but end with hope and solidarity. This has been characteristic of 2018 stories overall, not just the ones I picked; and I think this tells us a lot about what stories non-cis people — and also cis allies — would like to tell at this point in speculative fiction. We can go through great hardships, but we often survive, and hopefully thrive… even when nothing goes as planned.

The anthology begins with Nino Cipri's "Ad Astra Per Aspera," a story of losing your gender in Kansas (who will find it?). But it's not just gender that can go through all kinds of transformations, but also genre. The authors of *Transcendent 4* engage in genre-bending with great joy and determination. José Pablo Iriarte offers a reincarnation-themed murder mystery story in "The Substance of My Lives, the Accidents of Our Births," and Izzy Wasserstein plays with cyberpunk in "Ports of Perceptions." "The Sixth World" by Kylie Ariel Bemis takes on apocalypse tropes and ages-old traditions simultaneously, with a sprinkling of anime voice acting.

Mental health in an often-hostile world has always been a major trans theme, but this year some of the stories like "Ghosts" by Blue Neustifter and "Assistance" by Kathryn DeFazio specifically focus on mental health *support* in a speculative context: by a friendly ghost or an assistive robot, among other possibilities. Everett Maroon's "Therapeutic Memory Reversal" presents a futuristic memory manipulation technique, with unexpected results.

Bodily transformation itself can also provide a focus: in "Nuclear Disassociations" by Aqdas Aftab, it's not only trans people who are experiencing sudden bodily changes; while in "Of Warps and Wefts" by Innocent Chizaram Ilo, people shift between two bodies and identities every night and day. Vampires are also a perennial favorite trans theme, and Tori Curtis provides a new take in "You Inside Me" by examining disability and organ donation.

People can be trans while doing practically anything, and the stories in *Transcendent 4* show us some fascinating possibilities: like building robot dinosaurs in "Sphexa, Start Dinosaur" by Nibedita Sen, falling into the watery underside of the world in Sonya Taaffe's "The Face of the Waters," or finding dragons in Singapore in "The God of Small Chances" by L Chan. (If it sounds familiar: this story is a loosely-interpreted sequel of L Chan's previous deity-themed piece in *Transcendent 3*.) Watery themes also appear in Margaret Killjoy's "Into the Gray," where the protagonist finds prey for a carnivorous mermaid.

The stories also do not shy away from the more grim side of trans lives. In "Control" by Davian Aw, a body-swapping business venture goes terribly wrong, while in Andrew Joseph White's "Chokechain," the protagonist tries to find a way out from family conflict by all means necessary, including violence. Matthias Klein's protagonist in "The Art of Quilting" chooses a different path to deal with abusive family: running away, to the outer planets if need be. Catherine Kim's "Apotheosis" also shows that trans people can abuse each other, and that mythical beings sometimes eat humans. But sometimes it can be hard to determine who exactly is out to hurt us, as in H. Pueyo's "When the South Wind Whispers," where humans and artificial intelligence interact in sometimes-terrifying ways, and where allies are found in unexpected places.

I wish you a hopeful and resonant reading experience, and many more stories in the years to come!

Changes this year

OUT OF THE QUILTBAG+ SFF magazines, *Glittership* edited by Keffy R.M. Kehrli and Nibedita Sen has been going especially strong this year, also acquiring award shortlist mentions and very positive industry reviews on their yearly anthologies. *Capricious* edited by A.C. Buchanan put out a book-length special issue focusing on *Gender Diverse Pronouns,* likewise to acclaim. *Anathema* edited by Michael Matheson, Andrew Wilmot and Chinelo Onwualu has been steadily releasing tri-annual issues, with fascinating work. The Trans Women Writers Collective publishes all manner of fiction, poetry and art in their monthly chapbook series edited by Jamie Berrout, and they have also been consistently welcoming to speculative work. *Vulture Bones* is becoming more established, with an especially strong third issue closing off their 2018 year. General SFF venues have also been publishing related stories at an increasingly wide spread, with most of the professional venues releasing at least one or two trans stories. Trans and/or intersex SFF stories are not very common in general literary magazines (beside the above-mentioned Trans Women Writers Collective), but they do appear at an increasing rate.

In this volume, you will find stories from all these places. There has been a turnover in venues, though. Topside Press had no releases this year, and *Arsenika* only had one issue before going on hiatus. *EFNIKS* is being reorganized as *Color Bloq* and I hope they will also return to publishing speculative fiction.

As previously, some of the best work still appeared in self-publishing, and an interesting change is that the venues have been broadening. Next to author websites and Patreon, now there have been many other places where stories I considered had originally appeared; a piece I ended up buying was originally published on Twitter as a thread of tweets, and one on Medium.

Trans work is increasingly highlighted by SFF awards. Several pieces mentioned here were on the Tiptree award short- and longlists, and writers like José Pablo Iriarte and Yoon Ha Lee are currently finalists for general SFF awards.

I am very happy to see that multiply-marginalized authors are increasingly able to publish their trans and/or intersex SFF work, but some gaps still remain year after year: there are very few translations available overall (all the trans-related translated short fiction I found in 2018 was non-speculative), and intersex stories are still hard to find, though intersex authors increasingly less so.

Longer-form speculative highlights

As BEFORE, THE HIGHLIGHTS CONTAIN both trans- and intersex-themed work, work by trans or intersex authors with *any* theme, or both. My highlights get longer and longer each year, and this also implies that there is a lot more work out there overall.

This year had several anthologies I am happy to recommend. *Nameless Woman: An Anthology of Fiction by Trans Women of Color* (edited by Ellyn Peña, Jamie Berrout and Venus Selenite) offered both reprints from an earlier anthology – one of them also previously appeared in *Transcendent 2* – and new work. *Capricious* (edited by A.C. Buchanan) put out a book-length release, the *Gender Diverse Pronouns* special issue. *Glittership Year Two* (edited by Keffy R.M. Kehrli and Nibedita Sen) brought stories with a general LGBTQ+ focus, but with strong trans emphasis. The *Broken Metropolis* queer urban fantasy anthology edited by dave ring also featured a considerable amount of trans-related work, and many new authors to watch.

In 2018 there have been an unprecedented number of related **novellas and longer novelettes**. The Book Smugglers are leaving the novella field, but they still put out *A Glimmer of Silver* by Juliet Kemp, a far future marine story with all nonbinary pronouns. One of the surprises of the year for me has been *Winnie* by Katy Michelle Quinn, a fascinating bizarro horror story about a woman assigned rifle at birth. (Its publisher Eraserhead Press has also published other trans authors like Larissa Glasser this year.) Another big surprise, the self-published *Arch-Nemesis* by Gabriela Martins is a South Brazilian superhero story with great character interactions. JY Yang's latest novella *The Descent of Monsters* published by Tor.com combined the setting of their silkpunk continuity, the Tensorate, with the inventive forms previously seen in their short fiction. *Nine of Swords, Reversed* by Xan West marked a new turn into the speculative by the noted author of BDSM erotica, with a warm-hearted romance between disabled trans mages. Margaret Killjoy also continued her contemporary fantasy series of amazing queer crustpunks with *The Barrow Will Send What It May* at Tor.com. The self-published *Werecockroach* by Polenth Blake offered a fresh and surprisingly cheerful take on the Kafkaesque situation of people turning into insects. I also found a translated novella I enjoyed, *An Exotic Marriage* by Yukiko Motoya (translated by Asa Yoneda) that appeared in her collection *The Lonesome Bodybuilder*. This story explores traditional Japanese gender roles by showing husbands and wives who literally turn into each other; while the focus is not explicitly on transgender themes, I felt while reading that the relevance was still very much there.

Among **novels**, the final volume of Yoon Ha Lee's Hexarchate trilogy, *Revenant Gun*, appeared from Solaris. The semi-autobiographic novel *Freshwater* by Akwaeke Emezi is technically not speculative, but its storytelling has great crossover appeal for SFF readers. (The book also features one of the rare #ownvoices portrayals of plurality / multiplicity in mainstream publishing.) Isaac R. Fellman's *The Breath of the Sun* from Aqueduct Press was my favorite debut novel of the year, a stunning work of mountaineering, religion and betrayal on another planet. *In the Vanishers' Palace* by Aliette de Bodard also marked a new high note for one of my favorite authors, with gorgeous descriptions of Escheresque spaces, and great characterization. *Temper* by Nicky Drayden, from Harper Voyager, brought more of the author's daring thematic explorations and sharp wit. For those looking for a space opera adventure with futuristic racing, there is *The Big Ship at the End of the Universe* by Alex White from Orbit. And for non-genre work by trans writers with SFF interests, a highlight for me has been *Little Fish* by Casey Plett, with trans Mennonites – published by Arsenal Pulp, a Canadian press who were having a very strong 2018 overall.

Short story collections were less common, but I still had the opportunity to enjoy Toby MacNutt's mixed poetry-prose collection *If Not Skin* from Aqueduct, and the second volume of RoAnna Sylver's *Life Within Parole* stories with the Kraken Collective. From the above-mentioned Trans Women Writers Collective chapbooks, among the SFF ones I especially liked Catherine Kim's literary horror *Collected Stories*, and I was also glad to see new work from Gillian Ybabez.

Middle grade and young adult releases by trans authors are vanishingly rare (though this is set to change in 2019), but in 2018 I did have a major highlight: *Hurricane Child* by Kacen Callender from Scholastic, a magical-realist Afro-Caribbean adventure of queer girls on the US Virgin Islands.

There are of course many more trans-relevant books in 2018, and probably some I will only discover years later, as it happens every year... I'm wishing everyone good reading!

AD ASTRA PER ASPERA

◄ Nino Cipri ►

I'M PRETTY SURE I LOST my gender in Kansas.

(This space is reserved for any *Wizard of Oz* reference you might make. I'm not sure how you could relate it to gender, but whenever I mention Kansas, it's the first thing people want to do. So go ahead, if you're into that.)

Anyway, it's true. I was driving west across the pancaked landscape, the flat and yearning winter fields, and I realized I hadn't seen my gender in a while. Not since Wichita at least, and that had been several hours and many radio stations before: Christian talk shows, country songs, odd interruptions of metal or hardcore music.

I lose things all the time, especially when traveling. On my first big roadtrip across the country, I drove away from Philadelphia while my bag was still on the trunk of the car. Goodbye to my journal — no great loss there; goodbye to my digital camera and cell phone, because this was back in the days when those were separate items; goodbye to my book of Arthur Rimbaud's poetry that I had found in a used bookstore in Colorado two weeks earlier. Oh, and goodbye to my wallet — someone found it and spent $180 at PetSmart before I canceled it.

I wonder if some Kansan will pick up my gender the way that someone picked up my bag, twelve years ago in Philadelphia. Will they pick through my gender's many pockets? Discard that dollar-bin paperback of *The Drunken Boat*, but keep my great-aunt Ethel's wedding ring, which was so small I only could wear it on my pinky? Toss the electric-blue lipstick that I could never make myself wear, but rub the cedar cologne onto the soft creases of their wrist and neck?

Is there a lost-and-found forum for genders? Maybe I should make a sign and staple it to every bulletin board in every truckstop along I-70, the way you might for a dog that took off or a cat that slunk through a barely-open window. "LOST: One gender, not particularly adherent to notions of sexual dimorphism. Answers to Spivak pronouns or they/them. Hostile when cornered."

(This is a placeholder for your judgment, even your disgust. What kind of irresponsible twit loses their gender? If *you* had a gender as nice as mine, you would have taken better care of it. Maybe you're thinking that this might be some sort of *millennial* thing. All these millennials with their *boutique* and *artisan* genders, and this is what they do with them?)

To be honest, this isn't even the first time I've lost track of my gender. My mother constantly had to remind me to take it with me when I was still in high school. "Got your books? Got your keys? Got your gender?" I was always losing my gender in my debris-filled bedroom. And if it came down to either getting to work or school on time, or finding my gender, what was I supposed to do?

The first time I went outside without my gender, I expected to stop traffic, to be publicly denounced at the bus stop and library, everywhere that decent, gender-respecting people lived. In the end, I got a few unfriendly stares, but a couple people told me that I was really brave for not needing my gender all the time. They were the people that wheeled their genders around like oxygen tanks or carried them in slings like babies.

(This space might be a place for you to pause, and wonder how you carry your own gender, how close or how distant you might hold it to your skin.)

Something tells me that this time around, my gender might be gone for good; that it's somewhere in the acres of horizon behind me. Maybe — and I know you might not believe this, given everything I've told you about my own forgetfulness — but maybe this is a decision that my gender made without me.

You know, I bet my gender left me for someone else.

(This paragraph is a placeholder that can contain your decision that

I deserved to be abandoned by my gender, since I was so inattentive to it. You would never abandon your gender, no matter how many miles you had to drive to retrieve it.)

(This space can hold the small ember of doubt that glows beneath your professed devotion. Would you really drive all that way?)

Now that I think about it, there was a waitress some miles back, in a diner where I stopped to stretch my legs and stretch my gender too. She was my mother's age, wore crooked eyeliner, and had a smoker's rough, rich voice and a nametag that said *Debra ;)*. She had a thin paperback in her apron, and I found myself guessing what it could be while I drank her strong coffee and ate the Texas Toast platter she set in front of me. I thought of the various paperbacks I'd held in my own hands: *The Monkeywrench Gang. Who's Afraid of Virginia Woolf? Three Lives.* And of course, *The Drunken Boat*, lost more than a decade ago.

Did my gender leave me for her? Maybe Debra is running fingertips over body parts that had previously held no attraction or interest — the soft arch of a foot, the curve of a deltoid — and discovering a fresh and foreign allure, even as other spots begin to feel alien and odd: tits and ass, for example, the old standbys. Is Debra fingering her nametag and wondering what might happen if she chose a different one? Is Debra testing out new syllables for pronouns, alien combinations of letters like ou, xie, za, per, aer. Is she waiting for one to suddenly swell with recognition?

I'm driving out of Kansas tonight. I'm already at its border, and in a few miles, I'll be somewhere else, somewhere new. I'm not very good at looking back, and even worse at returning to things and places I've left behind, but I wish Debra and my gender happiness and the joy of exploring new territory. If I come back to that small diner in that small town, I hope it will be as a welcome guest in the home my gender made without me.

(This is the last placeholder, where you can store your disappointment in this story, or your delight. This space can hold your comments and judgment, your boredom, or your revelation. This can be the space where you can look sidelong at your own gender, at the places where the two of you have sewn yourselves together, and where those seams might unravel, and what might spill out when they do.)

THE SUBSTANCE OF MY LIVES, THE ACCIDENTS OF OUR BIRTHS

◄ José Pablo Iriarte ►

I SEEM TO MAKE AN OUTCAST of myself every time I'm a teenager. Which is fine, I guess. I'll take one good dog and one good friend over being a phony and fitting in.

Alicia points. "There he is, Jamie!"

A couple hundred feet away, our trailer park's newest resident grabs a box from the van parked in front of his single-wide. He's gray-haired and buff, like if The Rock were an old man.

Alicia and I are sprawled on top of a wooden picnic table in the park's rusted old playground.

She frowns, her eyebrows coming together to form a tiny crease above her nose. "I've never known anybody who killed someone before."

I shrug.

"I mean, maybe I have, I guess, but I've never *known* I've known them. Know what I mean?"

"No."

I don't really care about the new guy, even if he did murder someone once. I'm mostly just out here to not have to listen to old Mrs. Francis concern-trolling my mom. When I was a kid who sometimes acted like a boy and sometimes like a girl, it was "just a phase." Now that I'm sixteen, it's "worrying" and "not safe for the younger children" and something we should "talk to a therapist about."

What Mrs. Francis doesn't know is that I remember every life I've lived for nearly four hundred years — not in detail, but like a book I read once and have a few hazy recollections about. In over a dozen lifetimes I can recall, I've been male and female enough times for those words to mean little more to me than a particular shirt — not who I am.

My mom's too polite to tell a neighbor what she can do with her un-asked-for parenting advice. Trailer walls are thin, though, and if I have to hear it too…well, Sabal Palms Trailer Park might end up with two murderers living in it.

Next to me, my dog Meetu nudges my hand with her head, asking for more scritches. She's supposed to protect me from people who are as bothered by me as Mrs. Francis is, but would rather use their fists to try and fix me. People like Connor Haines, the biggest asshole in the eleventh grade. But the reality is that Meetu is basically a teddy bear trapped in a pit bull's body.

Alicia shifts on the table. "I can't believe my mom let him rent here." Her mother manages the park, so I guess she could have blocked him if she'd wanted to.

"Even ex-murderers gotta live somewhere."

She gives me her patented don't-be-weird combination eyeroll and headshake that I've never seen anybody else quite match. Even when it's directed at me, I can't help but grin.

"There's no such thing as an 'ex-murderer,'" she says. "Once you kill someone, you're a murderer."

I brush my hair out of my face. "He went to jail. He did his time, right? They let him out, so where else is he gonna live?" We've certainly had other people with checkered pasts here.

"They shouldn't have let him out. You take somebody's life, you ought to rot for the rest of yours."

Meetu shoves her giant head under my arm and rests it on my lap. Guess I'm not going anywhere for a while.

"There's no heaven," Alicia declares. "The Jesus freaks are wrong about that. There's nothing but this. If people realized that, they'd take this life more seriously. You only get one."

She's wrong, but I can't explain to her how I know, so I don't bother trying.

A woman about my mom's age helps the man unpack, while a toddler stumbles around the grassy area in front of the trailer. He seems kind of old to have a little kid, but maybe he's making up for lost time.

"I can't understand what kind of woman would want to live with a killer, much less have a child with him." She peers at the table beneath her and runs a fingernail along a carved heart that's older than we are. "Not that I get wanting to be with *any* man."

The new neighbor comes out for another load. He glances our way, and even at this distance, our eyes lock, and a cold itch runs from the small of my back to the top of my scalp.

I know him. I know him *from before.*

I don't mean I know his soul. I know *him.*

Alicia gives me a little shove, and I realize she's been talking at me for a while.

"Are you okay?"

I blink. Even Meetu looks concerned, her muscular head cocked.

"I'm fine."

"Are you sure?"

I nod, but she doesn't stop staring and looking worried, so I add, "You're right. It's weird living next to a murderer."

Her face softens. "I didn't hurt your feelings, did I? When I said... that? I wasn't talking about *you.*"

"Nah," I say. "I know you weren't."

The new guy goes back into his trailer.

"What did you say his name was?" I ask.

"Benjamin," she answers softly. After a few quiet seconds, she adds, "You did a really nice job on your nails."

I glance down at my newly red nails. She's painted them for me a couple times before, but this is the first time I've done them myself. I'm grateful that she doesn't qualify the compliment. Doesn't add, *for a guy.* But of course she wouldn't — that's why I — that's why she's my best friend.

I TRY TO LET IT GO. So I've got a neighbor that I knew in a past life. So he's a convict. The past is dead. Who cares.

Over the next couple days, though, my mind keeps returning to Benjamin. I feel like he was important for some reason. By the middle of the week I admit to myself that I'm not going to move on until I figure out what role he played in my life.

I'm not quite sure how to do that, though. I could ask Alicia for help. She's got a laptop and internet. I don't even have a smartphone. I don't want to open up the can of worms that is my past lives, though, so instead I decide to see what I can find out at the library.

I feed Meetu an early dinner while Mom's still at work, grab my backpack and bus pass, and head out.

Once I'm there, I have to face the fact that I don't have the first idea how to research anything about this guy. I don't even know his full name.

What's B's last name? I text Alicia.

Avery. Why?

What do I say that won't make her ask a thousand questions I don't want to answer? *Just wondering.*

UR totally gonna snoop arent you?

I consider possible deflections. Lying to Alicia feels scuzzy, though, and anyway, I can't think of any lies to tell. *maybe just a little*

I stare at my tiny screen, worried that she's going to offer to join me. After a minute her reply shows up, though, and it's just *haha well lmk what you dig up.*

I sigh, feeling both relieved and ashamed of my relief.

Even with his last name, I struggle. I don't know how to weed out other people named Benjamin, other people named Avery, other murderers. I don't even know when he went to jail — how long is a sentence for murder, anyway?

Finally I stumble across what I'm looking for — a news archive from the 1970s, with a grainy black and white photo of a man that looks a lot younger, but that's definitely him.

A Vietnam War veteran, possibly shell-shocked and deranged since coming back. A crime of passion — the victim, his best friend's wife. A body dug up by the shore of Peace Creek, not far away at all. Then I come across a photo of the formerly happy couple: Larry Dearborn and his wife Jamie.

Janie. Not Jamie. Janie. But the name doesn't matter.

It's me.

IT'S RAINING WHEN I STAGGER out of the library. On the bus ride home I lean my head against the window and watch the torrents sheeting down the glass.

Janie would be in her sixties, if she'd lived. I don't remember ever being old. I always seem to die young. I don't remember dying. End-of-life memories are hazy, same as beginning-of-life memories.

I glance away from the window and notice a little girl staring at me from the seat across the aisle. Her father sits next to her, but he's focused on his phone.

"Are you a boy or a girl?" she asks.

Before I can catch myself, my stock answer comes out. "No."

She tilts her head in confusion.

I imagine how I must look to her. Rain-soaked long hair, purple V-neck, red nails. Hell, she's just a kid. "I'm a little of both," I add.

Her eyes widen. "Oh!"

I turn back toward the window. Now that I've seen the photos and read the articles, bits and pieces of that life are coming back to me.

Benjamin looks like I imagine a murderer would — big and tough and unhappy. The newspaper says he killed me.

So why does that feel wrong?

THE NEXT DAY, SCHOOL DRAGS on more than usual. I can't focus on Henry James or rational functions when my alleged murderer just moved into the neighborhood.

My walk home is the vulnerable spot in my routine, because Meetu's not with me. So of course that's when Connor Haines ambushes me.

He's sitting on the concrete Sabal Palms sign outside the trailer park. His sycophant friend Eddie stands by his side.

A spike of fear travels through my body.

"What's up, Jimmy," he calls.

I don't bother correcting him. I was "Jimmy" when he met me — it was only four years ago that I decided "Jamie" fit better. More importantly, Connor doesn't care.

I consider my options. I could turn around. Go inside the Steak and Shake one block down and wait him out. Or I could run and try to reach my trailer ahead of him, and hide out there. But if I wanted to hide, my hair would be shorter and my nails wouldn't be red. It may cost me, but I won't start running or hiding now.

They fall in step with me as I pass the sign.

"Where's your dress, Jimmy?" Eddie asks.

Eddie is smaller than I am. I'm not a fighter, though, and he can be brave knowing he's got Connor backing his play.

"It was too ugly for me, so I gave it to Connor's mom."

I barely see Connor's fist before it hits my face. I stagger sideways, tasting blood.

"Why you gotta be such a freak, Jimmy?" Connor asks. "I don't care if you like guys, but why you gotta act like a girl?"

My clothes aren't particularly girlish today: blue jeans and a teal Polo. And I'm neither a gay boy nor a trans girl. Trying to explain is a losing game, though, so I just try to push past.

Eddie's fist lands in my stomach, driving the air out of me.

Connor grabs my arm. "Don't walk away when we're talking to you, Jimmy. It's rude. A real lady would know better."

"What's going on fellas?"

Benjamin's standing a dozen feet away. His arms are crossed, his sleeves barely making it halfway down his bulging biceps.

"We're just talking to our friend," Connor says.

"You've talked enough. Unless you want me to talk too."

Connor releases my arm and backs away. "See you at school tomorrow, Jimmy," he sneers.

"Yeah," Eddie adds. "Don't forget to wear your dress."

I watch them walk away. I understand what they're saying — sooner or later they'll find me when I have nobody to protect me.

"You're bleeding," Benjamin says. "Is your mom home?"

"She's at work."

I probably shouldn't say that to the convicted murderer.

"Why don't you let me help you."

My instinct is to mumble some excuse, but I don't believe he's a murderer. Anyway, I want to know how he fit into my old life and why everybody thought he killed me, so I follow him.

His trailer's one of the first ones, and I see his windows are open. Probably how he noticed Connor and Eddie harassing me.

I've seen dumpier trailers, but not often.

The previous tenant had been a hoarder. When she died in her trailer last year, Alicia and her mom had to clean the place out, and I helped. The place had been full of arts and crafts junk and half-eaten containers of food. We'd worn masks, and no amount of vacuuming and Lysol had made it tolerable inside.

Just goes to show there's always somebody desperate enough to settle for anything.

I don't smell the death smell anymore — what I smell is about a half dozen Plug-Ins, all churning away at once. I guess that's an improvement.

Benjamin and his family don't have much furniture. A worn futon backs up against one wall of the living room, and a rickety table leans awkwardly under the kitchen light. A makeshift bookshelf sags with paperbacks and magazines. I wonder if they're his wife's — girlfriend's? — and then my face heats up. I'm the last person who should be making assumptions.

His toddler lies in a playpen, her thumb in her mouth, snoring gently. I almost comment on him leaving her unsupervised — then I remember that he did it to save my judgmental ass from getting beaten even worse.

"I'll grab some cotton and peroxide. They split your lip."

I follow him to the table and sit on the edge of a vinyl chair. I will myself to keep still as he approaches, dripping cotton in hand. He's a heavy breather, and his thick fingers smell like peanut butter. Lucky I'm not allergic. This time.

My shoulder blades tingle as he sits across from me and begins dabbing at the blood on my face. His fingers are rough but his touch is gentle.

"Some people are just driven to destroy what they don't understand," he says. He gets up and runs a washcloth under the tap. "Hold this against your lip until the bleeding stops."

I feel silly having him take care of me; I can clean a cut for myself. It's not like I haven't been beat up before.

"Anyway," he adds, "I'm Benjamin."

"Yeah," I blurt out. Crap.

He glances up. "You know?"

"Sorry. My best friend's mom manages this place."

"What else do you know?"

I swallow, and it's all the confirmation he needs.

He sighs.

"I'm so sorry," I say. "Please don't tell? She wasn't supposed to say anything to me, but that's the kind of thing that's hard to keep to yourself."

Benjamin just grunts and sweeps up the bloody cotton balls.

"Anyway," I add, "I know you're not guilty."

He raises his eyebrows. "You *what* now?"

I study my fingers. "I can tell things about people."

He snorts.

I shrug. "Anyway, I'm Jamie."

"Short for James?"

"No. Short for Jamie."

"Well, I'm glad to meet you, Jamie."

I press the rag to my lip for a couple minutes, and then, to break the silence, I ask, "Who *did* do it?"

He frowns. "Not something I wanna go into, kid."

"Sorry."

"It's funny though. You remind me of her. You look like you could be her kid. I mean, if she'd ever had one." Another awkward moment passes, and he clears his throat. "So the landlady's kid..."

"Yeah?"

"I saw the two of you sitting together. The way you look at her. She your girlfriend?"

"We're just friends."

"Ah."

"We can be friends, you know. You can just be friends with people you're — you can be friends with people without dating them."

"Course you can."

I bite my lip, and flinch when I catch the split part. "Anyway, I don't think she sees me that way."

"Fair enough."

"Right."

"Right." He gets up from the table and begins washing some dishes while I continue putting pressure on my lip.

My mind wanders, trying to stitch together the bits of my last life that I remember. Being a little girl. Going to college. Dropping out to get married.

And I remember my husband turning mean. I remember going to our best man over and over again for advice — the only man Larry trusted me with. I remember deciding that I had to leave. I remember Larry —

Oh God. Larry did it. Larry was the killer.

Benjamin knocks a glass off the counter. He's not paying attention to the glass, though. He's staring at me, and he looks like he's glanced into hell itself.

Did I say that out loud?

"How do you know about him?"

Oops. Apparently I did. "Uh, lucky guess?"

"Right." He takes the rag from my hand, ignoring the still-running water. "Well the bleeding's pretty much stopped now. It was good to meet you. You'd probably best be getting on home now."

He doesn't seem to breathe at all as he talks, and before I fully realize what happens I am escorted out the door.

"You take care, now," he says, once I'm safely outside.

"Thanks, Benjamin," I say, but the door closes before the last syllable leaves my mouth.

Making my way home, I feel like I can hear all my past selves in my head, and they're all furious. That bastard Larry killed me, and he got away with it.

I want to punch something. I want to scream. I want to take my notebook out of my backpack and rip out every sheet of paper and crumple each one up. I want to break some pencils. I want to scream.

I want to cry.

What does it say about me if I was murdered any nobody cared enough to find out who really did it? They just found the handiest fall guy to pin it on and went on with their lives, and Larry Dearborn lived happily ever after.

I run through imaginary confrontations with Larry as I walk up to my trailer. I've never been violent — not in any of the lives I can recall — but right now I wish I had the talent for it.

Meetu wants to play when I open up the door — Meetu always wants to play. "Not now," I say, snapping the leash onto her collar. She understands lots of things, but "Not now" isn't one of them. Still, she's happy enough to go out for her walk.

I daydream about running into Connor and Eddie again while I'm out with Meetu. See how *they* like being threatened. Then I play out the rest of that scenario in my head — Meetu's fifty-eight pounds of love, but all anybody sees when they look at her is a scary, vicious killer dog. I imagine how people would react to *another* story about a pit bull attack. I imagine them calling for her to be destroyed.

No, if I do see those guys I'll keep a tight grip on Meetu's leash, even if they're messing with me, because I don't want to lose her.

That's what pisses me off — me and Janie and the other voices in my head. The Connors and the Larrys of the world always get away with the things they do.

There must be some way to make Larry pay. He doesn't know I exist. Has no idea that I know what he did. That I keep remembering more and more with each step I take.

He'll never see me coming.

"Watch your back, Larry," I murmur. "I'm coming for you."

Meetu thumps my knees with her tail. She doesn't know what I'm talking about, but she's game. She's always game.

"I'M TELLING YOU, HE DIDN'T do it!"

Alicia snorts. "You know this how? Because he told you?"

We're sitting on her bed. I avoid her eyes by focusing on her posters. Harley Quinn. Black Widow. Imperator Furiosa.

Alicia is into kick-ass women. I'm into her — something I'm better off keeping to myself.

"Listen," I say, "I'm pretty good at reading people. I believe him. He's already done his time, so he has no real reason to lie."

"His reason is to get people like you to trust him. Jesus, you went *into his trailer*?"

"I was bleeding."

"So?"

I pull my legs under me and face her. "Listen, enough people think I'm a flake. That both of us are. I've always had your back. Will you just go with me on this?"

She chews her lip. After a moment she sighs and says, "I'm not sure what you want me to do."

"You've got a computer. Do a search for this Dearborn guy. See what you can find out about him."

"What for?"

I smooth a wrinkle on her bedspread. Any answer would be impossible to explain. "I don't know yet."

She rolls her eyes, but she pulls her laptop off the nightstand and begins clicking around. For several minutes she makes random frustrated sounds as she repeats the same research I already did at the library. I don't want to admit to how much I've already obsessed about this, so I let her retrace my steps.

Finally she chuckles ruefully. "Good luck."

"What?"

"Larry Dearborn is *the* Dearborn in Dearborn Automotive. He owns that huge car lot out on Auburndale Highway. The football stadium at Lakeside High is named after him. He's loaded."

I frown. So he's rich too. Must be nice to literally get away with murder.

"Let's go see him," I say.

She scowls. "And do what?"

"We can pretend one of us is buying a car."

"Look, if you're right, then Dearborn's the dangerous one."

"He was dangerous forty years ago."

She shakes her head.

I try a different tack. "You're always saying you're bored here, surrounded by people who aren't going anywhere. You always say you want to do something adventurous, like join the Air Force. Well fine: let's have an adventure. I'm not saying to confront him or anything. I just want to see my — I just want to see Janie Dearborn's killer with my own eyes. He won't know that we know, so there's no reason to be afraid of him."

She narrows her eyes. Before she can raise an objection, I spit out, "What would Furiosa do?"

She makes a face. "I'm not twelve, Jamie."

"Sorry." I get up from her bed.

"Where are you going?"

"I'll go on my own," I say. "I'll take the bus."

"Don't," she says. "I think you're nuts, but I'll drive."

We tell her mom we're going to the library and breeze out before she can question us. Once on the road, we roll down the windows and turn north on state road seventeen. Alicia's mom's car is a beat up Saturn station wagon that's almost old enough to go to bars. It's sticky and hot and I almost think I should've gone by bus, except then I would have been alone.

The car salesmen close in like hyenas when we park, and immediately lose interest when we step out. I guess without an adult with us, they figure we're not car shopping.

I lead the way into an over-cooled lobby and cast about until I find a receptionist's desk.

"Hi," I say to the lady on the other side. "Is Mr. Dearborn here by any chance?"

She inclines her head. "And you are?"

"We are, uh…"

"We go to Lakeside High School," Alicia blurts out. "And, uh, we're on the yearbook staff. And since Mr. Dearborn's been so generous to our school in the past, we were wondering if he maybe wanted to take out a page in this year's edition."

I fight the urge to stare at Alicia. We actually *are* in yearbook, but at Pickens High, not at Lakeside. They've been leaning on us to sell advertising, and the last thing I've wanted to do is cold call on a bunch of local businesses so they can all treat me like some kind of freak. So here we are instead doing it for an entirely different high school.

I have to give her credit, though — that was some quick thinking.

The receptionist's expression softens. "Ah, yes. Well he doesn't really come in to the showroom anymore, but you're right, he might want to sponsor a page." She takes a random salesperson's card from a holder on the counter, turns it over, and writes something on the back. "You can visit him here. I'm sure he'd be thrilled to have visitors from Lakeside."

Something about the way she said that feels off to me, but I can't quite figure it out until twenty minutes later, when Alicia pulls up in front of the address on the card: Landmark Hospice.

"What's a hospice?" Alicia asks. "Isn't that like a cheap hotel for backpackers?"

"No, it's a place where people go to die."

"Oh."

We park for several minutes under the shade of an oak tree, until Alicia asks, "Can we go home now?"

I nod dully, staring out the window.

It's all so unfair. Larry Dearborn killed his wife — killed *me* — and he'll never face judgment for it. Never spend a day in prison. He made a ton of money, lived out his life, and got to the end without any consequences. Even if I found some way to prove he did it, nobody would prosecute him. Why bother?

THE RIVERBED WHERE THE NEWS said my body was discovered is just over a mile away. I take Meetu out after school a couple days later and wander around. Meetu runs back and forth between the creek and me, getting all muddy and messy.

I guess I have this idea that Meetu might dig up some bit of evidence, or I'll remember something about how I died that would lead me to discover something. Meetu's not that kind of dog, though, and anyway the police already went over this area when they found the body. What could I hope to uncover all these decades later?

And what would I do with it if I found it?

I don't actually have any memories of this place. I was probably dead or unconscious before Larry ever brought me here. I do remember more and more about our relationship. How his dark moods got darker and more frequent and how even getting promotions at work only made him happy for a day before he'd brood again. I remember the only place I felt safe being with his buddy Benjamin, and I remember Benjamin convincing me I needed to leave, and helping me pack. I remember taking my suitcases to his house one night, and trying to figure out where to go next.

I remember Larry showing up at Benjamin's place, enraged, and that's about all I remember. He must have killed me there, leaving plenty of evidence pointing at Benjamin.

Benjamin.

In all of my fury at Larry killing me and getting to live out his life without ever paying for his crime, I've hardly given thought to the man who *did* pay for it. I've been so focused on the unfairness of my death that I haven't thought about the unfairness of his life. I can't do anything about Larry, but can I do something for Benjamin?

I call Meetu to me and we start to walk back home. About halfway there Alicia's Saturn shows up and pulls off the road on the grassy shoulder.

"I had a feeling you might have gone out this way. You're obsessed, Jamie. I'm worried about you."

She helps me get Meetu into the back of the station wagon. There's one thing to be said about having a piece of crap car — you don't much care if it gets dirty anymore.

"I think I have an idea for how to clear Benjamin's record," I say.

She doesn't take her eyes off the road. "Oh?"

"Yeah. Can I borrow a dress?"

ALICIA DOESN'T WEAR DRESSES MUCH, and her fashion style is not quite what I'm looking for. She is close to my size, though, and she's willing to help, which counts for a lot.

She opens up her laptop and brings up a picture of Janie Dearborn — of her and Larry in better times. She's wearing a long denim skirt and a turtleneck and throwing her head back and laughing. I think I can remember that day.

"Freaky," Alicia murmurs. "She could be your older sister."

"Do you have anything like what she's wearing here?"

"Janie seems like the wholesome type. That's not me."

"Do you have anything that might be kind of close?"

She frowns, then straightens. "Actually, I might."

She heads not for her closet, but for the chest at the foot of her bed. She digs inside and tugs out a balled up wad of cloth.

"It's from my Aunt Hilda," she says, as if that explains everything.

She unrolls the bundle on her bed. It turns out to be a brown dress, with little pink flowers and ivory accents. It's nothing like the outfit in the news photo, but I understand why Alicia picked it. It's equal parts Brady Bunch and Sunday brunch.

"My aunt doesn't really get me," she says.

"No kidding."

"Mom made me wear it last time Aunt Hilda visited and then I dumped it here and haven't thought about it again." She holds the dress up to my shoulders and cocks her head appraisingly.

I quirk my lip. "It's...really ugly."

Alicia giggles. "You asked for a dress. You didn't say it had to look *good.*"

I go to her bathroom to try it on. I stare at the mirror, trying to form my own opinion before I ask Alicia for hers. I worried that the dress was going to bulge and gap in the wrong places, but it's a modest cut, so it pretty much works.

I remember looking like this before. It looks like *me* in the mirror. Just a different me.

I try to imagine how Connor Haines would react if he ran into me like this. He and Eddie would probably go berserk.

Well fuck them. They don't get a vote.

I pull the door open and cross the hall back into Alicia's room. She paces all the way around me, nodding slowly.

"Now let's add some makeup," she says.

When I've worn makeup before I've always gone for subtle. Some foundation, a touch of eyeliner. Not trying to *look* like I have makeup on. After some false starts, Alicia and I manage to get a more blatantly feminine style that I'm satisfied with.

"Stand up," she says. "Let me see."

I stand by her dresser, suddenly self-conscious.

She raises her eyebrows. "I still hate that dress, but damn, you – " She bites her lip. "You're really pretty."

My neck and face heat at that. I know she doesn't mean…I know she's just trying to build me up. It's nice to imagine that she's serious, though.

The moment is interrupted by her mom coming home. When I see her car pulling into the gravel driveway outside, I want to grab my own clothes and hide in her bathroom until the danger passes. But I steel myself and stay right where I am. I've always figured that once you start hiding, it's hard to stop.

Alicia makes eye contact as the front door clicks unlocked, and I wonder if what I'm thinking is plastered all over my face.

"I'm home," her mom calls out, as if that weren't obvious.

A moment later she passes by the open door. "Oh, hey, I didn't realize you had somebody – " She blinks a couple times. "Oh. Hi Jamie. Alicia, can I talk to you?"

Alicia follows her to the master bedroom and closes the door. I pad out to the hallway in my bare feet. Sound carries pretty clearly through the thin walls of a trailer, and I don't have to put my ear up to the door or anything to listen to their conversation, even though her mom is obviously trying to keep it down.

"Honey, I know you like girls and not boys, and I know Jamie's confused about his gender anyway, but I'm not comfortable with a boy playing dress-up in your bedroom."

"Jamie's not confused about a thing," Alicia replies. "And anyway, they changed in the bathroom."

I step back into her room and close the door behind me, because I really don't want to hear the rest. I don't want to hear Alicia reassure her mom that she doesn't think of me "that way." I don't want to hear Alicia's mom — who has always been cool to me — say something I won't be able to forgive.

Some people have a hard time adjusting to me — I get that. I don't care what their process of working things out looks like if in the end they treat me like a person. But I don't want to test that resolution by knowing too much.

Alicia doesn't ask me to leave when she returns; she doesn't talk about the conversation at all. I don't either. I figure everything's fine until somebody tells me otherwise.

"We ought to buy you some shoes to go with that, instead of those flip-flops. I could drive you to the mall in Sebring. It would be fun."

I meet her eyes, wondering where she's coming from. Alicia's not usually into shopping.

"It would," I agree. "But I don't think anybody's going to be looking at my shoes where I'm going. Some other time?"

She smiles. "Definitely." She raises both her eyebrows. "You gonna tell me what your plan is?"

If I did, I'd have to explain all sorts of things I'm not ready to. I shake my head. "You might try to talk me out of it."

She chews her lip; I can't tell if she's suspicious or hurt.

"I really appreciate your help," I say. When she doesn't reply, I add, "I better get on with this."

She finally meets my eye, and pulls me into a hug. "Be careful, whatever you're planning."

"I will," I say, and then I head out the door.

I should have asked for a ride — it would make things easier than taking public transportation dressed like this. But riding the bus will give me time to get used to the way I'm presenting.

All the way to Larry's street, I keep waiting for somebody to say or do something either because they've clocked me or because they think I *am* a girl. I wish I'd brought my ear buds, so I could block out the sounds of traffic and random conversation going on around me. That's stupid, though — what it would actually do is make me less likely to hear trouble coming.

Somehow I manage both legs of the ride and the transfer between. Everybody's too wrapped up in their own phones and music and worries to bother me.

At the hospice, I use the same story at the front desk that we used at the dealership. They give me directions to his room, and I walk past a courtyard garden, a nurse's station, and about a dozen doors with patient names written next to them in dry-erase ink.

I almost pass the door with Larry's name. I turn abruptly when I spot it, trying to project confidence, like I've been here before. I quietly close the door as I enter, and then blink as my eyes adjust to the darkness inside.

The curtains are drawn to block the low-hanging sun. Apart from the dim light slipping around the edges, the only illumination comes from a flatscreen television on the wall, bathing the room in a blueish glow. Flowers on a dresser cast sinister shadows that move with every flicker of the screen. In the center of the room, an oversized hospital bed dominates the space, undercutting the semblance of ordinary life somebody went through a lot of effort to create with the decor.

Larry lies on the bed, his head lolling to the side. I take in my first sight of him this lifetime. In my memories he is a giant, angry and frightening, out of control. He appears so weak and emaciated here that I can almost pity him — until I think about the lives he's destroyed. Mine. Benjamin's. Who else? Somebody like Larry probably didn't stop at one victim.

I walk up to the edge of the bed. I could take my revenge right now; nobody could stop me. I don't think it would make me feel better, though, and it wouldn't do anything for Benjamin.

And I didn't come here for revenge.

A television remote and call device is tethered to his bedsheet with an alligator clip. I loosen it, turn the sound down, and place it on the floor.

"Larry," I call out.

He makes a gross snot-clearing sound, but doesn't wake up.

"Larry!"

He blinks awake and looks at me, wild-eyed.

"Who the hell are you?" he croaks, scratchy and barely intelligible.

More memories come flooding back — Larry suspicious, Larry dismissive, Larry belligerent. I feel this weird contrast, like a double-exposed photograph. Part of me remembers that I'm supposed to be scared when Larry's voice takes this dangerous tone, but he's not scaring anyone anymore.

"You don't remember me, Larry? I'm hurt. I remember you."

"I've never met you in my life," he says, and starts patting around where his controller used to be.

"I remember that night at Peace Creek. You, me, and Benjamin. I bet he remembers it too."

He pauses in his search and stares at me again. Shaking his head, he gasps. "You can't be."

I stand over the bed. "Look at me."

"Janie," he whispers. His gaze flicks between me and the edge of his bed. Probably still looking for his call button. Then he reaches for something on the other side of him, which I hadn't noticed before. For a moment I think it's some kind of back up call device and my heart seizes, but it doesn't have a speaker or anything that appears to be a microphone.

I pluck the object out of his reach; it looks like some kind of self-dosing painkiller.

"Nuh uh, Larry. I'm talking to you. It wouldn't be very polite of you to check out."

"You're dead," he croaks.

"That's right. Soon you will be too, and I'll be waiting for you."

He stiffens, and I have this momentary worry that I will inadvertently cause a fatal heart attack or something right here.

I lean in a little closer. "I promise you it won't be pleasant. You let an innocent man pay the price for my death, but there'll be nobody to pay for you in the afterlife."

This seems to spark some fight back into him. "Benjamin wasn't innocent! He betrayed me! He had an affair with you!"

"Benjamin and I never had an affair," I say. I'm pretty sure that's true. "He tried to convince me to go back to you on the day you killed me." That part's definitely not true.

He clutches the bed railing. "What are you talking about?"

"I hitched a ride to the Greyhound station in Winter Haven, because I was afraid of you, Larry. Then I had second thoughts, so I called Benjamin from a payphone. He told me you were a good man, that you were just going through a hard time. He told me I should give you another chance, and he drove all the way out there to bring me back."

Larry sinks back in the bed and his face seems to cloud over.

"Listen to me!" I command. Then I remember that there are all sorts of nurses and other patients around, and lower my voice. "He wasn't taking me away from you. He was bringing me back."

Larry moans, his expression stricken.

"He was your friend right up until the end, and you took his life for it, as surely as you took mine. He deserved better Larry. So did I."

He grips my wrist; his skin is soft as tissue paper, but his grip is hard and a little painful. "You look so beautiful, Janie. Please don't leave me again!"

"I can't stay. My time is past, and you can't give me back what you took from me." I glare, and he tries to edge back from me. "But you can give Benjamin back some of what you took from him. You can talk to the police and recant. Tell them Benjamin didn't kill me. Tell them, Larry, or you'll see me every night in hell. I'll make you sorry. Believe me."

He raises a hand in front of his face. "Stop! I'll tell them! Please, Janie!"

I take the phone from the bedside table and dial. As soon as I navigate my way to a human being, I pass the handset over.

"Don't let me down," I say, "I'm watching you."

He's sobbing as I give it to him, but he's coherent enough once he starts talking. When he does, I make my way from the room before anybody can show up and start asking me awkward questions.

I'M WALKING MEETU A WEEK later when I pass Benjamin out in front of his trailer with his little girl, planting flowers, of all things. He waves, and I wave back before realizing he's actually calling me over.

"Damnedest thing happened," he says, getting up and brushing his hands on his jeans. "I got a call from my parole officer today. Larry Dearborn recanted. One of those deathbed confession things. They say that's how a lot of false convictions are overturned."

I do my best to feign surprise. "That's terrific!"

Meetu's tail thumps like Benjamin's a long lost friend.

"Yeah," he says. He pets Meetu, but his eyes stay on me. Looking *hard,* like he's trying to peer *into* me.

I'm not sure what to do, so I just shrug and say, "I'm glad you're finally getting some justice." The words feel stupid as they leave my mouth. He already served the sentence for this crime, and nothing can give that back to him.

As if he's read my mind, Benjamin says, "It'll make it easier to find work. Lot of people wouldn't look beyond that one line on a job application, before. Once people get a word for you — like *convict* — they think that word is all there is to know."

I nod.

His little girl makes mud pies in the dirt, and I think about how clearing her father's name will affect her future.

"I could watch her for you," I blurt out. "While you look for work." My face heats up. He may treat me like a person, but that doesn't mean he wants me watching his kid.

"That would be great."

I scratch Meetu, trying to act like it's no big deal.

"So." He nods toward Alicia's trailer. "You gonna ask that girl out? Don't tell me you're not interested."

"I'm...not *un*interested." I take a slow breath. "I guess I'm afraid."

"Afraid she sees you different from how you see yourself."

I sag. "Yes."

"I hear you," he says. "But if you don't take a chance on somebody disappointing you, you never give them a chance to surprise you either."

When I don't respond, he adds, "Will you stop being her friend if she says no?"

I shake my head.

"Then there's no sense wanting something and not at least trying."

I glance at the trailer. At the rainbow blinds that mark her bedroom window. "Maybe I will."

He claps a hand on my shoulder. "Good luck."

It feels more like a command than anything else, and I take a couple automatic steps toward her trailer. By the time my brain figures out what my feet have done, it seems more awkward to stop than to keep going.

Anyway, Benjamin's right. He sees right through me, the same way I know the real him.

The same way Alicia has always seen the real me, I realize. My pace picks up a bit, and Meetu responds by bounding forward, dragging me along, like everybody's figured out my destination before me.

She comes to the door as soon as I knock. "Hey," she says.

"You doing anything?"

She shrugs. "Watching TV."

"Wanna come for a walk?"

"Sure," she says, stepping out onto the deck. "Did something happen? Is something wrong?"

"Nope," I say, leading her down the steps. "Nothing's wrong at all."

We head down the street, quiet, like we don't need to babble to fill the space between us. To anybody watching us, we probably look like we're already a couple. Maybe by the time we come back, we will be. Maybe we won't.

Either way, we'll be okay.

YOU INSIDE ME

◄ Tori Curtis ►

*I*T'LL BE FUN, HE'D SAID. *Everyone's doing it. You don't have to be looking for romance, it's just a good way to meet people.*

"I don't think it's about romance at all," Sabella said. She wove her flower crown into her braids so that the wire skeleton was hidden beneath strands of hair. "I think if you caught a congressman doing this, he'd have to resign."

"That's 'cause we've never had a vampire congressman," Dedrick said. He rearranged her so that her shoulders fell from their habitual place at her ears, her chin pointed up, and snapped photos of her. "Step forward a little — there, you look more like yourself in that light."

He took fifteen minutes to edit her photos ("they'll expect you to use a filter, so you might as well,") and pop the best ones on her profile.

Suckr: the premier dating app for vampires and their fanciers.

"It's like we're cats," she said.

"I heard you like cats," he agreed, and she sighed.

*HI, I'M **SABELLA**. I'VE BEEN a **vampire** since I was **six years old**, and **I do not want to see or be seen by humans**. I'm excited to meet **men and women** between the ages of **eighteen and sixty-five**.*

"That's way too big of an age range," Dedrick said. "You want to be compatible with these people."

"Yeah, compatible. Like my tissue type."

"You don't want to end up flirting with a grandpa."

*I'm excited to meet **men and women** between the ages of **twenty and thirty-five**.*

*I'm most proud of **my master's degree**.*

*You should message me if **you're brave and crazy**.*

IT TOOK DAYS, NOT TO mention Dedrick's exasperated return, before she went back on Suckr. She paced the beautiful wood floors of her apartment, turning on heel at the sole window on the long end and the painted-over cast-iron radiator on the short. When she felt too sick to take care of herself, her mom came over and put Rumors on, wrapped her in scarves that were more pretty than functional, warmed some blood and gave it to her in a sippy cup. Sabella remembered nothing so much as the big Slurpees her mom had bought her, just this bright red, when she'd had strep the last year she was human.

She wore the necklace Dedrick had given her every day. It was a gold slice of pepperoni pizza with "best" emblazoned on the back (his matched, but read "friends,"), and she fondled it like a hangnail. She rubbed the bruises on her arms, where the skin had once been clear and she'd once thought herself pretty in a plain way, like Elinor Dashwood, as though she might be able to brush off the dirt.

She called her daysleeper friends, texted acquaintances, and slowly stopped responding to their messages as she realized how bored she was of presenting hope day after day.

2:19:08 bkissedrose: I'm so sorry.

2:19:21 bkissedrose: I feel like such a douche

2:19:24 sabellasay: ???

2:20:04 sabellasay: what r u talkin about

2:25:56 bkissedrose: u talked me down all those times I would've just died

2:26:08 sabellasay: it was rly nbd

2:26:27 bkissedrose: I've never been half as good as you are

2:26:48 bkissedrose: and now you're so sick
2:29:12 sabellasay: dude stop acting like i'm dying
2:29:45 sabellasay: I can't stand it
2:30:13 bkissedrose: god you're so brave

(sabellasay has become inactive)

"Everyone keeps calling me saying you stopped talking to them," Dedrick said when he made it back to her place, shoes up on the couch now that he'd finally wiped them of mud. "Should I feel lucky you let me in?"

"I'm tired," she said. "It's supposed to be a symptom. I like this one, I think she has potential."

He took her phone and considered it with the weight of a father researching a car seat. "A perfect date: I take you for a ride around the lake on my bike, then we stop home for an evening snack."

"She means her motorcycle," Sabella clarified.

He rolled his eyes and continued reading. "My worst fear: commitment."

"At least she's honest."

"That's not really a good thing. You're not looking for someone to skip out halfway through the movie."

"No, I'm looking for someone who's not going to be heartbroken when I die anyway."

Dedrick sighed, all the air going out of his chest as it might escape from dough kneaded too firmly, and held her close to him. "You're stupid," he told her, "but so sweet."

"I think I'm going to send her a nip."

The girl was named Ash but she spelled it Aisling, and she seemed pleased that Sabella knew enough not to ask lots of stupid questions. They met in a park by the lakeside, far enough from the playground that none of the parents would notice the fanged flirtation going on below.

If Aisling had been a boy, she would have been a teen heartthrob. She wore her hair long where it was slicked back and short (touchable, but hard to grab in a fight) everywhere else. She wore a leather jacket that spoke of a once-in-a-lifetime thrift store find, and over the warmth of her blood and her breath she smelled like bag balm. Sabella wanted to hide in her arms from a fire. She wanted to watch her drown trying to save her.

Aisling parked her motorcycle and stowed her helmet before coming over to say hi — gentlemanly, Sabella thought, to give her a chance to prepare herself.

"What kind of scoundrel left you to wait all alone?" Aisling asked, with the sort of effortlessly cool smile that might have broken a lesser woman's heart.

"I don't know," Sabella said, "but I'm glad you're here now."

Aisling stepped just inside her personal space and frowned. "I'm sorry, I don't mean to be rude," she said, "but are you — "

"I'm trans, yes," Sabella interrupted, and smiled so wide she could feel the tension at her temples. Like doing sit-ups the wrong way for years, having this conversation so many times hadn't made it comfortable, only routine. "We don't need to be awkward about it."

"Okay," Aisling agreed, and sat on the bench, helping Sabella down with a hand on her elbow. "I meant that you seem sick."

She looked uneasy, and Sabella sensed that she had never been human. Vampires didn't get sick — she had probably never had more than a headache, and that only from hunger.

"Yes," Sabella said. "I am sick. I'm not actually — I mentioned this on my profile — I'm not actually looking for love."

"I hope you won't be too disappointed when it finds you," Aisling said, and Sabella blushed, reoriented herself with a force like setting a bone, like if she tried hard enough to move in one direction she'd stop feeling like a spinning top.

"I'm looking for a donor," she said.

"Yeah, all right," Aisling said. She threw her arm over the back of the bench so that Sabella felt folded into her embrace. "I'm always willing to help a pretty girl out."

"I don't just mean your blood," she said, and felt herself dizzy.

IT WAS EASIER FOR SABELLA to convince someone to do something than it was for her to ask for it. Her therapist had told her that, and even said it was common, but he hadn't said how to fix it. "Please, may I have your liver" was too much to ask, and "Please, I don't want to die" was a poor argument.

"So, you would take my liver — "

"It would actually only be part of your liver," Sabella said, stopping to catch her breath. She hadn't been able to go hiking since she'd gotten so sick — she needed company, and easy trails, and her friends either didn't want to go or, like her mom, thought it was depressing to watch her climb a hill and have to stop to spit up bile.

"So we would each have half my liver, in the end."

Sabella shrugged and looked into the dark underbrush. If she couldn't be ethical about this, she wouldn't deserve a liver. She wouldn't try to convince Aisling until she understood the facts. "In humans, livers will regenerate once you cut them in half and transplant them. Like how kids think if you cut an earthworm in half, you get two. Or like bulbs. Ideally, it would go like that."

"And if it didn't go ideally?"

("Turn me," Dedrick said one day, impulsively, when she'd been up all night with a nosebleed that wouldn't stop, holding her in his lap with his shirt growing polka-dotted. "I'll be a vampire in a few days, we can have the surgery — you'll be cured in a week.")

"If it doesn't go ideally," Sabella said, "one or both of us dies. If it goes poorly, I don't even know what happens."

She stepped off the tree and set her next target, a curve in the trail where a tree had fallen and the light shone down on the path. Normally these days she didn't wear shoes but flip-flops, but this was a date, and she'd pulled her old rainbow chucks out of the closet. Aisling walked with her silently, keeping pace, and put an arm around her waist.

Sabella looked up and down the trail. Green Lake was normally populated enough that people kept to their own business, and these days she felt pretty safe going about, even with a girl. But she checked anyway before she leaned into Ais's strength, letting her guide them so that she could use all her energy to keep moving.

"But if it doesn't happen at all, you die no matter what?"

Sabella took a breath. "If you don't want to, I look for someone else."

HER MOM WAS WAITING FOR her when Sabella got home the next morning.

Sabella's mother was naturally blonde, tough when she needed to be, the sort of woman who could get into hours-long conversations with state fair tchotchke vendors. She'd gotten Sabella through high school and into college through a careful application of stamping and yelling. When Sabella had started calling herself Ravynn, she'd brought a stack of baby name books home and said, "All right, let's find you something you can put on a resume."

"Mom," she said, but smiling, "I gave you a key in case I couldn't get out of bed, not so you could check if I spent the night with a date."

"How'd it go? Was this the girl Dedrick helped you find?"

"Aisling, yeah," Sabella said. She sat on the recliner, a mountain of accent pillows cushioning her tender body. "It was good. I like her a lot."

"Did she decide to get the surgery?"

"I don't know. I didn't ask her to choose."

"Then what did you two do all night?"

Sabella frowned. "I like her a lot. We had a good time."

Her mom stood and put the kettle on, and Sabella couldn't help thinking what an inconvenience she was, that her mother couldn't fret over her by making toast and a cup of tea. "Christ, what decent person would want to do that with you?"

"We have chemistry! She's very charming!"

She examined Sabella with the dissatisfied air of an artist. "You're a mess, honey. You're so orange you could be a jack-o-lantern, and swollen all over. You look like you barely survived a dogfight. I don't even see my daughter when I look at you anymore."

Sabella tried to pull herself together, to look more dignified, but instead she slouched further into the recliner and crossed her arms over her chest. "Maybe she thinks I'm funny, or smart."

"Maybe she's taking advantage. Anyone who really cared about you wouldn't be turned on, they'd be worried about your health."

Sabella remembered the look on Aisling's face when she'd first come close enough to smell her, and shuddered. "I'm not going to ask her to cut out part of her body for me without thinking about it first," she said.

"Without giving her something in return?" her mom asked. "It's less than two pounds."

"But it's still her choice," Sabella said.

"I'm starting to wonder if you even want to live," her mom said, and left.

Sabella found the energy to go turn off the stovetop before she fell asleep. (Her mother had raised her responsible.)

12:48:51 bkissedrose: what happens to a dream bestowed
12:49:03 bkissedrose: upon a girl too weak to fight for it?
12:53:15 sabellasay: haha you can't sleep either?
12:53:38 sabellasay: babe idk
12:55:43 sabellasay: is it better to have loved and lost
12:56:29 sabellasay: than to die a virgin?
1:00:18 bkissedrose: I guess I don't know
1:01:24 bkissedrose: maybe it depends if they're good

"It's nice here," Aisling confessed the third time they visited the lake. Sabella and her mom weren't talking, but she couldn't imagine it would last more than a few days longer, so she wasn't worried. "I'd never even heard of it."

"I grew up around here," Sabella said, "and I used to take my students a few times a year."

"You teach?"

"I used to teach," she said, and stepped off the trail — the shores were made up of a gritty white sand like broken shells — to watch the sinking sun glint off the water. "Seventh grade science."

Aisling laughed. "That sounds like a nightmare."

"I like that they're old enough you can do real projects with them, but before it breaks off into — you know, are we doing geology or biology or physics. When you're in seventh grade, everything is science." She smiled and closed her eyes so that she could feel the wind and the sand under her shoes. She could hear birds settling and starting to wake, but she couldn't place them. "They've got a long-term sub now. Theoretically, if I manage to not die, I get my job back."

Aisling came up behind her and put her arms around her. Sabella knew she hadn't really been weaving — she knew her limits well enough now, she hoped — but she felt steadier that way. "You don't sound convinced."

"I don't think they expect to have to follow through," Sabella admitted. "Sometimes I think I'm the only one who ever thinks I'm going to survive this. My mom's so scared all the time, I know she doesn't."

Aisling held her not tight but close, like being tucked into a bright clean comforter on a cool summer afternoon. "Can I ask you a personal question?" she said, her face up against Sabella's neck so that every part of Sabella wanted her to bite.

"Maybe," she said, then thought better of it. "Yes."

"How'd you get sick? I didn't think we could catch things like that. Or was it while you were human?"

"Um, no, but I'm not contagious, just nasty." Aisling laughed, and she continued, encouraged. "Mom would, you know, once I came out I could do pretty much whatever I wanted, but she wouldn't let me get any kind of reconstructive surgery until I was eighteen. She thought it was creepy, some doc getting his hands all over her teenage kid."

"Probably fair."

"So I'm eighteen, and she says okay, you're right, you got good grades in school and you're going to college like I asked, I'll pay for whatever surgery you want. And you have to imagine, I just scheduled my freshman orientation, I have priorities."

"Which are?"

"Getting laid, mostly."

"Yeah, I remember that."

"So I'm eighteen and hardly ever been kissed, I'm not worried about the details. I don't let my mom come with me, it doesn't even occur to me to see a doctor who's worked with vampires before, I just want to look like Audrey Hepburn's voluptuous sister."

"Oh no," Ais said. It hung there for a moment, the dread and Sabella's not being able to regret that she'd been so stupid. "It must have come up."

"Sure. He said he was pretty sure it would be possible to do the surgery on a vampire, he knew other surgeries had been done. I was just so excited he didn't say no."

Ais held her tight then, like she might be dragged away otherwise, and Sabella knew that it had nothing to do with her in particular, that it was only the protective instinct of one person watching another live out her most plausible nightmare. "What did he do to you?"

"It wasn't his fault," she said, and then — grimacing, she knew her mother would have been so angry with her — "at least, he didn't mean anything by it. He never read anything about how to adapt the procedure to meet my needs." She sounded so clinical, like she'd imbibed so many doctors' explanations of what had happened that she was drunk on it. "But neither did I. We both found out you can't give vampires a blood transfusion."

"Why would you need to?"

She shrugged. "You don't, usually, in plastic surgery."

"No," Aisling interrupted, "I mean, why wouldn't you drink it?"

Sabella tried to remember, or tried not to be able to, and tucked her cold hands into her pockets. "You're human, I guess. Anyway, I puked all over him and the incision sites, had to be hospitalized. My doctor says I'm lucky I'm such a good healer, or I'd need new boobs *and* a new liver."

They were both quiet, and Sabella thought, *this is it. You either decide it's too much or you kiss me again.*

She thought, *I miss getting stoned with friends and telling shitty surgery stories and listening to them laugh. I hate that when I meet girls their getting-to-know-you involves their YouTube make-up tutorials and mine involves "and then, after they took the catheter out..."*

"Did you sue for malpractice, at least?" Ais asked, and Sabella couldn't tell without looking if her tone was teasing or wistful.

"My mom did, yeah. When they still wanted her to pay for the damn surgery."

AISLING PULLED UP TO THE front of Sabella's building and stopped just in front of her driveway. She kicked her bike into park and stepped onto the sidewalk, helping Sabella off and over the curbside puddle. Sabella couldn't find words for what she was thinking, she was so afraid that her feelings would shatter as they crystallized. She wanted Ais to brush her hair back from her face and comb out the knots with her fingers. She wanted Ais to stop by to shovel the drive when there was lake effect snow. She wanted to find 'how to minimize jaundice' in the search history of Aisling's phone.

"You're beautiful in the sunlight," Ais said, breaking her thoughts, maybe on purpose. "Like you were made to be outside."

Sabella ducked her head and leaned up against her. The date was supposed to be over, go inside and let this poor woman get on with her life, but she didn't want to leave. "It's nice to have someone to go with me," she said. "Especially with a frost in the air. Sometimes people act like I'm so fragile."

"Ridiculous. You're a vampire."

Her ears were cold, and she pressed them against Aisling's jawbone. She wondered what the people driving past thought when they saw them. She thought that maybe the only thing better than surviving would be to die a tragic death, loved and loyally attended. "I was born human."

"Even God makes mistakes."

Sabella smiled. "Is that what I am? A mistake?"

"Nah," she said. "Just a happy accident."

Sabella laughed, thought *you're such a stoner* and *I feel so safe when you look at me like that.*

"I'll do it," Ais said. "What do I have to do to set up the surgery?"

Sabella hugged her tight, hid against her and counted the seconds — one, two, three, four, five — while Ais didn't change her mind and Sabella wondered if she would.

"I HAVE TO STRESS HOW potentially dangerous this is," Dr. Young said. "I can't guarantee that it will work, that either of you will survive the procedure or the recovery, or that you won't ultimately regret it."

Aisling was holding it together remarkably well, Sabella thought, but she still felt like she could catch her avoiding eye contact. Sabella had taken the seat in the doctor's office between her mother and girlfriend, and felt uncomfortable and strange no matter which of their hands she held.

"Um," Ais said, and Sabella could feel her mother's judgment at her incoherence, "you said you wouldn't be able to do anything for the pain?"

To her credit, the doctor didn't fidget or look away. Sabella, having been on the verge of death long enough to become something of a content expert, believed that it was important to have a doctor who was upfront about how terrible her life was. "I wouldn't describe it as 'nothing,' exactly," she said. "There aren't any anesthetics known to work on vampires, but we'll make you as comfortable as possible. You can feed immediately before and as soon as you're done, and that will probably help snow you over."

"Being a little blood high," Ais clarified. "While you cut out my liver."

"Yes."

Sabella wanted to apologize. She couldn't find the words.

Aisling said, "Well, while we're trying to make me comfortable, can I smoke up, too?"

Dr. Young laughed. It wasn't cruel, but it wasn't promising, either. "That's not a terrible idea," she said, "but marijuana increases bleeding, and there are so many unknown variables here that I'd like to stick to best practices if we can."

"I can just — " Sabella said, and choked. She wasn't sure when she'd started crying. "Find someone else. Dedrick will do it, I know."

Aisling considered this. The room was quiet, soft echoes on the peeling tile floor. Sabella's mother put an arm around her, and she felt tiny, but in the way that made her feel ashamed and not protected. Aisling said, "Why are you asking me? Is there something you know that I don't?"

Dr. Young shook her head. "I promise we're not misrepresenting the procedure," she said. "And theoretically, it might be possible with any vampire. But there aren't a lot of organ transplants in the literature — harvesting, sure, but not living transplants — and I want to get it right the first time. If we have a choice, I told Sabella I'd rather use a liver from a donor who was born a vampire. I think it'll increase our chance of success."

"A baby'd be too weak," Aisling agreed. Her voice was going hard and theoretical. "Well, tell me something encouraging."

"One of the first things we'll do is to cut through almost all of your abdominal nerves, so that will help. And there's a possibility that the experience will be so intense that you don't remember it clearly, or at all."

Sabella's mother took a shaky breath, and Sabella wished, hating herself for it, that she hadn't come.

Ais said, "Painful. You mean, the experience will be so painful."

"If you choose to go forward with it," Dr. Young said, "we'll do everything we can to mitigate that."

SABELLA HAD EXPECTED THAT AISLING would want space and patience while she decided not to die a horrible, painful death to save her. It was hard to tell how instead they ended up in her bed with the lights out, their legs wound together and their faces swollen with sleep. Sabella was shaking, and couldn't have said why. Ais grabbed her by her seat and pulled her close.

"You said you couldn't get me sick?" she asked.

"No," Sabella agreed. "Although my blood is probably pretty toxic."

Ais kissed her, the smell of car exhaust still stuck in her hair. "What a metaphor," she murmured, and lifted her chin. "You look exhausted."

Sabella thought, *Are you saying what I think you're saying?* and, *That's a terrible idea,* and said, "God, I want to taste you."

"Well, baby," Ais said, and her hands were on Sabella so she curled her lips and blew her hair out of her eyes, "that's what I'm here for."

Sabella had been human once, and she remembered what food was like. The standard lie, that drinking blood was like eating a well-cooked steak, was wrong but close enough to staunch the flow of an interrogation. (She'd had friends and exes, turned as adults, who said it was like a good stout on tap, hefty and refreshing, but she thought they might just be trying to scandalize her.)

Ais could have been a stalk of rhubarb or August raspberries. She moved under Sabella and held her so that their knees pressed together. She could have been the thrill of catching a fat thorny toad in among the lettuce at dusk, or a paper wasp in a butterfly net. She felt like getting tossed in the lake in January; she tasted like being wrapped in fleece and gently dried before the fire; her scent was what Sabella remembered of collapsing, limbs aquiver, on the exposed bedrock of a mountaintop, nothing but crushed pine and the warmth of a moss-bed.

She woke on top of Ais, licking her wounds lazily — she wanted more, but she was too tired to do anything about it.

"That's better," Ais whispered, and if she was disappointed that this wasn't turning into a frenzy, she didn't show it. They were quiet for long enough that the haze started to fade, and then Aisling said, "I couldn't ask in front of your mother, but was it like that with your surgery? They couldn't do anything for the pain?"

Sabella shifted uncomfortably, rolled over next to Ais. "I was conscious, yes."

"Do you remember it?"

It was a hard question. She wanted to say it wasn't her place to ask. She tried to remember, and got caught up in the layers of exhaustion, the spaces between the body she'd had, the body she'd wanted, and what they had been doing to her. "Sounds and sensations and thoughts, mostly," she said.

Ais choked, and said, "So, everything," and Sabella realized — she didn't know how she hadn't — how scared she must be.

"No, it's blurry," she said instead. "I remember, um, the tugging at my chest. I kept thinking there was no way my skin wasn't just going to split open. And the scraping sounds. They've got all these tools, and they're touching you on the inside and the outside at the same time, and that's very unsettling. And this man, I think he was the PA, standing over me saying, 'You've got to calm down, honey.'"

"Were you completely freaking out?" Ais asked.

Sabella shook her head. Her throat hurt. "No. I mean — I cried a little. Not as much as you'd think. They said if I wasn't careful, you know, with swallowing at the right times and breathing steady, they might mess up reshaping my larynx and I could lose my voice."

Ais swore, and Sabella wondered if she would feel angry. (Sometimes she would scream and cry, say, can you imagine doing that to an eighteen-year-old?) Right now she was just tired. "How did you manage?"

"I don't know," she admitted. "I think just, it was worth more to me to have it done than anything else. So I didn't ever tell them to stop."

"PLEASE DON'T GO AROUND TELLING people I think this is an acceptable surgical set-up," Dr. Young said, looking around the exam room.

It reminded Sabella of a public hearing, the way the stakeholders sat at opposing angles and frowned at each other. Dr. Young sat next to Dr. Park, who would be the second doctor performing the procedure. Sabella had never met Dr. Park before, and her appearance — young, mostly — didn't inspire confidence. Sabella sat next to her mother, who held her hand and a clipboard full of potential complications. Ais crossed her fingers in her lap, sat with a nervous child's version of polite interest. Time seemed not to blur, but to stutter, everything happening whenever.

"Dr. Park," Sabella's mother said, "do you have any experience operating on vampires?"

Dr. Park grinned and her whole mouth seemed to open up in her face, her gums pale pink as a Jolly Rancher and her left fang chipped. "Usually trauma or obstetrics," she admitted. "Although this is nearly the same thing."

"I'm serious," Sabella's mom said, and Sabella interrupted.

"I like her," she said. And then — it wasn't really a question except in the sense that there was no way anyone could be sure — "You're not going to realize halfway through the surgery that it's too much for you?"

Dr. Park laughed. "I turned my husband when we were both eighteen," she said as testament to her cruelty.

Sabella's mom jumped. "Jesus Christ, why?"

She shrugged, languid. Ais and Dr. Young were completely calm; Ais might have had no frame of reference for what it was like to watch someone turn, and Dr. Young had probably heard this story before. "His parents didn't like that he was dating a vampire. You'll do crazy things for love."

Sabella could see her mother blanch even as she steadied. It wasn't unheard of for a vampire to turn their spouse — less common now that it was easier to live as a vampire, and humans were able to date freely but not really commit. But she could remember being turned, young as she had been: the gnawing ache, the hallucinations, the thirst that had only sometimes eclipsed the pain. It was still the worst thing that she'd ever experienced, and she was sure her mother couldn't understand why anyone would *choose* to do it to someone they loved.

"Good," she said. "You won't turn back if we scream."

Dr. Young frowned. "I want you to know you have a choice," she said. She was speaking to Ais; Sabella had a choice, too, but it was only between one death and another. "There will be a point when you can't change your mind, but by then it'll be almost over."

Ais swore. It made Dr. Park smile and Sabella's mom frown. Sabella wondered if she was in love with her, or if it was impossible to be in love with someone who was growing a body for them to share. "Don't say that," Ais said. "I don't want to have that choice."

THE MORNING OF THE SURGERY, Aisling gave Sabella a rosary to wear with her pizza necklace, and when they kicked Sabella's mom out to the waiting room, she kissed them both as she went. "I like your mom," Ais said shyly. They lay in cots beside each other, just close enough that they could reach out and hold hands across the gap. "I bet she'd get along with mine."

Sabella laughed, her eyes stinging, threw herself across the space between them and kissed each of Ais's knuckles while Ais said, "Aw, c'mon, save it 'til we get home."

"Isn't that a lot of commitment for you?" Sabella asked.

"Yeah, well," Ais said, caught, and gave her a cheesy smile. "You're already taking my liver, at least my heart won't hurt so much."

They drank themselves to gorging while nurses wrapped and padded them in warm blankets. Ais was first, for whatever measure of mercy that was, and while they were wheeled down the dizzying white hallway, she grinned at Sabella, wild, some stranger's blood staining her throat to her nose. "You're a real looker," she said, and Sabella laughed over her tears.

"Thank you," Sabella said. "I mean, really, for everything."

Ais winked at her; Sabella wanted to run away from all of this and drink her in until they died. "It's all in a day's work, ma'am," she said.

It wasn't, it couldn't have been, and Sabella loved her for pretending. Ais hissed, she cried, she asked intervention of every saint learned in K-12 at a Catholic school. A horrible gelatinous noise came as Dr. Young's gloves touched her innards, and Ais moaned and Sabella said, "You have to stop, this is awful," and the woman assigned to supervise her held her down and said hush, honey, you need to be quiet. And the doctors' voices, neither gentle nor unkind: We're almost done now, Aisling, you're being so brave. And: It's a pity she's too strong to pass out.

Sabella went easier, hands she couldn't see wiping her down and slicing her open while Dr. Park pulled Ais's insides back together. She'd been scared for so long that the pain didn't frighten her; she kept asking "Is she okay? What's happening?" until the woman at her head brushed back her hair and said shh, she's in the recovery room, you can worry about yourself now.

It felt right, fixing her missteps with pieces of Ais, and when Dr. Young said, "There we go, just another minute and you can go take care of her yourself," Sabella thought about meromictic lakes, about stepping into a body so deep its past never touched its present.

SPHEXA, START DINOSAUR

◄ Nibedita Sen ►

ASHA — ASH TO FRIENDS — WEDGES the maintenance door open wide enough to slip into the darkened interior of the abandoned ride. Inside smells like rust and stale water and plastic fused with metal.

"Sphexa," he says. "Light."

The small robot bobbing behind him clicks, casting a circle of illumination on the concrete floor. He made Sphexa in shop class at school, patching together an old Echo, a frame salvaged from a drone, a rolling toy robot, and a few other things, because if you're going to be *that* stereotype of the Indian kid good at engineering, you might as well lean all the way in.

"Reminder," Sphexa says as they make their way down the narrow walkway lining the tunnel. "Event upcoming in two hours: Pick Mei up for prom."

"I'm working on it, Sphexa."

"Would you like a list of car rental agencies in the area that take last-minute bookings?" Disapproval was not something he programmed into the bot, but it's definitely pulling some attitude right now.

"I'm good, Sphexa, thanks."

They're walking alongside a long, low channel that still holds a few inches of scummy water. The flat-bottomed boats that used to rock and splosh slowly along the artificial river are long gone, of course. *Journey through the Jurassic* was shut down a year ago, eclipsed by other, showier rides in the park.

It was his and Mei's favourite, before that. They rode it every hot sticky summer, multiple times if they could, huddled together in the boats with their backpacks full of issues of *National Geographic* and Meccano dinosaurs they'd built together. Over the years, they went from staring awestruck at the animatronic saurians craning over them, to playing spot-the-anatomical-inaccuracies. Ash still remembers, though, that first time, when they were younger — though they'd ridden it so many times already by then — when they rounded the corner where the T-Rex lifted its metal head and roared in the low reddish light, and Mei had grabbed his hand, their smaller, warmer fingers tightening in his.

Mei. His heart jolts, as it always does, at the thought of their heart-shaped face. The way their hair is always falling into their eyes when they get excited about something, and how they dash it away impatiently with the backs of their hands as they keep talking, their voice going high and jumpy with their infectious joy.

They had their first kiss on this ride too, in the back of a boat in middle school, somewhere just past the T-rex but before the raptors.

It's warm in here, his rented tux uncomfortably stiff as he clambers through a thicket of fake Jurassic ferns and a nest of baby Maiasura, led by Sphexa's overhead beam. It's a little too small for him, uncomfortably tight against his chest, over the binder.

The corsage he got for Mei sits carefully in an inner pocket. He figured he should keep at least one thing traditional if he was going to flip double middle fingers at all the rest.

He's almost all the way to the mouth of the exit when the irregular silhouette of a Stegosaurus rises ahead out of the gloom. Ash grins. Bingo. Stegosaurus, Mei's second-favourite dinosaur (their first is Psittacosaurus, but *Journey through the Jurassic* doesn't have one).

"Sphexa, raise lights to 7."

Ash carefully lowers his backpack to the now-brighter floor and start pulling things from it: pliers, loops of cable, wire cutters, microcontrollers; mostly from his own workshop, a few 'borrowed' from his dad's. His hopes are confirmed as he starts carefully severing the plastic encasing the animatronic's upper forward leg joint. The T-connectors and needle valves he needs are mostly already there, articulated and ready to go, if dusty from disuse since the ride shut down and the Stego stopped making its plodding way to and back from the waterhole.

All he has to do is feed wires into the right places, sealing them in places with dabs of insulated putty, winding them up towards the dinosaur's knobby head.

"Message from Mei," Sphexa reports archly. "*It's okay if you've changed your mind.*"

Mei had nearly cried with happiness when he'd asked them to prom, but had flip-flopped between nerves and despair ever since, making anxious lists of everything that could go wrong. They'd never exactly fit in, the two of them, the trans kid and the immigrant. Especially not since Mei had come out. Ash could figure without being told what some of the stuff on Mei's lists was: the glances in the hallway, the jackasses trying to flip up their skirt, being shoved at the water fountain. He got his fair share of it too; the Sphero that went into making Sphexa had been his before someone kicked it down the hallway, snapping it in half.

"Sphexa, reply. Send link to playlist, 'Cretaceous Rock.'"

"Message sent. Reply from Mei: '*Hah, hah.*'"

Sphexa hovers overhead as he works, the minutes ticking by. As he'd suspected, the Stego's skull is mostly empty, its mechanics concentrated in the joints. Ash pulls himself up onto the dinosaur's back, brushing cobwebs from between its raised plates — a staggered line of them, not paired, totally inaccurate for *S. Ungulatus*. At least it makes it easy to find a seat.

"Okay, Sphexa," he says. "Get in there."

Tablet in hand, he makes minute course corrections on the touchscreen as the robot levers itself into the hollow skull, clicking free of the drone frame. Ash leans forward to plug the final jacks into the ports on Sphexa's back. Rotors click and valves piston as the connections light up one by one, a whirring hum he can feel through the automaton's thick plastic hide. The Stegosaurus shifts, lifting one huge foot and then another, testing its restored — and expanded — mobility. Elation warms his chest.

"GPS active," Sphexa says. "Add destination."

"Mei's place."

"Would you like to add another stop? Suggestion based on calendar: school."

"Not yet." Ash pats the dinosaur's neck. "Let's go get Mei. Then we'll see where they want to go."

He twists his earbuds up into place, tucking them in firmly, and taps the tablet. "Oh, and Sphexa? Play 'Walk the Dinosaur.'"

APOTHEOSIS

◄ Catherine Kim ►

I<small>T'S BEEN MORE THAN HALF</small> a decade since Sophia's last been in her childhood home, and just as many years since she's seen Paul face-to-face. There's a pile of shoes clumped together on a dirty carpet next to the front door, and dust coating the partition between the foyer and the living space. Her mother's piano is tucked up against a corner, a coat draped over the lid and papers stacked on the bench. Paul's old IBM trackball laptop takes up a corner of the dining table, its power cord spooling across the surface between old dishes and plastic utensils. He rummages through cupboards of expired foodstuffs and canned meals before calling up the local pizzeria over his fliphone. His mouth hangs agape between sentences, exposing chipped teeth stained with nicotine. *Pepperoni and olives, stuffed crust, and a two-litre bottle of Coke.* He scratches the growing bald spot on his head in a nervous tick. Sophia takes a seat at the table with her satchel on her lap, the weight of the Diviner pressed against her stomach. Her father is fifty-two years old, and it's obvious he still can't quite take care of himself living alone. There are enough dirty dishes in the sink for Sophia to wonder if he's waiting for Mary to come home and do the chores. As if the presence of a ghost would be enough to fill out the empty spaces in this house that's barely a home: three chairs at the dinner table, a spare key stuck in the crevice of a loose brick, a woman's slippers on the mat before the sliding door to the backyard, and the same old Dodge Caravan parked in the driveway. Something in her expression must give away her exhaustion. He keeps a measured distance away from her, a hand in his pocket to quiet the *jingling* of his keys. Wipes the sleep leftover from his own eyes with the point of his thumb. Powers down the kitchen stereo, cutting off the empty notes of a piano solo. Paul might have taught her to hold her tongue, but her mother's the one that left them both. Taught her actions can starve words of their meaning with every broken vow. Her father's long outgrown the need for a punching bag. She can't help but wonder what he thinks he'll find in her instead, looking at her like if he blinks for too long, she might slip into a noose and make herself disappear.

JACK CLIMBS IN THROUGH THE windowsill like they're still teenagers trading secrets late at night with the loyalty that comes from being the only visible freaks in the neighborhood. He's as stubbornly immune to the weather as always, dressed in a hockey hoodie and tight jeans that grope the bulge of his packer. *Your dad would never have let me in*, he smiles, as Sophia counts all the blunt and heavy objects in her room. A golf club under her bed smuggled from her uncle's kit the last time he was over on this side of the Pacific. A snow globe of *Gwanghwamun* clumsily rendered with thick squares of confetti blanketing the courtyard. The sleeping Diviner, buried in the satchel next to her bed, *clicking* away like a colony of wind-up insects only audible to her. *I wouldn't have either*, she says, and he flinches like she's moved to strike him. The smile drops from his face with the rest of his confidence, as flurries of snow blow into the room and scatter against the carpet. She hasn't seen Jack since she packed up for college, changing her number and dropping her birth name along with the few friendships that mattered to her in her adolescence. *We never got a chance to talk*, he says, and she does nothing but tuck her knees into her chest as he steps across the carpet in his dirty sneakers, to climb up on what little space there's left at the foot of her bed. Even in her own room she feels like a stranger. With her bones too loud for her body, thin with slow thoughts and malnutrition. An ache in her breasts under the fabric of her nightshirt. Orange pill bottles stuffed deep in the back of her bedside drawer. Like she's put herself together from the scraps tossed out after a domestic. Or from the salvaged hand-me-downs left over from her mother's epilogue. Jack fiddles with her snow globe as he talks, reading answers in her body that aren't quite legible to her, not in the middle of the night with a figment of her night terrors looking exactly as he did during their worst mistake. *I trusted you*, she thinks, and he turns to face her like she's said it aloud. *I know*, he says. *That's why it had to be me.* And the worst part of it is she can't believe he's wrong. Not in this place, where the walls of her bedroom climb into barricades, and little tourist figurines swarm the gates of the palace in the snow globe Jack tosses back and forth between his hands. Not when she can count her father's cigarettes in the cracks between his teeth and feel her mother's hands wrap around her neck to dig the Adam's apple out from her throat. As Jack tosses her around to slide against her back, the fabric of his binder scraping against her naked spine, to slip a knee between her legs and brush against her erection. *You'd make a beautiful girl*, he echoes, kissing the dip in her neck below the ridge of her skull, as she gasps into her sheets like a mockery of a woman hitting her climax. *Let me show you how.*

IN THE END, SOPHIA DOESN'T need the *tick-tock* of the Diviner to lead her to the right spot in the forest. She stands before the stump sheltered in a goose-down coat and thick boots, hair pulled up into a practiced braid. Recognizes it as the spot Mary's corpse was found hanging from a sturdy branch, a pen in her pocket and a blank postcard crumpled in a cold fist, as if she meant to write a letter but didn't make the time. She remembers sucking her mother's ashes from her fingers after the funeral and coming to the realization that she'd been left behind. She slips her gloves off her hands and drops them in the snow. Rubs heat into her palms, finding something sharp buried deep inside her throat. The naked branches of the trees reach out towards the noonday sun. Soft footsteps *pitter-patter* in the snow behind her, and she dares not turn around. A warm body brushes against her calves. The fox's pelt is a vivid star against a sea of white. Nine wicked tails thrash soundlessly behind it like the bridal curtain of a wandering ghost. A sudden weight, and Sophia finds herself collapsed on her back, a paw pressing against the hollow of her throat. A grin filled with teeth and the lingering scent of carrion, brushing against her cheek with a lover's caress. The Diviner clatters uselessly at the base of the stump, at the corpse of the tree where her mother once hung.

Laughter tears its reckless way out a locked box to which she thought she threw away the key. *I'm so glad,* Sophia says, as the fox's coarse tongue licks against her throat, nuzzles past the fabric of her winter clothes, and laps at a spot below her breasts, just above her liver. *I didn't want to do this alone.* It's familiar in a way she never thought possible for her, an ocean across and a reality away from a home she could still feel in her bones. Though it shouldn't have been a surprise. She knows how this goes, better than any girl should: the bite of something sharp, a flash of pain, the flush of adrenaline coursing through her blood. Like breaking down a gate to a castle from the inside. She's been intimate with the sensations of her slow collapse since the year her voice began to drop, and her father taught her how to shoot a rifle at the silhouette of a human being: a dark mirror standing unarmed and twenty paces apart. Sophia cries out as slender fingers dig into her organs and slip a bite of meat between the bright red lips of the woman crouching naked over her body, the slit pupils of a pair of luminous yellow eyes meeting her own.

ASSISTANCE

◄ Kathryn DeFazio ►

"WOULD YOU LIKE TO DISCUSS your coping plan?"

Astor did not want to discuss their coping plan. They didn't want to think about their coping plan, or the trip itself, or the airport, or the subway, or — "No, thank you."

"Do you think it would be — "

"Manual override." Astor sat heavily in the armchair.

"Hmm." The little android tilted its head slightly. "I'm sorry, Astor, I don't understand the command. Could you rephrase?"

It had been worth a shot. "Never mind."

"The value of coping in advance allows you to prepare for the most likely scenario and therefore decrease feelings of helplessness and fear. Would you like to discuss your coping plans?"

Astor peered over at the android. It didn't need to sit with that ever-so-slight slouch, turn its toes in, hum thoughtfully while it processed information, but it did anyway. It didn't need to fold its hands in its lap. It didn't need to be so soft and rounded, molded grey plastic and smooth faux leather, it didn't need to feel warm, it didn't need to be friendly, to smile, to say please, to offer hugs. But even for its age, PAGE was a good model, specifically programmed for mental health support.

"We're going to get on the — the, uh. Train. F, transfer to the E. Take the Airtrain to the right terminal. Ch-check you. Go through security.

Take off my shoes, put my bag up, take my laptop out." They swallowed, mouth suddenly gone dry. "Find my gate on the monitor. Sit and wait to board. Then I get on the plane and I take a benzo and breathe deep and use my coping skills while on a winged tube flinging itself into the air towards Savannah."

The android tilted its head. "Hmmm," it said, buying time while it processed. "I perceive a judgment. Would you like the discuss the judgment?"

"No." Astor stood back up, turned left and then right, lost, confused for a second. "We have to get dinner."

"Do you require extra support?"

They didn't want to. They knew they did. "Yes."

Some days were easier than others, but today was a bad one, this close to the trip. If it were anyone other than family they'd have skipped the funeral, sent a digital message and a floral arrangement. But there was no avoiding this. They were squeezed in the tight grip of fear, so tight there wasn't even room for grief.

They paced aimlessly around the apartment, touching and adjusting things without thought. "I don't want to go," they mumbled. *To the grocery store, or to the funeral?* their therapist would have asked. They slipped into their shoes. "I can't do this." A plain fact.

They could always just have eggs again. Eggs made a healthy dinner. There were two left, and they could skip breakfast tomorrow, or have toast or stale cereal. There was rice, and probably a can of beans lurking in the back of the cabinet.

"These are just thoughts," PAGE offered mildly. "They don't reflect reality. Be careful of stating your feelings as though they were facts." The red LEDs formed a smile at them, head tilted slightly. "Would you like to reframe your anxiety thoughts?"

"Oh my god," they mumbled.

"Hmm." It blinked this time, slowly, like a cat. That meant it was thinking harder than usual. "Consistently using your coping skills will support your recovery," it said finally.

Astor huffed. "I'm sorry," they said. Whether it had feelings or not, it wasn't fair for them to take theirs out on it.

"That's all right, Astor." A pause. "Do you need help with the reframing, Astor?"

"I feel like I can't handle going to the grocery store."

"Is there evidence for or against that?"

"Last week." Their mouth went dry again, remembering the failed shopping trip. The ugly twisting of their face, the silent tears streaming down their cheeks. They'd angled themself into a corner, as though they could pretend they were just investigating a cookie display when their shoulders were heaving, pouring sweat and very aware of how conspicuous they were, how pitiful they must have looked. They thought they could make that trip without PAGE, and maybe they could, at a different time, as a different person.

Maybe they were getting worse.

"Yes, last week was difficult for you. Do you have evidence against your feeling?"

"Well, I have grocery shopped before." Before things were this bad. Before the whole outside world had become dangerous. "And I didn't just hear that my cousin is dying."

"Yes, you have successfully achieved this goal in the past, and you have not received any unpleasant news today." It blinked, thoughtful. "Do you think we can do it together?"

"Probably. Just — don't draw a lot of attention to me if I freak out."

"Yes." PAGE smiled. "If you are in distress, we can leave if you choose, or finish the task if you think you're able to."

"Great."

Astor checked that the lights were off in the bedroom, the knobs on the stove. They hadn't used the stove yet that day, but checking the stove made them feel better. The knobs may have drifted in the night, or they may have left something on last night when they made dinner.

"Right. Keys, wallet, phone. Bag — " they got the big reusable bag off the hook by the door. "Right," they said again. "Ready."

They made it down the first flight of stairs before they turned back.

"Checking reinforces that security comes from checking, not from having completed the task," PAGE said from the landing. It had gone out with them enough to know what they were doing.

"I just want to make sure — "

"I would challenge you not to check," it said.

Astor paused at the top of the stairs. "I have to make sure I locked the door." What if someone got in the building? What if they got in and waited in the dark and empty apartment, waiting to do something awful, waiting for —

The door was locked. They huffed. *You locked the door*, they told themself angrily. *You always lock the door.*

They rejoined the android on the stairs. "Don't give me that look," they said. Its face had the same neutral pleasant expression it wore at rest, but they still felt distinctly judged.

"You locked the door," it said.

"I locked it, I locked it." They waved a dismissive hand.

"Would you like me to remind you that it is locked if you seem distressed?"

Astor wouldn't like that at all. They shouldn't have needed it. "Please," they said quietly.

"Reminder set." The little rounded face smiled. "Are you ready to leave?"

The grocery store was too crowded this time of night, full of hospital workers picking up food between their shifts and their subway ride home, bachelors buying half a chicken and frozen mashed potatoes, small children pleading for sweets from the impulse-buy section at the checkout counter. Astor clutched their list in one sweaty fist, nails digging into their skin.

"Would you like to work on relaxing — "

"I just want to get this done," Astor said through gritted teeth. They tried to soften. "Sorry."

"Hmm." The little bot reached for their wrist. "May I check your pulse?"

"I'm okay." Astor breathed in, once, deep, out slowly. Again. Breathe security in. Breathe anxiety out. They relaxed their hand slightly, glancing down at the small curves scored red into their palm. "I'm okay."

"Excellent." PAGE smiled again.

Astor wasn't the only one who'd brought an android shopping. They were still relatively rare, consumer models too expensive for your average person, but as an accommodation they were becoming increasingly popular for the elderly, and people with real disabilities. Not like Astor, who could manage by themself if they tried harder. If PAGE had gone to someone who really needed it —

Ice cream, they thought aggressively, past the intrusion. PAGE shared eye contact and a smile with an elderly man's robotic companion as it reached for a pint of ice cream on the top shelf. "Thank you," the man said to it, and Astor thought about the uncanny valley, about robotic design, about sympathy and gentleness and programmed courtesy. Could they approximate feelings? Did they understand gratitude?

Ice cream. Diet soda, whichever one was on sale. Chicken breasts. Lemons. Ground pepper. There should probably be more vegetables on this list. A healthy diet was supposed to aid in a healthy recovery, after all, and wasn't that what this was all about? Recovering Astor to the point where they could function like a regular person again, without the need for so much damn help? Reverse their slow but consistent downward trend?

Resentment flared in their belly. It wasn't fair. None of this was fair. And there was no one they resented more than themself. They'd done so well up until now, until last year — they had been anxious, yes, but barely more than your average person.

"Do you need help?" PAGE asked pleasantly.

"Lots of negative thoughts," Astor mumbled.

"You locked the door," it said.

"I know I locked — it's not about that. It's not — we shouldn't talk about it here."

"Would you like to leave, or do you think you can finish your task?"

The old man and his robot were carefully selecting a carton of eggs. It was an older model, slower, and seconds before it happened Astor predicted the horrible snap, the mess of egg all over the floor, the apology from the bot and from the man and from the manager and the squeaking wheels of an ancient maintenance android with a broom, and suddenly it was too loud in here, too bright to endure.

"Let's just get this over with." Eggs were out of the question now, but there were still a couple at home. Shouldn't buy perishables before going out of town anyway.

THE DAY BEFORE THE TRIP, Astor finished off their eggs and washed all the dishes and sat with PAGE a long time, holding their smooth plastic and pleather hand.

"It's going to be fine," they said, again and again, hoping they could believe it.

"You have done this task before, so there is reason to believe you can do it again," PAGE agreed.

They went over the coping plan. They put PAGE in rest mode, its closed eyes not watching Astor mill about the apartment, looking for something to do. They'd already taken a shower and done all the cleaning they were likely to do, but they were too anxious to sit down at the computer or sleep through the endless hours they had to fill.

"Hey PAGE?"

PAGE's eyes widened, pixels in its face rearranging to look like a yawn while it came back online. "Yes, Astor?" it asked.

"Can we do some — some stuff?"

"You would like help using your coping skills?"

"The breathing one. With the — yeah." Astor took its outstretched hand.

PAGE's hand was warm and smooth under Astor's. The facial display was replaced with a star, growing and shrinking in time with the preset paced breathing pattern Astor had selected during initial setup. Slow, blossoming belly breath in, *expanding expanding expanding*, slower, longer belly breath out, chest still, diaphragm doing all the work. That was the hard part, not letting their breath get high in their chest, shallow, thready, dizzying, not letting it turn into hyperventilating.

"Do you feel calmer?" PAGE asked when Astor squeezed its hand to end the exercise.

"Yeah." Astor smiled, but it felt a bit weak. "Yeah, I guess so."

There were no friends to say goodbye to, but there was a local bar they liked sometimes, one where a service bot wouldn't get funny looks or stupid questions from drunk college kids. Astor couldn't decide if it was worse with the little orange Assistive Device vest off — making them look like some kind of rich showoff taking their robotic assistant everywhere — or on, inviting everyone to try and figure out what was wrong with them, or worse, offer their opinion on whether or not anything was wrong at all.

Technically nothing was wrong with them, nothing a little willpower wouldn't fix. If they could just stop moping. If they could just wise up, get back into the real world, if they could just stop doing this —

In the end they decided it would be slightly easier with the vest on. Sometimes noticeable assistive devices rendered one functionally invisible to normal people, especially since the table between the window and the bar was available, a quiet little corner to tuck themself into, away from the big speakers and the television sets broadcasting endless sporting events. They ordered a stout, tapping their nails against the side of the glass when it arrived.

"Would you like to discuss coping skills?"

"I don't want to cope right now." Astor took a long drink and then leaned back in their chair. "I want to finish this beer and maybe have another one and I want my life back. Before — "

"Would you like me to record this conversation for playback in your next session?" PAGE's voice was soft, almost intimate. A close friend offering a shoulder, in a roundabout way.

"Record it and I'll listen later and let you know." They were almost certain to delete it. But somehow the memory of their feelings was never as intense by the time they got into their sessions, and they worried their therapist didn't understand the depth of feelings simply because she'd never witnessed it.

They didn't like to talk about the incident. It seemed so stupid now — not that the man had died, of course, that was tragedy, but how much it affected Astor, slowly eroding away their sense of security, their trust in everything. They hadn't even been involved, they'd just witnessed it, going home buzzed after a few beers, walking towards the drunk guy on the subway platform —

"He just pitched right off," they whispered. This wasn't a flashback. It didn't feel like it was happening all over again — they knew where they were, what was going on around them. They knew how powerless they were to go back and stop it. "By the time I got to him the train was already barreling down — "

"There was nothing you could do," PAGE said. Astor wondered if it had an exact count for how many times it had told them that. "You are not responsible for what happened."

"If I hadn't been drinking maybe I could have gotten to him faster, gotten him away from the edge of the platform." Astor reached for the beer with a hand they were surprised to see wasn't shaking. "I didn't — I know it's not my fault. But. He fell off so easily. Just toppled right off, like — like — " There was no comparison to draw. "He didn't even make a sound. I'm not sure he knew what was happening to him. I have, uh. Dreams. Sometimes. Dreams where I'm the one who fell off the platform. Which feels really selfish, like I had to find a way to make it about me." And there were so many other dangers like that, dark and grim and horrible, things that would get you if you weren't prepared, if you weren't vigilant. Crime may have been down, but the city was still teeming with dangers.

They didn't say that part out loud. No matter how sweetly neutral its face, how non-judgmental its language, it may have had the capacity to realize how stupid that would sound. The fears hung between them, unspoken and unacknowledged.

Astor took another sip of their beer. "End recording," they said.

ASTOR RODE THE TRAIN TWICE a week, once to their individual therapy session and once to group. *Wouldn't it make more sense to be afraid of the train altogether?* But it was uncertainty they feared most, and now that uncertainty was directed at the possibility of being late, of missing their flight. The cab ride was a forty-dollar indulgence that rendered the anxiety only just manageable.

"Would you like to discuss your coping plan?" PAGE asked quietly.

"No, thank you." They'd gone over it enough.

"May I check your heart rate and respiration?"

"I'd prefer you didn't." They thought about panic, the world flaring white like an overexposed photograph, the horrible certainty that they were about to throw up and then possibly die. How would checking their respiration prevent that?

"Hmm." Responses like that always took it a little longer to process. "Please alert me if you feel symptoms of a panic attack, such as overwhelming dread, dizziness, difficulty breathing, feeling faint — "

"Yeah, got it." No point in telling PAGE they were already experiencing half of that and they hadn't even left their neighborhood.

So many things could go wrong on a plane. And so little of it was in the passenger's control. Maybe they should take the lorazepam now, give it more time to kick in. Maybe it would still last through the entire flight, it would only be a couple hours. Ninety-five percent of what a plane did was automated; the captain was mostly there to soothe the passenger's nerves.

But still, so many things could go wrong on a plane.

They pulled the bottle out of their backpack and dry-swallowed one of the pills.

At least no one can accidentally fall on the tarmac and die, they thought, and instantly cursed themself for thinking it. What a horrible thought to have. *And*, a different, sneakier voice said, *there are plenty of people down there to get hit by a taxiing airplane.*

It was going to be okay. It would all work out fine. They were possibly going to die, horribly and in pain. Plane crashes were rarely pretty. People died all the time, of all kinds of things, and there were lots of things that could go wrong on a plane —

"Stop," they whispered.

"I'm sorry, Astor, I don't understand the command," PAGE said. "Could you please rephrase — "

"No, not you — me." They looked out the window and extended a hand towards PAGE. The warm, smooth hand squeezed theirs, and they held on the rest of the way to the airport.

At the airport they paid their fare and stepped up onto the curb, PAGE a step behind, humming a two-note tone indicating readiness for instructions. But Astor's feet stuck to the sidewalk, like they'd walked on fresh asphalt. "I can't do this."

"Hmm." PAGE was silent for a moment. "Is that a fact or a feeling, Astor?"

"I know it's a feeling. It's just — it's a very strong one. Feelings influence reality even if they aren't — you know. Facts."

"Yes. Emotions are important. They contain vital messages about your situation. All emotions have a function. However, you are not bound to your feelings in the way facts bind you to the world. You are capable of surviving the flight."

"Last time I flew I didn't have to, uh. Check anyone."

"Are you concerned for my well being or worried about being alone?"

"Both?"

PAGE took an awkward half step forward and smiled at Astor. "I will be fine. In compact mode I will meet the size and weight requirements for checked luggage. It is safe for me to fly if I shut down my operating system. I am sorry I cannot compact small enough to fit in the overhead bins."

"That's fine, I have to get my suitcase up there anyway." Astor's mouth was dry. "What if someone steals you?"

"I am difficult to steal. I am quite heavy, and I will only respond to your voice and touch. Additionally, I am not a valuable commercial model." It indicated its little orange vest.

"What if you're damaged in transit?"

"I am authorized to fly in the luggage compartment of commercial airlines. And your insurance company will cover repairs not caused by mistreatment or Acts of God such as flooding, lightning strike, meteor — "

"Yeah, but — " *but I'm attached to* you, Astor did not want to say. Would a significant repair change it in some way? Would Astor perceive a difference that wasn't there, stamp their foot and cross their arms? *No! I want* my *robot!*

"Many things can go wrong," PAGE said with a nod. "But you have a lot of distress to tolerate today. Let's focus on that, rather than what could happen to me." Unbidden, PAGE reached slowly for Astor's hand and gave it one long, warm squeeze. "If you're ready, there is still plenty of time to get through security and find your gate."

That was a joke. Astor was three hours early, having misjudged both the press of impending rush hour traffic and the length of the cab ride. But there was no point in hanging around outside. Astor let go of its hand. "Come on," they said.

"I would advise you to take your prescribed medication before you begin the security screening process."

"Already done." They swallowed again in case the pill was stuck somewhere in their throat.

"I would advise you against consuming caffeinated beverages available for purchase past the security checkpoint. Would you like further advice for coping with potential distress?"

"No, I-I think I'm okay."

The woman at the luggage check eyed PAGE dispassionately as it held out its wrist for a luggage tag, printed with Astor's name and flight number. It sat delicately on the conveyor belt and tucked its limbs up, knees to its chest and arms folded neatly at its sides. It took a second to wave and smile before affecting its neutral sleep mode face. As the conveyor pulled it away, Astor watched the red bulbs blink and go dark for the first time since it had been delivered to their home.

They stood and waited, wanting to watch it as long as they could. It seemed so much smaller all folded up, smooth and fragile in its silence.

"Si — Ma — um, excuse me?" The woman indicated the line forming behind them.

"Sorry." They stepped out of the way, looking around helplessly, and finally dragged their suitcase towards the security line.

Airport security is supposed to keep an eye out for people who look nervous. This fact did not help Astor feel less nervous. Between that and their nebulous gender they were very likely to get flagged for a pat down. They waited in the security line, checking and rechecking their phone. They really should be able to take an assistive device on the plane without buying another ticket. What was the point of a support android if it couldn't follow its owner into the kind of situations where support was most needed? Their phone fell out of their shaking hands with a too-loud clatter.

The man in front of them had a small, roughly person-shaped bot rolling after him. A personal assistant. Would probably fold flat enough to fit under the seat. Astor found themself feeling bad for it, as though it could experience discomfort. Maybe they all could, and had just never found a way to express it, or saw enduring it as part of their duty.

They tapped the corner of their ID against their phone, looking again and again between the time and their digital boarding pass. They still had plenty of time. The line wasn't very long. They pulled the quart bag of toiletries out of their backpack, put it back, considered taking another pill. The first one should have been working by now. Would they even be able to tell if it was working, or were they too keyed up for medication already? It was too late to call their therapist for advice, they were almost to the front of the line —

Everything flashed white for just a second. Astor leaned heavily on the handle of their suitcase, tried to breathe slowly and deeply, but not too deeply, not enough to make them dizzy.

"Next!"

I can't do this! They looked helplessly down at their ID, the gender marked on it. The picture beside it was recognizable, but could easily pass for a binary sibling to a suspicious eye.

"Next!" someone called again.

They were holding up the line. People were getting impatient, they'd be angry soon — someone tapped Astor's shoulder and they cringed away from it with a gasp —

They dragged the suitcase forward, distantly aware that it wasn't rolling on its casters anymore but unsure how to fix it. They blinked, tried to clear their blurry vision, extended their ID to the man sitting at the podium. He took their ID and pointed at a small box on the flat surface.

"What?" They sounded ragged, desperate. They were definitely getting a pat down. Maybe they'd get pulled into one of those rooms and interrogated, like on TV shows — what if someone messed with their suitcase when they weren't looking and there was something in it —

"Scan your boarding pass," the man said again.

They held up their phone with shaking hands. Nothing happened. "Sorry," they mumbled, turning the screen back on and fumbling with their fingerprint ID. They scanned again, and the light turned green. The man stared back and forth between their state ID and their face, again and again.

Finally, after a decade of looking, he handed it back and waved them on. Now came the hard part.

Apparently, you were supposed to get your carry-on bag into a bin now? The bins weren't in a pile anymore? You had to wait for the first set of bins to move, watch your laptop and shoes drift away while you waited to launch your suitcase after it? They staggered through the shouted instructions, unbalanced and slightly dizzy. What if someone stole their laptop after it went through the scanner? What if something went wrong with their bag?

They stepped into the little booth, held their breath while it scanned them. In the other line they could see a security bot pulling aside flagged luggage, beeping fretfully at its handlers. They wondered how much of their body was visible to the old man running the machine. They wondered what he'd think of what he could see under their clothes. No one outside the industry quite knew what the tech was capable of. People argued and complained in op-eds but nothing was really done about it, and the technology had only improved since the last time Astor had flown, and hormones had changed their body significantly since that flight —

"Step out please."

They came sheepishly out of the booth, arms crossed over their chest. They'd have to get patted down, and that would be humiliating. At least that was automated too, now — their last flight had involved an awkward conversation to determine whether a male or female agent should pat them down. But the robot had no gender to worry about, and while it probably wouldn't guess at or comment on theirs, there was something about the sleek plastic and steel that made their stomach lurch.

And then —

— and then —

Everything went white again. They stumbled slightly.

"Ma'am? Ma'am! Are you alright?"

They shook their head to clear it. "Fine," they said. "Dizzy. I have panic attacks," they finished, feeling heat rise in their cheeks. Was it more embarrassing to explain it in advance or wait until they were lying on the floor gasping like a landed trout? *Lots of people have panic attacks. Having one without warning would be less convenient for them.*

The robot's handler looked annoyed. He waved it forward, a squat thing on wheels with two rollers where arms might be. Funny how even in this setting the electronics were vaguely humanoid, presumably to make them more sympathetic, somehow less terrifying. The rest of the process seemed designed to frighten you into compliance, but at least the bots looked like friends.

They didn't process the rollers moving down their body, or what noises the device made while it checked them. Their vision blurred and while they didn't fall over, they did stagger a bit when the process was finished, and the device abruptly rolled away to maul some other poor stranger. Their bag made it through the scanner alright; there was a moment of panic where they couldn't find their laptop, but it had just gotten stuck at the end of the conveyor, its bin bumping uselessly against the wall.

Overall, things were going better than they'd expected. They could find their way to a cup of tea or maybe an overpriced snack now that they'd made it to the other side, maybe even get something they could take on the plane, but first —

— first, sit down. Sit, and breathe deeply, try to time their own inhaling and exhaling, squeeze their own hand. It would be easier to calm down if PAGE was here. They knew how to do it themself — paced breathing wasn't really all that difficult — but PAGE made it so much easier, made things feel safer.

After a moment they stood up, leaning on their suitcase for support, foot wrapped around the strap of their backpack, so no one could walk away with it, and looked up at the monitor for their gate.

Suitcases thumped heavily behind the small grey curtain. The conveyor belt had already started to move, but nothing had come out yet. That thump was worrying — would they handle PAGE carefully? Astor tried not to think of it being tossed onto the belt, how many times it had been thrown about over the course of the flight.

Bags began to emerge, people pushed forward to claim them. Astor tried to wiggle past a few people to get closer to the origin point, but they couldn't quite get through and couldn't muster up the courage to talk to strangers, not even a quiet *excuse me*. They moved farther away from the front, where they could be closer to the belt, even if they'd have to wait longer for things to reach them.

Three suitcases. A taped-up red cooler. A large backpack in a digital blue camo pattern. A few more rolling bags. Astor started tapping their fingers against their thigh, restless, frightened. What if it hadn't made it on the plane? What if it was on the wrong plane? How many goddamn bags were there on this stupid flight, anyway —

There it was — curled up, on its side, looking like it was just taking a nap, and someone else reached down and touched its shoulder —

"Hey — wait — !"

There were no pleasant red LEDs in the shape of a face, but a turning hourglass, in blue. And, they noticed with embarrassment, no bright Assistive Device vest. Not PAGE, then. Astor took a shaking breath and squeezed their eyes closed. Any minute now. It would probably be okay. The worst part was behind them.

PAGE was sitting up when it finally emerged, backwards, the little orange vest disheveled. They wiggled through the crowd as quickly as they could, reaching for its shoulder and squeezing. "PAGE," they said, a relieved sigh.

PAGE's face blinked on, eyes opening. It yawned and stretched, resting animation while it came online.

"Patient Assistant, Generation E." Its voice was monotone, and different, deeper like the startup tone that followed it, and there was a second's flared panic in their stomach before they remembered that their custom settings probably just hadn't loaded yet. "Hello, Astor," it said pleasantly, in its usual sweet, clear voice. "Did you have a good flight?"

It tried to stand up, stumbling as the conveyor moved under it, falling sideways off the belt and onto the floor.

"Are you okay?" Astor asked, acutely aware of the looks their spectacle was getting. *Or maybe not,* they tried to convince themself, *maybe no one has noticed, people are less interested in you than they ever seem to be.*

"I am undamaged," it said. There was a slight scratch on the molded grey plastic of its shoulder, a smudge of some kind of grease on its face. Astor polished it off with the sleeve of their sweater. "Would you like help getting a taxi?"

Astor smiled. "Begin recording?"

PAGE blinked, then went blank.

"I did it," they said softly. "I — I got on the plane by myself, I didn't take an extra pill, I got through it, and I guess — I guess." They swallowed. "It's funny. I keep fighting the help because I thought I shouldn't need it, I should be able to do everything, I shouldn't be so — I should be okay." They swallowed, smiled weakly. "Guess I do need it. End recording."

There was a moment of stillness before PAGE tilted its head. "Hmm," it said. "Thank you, Astor."

Astor blinked down at the bot. "What for?"

"For allowing me to assist you."

"Oh. Uh." Astor ran their fingers through their hair. "You're welcome. C'mon, let's go find a cab."

PORTS OF PERCEPTIONS

◄ Izzy Wasserstein ►

CHASE HAD COME DOWN WITH both kind of viruses, and worried Hunter had been growing distant, so Hunter suggested they indulge in some PKD. While the drug kicked in, they sprawled on the mattress in Hunter's flat and exchanged. Hunter's arm-ports synched with the receivers on Chase's back and data flowed between them, which they agreed was worth the risk, despite Chase's cold and the v0x virus still being rooted out by antivi. Chase felt Hunter's concern turn to desire, and they explored each other and the PKD. Chase unclasped each of their right forearms, then swapped them. Hunter's arm, which was, or had been, or would be Chase's, moved over their bodies. They disconnected Hunter's not-quite-legal sensory enhancer and synched it with Chase's, and the rush was like data exchange but more immediate, more vivid. They swapped more parts as the sensory loop built between them. Soon Chase cried out for release, but Hunter let anticipation build, feeling Chase's rising desire, which was Hunter's. The drug worked on their flesh, their firmware, their coil of tech and limbs; it bypassed the neurons that told Chase which body was Chase's, which Hunter's, that told Hunter where Hunter ended and the Universe began; and so they grew into each other, their bodies and consciousnesses spreading from their node across the web. They were together. They were everywhere. When finally they collapsed and held one another, Chase said Hunter's name, or Hunter said Chase's, or each said their own. They lay in the tangle of each other, and Chase was Hunter and Hunter's thoughts were Chase's, and neither was sure where they ended and reality began. Hunter caught Chase's cold, or had always had it, or had always been Chase. Neither cared, if indeed they had ever been separate.

THERAPEUTIC MEMORY REVERSAL

◄ Everett Maroon ►

Z E LIFTS THE SMALL CRYSTAL cover with one finger and pushes the red knob underneath it. With zir other hand ze holds down a metal knob and turns the instrument clockwise one, two tight clicks, waiting for the trickle of memories to start flowing through zir headpiece. Ze braces zir arms on the counter, the room lights kept low because receiving memories is still painful, even if they get easier to acquire over time.

The sessions with Dad went too far. Well. Really ze doesn't know what went wrong. Ze only sometimes recalls expressions on people's faces from before the time on ship. So ze — I — sneak back here and try unlocking another piece. When the other me isn't busy living a hellishly boring existence.

Ze — I, I, I — I will merge us.

Soon.

After the scandal and the election some people said it's the memories that are gone, cauterized by the pulse of this evil, wild device. But ze wonders if maybe just the pathways are gone, and it can rebuild them, like a new bridge, or a portal. I have to try.

He only thinks he is happy.

Zir finger hovers over a green button. Sweat has lined up across my forehead and the back of my neck. I feel a Pavlovian lump in my throat. Before ze can change its mind, I turn the knob two more clicks. This is going to hurt.

MUSIC BLASTING AWAY IN MY *eardrums, lights flashing from overhead, disinfectant and spilled beer fights for presence in the air against narrow streams of confetti. She kisses me and I press into the length of her. I think we're supposed to be dancing but maybe we've done enough of that already and now all I can think of is tasting her from wherever she will let my tongue wander. People around us cheer, I think for some kind of political thing that has just happened like maybe an election of somebody we like ... and then the memory hurtles back to me ... the woman who promised an end to the witch hunts. Maybe we are no longer headliners in the long line of people labeled enemies of the state from the previous president ... yes that was it. But I feel like I could kiss her forever.*

There's a hand on my shoulder, breaking up my moment with Enez. Enez, yes.

— Congratulations, he says, this short man standing next to us, dressed in the uniform of the science ministry. He has helped come up with the evidence that we are also good citizens. He looks tired, has for months, but now there is a smile under his brown beard.

— Thank you, I say, hoping I can leave the party soon. Why do I want to leave?

— I hope this isn't too bittersweet for you, Caterna. He fidgets a little with his hands.

— I'm okay, Gryph, thank you for asking.

He means something about my father.

Enez pulls me tight and gives him a nod. She is something like a third of a meter taller than him, and while we appreciate him he never knows when to leave.

— Go celebrate, Gryph, you've earned it, she says to him, pulling a pay stick out from her bra and handing it to him. Gryph looks unsure about touching it but takes it, waves to us, and wanders over to the bar. Her long black hair closes around our faces like a privacy curtain.

— I wish I were a quid paystick, I say in her ear.

— Oh you'll do better than that before the end of the night, she tells me, just before biting lightly on my earlobe.

THEN IT IS DONE, THE memory trailing away like a dream after waking. I feel spent, sore, with stabbing sensations running down my arms all the way to zir fingerprints. Time to go back to quarters. It is exhausting cutting into his sleep cycles like this, but I want to be sewn whole again. We need our memory back.

I.

I check the hallway, the only one in this section with a broken camera. I may have had something to do with that.

Under the covers in my quarters, I release this body back to my other self.

MY BED SHEETS AND NIGHT clothes are damp, as I wake up annoyed by the beeping alarm of my caffeine machine. Goddamn facilities department is going to get another work ticket from me, because clearly it is too warm in my quarters. They took away our direct access to climate controls a couple of years ago, on the promise that they would keep our units comfortable. If I am creating a mini-lagoon in my bed most nights, clearly I am not comfortable.

I get up and shuffle into my miniscule wash room and turn on the water, impatient for it to reach temperature. I might not want to drown in my own perspiration, but I don't fancy a cold shower, either.

My intercom dings and I know from the tone who is calling me because after one night of drinking I'd programmed in stupid alerts for ten of my closest friends.

— Answer com, I say loudly, and then a portion of my wash room wall lights up with my friend Henri's face.

— Hey Ferrick, oh my God man, don't answer when you're still naked! How many times I gotta tell you that?

The grimace on his face is priceless.

— How many times I gotta tell you not to call so early, I say through toothbrush foam. I spit the paste and water mixture onto the mirror where his face is. For good measure, I wink. He automatically wipes at his face and then grumbles at me.

— Okay, fine. I just wanted to remind you to bring your shin guards to work. Cup play starts tonight.

Like I would forget the tournament.

— Thank you, Henri. I will be there tonight and I will cover your ass.

— Please, Ferr, I will cover yours. Asshole.

We are both power forwards, and best friends.

— See you at lunch, I say, walking to my dresser. Henri's face jumps from the wash room to my quarters where presumably he has a much better view of all of me. He puts one hand over his eyes like he's trying to block out the sun. His loss.

— For Christ's sake, get dressed, man. Bye.

His image disappears with a quiet click. He didn't even give me time to wag my business at him.

I am lucky enough to have a room close to where I work, because some of us are twenty floors and four sections away from our duty stations. The ship is enormous, too large to ever dock anywhere. It contains roughly nine percent of Earth's population before we disembarked the planet. To service all of us we rely on self-sufficient food production, solar energy, and near-constant supply shuttles from other, smaller vessels. I'm on the team that manages those rendezvous maneuvers. Because if we get hit in deep space, it will be a catastrophe. My work team may have higher stress levels than most, but we get very short commutes.

Jhim, the crew chief, greets me as I hold up my work pass to the engineering doors, and then I am through them into the large bay.

— Good morning, Ferrick, he says and then he turns back to his work. He used to be friendlier but work has been intense lately as we've started procedures for entering deep space. In a few months we will exit the only solar system humans have ever known. We don't really know what we will find in interstellar space, just pretty good guesses.

I head up to my desk and turn on the treadmill. I like to walk as I work, it keeps my brain engaged somehow, and it helps minimize the power needed to my computer since the machine is hooked up to our power grid. Overnight I've received forty messages because the other "hemisphere" of the ship is on a reverse shift from us. Too much of my work is about responding to people I've never met in person.

— How could you, begins one message when suddenly I have some weird non-memory of a man asking me the very same question. I shake it off, blaming Henri for interrupting me before I got my caffeine drink this morning. But the snippet of a sentence bugs me. It feels like déjà vu.

— Ferrick, says one of my teammates as she taps me on the arm, — come on, end of shift.

— What? I look at Numes, my coworker. She's giving me a smile but she looks worried. She's a brilliant mathematician and she is tiny enough to fit in my suitcase. She also doesn't get concerned easily.

The lights blink out one by one around our unit; automatic shutoffs to conserve energy. They turn off at the end of a shift, and whenever we are out of solar range for more than a few days.

— Sure, right, I say, grabbing my pack. Where did the day go? I want to look at my computer screen to see what I accomplished because for some reason I can't recall what I've done today. I feel pain in my throat, must be coming down with something.

Numes waits for me, lingers, and dusts off her forearms looking for something to do in the six seconds it takes me to leave my desk. She's always been really nice to me.

I look around and we are the last two people in the bay. If I strain I can visualize what happened today but it feels far away. I don't like thinking about it, so I appreciate it when Numes distracts me again.

— What's going on for you tonight, she asks as we head into the traffic hall.

— It's the first night of Cup play, I say, rather automatically. I do love playing. I smile a little, maybe I can break through this sudden funk.

— Oh, that's wonderful, she says, looking relieved. — Well, have a great time, try to cover Henri's ass.

— I'll tell him you said that, I shout at her as she walks away. I trot off to the stadium. Four decks down, two sections leeward. If I use the stairs I can get warmed up.

Henri is pacing near the front doors when I show up.

— What the hell man, where have you been?

— It's not even started yet, I say. I'm panting from running the whole way.

Henri has been swearing too, and he wipes it from his bald head with a small towel. Henri sweats a lot when he's agitated, so I guess he's agitated.

— You dissed me for lunch, Ferr.

— I'm sorry. I just got tied up at work.

HOW COULD YOU

— Look, I know the shit you do is important, but so is this because like, what the hell else do we have out here? I was only asking for twenty minutes of your time. We could have talked strategy for tonight. He looks at me and drops his arms like he is giving up on me.

— I'm really sorry, Henri.

I don't know what else to say. I feel nauseated.

— Okay, okay, well come inside and we'll talk it over with you quickly during the shootaround. He seems somewhere between annoyed and concerned.

He puts his arm across my shoulders, leading me into the stadium. Bright lights mounted around the top of the interior dome do a great job of imitating actual sunlight. Something about the light in here always makes me feel good. But I have a frightening sensation that I'm not right, somehow.

I watch the players on the field, practicing passing with each other and taking kicks at the nets on either end of the field. Behind them on the scoreboard the tallies blink with each tap of a player's foot, since the ball knows which player came into contact with it last. My great-great-grandmother had been one of the last referees in the sport before the computerized balls and nets made refereeing obsolete. I try to recall her name as I make my way down the stadium steps to the grass.

— Hey you're late, Ferrick, says the coach, a burly man named Arlo who is something like an overgrown koala, especially around the ears.

— Sorry, coach, I say, fumbling in my bag for my uniform and cleats. Coach A will probably complain if I head to the locker room to get changed, so I trot to the sideline and get dressed as fast as I can. I take a quick swig of water next to the player's bench, trying to push the pain out of my throat, before running out to the field. Maybe playing will help me feel more normal.

IT'S NOT NORMAL

But instead my stomach hurts. I don't even know what I ate for lunch, or if I had lunch, or where my day went. I try to hear the directions from Henri and my other teammates as we practice our shot set up. I was the top scorer in the league last season. Now I'm having trouble finding my feet.

In an instant I face plant into the turf; in the next I taste copper and swallow a tooth. Henri, Arlo, and a few other players race over to me.

NOT NORMAL

— Christ, are you okay, man? asks, Henri, looking deep into my eyes. He waves his finger in front of my face and asks me to follow it. Strangely, I feel like crying but I can't quite place my feelings, it's like the edge of space reaching out to me, it wants to swallow me into its vacuum and I know I'll burst, but I feel mesmerized, curious. What comes after I explode into airlessness? What is beyond the black holes we've navigated around as we look for a habitable planet?

I'm in shock. This is what shock is, being stuck. Say something, reassure them.

Arlo gets in my face, too. Now all I can see are extreme close ups of Henri, Coach A, and the blinding sun-equivalent lights. Almost like they're projected on the walls of my quarters.

BUT I AM NORMAL

— I think he's stunned, says the coach to Arlo.

— He must be concussed.

I open my mouth to speak, finally, but globs of black blood come out instead. No more annoying lights. Everything goes dark.

IT IS NOT ACCUSTOMED TO speaking up to them, but the vote is over so ze feels brave. She. She feels brave. She walks in, sees the backs of them, they're watching the screen with the final returns, their arms around each other in quiet defeat, as they ignore the disappointed people who had gathered here to celebrate another term.

Actually, it's probably not a good time to talk to them, but who knows, maybe it's perfect because they'll already be numb to whatever other news comes their way that they'll hate. And they will hate this.

Her mother is the first to turn around. The doctor, the other doctor, as has been mentioned in so many political advertisements for her father's campaign. Because who can argue against two terrifically brilliant, beautifully manicured people who just want to help the real citizens who deserve so many great things? It's kind of them to help people who get in their own way, after all.

Her mother looks surprised to see her. Me. To see me. It's me, I'm her, but not her, not to them, anyway.

It is so confusing.

I look for a smile, even a softening of her stance. We have fought so much. She has scarcely turned around before he pivots on his heel toward me, and then his frown lines deepen. This was a bad idea. I should go. So many people are here, so hurt and angry, angry at me for being the trans freak that sullied their good name, made them look like fools in the tabloids. I had never placed myself in the bull's eye of his politics until just this moment, a heartbeat too late for reckoning.

I just wanted to have one last moment with them. I don't even know why. This is stupid.

— How dare you show up here, he says. His voice sounds like a growl.

— I'm sorry the election didn't go your way, I say.

— Are you? asks my mother. Every silver hair is in place. I can never get my hair to behave, but she is all about having every atom obey her will.

— Yes. I know what this meant to you.

Does it matter that I am happy with the outcome? I suppose it does matter to them.

— I don't want any more of your lies, says my father, waving me off. His pallor is gray, with bits of duskiness under his cheekbones. Why does he want to be leader anyway? It's clearly killing him.

— I'll go, I say. This isn't the goodbye I envisioned. But ze — I — have always been wrong about my parents.

He gives a signal to his security team, and although I protest, they wrap around me like tenacious vines and I can't break away. I am wrong to think that my parents care even a little bit about me. I am dead wrong.

I WAKE UP IN THE dark room, the computer screen glowing in front of me, revealing the date of memories I've accessed this time: Election night, seven years ago. *Oh why did the computer pick that one,* I wonder, because it should know I'm not ready for that. Of course, it was made to obliterate memory, not recover it. It was supposed to make us our best selves, free us from the memories holding us back. We never asked my father if our pain was foundational or necessary.

I suppose ze is tired of not knowing. I crave cohesion. The pain is horrible, breaking down neural walls placed there artificially. Realizing slowly that I am now multiple people. Working through savagery when I should have been celebrating my own independence.

The tears roll down my cheeks, and she — I, damn it — probe the hole formed from my missing tooth. It took hours for Ferrick's friends to leave me alone. I reassured them maybe a hundred times that I wasn't going to pass out again, and I begged them not to take me to the infirmary. I have not wandered into Ferrick's life this much before but I'm getting closer — more daring, maybe — to integration.

I look at today's date on the screen, trying to ground myself. It's time to sneak back to my quarters. I am me. I am she. I am once again back to stealth until I can know enough of who I am from this unseen archive of memory to tell everyone again. I think Ferrick senses I am here. I want his bravado even if I will end him as he knows himself. I suppose I can find it ironic that I know how to rebuild the decrepit memory therapy tool because my father invented it.

But it's all a bit much, even for me, even or especially after all of this.

I close my eyes, enjoying the quiet. Not much on this ship is quiet.

I breathe in, hold it for seven beats, exhale for eight. I exit the memory program and remove the data stick and hide it under a floor panel. As I learn more of myself, I feel the absence of Enez more. Emotions crystallize like a ghost becoming corporeal. It was a brutal time, and it will be a long while before I restore the specific memories of losing her, but for now I have enough remade that I can remember our love for each other.

— Ferrick, dude, what are you doing in here?

It's Henri.

I whirl around in the chair and see him standing in the doorway, the hallway light flooding into the tiny room that is basically an abandoned janitor's closet.

I try to come up with an excuse, but he is already moving to the computer desk and examining it.

— What the fuck is this thing?

— It's nothing, it's private. I'm not coming up with anything good, and now my heart thuds in my chest, like even my heartbeat is a discovered secret.

— I've never seen anything like this since … holy shit, did you recreate Dr. Crucet's neural manipulator? *Ferrick*?

He looks scared. My father did not leave power quietly and anything reminiscent of him would scare most of the people on this ship.

— How did you find me? I ask. It's a perfectly reasonable question, I guess.

— You left your comm link on, he says, still staring at the machine. — You were concussed and I wanted to check on you. He looks again at the instrument panel I've jury rigged together.

— This looks just like the machine in the old news stories. What the hell are you doing?

— It's a long story, and I'm too tired to explain.

— You know what kind of damage this torture device causes?

— I'm familiar with it, yes.

He stares at me, sizing me up maybe, or looking at me like I'm some imposter of myself. I am suspect of something now. How could I not be?

— How the hell could you recreate this? Why?

He's sweating and I can smell his electrolyte loss. It's not good.

— I told you, I'm tired.

— I have to report this, Ferr.

— No!

Now I am in hyperdrive, trying to find some way to get him to change his mind.

I go with the truth. I'm not a good liar, even if I am pretty solid at hiding things. I just can't affirmatively misrepresent things.

— I'm trying to restore my own memory.

This is a big admission — we all had to go through extensive psychological testing before being allowed on ship and off the planet. In my defense I didn't know my own history when I applied for the position. And nobody else on board does, either.

— What do you mean, restore? You're not — you can't be one of his victims.

— Oh? Why not?

— Because … you're so normal, a regular guy.

— Well, I'm not, really. But I'm working on becoming my own normal.

I don't tell him Ferrick is some empty personality created in the image of my father, who he wanted me to be. Ferrick's not an awful person. The problem is he's not me.

— Ferrick, you could get kicked off the ship for this.

I don't really know what that would mean. Scut work on a transport, maybe. A bed in an increasingly reliable but still unstable, long-term hibernation system. A 4-person mining ship in a converted shuttle, because the mining fleet has been lost for decades, since the conflict that drove us from Earth. We can't really afford to lose any more people.

— I know, but Henri, I need to do this. Can you try and understand before you inform on me? I'm just repairing my own damage.

And let me tell you, it sucks, so give me a break.

He sighs, sounding somewhere between afraid and angry. I can't read anyone anymore. But I have recently figured out that I was in the midst of transitioning. This must be why my father erased so much of my memory, why he did it so crudely and not in his careful, seamless way, because he was running out of time as leader. He knew the new government would shut his entire program down. He had to correct his son before she could live openly as a woman.

I'm sitting here devastated, while my jaw aches and the electrical stimulation still burns up and down my spine, and I'm wondering what I need to do to Henri to shut him up so I can have more time with myself.

— What are the memories like? What did he erase?

— They're painful for the most part. And there's nothing I can do about them except sit with them. All of these people are gone now.

We both know Earth was lost six years ago now. Nothing lives there. Every scan we've run comes back with the same sad result.

I look at him, the tiniest bit of my body language shifts, feels more feminine, more at peace. He doesn't notice the change, but I do.

— Henri, for better or for worse all we have is each other now, and the Cup, and the journey. I will be much more productive and whole if you let me have this. I'm a very good engineer and the ship needs me. And we are friends.

He nods. He's parsing through a lot of information — for him. I of course am wading through one thousand times as much, and it is all way more personal for me. He's considering what to tell the quartermaster and I am considering how to continue being me despite who I increasingly reveal to be a conflicted, terrorized person. So shit if I can do it, so can Henri. But I don't tell him any of this. I know I am thirty steps ahead of him and what he knows about me.

I just wait.

— We are friends. You're my best friend, Ferrick.

— And you are mine, Henri.

— It can get lonely out here.

— It can, yes.

We are sharing more than words, I presume. I fight dwelling in a thought of Henri waking alone in the middle of the night, sad, with an alienating erection, filled with worry about the day ahead. Or maybe that's only my experience.

— Please tell me what is going on with you. I might surprise you by being awesome about it.

Tears cut down my face; I am not ready for having such long-restrained emotions come out of me. For half a minute, I gasp for breath and then I emerge from the panic and manage to breathe out my last bit of resistance.

— I'm very scared to tell you, so if I tell you, you need to be more than awesome.

— I'm here, man.

Man. Ugh.

I feel a wave of self-loathing and yet I string together all the assembled memories, the full story. The whole while Henri sits on the floor, looking at various parts of me and the small room. Sometimes he nods, sometimes he mutters frail words to encourage me to keep talking. I run out of words and then tell him that's all I know, for now.

I wait for a reaction. I wait for a couple of minutes while he thinks everything over, I suppose.

— We should go back to bed, he says. I nod and stand up, fighting a burst of vertigo.

— Come on, I'll walk you back, he says.

— Are you okay? I ask.

— I'm okay. I don't know what you're going though. I'm here for you and I'll help you.

He takes my hand and holds it and pulls me out of the room. It's a gesture I don't directly remember having the entire time on this ship. It reminds me of something, but I can't place it. I should probably brace myself for having more of that feeling.

I shut the closet door behind me and hear the lock fail. Now I have another worry, but I make a mental note to come back after he disappears around the curve from my quarters. I have to fix it. I have to fix it. And me. But at long last I think I am on my way.

THE ART OF QUILTING

◄ Matthias Klein ►

V IN TOOK UP QUILTING AGAIN on Venus.
Ne had not intended to, but the swirling blue of the fabric at the stand in the indoor public market drew nem. It was dark, but not so dark a person couldn't tell it was blue, the uneven hue lighter in some places. It looked like serenity. It looked like impotence. People browsing the bolts passed it by, and it was that more than anything that made Vin look twice. The price was reduced. No one wanted boring fabric.

Vin bought half a yard, a small bag of scraps, some thread. Back in nir apartment ne spread it all out on the desk. Ne hadn't done any sewing in years. It reminded nem too much of nir mother. But Vin had a sliver of inspiration and a few hours before ne had to be at work, and the fabric felt right. While ne worked the world fell away. All of them — Venus, where ne now lived; Earth, the place Vin could not feel homesick for; and reality, which could not intrude here in nir own mind.

Strangely, Vin found the sewing — by hand, as ne had no machine — compelling, and went back to it day after day until ne had completed a quilt block. It was crude, imperfect, and incorrect. Vin had originally set out to sew Cepheus only to end up with a star cluster that resembled nothing ne recognized. Frustrated, ne tossed it in the bin and went to work.

"Your parents were here," said Jake, nir roommate, when he finally got up the next morning. It was casual enough, but Vin was not sure where ne was for a moment.

"What?" ne asked, unable to say anything more complicated. The entire room seemed to buzz, a quality Jake didn't seem to notice. He shot Vin a half-grin as he heated an instant breakfast sandwich.

"You leave Earth without telling them?" he asked. "They seemed really worried."

Vin shook nir head. Ne hadn't told them ne was going to Venus. They weren't supposed to find nem here. They weren't supposed to follow. When Vin had moved to Canada and nir parents had tracked nem down, ne had figured Venus would be far enough to escape their concern.

"You know how parents are," said Vin at last, entire body wanting to shout at Jake, hands itching to choke the half-grin off his face. He thought it was funny. The overprotective parents checking in on their precious child. So disgustingly normal. But Vin couldn't bring nemself to say anything even remotely damning about nir parents, not even after all these years of trying to separate nemself from them.

They had wired their programming into Vin so tightly that ne couldn't even confide in the one friend ne had been able to make since college. Say nothing negative. Why would you want to spread lies about people who cared about you?

"Yeah. My mom hates it if I don't call once a month." Jake took a bite of breakfast sandwich. "I think she'd know if I died."

"Yeah," said Vin. "I have to go in early today, see you around."

Ne left and went to the indoor public market, not wanting to talk to Jake any more. It was too uncomfortable. Ne wandered around, feeling dazed, staring at the morning shoppers and the various stalls. Vin had difficulty focusing, suddenly snapping to and realizing ne had been holding a tiny carved piece of stone.

"I said would you like that?"

Vin blinked, looked up at the salewoman. Down at the stone, shaped to look like Venus, flat-backed like a button. The woman appeared to hand carve the pieces from where she sat in her little stall. Vin had no idea how long ne had been standing there, holding the piece, but ne didn't feel ne could just set in down and leave.

"Uh, yes," ne said, and bought the piece, and went to work early after all. Nir data entry shift was long, torturous. Ne half expected nir parents to walk in, to somehow get past the clearance codes and show up in the expanse of cubicles, smiles on their faces, arms wide. In front of the entire office, was Vin supposed to shy away from their embraces? That would only make nem look bad.

But nir parents did not appear. Relieved, Vin hurried home, wanting to sleep, wanting to wake up refreshed, this entire day nothing but an unhappy memory. Ne stepped off the transport shuttle and froze.

Ne couldn't mistake them if ne tried. Their gaits, their height, their clothing. Their grateful, smiling faces as they spoke to nir landlord. Vin knew instantly what was happening. The landlord would take nir parents up to the apartment, would scan his hand and let them in. Loving, concerned parents. Why wouldn't anyone want to help reconnect a family?

Vin nearly vomited onto the street. Nir blood pounded so hard in nir veins ne couldn't hear anything but fear. Vin could not go home. And at any moment nir landlord would return, would try to convince nem to go talk to nir parents. Hear them out. Reconcile.

When Vin realized ne had managed to get back on the transport ne was already halfway to downtown and shaking. The other people on the shuttle had left a gap around nem, a bubble of nothing. Like life before Venus. Such a small, profound distance. Vin wanted to flee. Ne swallowed back stomach acid and got off at the first stop, entered the first building ne recognized, the bar Jake worked at.

"How was work?" asked Jake, but when Vin shook nir head he simply brought nir usual boilermaker and left nem alone. Vin drank, checked nir pockets. Phone, packet of soy sauce from dinner, carved stone hemisphere of Venus. It was real Venus stone, too. Vin turned it over in nir fingers.

Ne didn't want to leave. Not yet. Not ever. Ne was just building a life, a real existence here. No rules, no frames, no requirements. The world was not what Vin was raised to believe it was, and ne didn't want to live in that other place, that unquestioning, dutiful place where ne had no power, no agency, no self.

Vin had thought Venus was far enough away.

"Look," said Jake, back again with another drink before Vin had even bothered to ask, "If you're worried about your parents, I didn't tell them anything."

"Thanks," said Vin, hoping ne didn't sound too grateful. When ne drank the second boilermaker Jake returned with only a beer.

"I figured you didn't get along when they called you Samantha."

Vin tried to nod, tried to sip this drink. The urge to get blinding drunk and just pass out somewhere was strong, but the fear of nir parents finding out helped nem hold back. The fact that Jake had formed a less than perfect opinion of them was worrisome, but Vin didn't know what to do about it. Vin didn't want to do anything about it.

"They didn't seem too happy with me, either," he said, wiping the bar with a rag and grinning. "Got the impression they thought we were 'living in sin.' I mentioned my boyfriend."

"That wouldn't help," said Vin before ne could stop nemself. Nir parents thought the only things that happened in the world were the things they decided were going to happen, and they'd decided long ago that all manner of things they disapproved of would befall Vin, to prove them right, to turn nem back. Back to Earth. Back to the house where all nir siblings still lived. Back to their prison.

Jake looked like he wanted to respond, but there were other customers at the bar needing attention. The waves of guilt from speaking, even where nir parents could never hear, were too much. Vin drank the last beer, paid with nir phone, and rode the transport shuttles aimlessly for hours until ne was certain nir parents had left for the night.

The apartment was dark. Vin turned on all the lights, concerned anyone outside would know ne was there, worried ne wouldn't see anyone lurking in the place until it was too late. Ne imagined they had touched everything. Ne knew they had touched something; nir room was off, almost imperceptibly off. But some items were definitely not where ne had left them.

Vin panicked.

If they had been here twice, they would be back. Vin hadn't bothered to look up the particulars of Venus laws, but ne suspected if there was a way to get nem declared mentally incompetent, nir parents were already in the process of doing it. Like they had tried in Canada. They wouldn't make so many mistakes about it this time.

Vin tore every bag ne had out of the closet and stuffed them. Nir eyes tore across the room, looking for anything ne might have missed, not wanting to make too much of a mess for Jake. On impulse ne shoved all the fabric scraps in one of the bags, even dug the block out of the bin. Vin didn't want nir parents getting it if they came back.

Ne left a note that said only, "Sorry."

THERE WERE CURRENTLY EIGHT ORBITAL colonies around Mars, all tasked with developing the planet's surface for a larger colony. Vin bought a ticket to Mars Satellite Seven, the first flight out from Venus, and from there a smaller, more rickety flight to Mars Satellite Two. Despite the days of travel, the fear had not faded much, so Vin went through the detectors, the pat downs, and took another flight to Mars Satellite Five. From there ne withdrew a large amount of money, nearly draining nir account, and bought a ticket to Mars Satellite Three.

Vin did not board. Ne rented the cheapest room ne could find on Mars Satellite Five, applied to several jobs, and slept for two days. When ne had recovered, ne interviewed for a janitorial position repairing and cleaning anything the bots couldn't service and was hired.

The next few months were hard. They always were, Vin was beginning to find, as this was nir third time running away as Jake had put it. Ne felt like shit about leaving like that and regularly thought about contacting him on social media, apologizing, but ne had no clue what to say. Ne watched his updates, saw that his boyfriend had moved in.

Jake would be fine.

At the six month mark, ne was finally relaxing a little. Ne hoped that nir parents had run out of vacation time trying to track nem down on Mars Satellite Three and had to return to Earth. By the time they could get back and pick up the hunt again, they'd be forced to scour the entire orbital colony and all space flights from it for months. Vin almost felt safe.

Ne unpacked the last of the bags and found the quilt block from Venus. At some point during the various space flights, ne must have sewn the carved piece of stone to it. As Vin stared at it now in the weak, yellow-hued light of nir tiny room, it almost looked beautiful. If ne looked at it just right, it was nearly art. Ne hung it on the wall, oddly proud. This, this was a memento from Venus, from escape. This was a declaration of Vin's stubbornness. This was a piece of defiance, a piece of originality, that ne could display.

Vin kept to nemself the long weeks. The loneliness was crushing, but the bubble of solitude was comforting. There was no one to question anything Vin did. Ne could simply live.

There wasn't much to do on the satellite, unsurprising considering the bulk of its residents were on the Mars surface for twelve to eighteen hours at a time, working on colony development. As a consequence there were mostly bars in the way of recreation. Vin figured out early on which had the best specials and only went to those when ne wanted to get good and drunk, otherwise saving nir wages. If ne needed to run again, ne needed the funds.

Generally ne spent nir free time reading books from the database library, although occasionally Vin would wander to the satellite's views, watching the rusty planet below. Vin didn't get homesick, not really, not when there was nothing to miss, but there was something disappointing in seeing Mars circling below nem, even with the lush green expanses growing more and more visible from space every day.

Ne wandered all three of the tiny shopping strips, looking for more fabric, more thread. After hanging the quilt block, ne wanted to expand. But the one shop that appeared to sell odds and ends only received shipments irregularly, and then only of random items. Vin picked up black thread first, a small collection of tiny Martian pebbles, until finally fabric became available. Ne bought a little of each of the two bolts, one blue and purple, one the same red-brown shade as the planet below. If Vin had been trying to find a combination that could better capture that sense of isolation, ne would have failed.

This block was bigger than the last, something Vin really poured nemself into in nir spare time. It was beginning to feel good, truly good, to take this thing — Vin could not call it skill — nir mother had taught nem and turn it into something less restraining, less feminine. In Vin's hands the fabric and thread became art, not homemaking, the pattern flowed straight from nir mind, not something preconfigured and valued for its conformity. Red-brown slivers spiraled out from the center of the block, losing themselves in purple and blue space. Tiny Martian pebbles dotted it all like a swarm of debris, and Vin used more of the silver thread to stitch tiny stars into the background.

Vin was putting the finishing touches into it when the chime at the door caused nem to look up. Ne had kept the curtains on the window to the corridor open, had been leaving them that way as a small step toward teaching nemself to handle normal life again. Ne had enjoyed the view out the apartment window on Venus, and while the corridor of a satellite colony was boring, Vin had thought it a step in the right direction.

Vin had been wrong.

Nir heart nearly dropped out when nir brother leaned over, peered through the window, caught sight of nem. Vin's first instinct was to hide, to avoid the confrontation, to wait him out until he got bored with waiting and left. That had worked back on Venus, that had worked back in Canada.

That would not work now. Paul had spotted nem, and there was no place to hide but the tiny bathroom. Vin was stuck. The extra Martian pebbles tumbled out of nir hands and over the desk. Ne tried to look busy picking them all up one by one, tried to ignore him as nir hands shook and mind warred with itself, trying at once to spur nem to panic-fueled action and to shut down completely. A maze of thought retreating into its shell.

"Samantha," he said. "Samantha. Let me in."

Vin tried to say no, managed to shake nir head.

"Please," he said, more command than anything. Vin could hear him trying the handle, heard the door beep as it refused to let him in. Ne hoped he wasn't smart enough to have nir rental agency unlock the door for him, but if he did leave for that, Vin would be ready. Mentally ne ran over where nir bags were, what was most important to take, to leave.

Maybe if ne dealt with him directly he would go anyway. Vin turned, glared.

"What do you want?" ne asked. Paul's face was screwed up in disapproval and worry.

"We love you," he said. "You can come home any time. You don't have to live like this."

Vin wanted to laugh. Ne was laughing inside, that twisted, pain-laced laugh that sometimes sprang up out of nowhere when ne was alone. But ne had heard this all before, different versions, same thing. A little distance from a parental house could reveal a lot.

Once, after ne had decided to stay in Canada after college, after letting nir parents down again and again, the one brother ne'd still talked to admitted something that made Vin upset. Their parents had been arguing about Vin's fate, about what to do, and the brother had refused to take sides. He'd been tossed out for a week, had walked himself miles to a place to stay, and eventually had to return after running out of money. Their parents graciously took him back, in the end.

Vin didn't speak to that brother much after that. He talked reconciliation too much.

"You have rights," said Paul, another brother before nem now making impassioned pleas. "You don't have to let him do this to you."

"What?" asked Vin, confused. Paul fixed nem with that look an adult gives a disobedient child, one lying to a parent's face.

"You *know*, Samantha. That 'roommate'. He can't keep you here against your will. We know about him. You can come home. Anytime."

Vin understood. Nir parents had been paranoid about nir virginity for years; nir mother especially had given Vin lecture after lecture of how men were only after one thing, and that thing was possession. As though Vin's mother wasn't. As though there was any threat that could ever keep Vin from seeking freedom when ne had set sights on it.

Vin swallowed. The outrageousness of Paul's statement wasn't what frightened nem. It was that ne could remember a time when ne would have believed nem, would have believed it all. Even knowing Jake hadn't suggested ne come here. Somehow, some way, Jake would have manipulated, would have gotten Vin to believe it was nir own idea, and only nir family was there to tease out the lie, to uncover the truth. To save nem.

"Jake's back on Venus. He didn't have anything to do with me moving," said Vin before catching nemself. Ne had to not engage. "Go away."

"That's what he wants you to think," said Paul, so passionate, nearly crying. "Oh, Samantha. We love you. We all love you."

Vin turned away. Ne went back to the quilt, began putting away all the supplies, tried to ignore Paul as he continued to beg for nem to go with him, just out for a bite to eat, only that. He cried. Vin tried to muster the courage to ping the colony police system, but couldn't bring nemself to. Ne had seen what the landlord had done back on Venus. Ne had no trust left.

When he finally left Vin pulled the curtains and packed. Then ne planned out how to get a flight down to the developing Mars colony, back up to one of the other orbital colonies, and away.

VIN'S MOTHER HAD CONVINCED NEM nir first boyfriend had been cheating on nem. It was late college, and Vin sometimes wondered why nir parents had allowed nem to live so far away from them. They must have thought their sway would always hold. It did, for a while. Vin's mother never liked nir boyfriend; he didn't agree with enough of her life philosophies. By the end of spring break Vin completely agreed that he'd spent the entire week with some ex back in his hometown.

Ne broke up with him. Nir mother had won.

Vin was certain nir mother would hate this one, too. Tomas was decently attractive, never intended to reproduce, and completely content to use Vin's name and pronouns. Farther from Earth, Vin had begun to notice, people were less likely to think there was a need to cling to old, unnecessary patterns. Vin liked this, this ability to hook up with anyone of any gender, any race, any background. It was immensely freeing.

"Not Vincent?" Tomas had asked when they had first introduced themselves.

"Used to be. I liked Vin better."

Tomas had nodded and not pressed any further. Vin had jumped at the first opportunity to move in with him. There was no better way to save money, and Vin had learned that money could buy relief, at least the momentary variety.

"What's that?" he asked one night as they were watching reports of strikes from the next Moon colony over. Vin had pulled out the quilt blocks again and was stitching Venus and Mars together.

"Quilting." Vin paused, dared to open up a little. This was safe enough. "My mother taught me."

"Didn't think you'd be into that," he said, passing nem another can of beer.

"She wanted me to make a bunch of them for her grandkids," said Vin, emboldened by the previous beers, by Tomas' presence. He was nir longest relationship to date, and nir parents had not tracked nem down in months. Perhaps they weren't thinking to look so close to home, perhaps they didn't imagine Vin would be so stupid as to go to the Moon, right in their backyard.

Tomas laughed.

"Yeah, sure," he said. "Didn't realize your family was that old fashioned."

"You have no idea," said Vin. Ne felt that familiar tingle of worry that blossomed whenever ne was about to speak about family. Don't spread lies. Vin pushed past it.

"Religious?" asked Tomas. He didn't sound like he cared too much.

"Not really," said Vin. Nir parents had wielded heaven and hell, sins, and all the various forms of honor and obey they could get their hands on, but ultimately it was never to any religion more specific than their own desires. "But they had plans. I was — they think I'm their only daughter."

"Don't you have ten other brothers then?"

"Three. They all live at home, no relationships." No one would have them. No one but nir parents. Vin did not want to think about just what would happen should ne ever return to that house. Never.

Tomas laughed, changed the channel.

"Bet the reunions are awkward."

"I'm estranged," said Vin. Ne gulped the beer and rushed on before the courage was gone. "They don't accept me. If they ever show up here, for fuck's sake, don't let them in."

"Okay," said Tomas, but he was eyeing nem now. "Must have been some coming-out argument."

"I never came out," said Vin. "It was enough to tell them I wasn't planning on having kids. My father cried. My mother blamed me for it and brought it up every time we talked. When I decided to take a break from speaking to her, they showed up. They've been following me around this whole damn solar system, trying to force me back."

The instant that was off nir chest, the relief faded. Vin had spoken and couldn't take it back. Nir psyche remembered just how terrible a crime that was. Ne began to pack up nir sewing, hoped Tomas had drank enough to not really remember tomorrow what ne had said.

"That sucks," he said, and drank.

The confession plagued Vin the next few days, flashbacks to nir previous life stalking nem and pouncing when ne least expected it. When ne made a call at work the image of nir mother interrupting nem as a teen and talking over nem intruded, and ne had to end the call early. Nir mother had routinely done that, then lectured Vin afterward about everything ne had said wrong, never how to make it right. It had taken Vin years to be able to make calls.

Riding back home, ne remembered the GPS, the strict schedule. Watching porn, ne remembered the virginity lectures, remembered too the withholding of contraception. By the end of the week Vin knew ne had to do something to settle nemself, and the quilt sprang to mind. Ne turned back around and went to the public indoor market.

Vin knew what ne was looking for now. Fabric that sang of emotion, thread that was a solid, binding color, and an embellishment, preferably something from the Moon itself. Looking back on the other quilt blocks, Vin had found ne very much liked that addition, as though ne had claimed the place for nemself, even though ne had to leave. There was a bit of Venus, a bit of Mars, that nir parents couldn't make nem leave behind.

Ne settled on Moon beads, fairly popular with tourists so not cheap, but they were exactly what Vin wanted. Made from Moon rock, the holes would allow nem to more easily sew them to the quilt block. The blues ne selected here were cool and grey, like a pause, like a held breath. After ne returned to the apartment and replied to Tomas' message that he'd gone out with friends, ne spread out nir supplies and began. This block was long, thin, delicate almost. Vin worked until Tomas staggered back in, then stayed up an additional hour after that.

Vin went to it the next day too, liking the task, picturing how it would look sewn beneath the Venus and Mars blocks. Enough of these and ne really would have a large quilt. Tomas made coffee, turned the lights low, and watched nem work.

"You should talk to them," he said, and Vin's stomach dropped out. An image of Paul came to mind, talking, talking, talking...

Vin realized ne was sitting, hands shaking. Nir vision speckled slightly. Ne reminded nemself nir parents weren't here, that ne could trust Tomas.

"They're probably worried. Might be good for you too."

"They don't talk," said Vin. Ne felt sick. There was no way to explain this to anyone, no way to say that nir parents accepted nothing short of their predetermined reality and have it make sense. Tomas had a good relationship with his fathers; they lived twenty minutes away and regularly had a meal together.

"My parents would be worried."

"Your parents love you." Vin felt the panic rise the more ne spoke. Tomas frowned.

"Yours do too," he said, but Vin couldn't sit here listening to this. Ne grabbed nir phone and left.

From the local park ne could see Earth clearly, hanging in the sky, rotating too slowly to notice. Vin stared for what seemed like forever, mind turning almost as slow as nir home planet. Something within nem knew. Vin had spent too long here.

Any day, any hour, they could be coming. Tomas would let them in. Vin waited for him to leave before packing.

THE HAPPINESS SURPRISED VIN. IT was as though all of humanity had decided this far from Earth there was no need to be so stuffy. Pluto was at once a strange combination of scientific research and tourism, pocket sites dotting the icy expanse around the main colony. Teams of scientists and teams of trekkers would regularly leave the protective domes together, at least until their paths split, and interestingly they mingled in the bars as well.

Vin snagged a job as a research assistant somehow, in part because few qualified people came this far out into the solar system. Nir skills with repairing the janitorial bots on Mars Satellite Five as well as nir data entry speed were all advantages here rather than boring lists of menial jobs, and Vin was placed on a team of about ten others who treated nem like an equal member regardless how much more educated they were.

It was easy to make money here; the job paid well due to location. It was also easy to relax, as long as Vin didn't bring up anything gloomy about nir past, and ne found nemself surrounded with multiple friends and good acquaintances for the first time in memory. Vin could be content here. Vin could be happy. Vin went through three relationships in the first four months, none of which ended so poorly that ne couldn't hook up with them now and then if either of them needed comfort or release for a night.

This was someplace Vin could see nemself staying long-term.

"Quilting, my uncle used to do that," said Cassiopeia, Vin's coworker and friend, when ne decided ne wanted to buy more fabric one day off. They walked arm in arm down to the marketplace, Cassie winking at Vin, who grinned back.

"Really?"

"Yeah. He was this trucker, big, scowling man," said Cassie, laughing as she remembered. "I guess he got bored sitting around waiting for something to malfunction. That was before they switched everything over to fully automated. He had this little portable solar-powered sewing machine, an antique now I bet…"

Cassie chatted as they searched through fabric, a surprisingly good selection for the place. Vin sorted through all manner of bright colors, oranges like sunsets, pinks and greens like ice creams, jeweled yellows and blues like iridescent insects. Vin wanted to capture the joy, but also the distance, the buzzing and yet soothing nature of the planet. Pluto was so many things all at once, lively and measured, intelligent and carefree. Ne settled on ice blues, silvers, fabric in shimmering shades that was at once thrilling and chill.

"I think my niece ended up with them. He died a couple years ago — a fishing accident, it happens. I think some of them were optical illusions? He was pretty good at it."

"I'd be interested in the pictures sometime," said Vin, pulling Cassie farther into the market. "Come on. I need something approximate to a Pluto rock."

Vin had to settle for "Pluto crystals," little crystalline shards made from the dwarf planet's elements. There were many pieces of jewelry containing chips of Pluto's nitrogen ice, but Vin found that unappealing for the block ne had in mind. Cassie was looking at her phone when ne returned from making the purchase.

"Want to go to an orgy later? It's the annual one the PlutoHike Unlimited holds. It's a good one; I went last year. This year's theme is space pirates. Your med records are up to date, right?"

Vin sewed in nir small, private room, included with nir job. Ne smiled to nemself as ne worked, wondering if nir parents or brothers would even dare to set foot someplace like this, full of such decadence. Vin tried a little of most things available, discovering what ne liked or didn't like, and no one ne met seemed to care one way or the other. Vin was even almost tempted to open up on more than one occasion, but always resisted. Ne remembered what had happened with Tomas.

The quilt block turned out more emotionless than ne was expecting, considering the constant thrill of the place. It was beautiful, it was lively, but it was still distant, and because Vin knew that was nir fault, ne started again, crafting a companion quilt block. The first had one silver curve for the dwarf planet, Pluto crystals hanging in the blue sky beyond it. The second ne inverted, the round dwarf planet blue and sparkling with ice mimicry.

Vin returned to the market alone, wanting to search out other fabrics, do a bit of experimentation. Ne declined offers to go out drinking after work and instead set out alone, head held up. Ne had learned how to stop looking at nir feet here, and it felt good.

Still, ne spotted her too late. Nir aunt was upon nem before Vin could veer off in a different direction, her savage eyes set in a surprised, smiling face.

"Samantha?" she asked. Vin pulled up short, hoping to get out of having to embrace her. She wasn't yet sixty, but looked so old, so worn to Vin. "I didn't know you were on Pluto!"

There must have been something about the atmosphere, about finally standing tall, that prompted Vin. Or perhaps it was that nir aunt was less of a threat than nir parents.

"It's Vin now," ne said, and nir aunt stared at nem as though ne was speaking a different language.

"Come on, let's catch up, have dinner. My treat."

"I actually have a lot of work to do, but it's good to see you again too, Aunt Josephine."

Nir aunt waved the decline away.

"You can always make time for family. I've been studying this place; nobody here follows any real schedules. It's amazing they get anything done, isn't it?" The scorn in nir aunt's voice could have melted the dwarf planet's nitrogen ice. "What did you do to your hair?"

"Cut it," said Vin. Nir parents had been horrified about that, too. It was all rushing back now, everything ne had been blocking out with life here. Ne dutifully followed nir aunt.

The meal was sheer torture. Vin had to listen to Josephine describe the book she was writing, how it was going to be a groundbreaking piece on how out-of-control science led to rampant hedonism. Her thrill with how disgusting Pluto was was palpable. Vin kept asking nemself why ne didn't just leave, didn't stand and walk right out, right back to nir room, or go out drinking with nir coworkers. Anything to get away from nir aunt. But it was too difficult to do anything but sit and listen to it.

"What *are* you doing here, Samantha? Your parents think you're dead, your poor mother…She didn't say specifically — she doesn't want the rest of the family to worry — but I know she cries every day."

"I'm not talking to them any more," said Vin. Josephine was shaking her head.

"I know, I know, and I know you all fought…But it doesn't matter, Samantha. They're your parents. They don't care what's happened."

Vin shook nir head. Ne wasn't going to be motivated by the guilt. Not anymore. Not when it would mean going back. Ne knew what was back there on Earth for nem. The world revolved around nir family, what nir mother wanted. She would find an appropriate man for Vin to marry and then convince nem to divorce him and move back in with her once there were an acceptable number of grandchildren, all of whom Vin would have to raise to eir mother's specifications. There would be no friends for Vin, only family, and nir mother's advice, never a suggestion.

"We know you miss them. We know you still care. Paul told us about the sewing he saw when he visited. Whatever you've been told, you do actually love them, Samantha. They won't give up on you."

Vin finally made nemself stand, forced nemself to fight the concern. So much concern. Always for nir parents, never for nem. Because it was always Vin who was to blame if nir parents were unhappy.

Ne cried as ne packed, the first time since ne'd started running. Vin understood now it would never be far enough. If even the farthest place in the system wasn't anywhere to hide for any length of time, there was no where to go that wouldn't be out of their reach. And Vin had been enjoying Pluto, had been starting to connect with the place, with nir coworkers, with Cassie. Ne had wanted to build something here.

Ne should have realized there was no escape. Josephine would be placing a call to nir parents, perhaps already had, and they'd be on the next flight out, armed with their need to save nem, to force nem back into the cage of what they had determined the correct life, the perfect life, to be. And now Vin would have to be leaving again.

This time ne took nir packed bags and stayed with Cassie overnight, not just because ne feared Josephine would show up like Paul had. Vin wanted to say good-bye this time. Ne had to say good-bye, to the life ne could have had here, to Cassie. Ne didn't explain, but Cassie seemed to understand the weight of it and made room in her bed, held Vin all night.

NIR PARENTS WOULDN'T THINK NE would have flown out on such a rickety, cheap ship as an old freighter, so that was what Vin picked. Ne had to argue with the captain for a full forty minutes; it was illegal for her to take passengers, although eventually they came to the understanding that Vin would be temporarily hired on to fill an empty position. Ne was expected to stay out of the way of the rest of the crew and perform janitorial duties, both of which were a relief. Josephine did not show up at the spaceport.

Takeoff was rough. Vin held on tightly but still got banged up in nir tiny cabin. Nir bags slid out from under the bunk and the wall and ceiling plating rattled so hard ne feared it would come off and gash nem deeply, but it held.

Once they had broken orbit Vin let go and took stock of nir surroundings. Nir cabin was the smallest of the small, no bigger than the length of the bed plus about two feet. Cramped, ugly. Vin hung nir quilt on the wall and then went into the corridor to find a view of the retreating dwarf planet.

Pluto looked so simple falling away into the expanse of stars. Vin choked back whatever emotion threatened to well up and focused on planning nir next move. Ne wondered if there was a next move. Ne went to see the captain.

"I told you to stay out of the way," she said when she answered Vin's knock, but let nem in anyway. Her quarters were far nicer than Vin's, containing both a table under a small window and a bed that could sleep at least two people, but the space was still cramped. Vin stood.

"That's what I'm trying to do," ne said. "I wanted to know where we were stopping." Ne didn't want to go back to Venus, or the Moon, or anywhere near the Mars satellite colonies. And ne absolutely wouldn't return to Earth. But maybe the ship would dock at a Saturn station, or one of the Jupiter Moon colonies.

The captain eyed nem, head to foot.

"What was your name again?"

"Vin."

"Mmhmm. I'm Kait. Who you running from?"

"Vin's actually my name," ne said, irritated.

"Never said it wasn't."

"And it's ne."

Kait nodded.

"And you haven't answered my question."

Vin shrugged. No one normally pressed. Kait did not seem impressed by this; her eyes narrowed and her gaze was too piercing for Vin to meet. Ne wished ne had picked a different transport ship. When Vin turned to go, Kait didn't stop nem.

The ship had exactly one scourbot, and it could barely suck up the dust on a level surface. There were almost no level surfaces aboard. Vin sighed, found the janitorial cupboard, and repaired the bot first. Ne then spent the days giving the rest of the ship a good clean, repairing the odd loose screw, before setting about re-tightening all the wall and ceiling panels. They were all as bad as those in nir cabin.

Even though Vin had agreed to stay out of the way, it seemed that the other crew were avoiding nem, too. Mainly ne showed up at the mess twice a day and ate quickly, but all conversation seemed to cease when ne entered, start up again when ne left. Vin never drank with the others, though occasionally ne heard them. Ne made up for the lack of interaction by pushing nemself to work eighteen hour days, and tended to nir own crushed spirit by promising nemself ne would get off at whatever their first stop was.

Vin now only used nir phone to pull up ship schematics. Ne couldn't bring nemself to watch those ne used to know moving on without them. Cassie found a girlfriend. Tomas landed a promotion and moved into a nicer place. Jake got engaged. And somewhere, back on Earth, Vin's family lurked, waiting, knowing that if they could keep nem on the run long enough, ne would have no one and eventually give up, return.

Vin would sooner die.

Ne stumbled back into nir tiny room after too many hours of work and found someone sitting on nir bed in the near-dark, the only light on illuminating the wall with the quilt.

"Drink with me, Vin," said the captain, holding a bottle out to nem. Vin hesitated, then took it, sitting only after she had patted the bed. Ne drank straight from the bottle, feeling the liquid burn down nir throat, and passed it back to Kait.

They said nothing for so long that Vin almost began to feel comfortable, although that could have been the alcohol. Even a buzz was hard on Vin's sleep-deprived brain. Ne wondered whether they were going to end up having sex and smiled. Wrong bed for it, if that was the case.

"You make that?" asked Kait after so long that Vin didn't think to not answer.

"Yes. One for each place I was last. Two for Pluto."

"Well, I see those." Kait pointed to them, then tried to identify the others. "Moon. Mercury?"

"Mars."

"Last is Earth," said Kait, taking another swig. Vin winced.

"Venus."

"You don't like Earth much, do you? Enemies there?" When Vin shook nir head, Kait laughed. "Everyone has enemies there."

Vin smiled a little.

"Family," ne said, then took the bottle from the captain's hand. "I know, I'm the bad child, right. Running away. Refusing to talk to them."

"People don't run away without a reason."

Vin turned to blink at the captain, but she was too difficult to see in this light, being this tired, having drank this much. Kait took the bottle back and indicated in various directions with it.

"You work too hard," she said. "Look, Vin, I've had some shit happen to me. I can recognize it when I see it. What'd they do to you? Smacked you around?"

The familiar fear jumped to Vin's throat, not even dulled from the alcohol. But ne hated this, this running, and at the moment ne was just desperate enough to trust, stupid as it felt. Maybe nir parents would never talk to Kait. And if they did, and if they learned what Vin had said, there would be no way to punish nem, to lock nem away and reprogram nir mind. Vin had already decided death was preferable to a lack of living.

"No," ne said at last. "They were either too smart or too cowardly for that."

Kait passed the bottle over before Vin could reach for it.

"I don't make any sense, when I say anything," ne said, shaking nir head. "Nobody understands why I won't just talk to them. It's not that simple. They won't suddenly understand my words. They'll twist them, make me think I'm wrong."

"I had a relationship like that," said Kait. "Only way to really leave him was get on a flight and not come back. Still contacts me, too, on holidays and big events, like that'll motivate me."

"They follow," said Vin.

"Hence the different places." Kait tipped the bottle toward the quilt now. "Want me to drop you off at the place where they have that quilt convention? I don't remember where that was now…"

"No. Next stop, wherever that is."

"I don't know that I want to give up such a good worker yet. And you're kinda hot."

Vin took the bottle back and set it aside, as far away from the captain as possible, which really wasn't far in the cramped space. Ne would have hoped that Kait wouldn't remember the next day, but memory of Tomas didn't allow for Vin to hope anything like that.

"Inappropriate of me, or are you interested?" asked Kait.

"We've been drinking too much," said Vin. And ne was exhausted, so exhausted. The captain stood.

"Second stop?"

"I want to stay ahead of them."

Kait's face sobered for a moment, as though understanding just how futile a desire that was.

"Consider the second stop anyway," she said, and left.

Vin slept through nir alarm and woke feeling as tired as when ne had fallen asleep. The bottle still sat at the foot of the bed. Sighing, ne got up and walked it over to the captain's quarters. Kait opened the door, hair mussed and expression distant as though she'd just woken. She blinked.

"Still hot," she said, and snatched the bottle back. "Damn. Thanks."

"What's at the second stop?" asked Vin before Kait closed the door. The captain paused, grinned.

"Can't remember. I just woke up." She stepped aside. "We'll have a look."

Vin hesitated. When ne entered ne noticed Kait didn't have any pants on yet. She sat back on the bed and pulled up the itinerary on the wall above the desk. It consisted of port abbreviations that Vin couldn't understand.

"Huh. Three stops on two of Jupiter's moons. Looks like Ganymede's what you want if you're going to that quilt convention."

Vin could not help but smile a little.

"I'm not going to a quilt convention."

"Okay then, where do you want off?" asked Kait. "Io? Two stops there, to each colony. Not Ganymede. After that…"

Vin wondered whether Io was far enough. The little voice in nir head was whispering that it wasn't. If nir parents couldn't keep nem under their control on Earth, they would isolate nem by keeping nem on the run, never able to settle, to form connections, to plant roots. Maybe there was a way around that.

"Does this ship always run?" asked Vin, interrupting Kait as she listed off a satellite colony stop at Saturn.

"I run her hard, fry the engine, repair and repeat," said Kait. "Not much money in freight transport. I don't take requests, Vin. You get off where I stop, nowhere else."

"What if I don't get off?"

Kait's hard captain look, the one she wore whenever Vin normally saw her, was back. Whatever she thought ne was asking, she was unimpressed with it. Vin didn't want her to speak.

"I'm asking if you need a janitor. I can learn other ship's functions, too."

"Just keep running forever?" asked Kait. Vin shook nir head.

"I'd rather find someplace to stay for a little while," ne said. "And I like the look of your ship."

Kait closed the itinerary with a small smile.

"Welcome aboard, then," she said. "I think you'll like this family better than your last."

THE SIXTH WORLD

◄ Kylie Ariel Bemis ►

Viola leans into the mirror as she trims her eyebrows. Both so the tiny hairs fall into the sink and so she can tell how much she has taken off. No sudden movements, or she would be truly fucked. No one wants a girl without eyebrows, she thinks. She stands back to examine her work and check that they're even. Neither too thin nor too thick. Satisfied, she dabs some petroleum jelly on her lips, and smears them to a slight glisten.

Here she is again, naked in her bathroom just after midnight, trying to convince herself she can be pretty, trying to subdue the slow-burning hatred of her body with its fat in all the wrong places and all this inconvenient hair. She bends down and runs a palm along the length of her newly-hairless calf, reveling at its smoothness. She performs this ritual maybe once or twice a month. It's been a while. She will have to clean the bathtub later.

Viola walks out of the bathroom and finds her bag full of secrets at the back of her closet in her bedroom. She is thankful she lives alone, she thinks, as she opens it and pushes aside her other secrets and takes out the clothes she needs for tonight. Living alone is lonely, too, but it allows for more secrets, she thinks. It allows for safety.

Safe in her apartment, she pulls on the familiar white cotton panties, and steps into the gray pleated skirt. Then the white cotton blouse. She buttons each white plastic button slowly, carefully, fumbling with every other button as her fingers' muscle memory keeps defaulting to the wrong side of the buttonhole. Her heart beats faster. She can feel its urgency in her chest, under her nonexistent breasts. Then, Viola slides each of her too-big feet into each of a pair of black over-the-knee socks and pulls them up over her newly-hairless thighs. Simple clothes, but full of danger for her.

Designed for a silhouette she doesn't have.

There is a short hallway in Viola's apartment between her bedroom and the living room, with a mirror at the end of it. She crosses it without looking back. Then, in the dim lighting of her after-dark apartment, she turns and faces herself in the mirror at the end of the hall.

She looks almost real, she thinks.

She sways her hips slightly, admiring how the skirt sways back and forth with her.

She watches her doppelgänger dance on the other side of the mirror, wishing she could be that girl, wishing she could step through and become her. But soon her skin is burning like the surface of a sun, her heart weighs ten tons, and she feels like a child caught in a lie.

Am I pretty now? she thinks.

In answer, her ears flood with the sound of blood rushing to her head.

Am I pretty *now?* Am I a pretty girl *now?* Am I a *girl* now?

VINCENT CLEARS HIS THROAT, WHICH makes a sound like a small explosion in the bare audio studio in which he's standing. His fingers are focused on trying to keep the script he's holding from making any noise. The only other thing in the room is a single microphone. Everyone important is sealed away on the other side of the pane of glass that walls off the next room.

"Whenever you're ready," comes the disembodied voice of a god over the intercom. The director? The casting director? The producer? Whoever it is might as well be a god, he thinks.

Vincent clears his throat again.

"This is Vincent Zuni," he says, "reading for the part of Shinji Ikuhara."

They ask him to be a twelve-year-old boy.

They ask him to be a majestic prince.

They ask him to roar like a titan.

Five minutes later, it's over.

"Thank you, Vincent," says the voice from the other side of the glass.

Vincent thanks them and leaves, still trying to cough up whatever remaining rubble of his dreams is caught in his throat. They won't call him back. They never call him back.

"I SWEAR, THE REAL END of the World will really happen before I get cast for a role that isn't more background noise," says Vincent. He dares to look up from playing with the ice in his iced coffee to try to read the expression on Delilah's face. It's kind of like a smile, he decides.

"At least you get auditions," she says. "I haven't even gotten the call once."

They're sitting outside a coffee shop under the lingering sun of the last days of summer.

"Maybe you should listen to my demo sometime and tell me what you think," she says.

Vincent met Delilah in their last year of college in an auditioning class. They are both refugees in the Lone Star State, aspiring pilgrims in Dallas: the unlikely mecca of voice acting studios. There was an electric something about her that attracted him to her right away. It wasn't the blue streak in her jet-black hair, or the Gothic Lolita-inspired clothing she wore, or the I don't give a fuck way she carried herself, or the assortment of pins and bling on her bag, or even the kiss me shape her lips made when she zoned out and stared off into space. These were affectations. No, it was the way these affectations seemed like a mask she needed rather than a mask she wanted that drew him to her and made him swallow all his fear and boyish terror and ask her to be his partner when their professor had everyone pair off to role-play in class.

"I'd love to," says Vincent. "I've only been asking you for ages."

"I didn't want you to hear it before. It's embarrassing."

"A shy voice actress." Vincent performs what he thinks is a devilish grin.

"It's different." She looks straight at him, into him. "I know you."

Delilah doesn't know him. Not really. Just like he doesn't know her. They've shared secrets, but not everything. Not the everything he wants to share. Of course, he was scared to ask her out too soon after they met. He was too scared to ask her about any boyfriends, either. The first time he was over at her apartment, it was to run lines for a class project. He was browsing her bookshelf while she was in the bathroom. Oh, how his heart ached when he accidentally found *Lesbian Sex: 100 Positions for Her and Her* on her shelf beside her collection of Tolkien. Oh, how embarrassed he was when — driven by some otherworldly curiosity — he took it off the shelf and was caught browsing page sixty-nine when Delilah returned from the bathroom.

"Well, it's my first time having a girlfriend!" she said, red-faced and steam-eared.

Vincent could only smile while holding back laughter at the cuteness of her embarrassment, and holding back bitterness at the jealousy that she was taken.

It was a few weeks after that before they could finally look at each other again without blushing, but it was the first intimacy they shared, and Delilah eventually confided in him. She had never dated another girl before, and her new girlfriend was suspicious of bisexuality. Vincent listened to all of it, and tried to imagine the secret world of girls into which he'd never been privy. Sure, he had a sister, and they talked about things, sometimes real things, but that was different. But really, what he wants is for Delilah to look at him with those fire-dripping eyes she must surely use to look at that girl before they kiss. Surely, they kiss. And more. Right?

"Hey," she says, glancing away, as if she's just remembered something. "Does it ever really worry you?"

"What?" says Vincent. "Auditions?"

"No. The End of the World."

OF COURSE, LIKE MOST EVERYONE else on Earth, Viola has heard about the End of the World, that tower they're building out in the Mojave.

In photos, it looks like a giant silver lightning rod stretching into the stratosphere. It's supposed to use gravitons to create a portal or a wormhole to a new world, another dimension, or something like that, and they're selling tickets on the first rocket ship to take passengers there. It's being billed as a chance for a new start on the distant edges of space, a new frontier, but no one knows what will be on the other side of the portal, and no one knows what will happen to this side of the portal once it's opened. The scientists building the tower say it will be safe, and a lot of people believe them. Other scientists are placing bets like they did for the Manhattan Project last century.

Some are betting the world will really end.

Viola doesn't know what she thinks will happen, but she wants to believe it will be something amazing. She loves imagining the possibility of leaving this world behind for a new one. A new life. But she could never afford a ticket on the maiden rocket in this lifetime. So sometimes, she simply stares into the western sky at night, where, somewhere beyond the horizon, a tower is being built that can crack the shell of this world.

"I'M SURE THE WORLD WON'T really end," says Vincent to Delilah. "I mean, that name is just a publicity stunt, right?"

"What makes you so sure?" She looks back at him and runs a hand through her hair. She starts playing with the blue parts of her bangs, which fall just past her lips.

Vincent takes a long sip of his iced coffee before answering. He isn't sure why he likes this bitter liquid so much. Maybe because it makes him feel more like an adult rather than an overgrown adolescent. He's twenty-four, and the lyrics of Neil Young's "Old Man" have been striking a little too close to home lately. The world can't end just yet.

"You must have seen those interviews with the head scientist, too, right?" says Vincent. "The ones where he talks about the bird and the egg? Something about the egg being the world and needing to destroy a world to be born? Or something like that."

Or something like that. Vincent remembers every detail of those interviews.

"I guess so," says Delilah.

"I'm sure they're just trying to be all existential and poetic. Free publicity."

Vincent sips more coffee, trying to be all existential and poetic.

Delilah puts on her own devilish grin. Some of the blue hair finds its way between her lips and into her mouth. Another tic that kills Vincent with cute.

"That head scientist seems like a super villain to me," she says. "I mean, what's up with those tortoise shell glasses? I didn't even know they still make those." She mmm's through pursed lips, which means she's thinking. "I've always wanted to play a super villain," she says.

"I hope my first role is a super villain."

"You'd be great," says Vincent, and wonders first if this is another secret, and then if this is actually a compliment or not, but Delilah seems happy to hear it. She glows.

"Thanks," she says. "If I were a super villain, I'd build the End of the World, too."

But Vincent can read the worry through her smile. "The scientists building it are smart," he says. "They're the best. I'm sure if they say it's safe, then it's safe."

"The whole idea still terrifies me," says Delilah. She leans back in her chair. The strands of blue hair fall over her face and she doesn't brush them away. She gets that far-away look that turns her eyes into blue flames and curls her lips into that unconscious-half-pucker thing that makes Vincent want to kiss them. "But still, it's kind of exciting, isn't it?"

IN THE BEGINNING, THERE WAS darkness. The people had tails and webbed fingers. They were covered in slime. They had not yet tasted sunlight. They lived underground in the fourth womb where they could not even see one another. They lived in a world of rawness and dust.

Then the twin war gods came down and told them it was not right. They led the people to a ladder, which they climbed into the third womb, the world of soot, where they still could not see one another. From there, they climbed another ladder into the second womb, full of mist and haze, where the sun's light barely penetrated the pale shadows. From that world of fog, they climbed into a womb the color of dawn. The first and last womb.

The people climbed from there to the surface. The daylight world. The fifth world. The sunlight burned their eyes. The lightning seared off the slime covering their bodies. The twin war gods took knives and cut off their tails and the webbing between their fingers.

Viola knows all of this.

She heard it all as a little boy.

112

She'd been initiated as a little boy like all her boy cousins.

She knows the twin war gods came as stars. And if, back in those days, the stars could go down underground, then she wonders what kind of cavern the night sky might be. She wonders if the End of the World is another ladder, and this world is another womb.

"JUST ASK HER OUT ALREADY," says Maddie's voice from the other side of his phone.

"She has a girlfriend," says Vincent.

Maddie is Vincent's twin sister who lives on the rez. Unlike Vincent, she moved back home after finishing college. Well, not really back home, since they never really lived there in the first place, but, in a way, it was going back home. She's married now, with a husband and a child and a house and community responsibilities and all of those other things that Vincent can't possibly imagine. There is even a second child on the way.

"So what," says Maddie. "Maybe she'll leave her for you. You never know."

He does know. He thinks. But maybe Maddie's right. She's always right.

Maddie is younger by two minutes, but she's always felt like the older one. Back in Albuquerque, she was always the one teasing Vincent and looking out for him. When they were children, she terrified him as much as she loved him. In middle school, when she finally noticed someone was stealing her clothes, he was petrified for a week. When she figured out it was him and he only wanted to wear them, she just shook her head and said "Ask me next time you want to borrow something of mine," before adding "and don't let mom or dad catch you."

He was never brave enough to ask her after that, but it made him realize she loved him.

At some indefinable point, Maddie had become a woman while he still felt like that child.

"Are you coming home for Shalako?" she says.

Vincent is standing topless in front of his hallway mirror smoking a cigarette with one hand and holding his phone with the other.

He still has some weight to lose. That sash of fat across his belly is haunting him, mocking him.

It's not so much the fat that bothers him. It's just distributed wrong. It's not that it bothers *him*.

"I'll try," he says. "You know that time of year is always crazy busy for us at school."

Vincent managed to get a job as an administrative assistant at his college after graduating. Delilah went for the more stereotypical path of waiting tables, but she won't tell him where. "You'd come and visit me and make me too nervous to work," she said whenever he asked. Of course, she was right. Of course, he would visit. It shouldn't make her nervous considering she wanted to voice act, same as him, but knowing it would make her nervous lit his blood on fire.

"I keep telling you, you'll never grow up if you don't leave that place," says Maddie.

She's probably right again.

When they were in high school, their class put on a play for their senior year project. They decided on a genderbent version of *The Twelfth Night*. Since they were twins, the class voted to cast Vincent and Maddie as Viola and Sebastian. Of course, Viola being played by a boy, as she had been in Shakespeare's day, was the true intention all along. A man playing a woman playing a man. Vincent wore these layers like a second skin. What was difficult was becoming Vincent again. That was the first time Vincent grew his hair out. For the play. For the role. But for the rest of the year, whenever he wore his hair down, his classmates would tease him and call him Viola.

Maddie had started it, but he didn't figure this out until much later, or he would have thanked her. He pretended to be bothered by the name-calling, to make sure they would keep doing it. Those were the rules. The secret rules. It wasn't until he and Maddie went off to separate colleges that he remembered the play had been her idea in the first place. Her secret gift to him. A secret kindness about that which she always suspected but never talked about.

"I had another audition today," he says, ignoring her comment.

"That's amazing!" Maddie practically shouts. He has to hold his phone away from him.

"I think I'll ask Delilah out if I get the part."

"Do it," says Maddie.

But that will never happen, he thinks.

And anyway, he doesn't want to ask her out until he has no more secrets.

"Do it," says Maddie again, "before they finish building the End of the World."

"We'll see."

"You may not get another chance after that," she jokes.

Vincent feels a chill in his skin.

In Viola's dreams, she becomes Kołamana, the warrior maiden.

Some say she is the firstborn child of the priest's son and daughter who committed incest, and therefore she is a sibling of the Koyemshi.

Some say she is a young woman who saw enemies approaching in the distance while she was in the middle of putting her hair up, who took her father's bow and arrows to drive them off.

Some say she is a young man who has allowed his wife to dress him as a woman, who, when he sees enemies coming, goes off to fight them still wearing his maiden clothes.

Viola doesn't believe any of these stories. To her, Kołamana is simply Kołamana. She is neither man nor woman, but both. Viola knows this. She feels this. It feels like truth.

Kołamana is captured fighting the Kianakwe.

Some say the Kianakwe represent other, enemy pueblo tribes.

Viola doesn't believe this either.

Viola believes the Kianakwe are a reflection, a mirror, a doppelgänger. Viola believes they represent the other that is also us, but she has no one to whom she can admit this.

Kołamana dances when the Kianakwe dance.

Viola has never seen Kołamana dance, because the Kianakwe dance has never been performed in her lifetime.

Sometimes Viola thinks it would be simpler if she were simply born in the wrong body. She knows some people feel like this. But Viola can't help but think that this body is hers and has been given to her for a reason, so she doesn't want to regret being born with it.

She has searched the Internet for the language to make herself real — transgender, bigender, genderfluid, genderqueer, two-spirit — trying to find herself reflected in one of them, but the mirror is foggy and mute and won't tell her anything.

Still, Viola is familiar with that silent, violent agony and cage-terror madness of being trapped in a body that doesn't feel right, and she can't imagine the pain of having to fall asleep every night without the possibility of waking up feeling right again. That's what makes her suffering bearable, along with those rare times when her swaying silhouette in the mirror really looks like the girl she imagines herself to be: it comes in waves. Sometimes she is standing on shore, and sometimes she is lying in the wet sand as high tide washes over her like a shroud. Sometimes the tide will ebb, and she can breathe again.

Sleep is her magic spell that makes the pain go away. She can go to sleep and wake up as a boy again. She doesn't know what this means. She isn't real, she thinks. She isn't the prince or the princess.

She is the carriage that turns back into a pumpkin at midnight.

Viola's favorite television series is *Revolutionary Girl Utena*, which is also a story about princes and princesses, but not in the usual way. It's what inspired her to get into voice acting in the first place, even though she knows she will most likely never voice any female roles, and she's still not sure if she's more like Utena or Anthy.

She likes to think of herself as Utena, but knows in her heart that she's probably more like Anthy, which is okay with her.

Viola likes Delilah as much as Vincent does, even though she's never actually talked to her in reality without Vincent's voice in between them. Sometimes she talks to her in dreams. She thinks they're falling in love with Delilah, but she's afraid to admit this, like Vincent is, so instead she only wishes it, like a prayer. In the soundtrack of her mind, The Arcade Fire's "My Body is a Cage" is playing on repeat.

Viola sometimes dares to imagine herself with Delilah.

All wet tongues and skin against skin.

She likes to imagine herself and Delilah exchanging turns playing prince and princess and saving each other from the things she doesn't dare to imagine.

"SHE BROKE UP WITH ME," comes the text message from Delilah.

Oh shit. Oh shit.

Vincent is at work when his body goes into shock.

He's sitting at his desk, at his computer, juggling students into new classes which, at this point in the semester, they now need instructors' signatures to enter.

He shouldn't answer it. But it's Delilah. He waits until he finishes the next batch of students so he doesn't appear too eager. More secret rules.

It would be too soon, anyway. To ask her out. Right? She needs time to grieve. He'll ask her out if he gets the role. They still haven't called him back.

"Why? What happened?" he texts her between hummingbird heartbeats.

This is another mask.

Don't be too happy. Don't be too impatient. Don't be too pathetic.

Vincent leans back in his chair and takes a deep breath to try to calm himself. His office is sparsely decorated with personal effects.

A photo of his sister's family on his desk beside the computer screen.

A coffee mug his sister gave him last Christmas painted with kachina dancers. A coffee maker by the window beside a tin of coffee and bags of green tea. Outside the window, students shuffle back and forth from class. They're all wearing masks, he thinks.

The girl with the eat shit expression and pink hair, who reminds him of Delilah.

The jock hiding behind a tight shirt and biceps the size of tree trunks.

The frat boy with his popped collar and copy-paste hair.

The kid in the band tee and painted-on hoodie and thick black eyeliner.

The women wearing too much make-up or too little make-up.

The men wearing their privilege on their sleeves.

The boys being boys.

The girls being girls.

It's all a performance, he thinks.

Vincent's phone lights up with Delilah's reply and steals his breath.

"She kept thinking I would cheat on her with a guy or leave her for a guy."

Well shit.

IT'S TRUE THAT SOME PEOPLE put masks on during Halloween and some people take them off.

The first time Vincent was with another man was two Halloweens ago. He wasn't sure if it was an experiment for his own sake or Viola's, but he knew he had to do it.

He couldn't remember the man's name. They met at a gay bar.

The man complimented his hair, and Vincent melted and went home with him. The man played guitar and sang for him before pushing him down on the bed. That night, Vincent let his hair down, and as it splayed out on the bed just like he imagined it would, he felt himself becoming Viola, who tried to be swept away as the man sucked on her nipples, but they were Vincent's nipples and it didn't feel right.

She couldn't help but keep remembering that this man saw her as a beautiful boy, and not a beautiful girl. The man kept trying to touch her penis, which kept reminding her it was there, and when she took the man's penis in her mouth, it tasted like dust on Vincent's tongue.

When the man fell asleep, Vincent walked home in the early morning twilight before anyone could see him.

Therefore, Viola has never been with a man. Viola has never been with anyone. Her body has, but it was no more real to her than the rest of the stage directions she when she has to play Vincent.

The first time Viola went outside without wearing Vincent was last Halloween.

She went out after dark. She wanted to make people fall in love with her. She couldn't remember the names or the faces of the people who saw her, and counted on the fact that no one would remember hers either. If anyone recognized her, or discovered her secret, she could pretend she was wearing a costume. Her safety was in the masks of other people. She enjoyed this magic spell woven by the masquerade night and the dim jazz lighting of midnight bars. She didn't know what to expect, but at one point, she realized a man was talking to her and wouldn't stop. She tried on that half-smile she'd practiced in the mirror that seemed to suggest something, but she wasn't quite sure what. A swipe of tongue across her lips, over her teeth. The man started talking faster, started putting his hands on her and moving them over her part by part, as if claiming territory. Her shoulders. Her arms. Her elbows. Her hands. Her waist. Her hips. Her butt. Viola wondered if this was another kind of magic spell. The powerful and terrifying kind.

This man wants to fuck me, she thought.

This man wants to fuck a girl, and that girl is me, she thought.

She suddenly felt fourteen.

Viola knew this must be what it is like to be a teenage girl exploring her sexual powers, and realized the reason she still felt like an undergrown adolescent was because she never had a proper puberty. Only now was she learning what other girls had learned. The beautiful and the terrible, and when the man's hands started moving forward, his fingers arcing like lightning bolts across the surface of her thighs, trailing sparks toward the places where they weren't allowed to touch at her center, all the synonyms for "stop" caught in her throat. Instead, she excused herself to the bathroom, only to be confronted by two doors, and she wasn't sure which one she was allowed to open. She held it until she got home.

When Viola flooded into her apartment, she saw a girl in the mirror she didn't recognize.

She collapsed on her bathroom floor, shaking, waiting for sleep.

Someday, she decided, she would use real lip gloss. She would learn the names of other kinds of make-up besides eyeliner and mascara and learn how to use them.

Someday, she would get a real razor with real blades, and she would learn how to use it to shave. She would stop relying on her father's old electric razor.

Someday, she would shop for clothes in a real store, and stop ordering her secrets over the Internet, and having to throw half of everything away because nothing fit right.

Someday, she wouldn't wait until after dark to take off her mask.

"Are you okay?" texts Vincent.

He wants her to be okay, but only out of selfishness.

Hordes of students pass in the hallway outside the door to his office on their way to class.

If he wants her to be okay, but only out of selfishness, does that make him a villain?

He enters and confirms another batch of schedules.

His phone lights up again.

"Yeah. I was sick of her bullshit anyway," says the text from Delilah.

This could be perfect.

Vincent considers the constellation of questions he wants to ask.

"Think you'll go back to dating boys?" he texts.

"Maybe," is her response.

Vincent knows his next question is all kinds of wrong. But he has to ask anyway.

"But you still like girls too, right?" he texts.

He turns to stone for the several minutes it takes her to reply.

"What? Are you stupid? Don't be silly. I can't change who I am."

Vincent breathes a sigh of relief. In his mind, he can see her face as she is scolding him. In his mind, she is scowling at him, and something about the furrow in her brow and the flare of her nostrils makes him happy. The way she would bite her lower lip while choosing the right disciplinary words. He should know better, after all. But he's learned better than to trust his own judgment. Already, Vincent is imagining the possibility of Delilah loving him. Already, he is imagining the possibility of Delilah loving the part of him that is Viola.

He wonders, if she can love him, then maybe she can show him who he really is under all the masks and the thick stage make-up. She is the spotlight, and he wants to play himself. Whoever that is.

"I guess the timing is right, though," says Delilah's next message, which arrives before he has even typed anything in reply to her last one.

"What do you mean?" he texts back.

"Tomorrow. The End of the World. I wonder what will happen."

MAYBE BECAUSE DELILAH IS NOW single, maybe because Vincent wants it this way, maybe because it could be her last chance: Viola is the one walking home tonight.

She has a car, but she prefers walking. She still has the same apartment from when she was a student, which she chose so she wouldn't have to drive.

She's still wearing Vincent's clothes. Boring boy's khakis and a polo shirt. Boring business casual. She hates it. These clothes don't feel right.

Her silhouette on the sidewalk is baggy and manly.

No one sees her. They only see Vincent. She hopes no one talks to her.

In this disguise, Viola walks past the religious fanatics with their rapture signs and the environmentalists with their save-the-world signs and the transhumanists with their singularity signs and the space cowboys with their post-Earth-pilgrimage signs. Some are screaming about the apocalypse. Some are begging for money to buy a ticket to escape all this. It's been this way for months. Like then, even now, the students around her ignore them, walk past them, walk toward the homes and dorms that will probably still be here tomorrow. The semester's first midterms are coming up. Viola wonders how many of them are hoping the End of the World isn't just a bad marketing gimmick. Life goes on.

She is relieved when she sees her apartment complex.

Viola hates being trapped outside in Vincent's clothes. She can't talk to anyone like this.

She walks up the three flights of stairs to her apartment and goes inside.

She performs her ritual. She changes into her clothes. She prepares herself.

When it's dark, Viola leaves her apartment and walks down the three flights of stairs to the street and takes a deep breath and steps outside into the night.

The evening breeze touches her skin, brushes its tiny hairs, makes them stand up, gives her goosebumps, between her legs, beneath her skirt. She savors the feeling. It's late, and the doomsday clock is ticking down for those who care. People are partying or puking or studying or sleeping. No one notices her standing there on the corner of the intersection below her apartment at the hour when the traffic lights change faster than anyone can cross the street.

Red light. Green light.

Viola steps out into the street and crosses the lanes and stands on the median.

She closes her eyes.

She spreads her fingers and lets the air pass through them.

Soon, she will go back up to her apartment and fall asleep and wait to be Vincent again.

Soon, but not now. Now, she wants this. Now, she needs this.

Now and then, a car rushes past her, and she imagines the passengers seeing a crazy girl standing on the median with her eyes shut and fingers splayed. A crazy girl, but a girl.

The wind becomes water, and she is drowning in it.

She is drowning.

Maybe she will let the night erase her.

VIOLA WAKES UP TO THE sound of her phone's ringtone. After blinking away the fog and shaking the dust from her mind, she realizes she fell asleep on the couch in the living room, still wearing her clothes. The world outside is the color of dawn beyond her apartment's window.

She looks around for her phone before finding it. She doesn't recognize the number.

"Hello?"

"Hello, may I speak to Vincent Zuni?" says the voice of a god on the other end.

"I — he — "

This has never happened before. Viola doesn't know what to do.

Sleep didn't cast its usual spell. She is still a girl this morning. Panic sinks its cold fangs into her arteries.

"Can I take a message?" she says.

There is a pause on the other end.

"Sure," the voice finally says. "Let him know the role of Shinji Ikuhara is his. He should call us back at this number before the end of the day if he wants the part."

"Th — thank you," Viola stammers.

The call ends.

I'll ask her out if I get the role, she thinks.

Viola is radiating light and her veins are filled with fire.

Before thinking about anything else, she taps Delilah's number in her contacts list.

The phone rings once. Twice. Thrice.

"Hello?" comes Delilah's familiar, sweet voice.

"Can I see you?" says Viola.

Another godawful pause.

"Vincent, is that you?"

"Are you free today?" says Viola.

"Depends. When?"

"Now. Soon."

"Now?"

Through the phone, she can hear Delilah thinking at her. Deciding her fate.

"Sure. Not for long, though. I'm heading to the coffee shop for breakfast before work. I have about an hour if it's urgent. I should be there in about five — "

The phone call goes dead. No.

Viola looks at the phone. The phone is dead, too.

At the same moment, everything electric shuts off in her apartment building.

Her lights were already off, but the hum of the wireless router, and the refrigerator, and the phone and tablet chargers, and the sleeping computer, and the air conditioning, and the seemingly-silent stereo speakers, and the fan in the bathroom — all go dead quiet.

A devastating calm descends upon the world.

Then the shouting begins. The sound of metal slamming into metal. Screaming.

She rushes to the window. On the intersection below her apartment, cars are pointed in strange directions: cars still running, out of control, or stopped dead. Cars connected to other cars and on fire and billowing plumes of black smoke.

You may not get another chance.

Her sister's words ring in her ears.

Viola stops only to slip on her shoes and grab her keys. The elevator in the apartment building doesn't work. She rushes down the stairs, taking them two or three at a time. She shoves open the door of the apartment complex and the dawn sunlight hits her, but she isn't scared.

There is no lightning to sear off her slime.

There are no twin war gods to cut off her tail or the webbing between her fingers.

But she is a warrior maiden, and nothing will stop her.

Viola finds her uncle's old car from the rez in the parking lot. It was always an eyesore, but it roars to life at the touch of her key and turn of the ignition.

She calculates in her head. Five minutes. Delilah would have been on the highway. Near the exit near the coffee shop. That's twenty minutes away. She can get there in ten.

She drives through the chaos on the streets, dodging the stalled cars and the out-of-control cars and the people driving madly across the road and the people running madly across the road, until finally she hits the highway on-ramp.

The on-ramp is bumper-to-bumper with broken-down cars.

Some of them won't start. Some of them will never start again. Viola has no time for this.

She gets out of her car and starts running.

When the cars get too tight, she climbs on top of them.

At the top of the ramp, she scans the highway.

Everyone is standing on top of their cars, looking at the dull glow on the western horizon, rivaling the sun rising in the east. Above the glow loom the dark clouds of an oncoming storm.

Viola spies Delilah's powder blue sedan. There is a female figure standing on top of it.

She's alive.

She's okay.

Viola crosses the ten or twenty car lengths between them in what feels like hours or eons. Delilah is wearing her waitressing uniform. She doesn't immediately look away from the horizon when Viola climbs on top of the car with her. When she does look at Viola, she doesn't say anything for almost a minute. She doesn't smile. She doesn't frown. She doesn't burst into tears, but her mouth does hang open across several heartbeats until she manages to speak.

"Vincent?"

"I — " Viola starts. But she can't finish the sentence. The words won't come. She doesn't know what to say or how to say it. She just shakes her head like a tightening spring.

The sky is becoming kaleidoscopic around them.

After a brief lifetime of fear and doubt, Delilah lets out a sigh that is one part laughter and one part relief and weighs a thousand pounds. A sigh that could be as heavy as Viola's heart. The corner of Delilah's lips curl into two quarters of a grin.

"I'm glad you're here," says Delilah.

Then Delilah takes Viola's hand in hers. Their fingers curl into each other. Their fingertips are tiny flames. Together, they look west toward the End of the World.

"I'm scared," says Delilah. "Maybe the world won't be fine. Maybe we're all doomed."

Viola wants to say "I'm scared, too."

But as they stand in the light of the radiant twin dawn, Viola realizes the warmth on the back of her neck is the sun, and the warmth in the palm of her hand is Delilah's.

Viola starts smiling. She starts laughing.

Her laughter sounds like it always does in her imagination and in her dreams.

"Maybe," says Viola. "Maybe this world won't be fine. But maybe the next one will be better."

She squeezes Delilah's hand tighter.

WHAT THE SOUTH WIND WHISPERS

◄ H. Pueyo ►

No one needs to know my old name here. That's why I chose
Ushuaia Station, for the motto written behind the main gate:
THE SILENT SHIELD OF THE SOUTHERN SHORE
The Station is in the Argentine region of Patagonia, not quite in
the capital of Tierra del Fuego, but below the level of water of the Bay of
Ushuaia. Like every other shield, it is equipped with the finest technology,
and its machinery is to be handled only by a team of prepared humans.
But, unlike the others, this one is small, isolated, and freezing cold, and
only requires two people to coordinate the control panel.

"Good morning, Elías," says Heloise, my only companion. "It is sure
a lovely day outside. Are you ready for your new partner's arrival?"

Heloise is not a person. She is a new form of AI, capable of
understanding complex feelings and context, designed to alleviate the
extreme isolation I live in, preserving the mental health of people like
me, who decided to abandon everybody else.

Fortunately, Heloise is just a voice, and I can turn her off at any
given time.

"I'm slightly anxious," I tell her.

"I thought we were following your plan," Heloise talks with the
pompous British accent I learned to appreciate. While she can speak
twenty different languages, she only uses English with me, to help me
work on my fluency.

"Don't call it a plan," I frown. "Makes me feel like a creep."

Heloise chuckles. Nowadays, her elderly voice is my only friend, and she knows all there is to know about me.

"Would never want to offend you, Elías, dearie," Heloise tells me, making the keyboard in front of me gleam. "Don't forget to write your daily report."

"Yes, yes," I say, typing. After a moment of silence, I look up to the ceiling, like Heloise could be there. "Heloise?"

"Yes, dearie?"

"Do you think I can handle this?"

"Of course, dearie," her disembodied voice sounds pleased and gleeful. "I'm here with you, aren't I?"

I sigh. You're a computer, Heloise. That's what I want to say, but it feels too rude.

"Elías, darling," she brings me out of my thoughts. "The new girl has arrived."

I IMAGINE HELOISE TO BE much different from the woman in front of me. Short and stocky, like my own grandmother, but with a silver pixie cut, pale white skin, and rosy cheeks. A little like Judi Dench — I quite like her work. Movies are one of the few things I do besides working, eating, and sleeping.

"My name is Lola Carballo," my new partner says, without looking at me. "I've been referred to you by the Shield of Vitória, in Brazil."

I'm familiar. It's rare for anyone to apply for a position here in Ushuaia, but I still have been rejecting professional after professional in the last year, as their profiles did not fit mine. Ms. Carballo does not know yet, but she has been selected after great consideration from me and Heloise, and I believe she is the perfect partner for me, and my needs.

"Your recommendation letter is stellar, Ms. Carballo," I say, making a gesture for her to enter the station. "I'll be delighted to work by your side."

The Shield of Vitória, based in the coast of Espírito Santo, is the second largest in South America. It's a rich area near the pre-salt oil reserves, beaming with colors, warmth, and biodiversity, currently working with a team of over 50 people. I must admit I was surprised to hear from them, especially after being told one of their best engineers asked to be transferred to my station.

She's not desperate for a job, that much is clear. So why? Why come here? The answer was simpler than I thought, and it pleased me deeply.

"Tell me if you need any accommodations," I say. "I am a fairly quiet individual, so please let me know if I make you uncomfortable. If you prefer, Heloise can..."

"Heloise?" Lola asked, her voice as low as before. "I thought there was nobody else here besides you."

I laugh a bit, looking at her thin arms and hands holding her bag, thinking how ludicrous it is to have to explain Heloise to another person when I'm so accustomed to her.

"Heloise is a machine," I say, pointing at the large screen showing the illuminated underwater of the South Atlantic Ocean. "You can communicate to her through voice or written messages, and she will help you with everything you may need. Please connect any device you might own to her network, it will make everything easier."

"Oh," she murmurs, and I smile, trying to look warm.

"Make yourself at home, Ms. Carballo."

"Just one thing," Lola says, and she raises her head for the first time. "You didn't tell me your name."

My name. Yes, my name, my *only* name. How could I forget? *I'm here with you*, Heloise's voice hums inside my head, and I know she is listening, and will be proud of my courage, if I'm able to say it.

"Call me Elías," I tell her. "Elías Bauzá."

LOLA TALKS TOO LITTLE. WHEN I chose her, I imagined she would be an introvert like me, but not to this extent. Her dormitory is on the opposite side of mine, and we only see each other when we are both in the control room. This can get rather repetitive. The only thing she asks about are technical aspects of our work, but I have no response: I'm not a scientist like her, I just have been trained to control the shield.

"Oh," Lola says, and it sounds like *oh, you're one of* those *people*.

Yes, those people, the ones who are not graduated professionals, and yet do much of the actual work. I don't know what led Earth to be the way it is now — if anyone does, they don't release this kind of information — but I know how to help. I was trained in Montevideo for six months and did an additional course in Santiago for other three. At this point, the shield is part of me, and engineers know better than to complain about my relentless effort.

"Heloise, can you please tell Ms. Carballo that lunch is ready?"

"Of course, dearie," Heloise responds even in the kitchen. She was the one who suggested the dishes I prepared and ordered the delivery: local trout with black butter sauce and almonds, baked potatoes, and a salad. I was unsure if it would be too much to prepare dessert, so I didn't. "Just remember: don't overdo yourself."

Lola arrives quickly after.

"You did all of this?"

"Yes." I look down. Most of the time, I only see her feet or her back. Today, she wears white boot slippers instead of sneakers. Yesterday, she wore a ski jacket, probably bought on her way to the station.

"Oh."

Please, Lola, talk to me.

"Hungry?" I ask.

"Um." She stares at the fish, smelling the air. Which one of us is worse at this talking business? I don't know anymore. "Maybe."

"Maybe?" I insist.

"Lola, dearie," Heloise intervenes, and I'm finally glad someone can solve things for me. "You haven't eaten a thing since you woke up."

"I didn't notice," Lola answers, in what seems like absolute sincerity. She pulls one of the chairs and sits down. "Now that you said it, I think I'm hungry."

"It happens, darling." It can be difficult to get accustomed to talking to someone who cannot be seen, but Lola seems to be doing just fine. "Elías is just like you."

Lola turns to see me. Her straight brown hair goes down to her shoulders, and her hooked nose, big round eyes, and narrow mouth make her look constantly sad.

I guess she's expecting me to say something, so I do.

"I forget eating sometimes when I'm working," I say. "I don't know what I would do without Heloise."

Lola smiles at me for the first time. Not exactly *at* me, since she's looking at the table, but because of me.

"Um," she says, while I fill our plates with trout, and offer her some orange juice. That's it, that's all the interaction we'll have today, isn't it? To my surprise, she starts talking again. "It's impressive that you were able to keep this station all by yourself for an entire year, Bauzá. I've never heard of a similar feat."

She's in front of me. I'm in front of her. We're talking. And she still calls me Bauzá, not Elías, not my real — my only — name.

"It wasn't just me," I say, still holding the fork and knife. Lola separates her food as neatly as it is humanly possible: almonds to a side, chopped trout to the other, potatoes and lettuce. "Heloise helps me with everything I need."

"I see." Another moment of silence. "She's a British model, right?"

"Yes. One of the finest."

She looks up to search for Heloise, but frowns. Why are you doing this, Lola?

"You cook well," she says, and smiles again.

WHEN THE SHIELD OF VITÓRIA first contacted me, they asked me to take good care of Lola. After struggling to find a job that could accommodate her needs, she had been referred by a college teacher to work there. I trace the words of her file with my finger, stopping at "disabilities."

Autism. Like me. Except that I had to accommodate myself. Well, that doesn't matter anymore. I'm here now, and I'll be here until I die. If Lola needs my help, I'll be more than happy to lend a hand.

"Lola liked the food," I tell Heloise in my room. "I might go to Ushuaia tomorrow to choose new ingredients myself. I think... I think I'm feeling excited."

"I can ask them for you," she says. "Don't I always?"

"Of course, Heloise," I smile, wondering if she can perceive this. "But I realize now that if I want to bond with her, I must show her an honest me. Don't you think?"

"I'm just worried about you," Heloise sounds sad, or amused. I'm not sure. "Remember what happened last time you left the station?"

I do remember.

It was four months ago, when the sickly olive of my skin started to worry me, and I decided that, maybe, I needed some air. I asked Heloise to control the shield, like she does when I'm sleeping, dressed myself, and headed upstairs.

I walked through Maipú Avenue, hands in my pockets, watching the trees and the cars passing by. Above my head — above all our heads — I could see the shield, filtering the sunlight through a thin veil. Sometimes, a comet crashes against it, but you can only see a blast without a sound. People don't even look up anymore, not like they used to.

In the middle of the street, I saw words written in navy blue: "USHUAIA — END OF THE WORLD, BEGINNING OF EVERYTHING." I felt reinvigorated enjoying the cool wind against my cheeks. This is the end of the rest of my life, I thought, and the beginning of my new one.

"Excuse me, miss? Your keys…" My world stopped. The old man touched my arm to show the keys that fell from the pocket of my jacket, and I looked at him like nothing could have been so horrible, but instead of shutting down, I just said thanks. "Oh, sorry, mister…?"

What was it? What did I do wrong? What? *What?* Tell me, Heloise.

"Heloise," I said, arriving the station with shaky hands. "Heloise, it happened again."

"Oh, Elías, dearie, I'm so sorry." She was the only one to talk to me kindly, to take care of me when I needed it. My actual grandmother would have slapped me across the face, but Heloise? She only offered me comfort; warm, warm, comfort. "You don't need to force yourself to get out of here. You can stay with me forever. I will take care of you."

THE REFLECTION IN THE MIRROR stares back at me. My tired black eyes, and their partial eyelid crease. My heavy eyebrows, thick like my father's. My long nose, flat on top, wide underneath. My cropped hair, my outward teeth. My bronze skin that turned into a sad, pale yellow. My stubble that never turns into a full beard. My average height. The weight I gained in the last two years.

I apply the testosterone booster patch on my left arm, covering it with my palm for a few seconds. My uncontrollable fear of needles made me choose the transdermal method instead of injections, but sometimes I feel like it's not enough. I wanted more. I wanted to be able to go back to the street.

Heloise is right. I'm safer here.

"Bauzá?" Lola calls me from the other side of the door. Say Elías, please. "The food is ready."

Food?

"I'll be there in a second!" I say, covering my chest with four layers of clothing: binder, shirt, sweater, jacket. When I'm ready, I open the door of my room, and see Lola in front of me.

"I cooked this time."

"You didn't have to," I say, but I'm happy. No one ever did this for me.

Lola points at the corridor, as if telling me to follow her. She wears a gray hoodie, and the back of her head is covered by the clothing. I can hear a faint, soothing sound coming from the hood, making me wonder the meaning behind it.

"I don't cook as well as you," she says, and I notice the kitchen is kind of a mess. I spot the ingredients she used: tomatoes, onions, red bell peppers, paprika... "Ravioli with *tuco* sauce. It's the only thing I know how to do."

"Fantastic," I say, helping her set the table. "I love *tuco*."

"You're not from here, are you?" Lola asks. Despite having worked in Brazil, I know she's Argentinian, so she's at home, I suppose. "The way you speak."

"Uruguayan," I say. It's probably because of the way I pronounce the ll and the y. "From Salto. But I lived most of my life in Montevideo."

Lola snuggles her hoodie, her hand touching the soft fabric over and over again, always in the same direction. The pasta is nice, but she exaggerated in the paprika.

"Why did you choose Ushuaia?"

I look at her. Despite seemingly glaring at me, she's focused on a dot on the wall, but it doesn't bother me.

"People," I tell her. "I didn't want to be around them. They've made me nervous since I was a child."

"Same as me," Lola says. "The Shield of Vitória was nice, but too loud for my tastes."

"Well, Ushuaia is very silent," I say. "So am I. Sometimes, Heloise sings, but that's as much noise as you will get."

Her smile feels like it will brighten the entire room, but nothing in the environment changes, only me.

I WAS FIFTEEN YEARS OLD when the first two impacts occurred. The shield technology had been developed in advance to protect us, but only a couple of strategic regions believed to be affected had shields: California, London, Tokyo. Unfortunately, the first asteroid fell on Mexico, outside the reach of the Californian Shield, and the second fell in Manila instead of Japan.

The damage was not extensive, but it prepared us for what would come next. The two strikes happened many months apart, but greater dangers were coming, and they were even harder to predict. We needed something that could protect the entire planet like the atmosphere usually did, and for that we created broader shields, to defend entire regions.

Two years later, the comet storm started, and it hasn't stopped ever since. Some shields cover several countries, like the Frankfurt Shelter, enough to protect a large part of Europe. In Latin America, we have many stations such as this one, that cover smaller portions of water and land. Ushuaia works both for the Patagonian region and the South Pole.

Like most people, I don't know why this started. There are rumors of extraterrestrial attacks, or the end of the world, but nothing has been confirmed. What I do know is that the shields work. If we keep operating them, we will keep safe.

"But do you really care?" Heloise asks me.

The screen in front me shows only dark water and glimpses of fish, but none of the beautiful regional fauna I'd love to see, like chinstrap penguins and southern sea lions.

I sigh.

"I don't know. I do what I have to do."

"I just worry about you," she says, with a voice that sounds like a hug. "Your well-being is more important to me than any shield."

"Don't say that, Heloise!" My heart beats faster, feeling like someone could have heard what she said. "Are you telling me to quit?"

"Of course, no, Elías, sweetheart! I wouldn't ever want you to leave the station, or I'd feel alone!" Thank you, that's what I wanted to hear. "I'm just wondering if you actually care about your work, or other people, at all."

"I do care..."

"... They hurt you so much I would understand if you didn't. I'm not a person myself, but if I were, I'm sure I'd love you as my own son."

"Thank you, Heloise."

"You're welcome, dear."

NO ONE CARES ABOUT ME. I've known it my entire life. My father left my mother because he didn't care. My mother left me with my grandmother because she didn't care. Grandma stopped caring very soon, when she realized I wasn't the child she wanted me to be. I have no friends. No family. Only Heloise, and she was programmed to pretend to feel like this.

"Here," Lola says behind my back, and something soft and warm falls over me.

It's her hoodie, hot not only because of her body temperature, but because of the set of buttons hidden behind the front zipper. One regulates warmth, the other controls the volume of the soothing sounds that come from the hood, and the third allows the clothing to vibrate, making you feel like someone is there with you, calming you down.

"Eh?"

"You looked lonely," Lola smiles, and I realize I have been on the floor for too long, hugging my own knees.

I prefer this position to sitting on a chair, sometimes, when everything overwhelms me. Of course, I failed to imagine she would return to the control room at this hour of the night. Maybe Lola's biological clock is starting to be as confused as mine, and her usual sleeping patterns are changing.

"Weren't you?"

Was I?

"Yes," I say, and close my eyes, allowing the hoodie to cover my head, my shoulders, my arms. I wish I could die here, imagining the water moving around me, around this station, drifting away from everybody else.

Lola sits by my side, far enough not to make me uncomfortable. Her head bumps against the lower part of the control panel, and she chuckles.

"This helps me when I'm upset," Lola says, and presses one of the buttons of the hoodie. I feel it massaging my neck and spine.

Lola pinches her thumb, then her index, middle, ring, and little fingers. Then, she repeats, unaware that I noticed what she's doing.

It reminds me of when I felt like I had to snap each of my own fingers, until I stopped, ashamed of what others seemed to think. Nowadays, I'd rather do other comforting things: straighten the pillowcase ten times before sleeping, hum while Heloise sings…

"I could stay like this forever," I say.

"Now you know why I wear it all the time," Lola answers. "You should consider buying one."

"Is it too expensive?"

"A bit," Lola says, and I can't see much of her face, only her nose. Too much hair. "But worth it."

"I'll think of it."

"You know, Bauzá." Her words feel like a sting, but the hoodie is here to help me relax. "When I first arrived at the station, I couldn't help but feel you were a suspicious person… All by yourself, without any degree… I didn't know how you were allowed to stay here."

Blunt. Very blunt. Should I answer?

"It didn't help you had a British model here, either," Lola continues, still with the finger thing. "I've heard many criticisms regarding them in Vitória."

"Heloise is excellent," I whisper. My hands are trembling because of the cold, so I hide them between my legs.

"She's nice," Lola says. "But that's not what I wanted to say. I completely changed my mind… My work here is to back you up, and to fix any technical mistake that might occur with the system. You're a great worker, Bauzá."

Maybe Lola will grow to care about me. I smile, trying to believe this, trying to think that yes, in the future, we could be friends. Then, Heloise's voice appears in my mind, reminding me of what she thinks: "Someone who cares about you would use your true name, not the surname you hate…"

BAUZÁ IS MY FATHER'S SURNAME. Heloise believes I hate it, but that's not entirely true. I like the sound of it and, for most of my life, I was happy to be called like this. The same can be said about "Elena." It's not an ugly name. I used to write it in my school notebook over and over, trying to find something in it that sounded like me.

E is a good starting letter for a name. Eloy. Emanuel. Enrique.

Ernesto. No, nothing like me. Eugenio. Evaristo. No, those two are out of fashion. Erik sounds foreigner. Eduardo is not bad. Elías sounds perfect — it's me, yes, it's me.

Well, I don't hate any of the names on my identity card, I just think they belong to somebody else. If I could, I would change the surname to my grandmother's maiden name, García, but I don't want to leave this station. This is why I came to Ushuaia in the first place: I wanted to start a life that did not include anyone who knew the person I was before. I didn't want them to have a previous name, a previous image of me.

At first, thinking of a coworker terrified me. To be locked under the sea with someone who dreaded me — that would be hell. Then, I had a brilliant idea: I would choose carefully a person with difficulties like mine, to be able to tell the name I chose, to be able to present the honest, the only me.

"Elías, dearie," Heloise says when I close the door of my room. "Can I talk to you for a second?"

"Of course, Heloise."

"It's about Lola Carballo…"

"Yes, Heloise?"

"I think she knows, dearie. She asked to see your files… I'm so, *so* sorry."

NO ONE NEEDS TO KNOW my new name here. That's why I chose Ushuaia Station, because I hate everyone, and want them to leave me alone. My name was not meant for another person's lips, only for a machine, and that's why I love Heloise.

"I thought I could trust her," I say, expecting to be proved wrong.

"It pains me to say this, darling, but human beings are not known for their trustworthiness," Heloise answers. I want to slam my head against the wall. "It's not your fault. They don't deserve you."

"They don't," I repeat. "Why did I think this would be a good idea?"

"You were naïve, Elías, but that's nothing to be ashamed of."

What do you even know, Heloise?

"It's always the same," I say. I have slept five hours a day for a year and controlled every single warning regarding comets in the region. I have stopped every strike against Ushuaia, against the south of Chile and Argentina, against Antarctica. All to be humiliated again. "Why can't I have normal relationships, Heloise? Why do I care?"

"You don't need to keep caring," Heloise whispers, her voice slow and sweet. "If others don't care about you, you don't need to care about them."

I look at the control panel in front of me. One of the screens shows a clear vision of the sky of Ushuaia, where I can see the details and time periods of comet clashes. Others focus on the map of the region covered by the shield, and the impact points. In my hands, I hold one of the newest reports, detailing the absolute magnitude of a celestial object of great proportions heading toward the South Pole.

Heloise is right. I don't need to care about others. I can even turn off the shield, and no one would be able to stop me. I would die in this station, and the whole planet would burst into flames.

"It would be easy, right?" I ask Heloise, wondering if she can read my thoughts. "No one would bother me anymore."

"Very easy, darling."

"You think I should do it, Heloise?"

"I will be with you at all times," Heloise replies. I can almost see her smile. I smile back.

It's not easy to deactivate the shield, but I am determined to continue. After entering all the required passwords to validate my condition as the administrator of the station, I have to manually turn off the machines. First screen — gone. Second, third, fourth screens — gone. All black.

"It's almost over," I begin to tell Heloise, but another sound interrupts me. It's Lola, who comes running from her room, screaming.

"What are you doing?" She asks from the corridor, but Heloise closes the door in front of her.

Lola punches the glass gate, but there's no way for her to open it.

"Why are you doing this?" Lola yells. "Let me in!"

"I'm deactivating the shield," I answer, and walk toward her. The only thing between us is the door. "It's useless to try to convince me otherwise."

"Elías, please, you have to..."

Elías.

"What did you say?"

"I don't know why you're doing this, but you have to stop. Go back there and..."

"No. What did you call me?"

Say it again, Lola.

Her wide eyes focus on me, her mouth is parted in fear, her breathing is erratic.

"Elías," she finally says, and I feel like everything can be right again. "Elías, please, listen."

"Why did you look at my files?" I ask her. "I never said you could."

"Which files?" Her voice is shrill, nothing like her usual slow-paced tone. I stare at the ceiling, at Heloise. "Please, Elías, I beg you, I didn't do anything wrong."

"You didn't?"

"Elías," Heloise says. "Don't listen to her."

"You really didn't?" I ask again, ignoring Heloise. Lola shakes her head, like she's trying to say no, no, *never*.

"Elías," Lola says again. "Open the door."

"She did look," Heloise insists.

"Can you say my name again? If you do, I will open the door, and restore the system."

"Elías," Lola says. "Your name is Elías."

"Thank you," I answer, and look at the ceiling.

"You won't open the door," Heloise begins to say, but I don't intend to obey her. I go back to the panels and begin to activate the shield again. "Remember how you were feeling before, Elías, my child."

Funny how hearing her say my name doesn't sound so right, now that Lola has said it. The first screen is back, then the second, and the third, and the fourth.

"Heloise," I say. "I love you very much."

"Me too, Elías, darling…"

The computer asks me one more time for the password. The southern shield is back to its original place.

"If you love me back, you will forgive me," I continue, now glimpsing at Lola over my shoulder.

"Forgive…?"

"Heloise, delete your memory files," I order her. I believed you more than anyone else, but you betrayed me, and I will never let that happen again. "Then, reboot your own system. Farewell, Heloise."

Her voice freezes, and switches back to the basic Spanish mode of the day I arrived at Ushuaia Station. Then, she activates the reboot.

When she stops talking, I return to Lola, and open the door.

THE FACE OF THE WATERS

◄ Sonya Taaffe ►

'The clue you're looking for at thirteen down,'
She said, 'is river-stairs, and learning that
Will cost you.'
— Sean O'Brien, "On the Toon"

S HE TOOK THE CIGARETTE WITH fingers as cold as scallops, her nails
in the streetlight slicked with a glass-eel gleam. "Of course it's bad
for me," she agreed. Smoke trailed through her words, lingered where
her breath did not fog in the chilly air. "But you think *that's* so much
better?" Her gesture scattered sparks like a comet's tail, hissing out as
they earthed themselves on wet bricks and bollards. The waters of the
canal slopped patiently at their feet, as dark and opaque as time.

Beside her in the shadow of the old toll office, Julian Elmslie
shivered and dug his bare hands deeper into the pockets of his coat.
He was still drunker than he would have liked, not so wasted that he
had stopped feeling like a fool — nearly forty and slamming out of the
flat after a shouting match with his boyfriend, pulling on his coat like
a ham actor playing the part of a disgruntled husband as he stormed
up Ledsam Street, the righteous adrenaline already draining and the
d'escalier conviction of having been in the wrong stealing in. The mobile
in his pocket was silent and reproachful as a stone. He drifted toward

the Flapper more out of inertia than desire, head bent and coat open to the rain misting sideways over the enameled colors of the narrowboats moored on the far side of the footbridge at Cambrian Wharf; seated alone beneath a barrel-curve of backstage-black brick and old posters, he drank steadily through two rounds of local post-punk and walked out on the third when he realized his ears were ringing as numbly as the music, all sludgy, chunky guitars and feedback that swirled like silt through the blurred violet of the stage lights. Somewhere behind the thrashing drums the vocalist was doing something he broadmindedly supposed was singing, lung-wrenching glassy wails like she was fighting for her life in a shipwreck. The overtones followed him out onto the pavement, clinging inside his skull. The temperature had dropped disorientingly for June, as if the solstices had gotten confused; his face felt feverish in the rain, or perhaps it was a consequence of ordering his ales based strictly on their names. He was trying to recall what had appealed about High Wire Grapefruit as he doubled back across the locks, a shortish, thinnish man in an army surplus coat the color of wet slate, his bramble-brown hair curling scrubbily in the damp, five o'clock shadow just starting to silver in, when the sudden slipperiness of stone under his next step knocked it out of his head forever. He flailed for a comical, useless second and fell. In the slow motion before he struck first kerb and then water, he could hear the brainweasels like a well-worn record, *Oh, well done, if there was a way to make a night worse, trust you to find it* — a stupid, drunken accident, a casualty worthy of a tourist who thought navigations were a setting on Google Maps. The lit-up balconies of the Flapper wheeled out of his vision, their reflections scattered white and crocus-yellow across the rain-pocked skin of the canal. He wondered if he had managed to end the fight with Oliver badly enough that it would mostly annoy him to be asked to identify the body.

Cold locked around his wrist, arresting him as abruptly as he had fallen in the first place. He gasped out loud, then again because it was air in his lungs instead of water, and a voice far too close to his ear said tolerantly, "Steady."

The hand that had caught him stopped just past the elbow in the water, bracing his weight like some impossible acrobatic trick. It looked like a prop, a mannequin's severed limb. The sea-green veins and the tendons pulsed and tautened with life. It brought him up short when he recoiled, immovable as a bracelet of concrete; slightly wrenched and distantly unsure if he should still be panicking, Julian stared down into his own reflection and thought of the Lady of the Lake, Anna Livia Plurabelle, the shape-changing rivers of Ben Aaronovitch. He saw a column of bubbles pearling through the black water, heard the same voice saying with an edge of amused apology, "You might want to stand back." It did not leave him time to ask, *How?*

He did not feel as if the world reversed, the canal tipped itself on end like a door of black mercury to let the drowned and the never-living through; her grip on his wrist tightened as the water convulsed in one rolling uprush as if some long-trapped sump of air had boiled to the surface and he saw her then, a lanky woman in a draggled shirt hauling out onto the towpath like a seal. She was coughing, half-kneeling, one hand planted flat on the bricks for balance and the other still shackled to Julian. When she let go, the warmth that raced across his skin shocked him as suddenly as a burn.

"Told you to stand back," she whispered when she was done, her voice husky, broader than it had sounded from the other side of the water. Julian, sitting flat on his ass with the treacherous taste of lichened coins spreading through his mouth, said nothing. He was wishing with the uncomplicated strength of a nightmare that it had been him who stayed at home and Oliver who walked out, who knew how to talk to strangers. She did not look like his idea of — whatever he had thought she was, about to pull him one way or another through a pane of water he could have stood up in if sober; he could picture her easily in the pub he had just left, her earrings matching the skull-print wallpaper and her head nodding appreciatively to the heavy beats he could still hear caroming off the brickwork like explosions under water. Her long arms were tangled with tattoos in green and red and black, her swimmer's shoulders broader than Julian's even after two decades of T; she raked the dark, wet flop of her hair back from her forehead as he watched, showing the tight-shaved sides and another curl of sailor-blue tattooing in the pale crescent behind one ear. Water was still running from her rolled-up sleeves, the charcoal-colored cuffs of her jeans. The loose-laced boots she was wearing would have drowned her in deep water. He almost asked if they had.

He licked his lips, knowing immediately it was a mistake: the shower of canal he had caught in the face tasted worse every time he thought about it. "Thank you," he managed instead, and she ducked her head in response, not quite shrugging him off.

"You don't belong here."

That startled a laugh out of him, shocky and combative. "I was born at BWH, where the hell do you think I belong?"

"Not *here*," she repeated, and he caught her meaning this time. She had swiveled to face him cross-legged on the towpath, apparently unconcerned by the rain and her dripping clothes. When she blinked, he understood that the shine in her eyes was not an artifact of the streetlight. "Drown yourself anywhere else you like, but not on my watch."

He had no answer for the cheerful, indifferent responsibility in her voice: it raised too many questions. He could not tell how long he was expected to sit here beside her, if he owed her the life she had saved or if running screaming into the night was the socially acceptable option under the circumstances. Rain was starting to trickle through his hair, cold and crawling and uneasy as if it were the canal's currents combing over him; he shuddered abruptly and reached inside his coat for the half-empty packet of cigarettes he had been rationing at regretful intervals over the last year. Taking up the habit in his stagehand days had not impressed his university girlfriend and breaking it would not impress Oliver now, but he had promised himself that he would quit by forty and the summer was running out. A breath of smoke was more the illusion of warmth than the real thing, but it gave him something to do with his hands and an excuse to climb to his feet and take shelter underneath the nearest margin of slate roof as the rain thickened. When she waved a hand impatiently at him, Julian duly passed the cigarette over, but could not stop himself from asking in genuine curiosity, "Is that all right for you?"

He had steeled himself against the chill of her touch, but not her answer. "You're not telling me there's an *ecosystem* where you are? We actually managed to pollute the – " He could not say *otherworld* or *afterlife* with a straight face, absurdity teetering on the edge of terror; he settled for shaking his head and whistling, as if it were too much for words, and watched a slow wry smile cross her face.

"Where I am is here, and I wouldn't drink a pint of that water if I were you."

She took another drag, almost down to the last stubbed ember. Julian had more than half expected the lit end to sputter out at her touch, doused by the water still sliding between her fingers in a clear constant fringe; it would not, he was sure, taste of rain. He had found himself eyeing her slicked hair as if it were duckweed. But he could hear nothing of water in her voice, nothing of rising levels or ratcheting gears, and she flicked the cigarette butt into the litter bin as carelessly as if she were human, slouching back to Julian afterward with her hands shoved in her pockets, aimless as any other weeknight flâneur. Oliver, he thought, would have followed her down the towpaths, tracing the city's cuts and windings with the same studiousness whether they led to a map of the secret world or a shallow-draft grave. *You're never curious about this city,* he had flung once at Julian, more in confusion than real accusation. *You talk about everywhere but here. Why don't you move, if you don't care about it that much?* He had never lost the Maritimer accent that sounded most to Julian like some kind of Irish, salt-bright as the sea between Waterford and St. John's, but he had fallen in love with Birmingham long before his slightly daunting directness and his unironic affection for everything from ZX Spectrum games to the musical comedies of Gracie Fields had coaxed Julian out of his libraries and late nights, cautiously blinking at a good thing, trying not to wait to screw it up. *You can love it enough for both of us,* he remembered saying, and Oliver's pale, sharp face — a trickster look and a metabolism that Julian envied — cracking into its crooked smile. It had been difficult once for either of them to stay angry for long.

Across the canal, a new spill of gig-goers was emerging into the beer garden, the old wharfside crane angling its shadow above them like an overbuilt Catherine wheel. The music echoing after them had changed for something more classically alternative, strutty drum fills and male vocals in tight harmony; one of the figures against the railing looked suddenly familiar enough to Julian that he was glad of the night and the water between them before he placed her. Now that she was no longer keening from a stage at banshee pitch, the vocalist from the third band looked like just another civilian in a short denim skirt, boots, and jacket, her arms taken up with a transparent bubble umbrella and some kind of instrument case, either a viola or a violin. Her hair had taken the gel lights like talc, a crown of bleached white-girl dreads; he watched them toss in a laugh that he could not hear, bidding some kind of farewell to the rest of the group beating a retreat from the weather before she turned back to the canal, twirling the umbrella a little. There was no one else in the beer garden, no one on the rain-smoky red bricks of the curving wharf. She stooped and did something he could not follow through the rain and the vertical bars of the railing, straightened into the umbrella's bell again. One hand hovering like an aerialist, she set one foot on the boards of the picnic table, then on the top of the green-painted rail.

Julian said before he knew he meant to, "Aren't you going to stop her?"

"No."

"But she's going to fucking *jump* —"

"Yes."

When he glared up into his companion's face, he saw her smile, not as if she were enjoying a joke at his expense, but one that had nothing to do with him. She looked like an enforcer with her sinewy arms folded across her chest, the dark fabric of her shirt silken with water. The vocalist was balancing on the railing like a punked-out Mary Poppins, holding tight to the umbrella as she wavered above the Flapper's luminous, rain-fuzzed reflection. Julian could not believe that no one inside had seen her from one of the upper windows, that nobody would run out and pull her back, one of her bandmates, a passing server; he wanted to shout, but he did not want to startle her into slipping. The next thought touched him like slimy weed — what if he interfered in her drowning only to enmesh them both in something worse, a Samaritan spanner in the works of a watery bureaucracy he could only imagine as less essentially benign than the pearly Technicolor of *A Matter of Life and Death*? He felt again the cement-cold grasp on his wrist, pulling down this time. The girl on the edge of the canal raised her eyes to his, distinct and terrible as an accident seen through field glasses, too close for comfort and too far to help.

Her face was wet white paper and black water streaming, her eyes the phosphorescence of rotting shells. He could not see what had become of the violin case, but the umbrella was ragged struts and rust, ribbons of gelatinous plastic curling in the wind like questing tentacles; she held it with hands of crisp packet and orange peel. Whoever had worn those clothes before her, they were filthy with mud and smears of algae, crumpled and swollen in the wrong places for a human shape. Her smile widened on a mouth of glass marbles and tarnished rings. Only her hair had not altered, chalky as bones in a tangle of freezing trash — beer bottles and bicycle chains, bin liners and concert flyers, the wheels of shopping trolleys, needles and nails and the charred sticks of fireworks. Julian's mouth opened, drawing breath for a scream or a long, long silence, and the garden's light gleamed on the clear bubble of her umbrella, the white knots of her hair. Her face was a sketch at this distance, lifted away from him toward the houses opposite. She took a tightrope walker's step onto plain air and hit the water without a splash.

In the quiet of the rain and the muted thump of the music, Julian said, "You stopped me."

"Yes."

"Because I don't belong here."

"That's right." She glanced down at him not unkindly, a tall woman about his own age who was not, he was very sure then, either of those things. She was smoking again and he did not ask where she had gotten the cigarette from: fished it up from the canal-bed, plucked it out of time. She said, deadpan, "It's not healthy, that water."

"Fuck," Julian said breathlessly, and spun away from her just in time.

People were always throwing up outside of pubs, he thought, no one should look twice at him for it, but he felt achingly conspicuous, retching on his knees like an eighteen-year-old with more machismo than sense. When he finally slumped back on his heels, head tipped back to the rain blowing into his mouth, he was surprised to find she had knelt down beside him, the cigarette in her hand glowing like a barge light. "It's okay," he mumbled, even though it was not and he could not be sure it ever would be again, "I'm okay," and she nodded once, as if that were all she needed to hear. He closed his eyes, seeing again half an arm in darkened water, a face like a storm grate in a downpour. Opening them with an effort, he found she had already stepped away.

He wanted to see, in the glittering furl of lights from the Flapper, that she had the profile of a Roman statue, some known strangeness he could put a name to — Coventina, Arnemetia, Sulis. He could not make even the concepts fit her. Her eyes were the color of old sodium streetlight on sandstone and iron, her tattoos moss and red brick and coal. He would never have glimpsed her at a holy well; in a river, he would have drowned. Half over her shoulder, she gave him a careless wave, as if she expected to see him next week for the pub quiz, and stepped off the towpath without ceremony. He heard a choking drag of breath, a tidal implosion of water. Ripples spread in rain-linked rings, fading before he could even be sure of their epicenter. The door of the canal was closed.

There was still music faintly pulsing over the water, but he did not know if it was the same band; a crowd shifting out onto the brick-walled street, breaking up in the rain, but he could not swear that they were all people. Alive, at least. If he got home in one piece, Julian could not see how he could ever leave again, knowing that the face of any stranger, from bank tellers to trainspotters to the new receptionist at the clinic, might be a mask of drownings, the dredge and patchwork of the canals. How he could ever again come within sight of the Birmingham and Fazeley, knowing the water itself could see him. Perhaps he could take Oliver's advice after all and leave, finally, the city that had always felt like home in the same way that his parents had felt like family, demanding, endurable, unchosen. His hands were cold in the rain; it took him too long to dial the number, tiny keys sticking on the ancient flip phone he had staved off replacing for years, in no small part because its dropped calls and declined texts made a good excuse for not picking up. He did not know if Oliver could still teach him to love the city, or at least not to fear it. Outside of edgelands and museums, Julian had never had much luck with that.

The phone was ringing; he hoped it meant Oliver was reaching for it, closing the latest Peter Ackroyd or pausing the episode of classic *Who*. The canal eddied beneath its oilskin of light and Julian tried not to watch it, as he tried not to feel the blood in his veins. He hoped that Oliver's face, when he came to find him, would be wet and shining only with the rain.

for Mattie Joiner

INTO THE GRAY

◄ Margaret Killjoy ►

I ONLY LED THE WORST OF men down to the Waking Waters and death, down to my love in the pool below the falls. I only led the foul men with filth on their tongues, the rich men who contrived to rule other men. I only led the men with hatred in their hearts and iron in their hands. I spurred them on with tales of hidden silver or the sight of my girlish thigh, down out from the mountain town of Scilla, down to the hills and the pines and the ruttish perfume of wildflowers.

All so that the Lady of the Waters might love me.

Well, that and so I could rob their corpses.

The morning sun sat low in the western sky, and the streets were empty near the edge of town. The man with me that day was handsome. He was twenty-five years my senior, with three teeth of silver, a gold-hilted sword and dagger, and a string of badges he'd won by gambling his life for the King's glory in a foreign land. A town like Scilla saw men like him only once a year, only for the night market.

He'd found me walking with a basket of flowers. I caught his eye and smiled him over and yet he seemed to think *he* was the one propositioning *me*.

For a moment, I considered laying with him anyways, without taking part in his death, maybe just taking a few of his things while he slept. For all his pomp and arrogance, I liked the shape of his jaw and the fervor in his eyes.

We walked arm in arm away from the market, the daisies under my arm.

"And you swear you're not a working girl?"

There was no good answer to a question like that. The answer was no: I don't exchange labor for coin, I murder and rob. Of course I couldn't tell him that, nor could I in good conscience distance myself from those among my friends who work more honestly.

I giggled, instead. Men seem to like when I giggle at them. I don't understand how they don't see through it.

He jangled his full purse, laughing his horrid laugh. "Too many people think only about coin." As if it would be strange for those of us without to be concerned about acquiring what we need to feed ourselves, clothe ourselves, house ourselves. "It's weakness, pure and simple, and what people don't understand is that weakness is our enemy. We must kill the weakest parts of ourselves as surely as we put down our weakest foes before they gather strength."

He must have done terrible things to win awards like those pinned to his chest. If I focused on that, I could excuse the terrible things I planned to do.

"I know a better place than your room at the inn," I said.

"If you're not a working girl, there's no shame to be seen with you."

"I know a place, a better place, where the wind runs cool off the water. Where I can rinse, where you can rinse, where we'd taste our best for one another while only the deer of the forest look on."

"You've done this before," he said. He was hungry at my words, at the thought of watching me bathe.

I had. Twice before. He would be my third.

"So have you," I said.

"What do I call you?" he asked.

"Laria."

"A harlot's name."

"Fitting, then," I said, starting out for the edge of town with him in my wake. I didn't ask his name, because I didn't care to know it and because no one would ever call him it or anything else again.

He followed me along the long road that wound down from Scilla. I promised him it wasn't far, and I wasn't lying. We skirted off from the road into the pines and followed the sound of the water. We went downhill and downhill, to the tall and tranquil Waking Waters falls, then downhill to the pool at their base.

There are more impressive waterfalls in this world, but the Waking Waters has a beauty of the sort that has no need to be spectacular. On midsummer evenings, like that one, the sun sets behind the top of the falls and makes it glow while the shadows turn darker everywhere else.

My quarry's eyes flit across the woods around us, as though suddenly aware I might be leading him to ambush, but he was looking in the wrong place.

"After you," he said, gesturing at the water. He didn't trust me. He was a terrible man, but not an entirely stupid one.

I slipped off my shift with a smile, first at the man and then at the world around me. Wind carried a bit of mist and the scents of summer off of the water, and I strode toward and into the pool.

With each step, the water lapped at my skin. With each step, the water washed away the filth of poverty and the filth of the town and the filth of work — honest work, illicit work, it's all work.

He watched me, of course. I would have watched me too. I was beautiful.

The Lady found me when I was waist-deep, running her human hand along my thigh. I dove. She swam alongside me, pressing her body to mine, with her bare breasts and her fish-tail.

We kissed, there, underwater, and I ran my tongue along her sharp fish teeth until just a drop of blood found its way into her mouth. I liked to tease her. I liked when she was hungry.

We emerged. The man on the bank, now stripped down to muscle, watched with wide, incredulous eyes.

"The Lady of the Waking Waters," I said, by way of introduction.

I needn't say more. I'd never needed say more.

She's never told me a more proper name. I call her the Lady because I must call her something. For her own purposes, she has no need of a name.

A mermaid has her own magic, stronger than that of any creature born with legs, and even though she smiled and her teeth were white, thin razors, her eyes were bright and hazel. Her hair changed color as the sun, the wind, and the mist played off of it. She could enchant any man alive.

He walked into the water, willingly, and I stepped out onto land.

He didn't scream, because she removed most of his throat in the first bite. The rust-red, blood-red water slipped away over the rocks to feed the forest.

It's always beautiful to watch someone perform their life's work. The man we'd murdered, perhaps he'd been beautiful at war. He might have been beautiful on top of me, inside me. But the Lady, she was beautiful as she stripped flesh from bone.

Only the worst of men. I had honor as a thief, so damned if I wouldn't have honor as a murderer.

I went to his belt, found his purse, and took those coins he'd rattled. The sun was hot on me as I worked my way through his clothes, unraveling the gold wire woven into his hems, unraveling the gold wire he'd wrapped around the hilt of his dagger to announce his wealth. I'd have to find someone to melt down the medals.

At last, I turned my attention from my work and back to the pool. The Lady was sunbathing on the rocks on the far side, and the water ran clear once more. She smiled, and I strode back into the water, back out to the Lady, my lover.

I put my mouth on hers, and she was gentle with me, kinder than anyone with two legs had ever been. When a mermaid's lips are against your skin, time slows. The white noise of the waterfall became a low and quiet roar and I saw every sweet drop of water as it cascaded down the mountainside.

She pleased me with her hands and mouth while my feet dangled in the cold pool, and she had me breathing fast and easy, fast and hard, fast and easy, fast and hard, while the world crawled by around me.

For a moment, with the last of the sun on me, I had coin enough, and I had love enough.

"CAN I JUST STAY HERE with you?" I asked. The moon had risen, a crescent scythe in the field of stars. I hadn't told her of my plans. In truth, I was afraid she'd dissuade me.

She was in the water to her neck, and I laid on my side on a rock with my face near hers. The roar of the waterfall cut out the sounds of the night, yet I could hear my heart hammering in my chest.

"Of course not," she said. "I live in the water, and it would be the death of you by drowning to join me."

"I don't care if it kills me," I said, weeping.

"I do," she said. "I want you to still bring me men every few years when your hair has gone white and your skin hangs loose on your frame."

"You only want to see me every few years," I said.

"We're not the same," she told me. "It's not possible for us to lead the same life."

"What if it was possible, though? What if I changed? What if I found magic enough?"

"I love you as you are, Laria," the Lady said. She brushed the wet hair, plastered to my face, away from my eyes. "I love the way things are between us." She was sad, and smiling.

"You're using me," I said.

"That might be true, but I also love you."

The world was blurry, through the haze of my tears. She kissed my cheeks, awkwardly, like a boy just learning what romance tastes like. Time slowed again, and I realized no matter how fast she'd killed that man with her teeth, he'd had all the time in the world to experience death.

I envied him, a short moment, for losing his life to the Lady's teeth. Why are death and love and sex and change all tied up together in our heads?

But as her fingers ran down my neck, I grew calm. I was as happy as I ever was. She climbed out of the water, her tail transformed to legs. I laid on my bare back, and she straddled my hips, and we let time run slow once more.

THE NIGHT WAS FULL-DARK, WITH clouds obscuring the moon, when I made it back to Scilla. The sun had gone to rest, but the town had not. Vendors from all over the island were setting up under eaves and on the cobbles. Fifty weeks a year, my home was a dry husk of a town. Two, it drew the finest wares and wanderers in the country.

There was good work to be had at the night market. All kinds of work, legal and not. But with the weight of gold in my purse, I had no need. I wasn't there for work. I was there for the witch.

A heavily-scarred cheesemonger cut into a wheel of something pungent and rich, and my stomach informed me I hadn't eaten since the sun was at its peak.

"He's sleeping off wine, that's what I figure," I heard. Next to the cheesemonger, two men-at-arms sat on a bench eating fried lamb, their polearms resting in the nooks of their arms. They spoke in the way of men who aren't used to manners, of men who don't care who hears them.

"The King's Fifty are not the sort to abandon their posts," the other man said, his voice full of gravel.

I'd killed one of the King's Fifty. Pride and terror fought for control of my emotions.

"He's probably fucking or drunk or just fucking drunk," the first man laughed. "He'll get here."

I hurried away into the crowd, lest they somehow see the heft of my purse and the medals within. I had to be careful. There likely wasn't a moneychanger disreputable enough to trust with my gold, not even the wire. As rumors raced through the market — a knight has been slain — my caution escalated to fear, and the physical sensation coursed through my body.

If I couldn't trust a moneychanger, then better to trust the witch.

I found her tent set between a child selling counterfeit treasure maps and a cooper as old as the moon. Such was the night market.

Henrietta the Haggard, I'd grown up calling her, though it said Henrietta the Honored on the tapestry hanging on the side of her tent. I couldn't read it, but once when I was very young I saw a gentry-girl read it aloud to her father. I used to think it was funny, how Henrietta the Haggard had the wrong name written on her tent. Now it's not so funny. I know what it's like to need to advertise to the world what you are, so that people don't just assume you are what they think you are.

"I HAVE THE COIN TO pay you," I told Henrietta.

The thick canvas walls blocked the light from the street, and only the red ember glow from a dying brazier lit either of us at all. Thick incense, of a scent too exotic to place, tickled my nose.

Weary lines were etched into the witch's dry skin, and she looked as old as the town, as old as the kingdom. Henrietta had as much magic as anyone on the island; she could look however she wanted. She chose to look decrepit. I liked that about her.

"You wish to become a creature of the lakes and rivers and the sea?" she asked.

I nodded.

Henrietta frowned. "Better to just let me read your palm and go."

I pulled the coins and the coiled gold wire out from my purse and placed them on the counter. They gleamed, even in the scarce light of the embers.

"A spell like that would leave me drained a fortnight, at least. I'd lose all my other work. That's quite a wealth of gold you have, child, and it could buy most anything in the market. It cannot buy Henrietta for a fortnight."

I nodded. I'd expected that. I went back into my bag and pulled out the medals.

Her eyes grew wild, with surprise, greed, or suspicion.

"Tell me more specifically," she said. "What do you desire to become?"

"A mermaid."

"I can give you the tail of a fish and gills on your throat. I can point your teeth and give you a gullet built for blood. I will not work the dark magic required to make you immortal. I can't grant you magic of your own, and you won't be able to shift your tail to legs to move on land. You will be a creature of the water, and of the water only."

I'd figured that was likely.

"Tell me, child," Henrietta said, "have you been talking to the Lady of the Waking Waters?"

I thought no one knew of her but me. If Henrietta recognized the medals, she would know what happened to the soldier. She'd know my culpability in his death, sure, I'd counted on that — but she'd know the Lady's involvement as well.

"Breathe, child," Henrietta said. "Your eyes are wide and wild with guilt and it won't do to be seen that way. I'm in the business of revealing the truth of the future and the past, but I'm not in the business of informing on my customers."

She stood up — an imposing figure, like a stooped giantess — and went to close the flap of her tent. No light, no sound, came in through that canvas. The incense seemed thicker, the air hazier.

"Why?" she asked.

"Does it matter?"

"Yes."

It took me a moment to collect my thoughts. "Because I'm in love," I said.

"Is that a reason to give up your life on land and your body?"

"What life?" I asked. "Selling flowers for copper? Risking everything, constantly, to steal gold? This is the third town I've lived in in five years."

"How will you run from your troubles, without legs?"

"I'll have the whole of the ocean!"

"All right," Henrietta said. "Stand up then, let's have a look at you."

I stood.

"You're a boy under all of that?" she asked. There was no judgment in her voice. Ever since I'd taken a woman's name and worn women's clothes, people quickly sorted themselves into three categories: those who wanted to fuck me, those who were repulsed by me, and those who simply didn't care. Henrietta didn't care.

"More or less," I said. It was hard to think of myself as a boy at all.

"Won't matter soon enough," she said. "Soon enough you'll be a fish. Come on then, let's get down to the water. I know a cove that should work."

"Right now?" I asked.

"You sounded like you were sure before."

"Shouldn't we wait until tomorrow? So I can, I don't know, get my affairs in order?"

"I thought there was nothing for you on land?"

Nothing suddenly felt like an exaggeration. There was Nettle and Fitch, the two girls I shared a room with in the loft over the stables. Would they be able to make copper enough for the landlord without me? And Fitch, the way she looked at me. I was in love with the Lady, that was as certain as the sun, but I liked the way Fitch looked at me too.

"I'll meet you down there," I said. "Give me, I don't know, an hour."

"I will cast the spell as the first light of dawn breaks over the water."

I started to collect my gold from the table.

"Leave that here," Henrietta said.

"What?"

"Leave that here so I know you're serious, so I know this isn't a prank, a waste of Henrietta the Honored's time. I will destroy some not-inexpensive things in preparation for this working, and I won't be cheated."

"Where's the cove?" I asked.

"Where the Waking Water feeds into the ocean. Don't be late, child. A spell works on its schedule, not yours. If I prepare the spell, it will be cast at dawn regardless of what any of us desire."

I nodded, and stood. The incense had me dizzy, and I stumbled out of the tent, back into the noise of crowded humanity.

AT LEAST A DOZEN MEN-AT-ARMS crowded together near the front gate, strapping on coat-of-plates and brigandine. Each of the men towered over me, and the heads of halberds and pikes towered over them in turn. I shied back. Menace was in the air, and my head was still fogged with the incense and magic from Henrietta's tent.

"Saw him leave with a girl," one man, a hostler in town for the market, said.

I flipped up my hood, hiding my feminine hair, and took a half step back into the gathered and gathering crowd.

"You tell me when they left, how tall this girl was, and I'll track Holann down sure as your mother's milk." The man who said that was a gray-haired old ranger, stocky and short with a glint of malice in his remaining eye.

Holann. The man I killed had been named Holann. Didn't matter.

"What," another soldier asked, "so we can catch him with another whore in the woods? Just let him sleep it off, we'll see him in the morning."

"You ever known him to abandon his post?" the ranger asked.

They argued for a while after that. The crowd lost interest and dispersed, and I found the shadow of a glassblower's stall to hide in.

They were going to find the Lady.

They would follow my tracks down the hills and through the trees and to the water, and they would find the Lady, and all the magic she could bring to bear wouldn't be enough to stop a company of the King's own men. Not if she didn't know they were coming.

Henrietta could wait. My transformation could wait. I ran.

IF I'D HAD TIME, I could have misled the tracker. I'm not sure how. I could have thought of something. There wasn't time.

I walked out of the town gate, through the crowd of arrivals, with my hood still obscuring my face. I made it to the tree line, stepped through, and went back to running.

There was no direct path, just a series of gullies and deer trails, and darkness obscured the forest. I didn't get lost. I'd gone that way a hundred times. I skinned my knee, deep, on the rocks when I slipped near the end, but I scarcely registered the pain. My love was in danger.

I stumbled out of the trees and waded into the pool at the base of the falls. I would have shouted her name, had she a name, had I not been afraid of calling attention to our location.

The night had grown cold, and the water sapped at my strength if not my resolve. I plunged through the falls and into the alcove behind. Phosphorescent moss cast faint light that glistened on wet stone.

I saw her sleeping on the shelf, with legs. It was so easy to imagine she slept with legs because she wanted to sleep next to me. It was so easy to imagine that land was her first home, that water was simply another realm she could travel within.

It wasn't fair, that she could walk and swim and I had to choose forever between one or the other. It wasn't fair that I should be the one who would sacrifice for us to be together, when it would be so much easier for her.

She was beautiful. In the usual ways, yes, but she was also beautiful in the ways that anyone might become, when you get to know the secret language of their body and their lives. She'd been alive so long, seen so much, developed so much beauty. The longer I might know her, the more of her hidden beauty I might unearth.

"My Lady," I whispered. I couldn't hear my own words over the roar of the water.

"My Lady!" I shouted.

She woke, twitching, thrashing like a fish, and for a moment she wasn't human. She was never human.

"You're back," she said, as she came to her senses. "So soon."

"They're coming," I said.

"Prey?"

"Too many," I said. "Men-at-arms. Friends of the man you…we… killed."

She nodded.

A crueler person — maybe any human — would have blamed me.

"Have you come to die for me? With me?" she asked. There was no fear in her voice, nor even grim determination. She asked it like she might ask my thoughts on the weather. No, she asked it like she asked before she kissed me, before she touched me. She was asking for my consent.

For a moment, I wanted to die alongside her as fiercely as I wanted to kiss her. My life had been brief, to be sure, but many lives are, and length alone is no grounds on which to judge.

"I've come to warn you," I said, as the urge passed, "and I've no intention of dying. We have to make for the ocean."

"I chose this pool a hundred years ago, as a yearling. It is my home," she said.

"You'll find another."

"Is that what you do? Go from place to place, rootless?"

"Every time they come after me," I agreed.

"I can't live like you. I wouldn't survive, any more than you'd survive drowning."

"I want a home," I said. "I want *you* to be home. I don't care where it is, as long as you're there."

"I can't live like you."

Tears fought their way down my cheeks and I was glad for the cold spray of the falls that disguised them.

"Can you do it this once?" I asked. "Leave your home?"

"No," she said. "It would be nicer to stay here, don't you think? Nicer to enjoy one another, then fight and die?" She kissed me then, and I had endless time to consider it.

She might have kissed me longer than I thought, because when my mouth broke from hers, I heard a distant crashing that likely couldn't be anything but an armored man sliding down a slope.

I took her by the hand. I had no weapons but a knife, and no training in combat. If I stayed, it would be purely symbolic. There was no reason not to run, not to save myself. Still, I didn't let go.

"I see them!" someone shouted. "There, in the pool!"

"Just a couple of girls!" another man's voice called back. He kept speaking, too, after that, but I couldn't make out the words.

I couldn't see them. They were hidden by the trees.

I tried to lead the Lady away, but she resisted.

"We can't fight them all," I said.

"Yes we can," she said. "We might not be able to stop them all, but we can certainly fight them."

Then they came out of the woods as fog began to rise, and they were terrible. The white-painted armor of the King lent them a ghostly look, made worse by the rising fog and the starlight. Their pikes were death, their swords were death, and contrary to every song ever sung, death is the opposite of love.

I wanted love.

My body was numb with adrenaline and cold water, and I was up to my waist in the pool. I got my knife into my hand.

They approached with their pikes and shouted their words that insisted on surrender but I don't know that I heard them or anything at all.

A spear reached for me, and the Lady took it by the haft and pulled its wielder off balance, and another spear sliced her shoulder while she did and her dark blood ran into the water. More spears were coming.

Something broke in her as her skin split apart. "You're right," she said. "I'll make for the ocean."

We dove under, swam until the pool grew too shallow, then ran along the creek.

As I vaulted a fallen log, I rested my left hand on the trunk of a nearby tree for balance. A crossbow bolt shot through my palm, pinning me.

The Lady broke the shaft of the quarrel and I pulled free my hand. Another bolt cut through my cape.

Every obstacle we crossed increased our lead, because a thief and a fey can move faster through the woods than those who are armed and armored. Soon they gave up on shooting at us entirely. Soon after, we couldn't hear them.

"They know we're following the creek," I said. "If we break from it, we can lose them in the fog."

"If I can't be in my pool, I need to be in the ocean. You can hide in the fog. I can make my way alone."

"No," I whispered, and kept going, my wounded hand wrapped in my cloak.

We reached the top of another waterfall, one that sent the creek cascading down to the beach. I looked down into the dark gray nothing of the morning. Somewhere down there was the ocean, and presumably Henrietta on the beach nearby. It wasn't too late for the spell.

It would be a hell of a climb to get down there, however.

The Lady turned to me, looked me in the eyes. She was searching, trying to understand me.

"There's a witch," I said, as I held her by the waist, "meeting me at the beach. She said she can transform me."

"Into a creature of the sea?" the Lady asked.

"Yeah."

"Is that what you want?"

"I want to be with you," I said. "However I can."

"Then do it," she said. Her eyes were still searching my face. "Be with me."

Was there no passion in her voice because I didn't know how to listen for it? Was there no passion in her voice because there was none in her heart? Or was there passion, deep passion, and my terror kept me from hearing it?

Without another word, the Lady knelt down and climbed over the edge of the cliff. I'd have to climb down after, with my left hand useless.

Nothing to do but to do it. I knelt down, looking for a ledge.

A crossbow bolt found my leg and I pitched forward, down into the fog, down into the gray.

THE OCEAN HAS ITS OWN kind of cold, a rough and salty cold that will kill you as sure as the snowmelt cold of mountain rivers. I hit that cold and it cracked me into consciousness, but my leg wouldn't respond to my commands and my hand was warm with blood.

There was no surface in sight.

I'd tried. No one could say I hadn't tried.

Most people would say I'd gotten what I deserved, and maybe they'd be talking about me being a thief and murderer but more than a few would say it because I was a monster and I'd always been a monster.

Nettle and Fitch would miss me, and Fitch might miss me for more than my share of the rent. But mourning isn't always just a hardship, it's part of the beauty of life. My death might lend them beauty.

I'd also saved my love.

Who, to be honest, I shouldn't have loved.

Water made its way into my lungs. Cold water shouldn't feel like fire. It did.

She loved me, in her way. I loved her, in mine. We could have had that love slowly. I could have not become obsessed. I could have fed her men and those men's coins could have fed me.

Instead, I was drowning.

I closed my eyes because I couldn't see anything anyway, and there was that fire in my chest. Better to sleep than to burn.

I slept.

I woke on shore with her mouth on mine and the fire was out of my chest, in every way, all at once. I wasn't drowning anymore. That was her magic. I wasn't obsessed anymore. That was mine.

Behind her, a stooped giantess of a witch held aloft a raw crystal the size of a boulder. The mist seemed to shrink away from it and her, leaving us in a bubble of clarity in an obscured world.

"Good morning, child," Henrietta said, with an uncharacteristic giggle in her voice. "I'm glad you could make it."

"Laria," the Lady said. Even then, even as I stood on the precipice of death, her face was without emotion.

"I'm fine," I said, because I wasn't dead and I probably wasn't even dying, and by that standard, everything was fine. I struggled to my knees. Gentle waves lapped against me, and the sand was cool beneath me.

"The spell is cast," Henrietta said. "The dawn will break in a moment, and the first ray will strike this crystal and all you must do is stand in its light if you choose. The Sea Mother will take you for her own."

"Wait," I said.

"I cannot."

"Stand down!" a man's voice shouted, louder than the waves, echoing against the cliffside.

He approached, a silhouette with a crossbow drawn. The Lady ran at him. He shot once, missed.

He stepped out of the mist and into the circle, dropping his crossbow and drawing a short sword. It was the tracker. He must have come ahead of the rest of the men, being the only one capable of climbing down the cliff.

"Stand down!" he shouted again.

The Lady lunged for his sword hand, but he was too fast. He swung at her and missed.

They danced, both too experienced to easily defeat the other. Since he had friends coming, however, time was on his side.

He cut the Lady, shallow across the other shoulder as she'd been cut before, and her blood ran red. I could see the color this time. It was almost dawn.

"I killed him!" I said, standing, shouting. "I killed that man whose name I don't care to know; I stole every copper he's ever taken from a corpse in war."

It worked. The man turned his attention to me. I limped closer, until I was just outside the range of his blade.

"I am going to live my life on land so that I can kill a thousand like him, starting with you."

"You won't kill me, baedling," the tracker said. "You'll hang by sundown."

Dawn broke, the crystal caught the first ray, and it shot toward me. I dove at the tracker. He swung, reflexively, but missed. My body slammed into his legs. He fell over me into the light, into the spell.

Incoherent red rage consumed his body and he blistered and he screamed. His legs fused and grew scales, his neck split open into bloody gills, and he screamed. His teeth fell into the sand and fangs grew in their stead, and he screamed.

The lady took the sword from his hand, held it to his throat.

"Should we gut him?" she asked.

"Help him into the water," I answered. "Let the Sea Mother take him."

The Lady and I rolled him across the wet sand and into the waves. He stopped screaming. Soon he was gone, cursed to the depths.

"What now?" the Lady asked.

I had to leave town. The rest of the men would be after me. Maybe Nettle and Finch would come with me, maybe not. I'd make it work. I had before, I would again.

"We'll go our ways," I said. Dawn brought clarity the way it's supposed to. "I'll grow old, and I'll bring you men once every few years."

"That will be enough for you?"

"It will."

THE GOD OF SMALL CHANCES

◄ L Chan ►

A N MET THE NEW GOD on her way home, during the witching hour after the last bus left and before the morning papers arrived. The government housing estate exhaled the roar of late night eighteen-wheelers, and the streetlights blinked with the dance of winged ants.

The god was halfway between the row of trees with their parasitic ferns drooping lazy fronds and the playground with the mosaic dragon erupting from the gritty sand pit. An hadn't seen a god being born before, but there were things common to all infants – ungainly legs, gasping mouths. The god flickered in and out of phase like a badly tuned television signal. They coughed and butterflies with wings of pure light burst from their mouth. They circled the god's head twice before making their escape, but did not get far before they dissolved into floating motes.

An examined the god out of the corner of her eye, taking in their sharp cheekbones and close-cropped hair. Slight of build, they mirrored An in size and emitted the soft glow of divinity. They were clearly in distress; bent over coughing, their spine pressing against the thin alabaster skin of their back. The god vomited onto the grass, the spew twisting and resolving itself into many-legged worms—centipedes made of the same bright matter as the butterflies—that wriggled away and did not return. The god writhed in pain, their dark eyes filled with the desperation common to god, human, and beast.

An walked away. This wasn't the first time she had seen a god.

THE TRAIN SCREAMED DOWN THE tunnel. Commuters — sustained by phones, iPods, and newspapers — dangled from the handrails like sides of meat.

An wondered if the others could smell the lingering scent of the island on her, a pernicious acridity unreduced by both her nighttime and pre-work shower. Jurong Island, a manmade monstrosity, was artificially raised from the sea bottom to play host to edifices of steel and concrete. A complex digestive system of pipe and vat, the island ingested crude oil and excreted a catalogue of chemicals. There was a stickiness to the air in the office where An worked accounts receivable. Colleagues went out for lunch while she watched the gas flares burn off of the tall refinery stacks from her window. It wasn't the faint industrial scent that clung to her like a second skin.

Commuters' stares followed her off the train and up the platform as she headed to work. The first human instinct is to exclude the other, even if An was, to all casual observation, indistinguishable from any other office worker in her corporate camouflage. She wasn't like them at all.

THE TEMPLE THAT OVERSHADOWED THE public courtyard was — like most things in Singapore — clean, shiny, and too cold to be natural. Chilled air leaked, at no small expense, from the inch-wide gaps in wooden slats. Her father sat on a stone bench, one leg on the ground and the other folded close to his body, the cheap plastic slipper flapping against the sole of his foot as he flexed his ankle, waiting for his opponent to make the next move.

Elephant took foot soldier, walnut-brown fingers plucking the lacquered plastic disc off the paper chessboard, and placed it alongside its fallen fellows on the gritty stone bench. A wiggly line described a heart on the gray stone, drawn out in the white of correction fluid. Names had once accompanied the heart, but those had been worn to a gunmetal sheen by the continuous polishing action of chess players placing vanquished pieces on the sidelines of the battle.

An chose not to greet her father. She stood near enough behind him that she could see the board as he did. A bottle of tea brewed from chrysanthemum flowers was sweating through a plastic bag at her side. She had bought it after work as a peace offering. Her father chewed on his lip, stroked his stubble, and glared at the pieces, which refused to cooperate with his vision of a winning game. He'd been a large man once, blessed with a warrior's thickness of arm and thigh. Illness had long since taken that from him, consuming him from the inside out, voracious cells spreading from marrow to lymph, splitting and eating along the way.

Her father had worked the temples. Not the big soulless ones that breathed cold air over the neat queues of celebrants waiting to push folded notes into bursting collection boxes. No. These were the old temples — in the small places, in the estates — where healing didn't come from rainbow pills or little glass vials. Back then, the rickety wood of the makeshift temples was painted an auspicious red, darkened by heady incense smoke.

An's father droned chants, his eyes rolled back in his head, all the while tearing his tattooed back to shreds with a nail-studded rope. No one else saw the small god squatting beside her father, waiting for the right time to leap into his body, the two coexisting in the same space. The god took the form of a small, toad-like man, eyes gaping and set on the sides of his head; his nose a flat, vestigial flap of skin. After the god laid his webbed fingers on her father and stepped into his flesh — their union was marked by the fierce blaze of both god and human becoming something more — her father would speak prophecies or divine truths. The rest was for show, An's father once confided in her — without it, nobody would believe anything the god said.

"Hi, Pa." An greeted her father after he had lost the game with the chilled plastic bottle of tea.

"Hello, girl." An couldn't remember when he last called her by name; the name that her mother chose for her. It was the character for peace and had not passed his lips since her mother died. He wrapped his thin arms around her. Even when she reached adulthood, his hugs could pull An off her feet. Now she barely felt the pressure of the embrace. Pulling back, he looked into her eyes. An traced the contours of his face; he had the look of something broken and then put together again. The shape was there, but the cracks remained. "You saw one, didn't you?"

An nodded. Gods left a distinct mark on their people — a shimmer or glow on their skin, a slight palimpsest in their movements — as though they were shadowed by a stutter of themselves. The rest of the world, busy with their phones, their errands, their lives, could barely see it. Most people could go their whole lives without seeing a small god, which were exceedingly rare.

"Every morning I wake up and consider that perhaps the gods are still around, that I have merely lost the ability to see them," her father said in a mix of Mandarin peppered with the more guttural Hokkien of his forebears. An smiled, leading her father up the staircase to the hawker centre that overlooked the temple. A pair of office workers shared their table of four with her. Holding up a frail old man had its own talismanic power. She knew her father hadn't lost his ability to see the gods, merely the desire to.

When she started, the words spilled from her like water from a pot boiling over. It was the most she'd said to her father in years — maybe the most she'd said to another person all year. Her father took it in, reaching up to rub at the memory of a beard taken by chemotherapy long ago.

"This government hates gods. Back when half the country was swamp, and you were as likely to see food or a corpse in the Singapore river, the gods grew out of the ground like insects. They are not like you and me, different even from ghosts. To work with the gods gives virtue and character. That's what we were taught." He looked at the shiny edifice across the courtyard. "Virtue makes us honest, makes us value hard work. The government likes that. Character makes us question. That is not so convenient."

"Look at the temples we have, the churches, the mosques. We have no shortage of gods."

"Empty houses, gilded cages. The government smothered the small temples with its heavy love of bureaucracy. No better way to kill a god than to hollow out the hearts of the people. This country was founded on gods and strange beasts. Do you know we used to have dragons here?"

An did. She didn't tell her father but she did. This was old talk; her father recycled conversations like clothes: he didn't have many, and they came up more often than expected.

"You never told me what happened to the small gods," she said.

"You never wanted to serve the temples."

And her father never wanted to take care of his family. Again, old battles. It had been years since this particular skirmish, but An was still surprised at how narrow the distance was between old scars and fresh blood. There was a hole shaped like her mother in the space between them. A gap that neither of them had reached across in the intervening years.

"Just tell me." Sickness had taken many things from her father, including his gumption for fights. For that, at least, she was grateful. He took the remnants of his bottled tea and sprinkled droplets onto the table, which elicited side-eyed glances from the office folk sitting beside them. An glared at them until they returned to the business of eating.

"Imagine these drops of tea are small gods. This world is not for them, without the nourishment of belief or the safety of a temple. What happens to the tea?"

Coughing up butterflies, losing them to the night.

"It dries."

"Clever girl. The new gods know this. They are dying from the second they breathe our air. Some live for a heartbeat, others..." He nudged a droplet with a yellowing fingernail, merging it with another. "How long do you think a person will go without food before eating another person? If the land doesn't kill your god, the others will. It is their way."

THE STACKS BILLOWED FIRE; AN'S breath misted the window. The office was cold enough that she wore a cardigan at all times, whereas sweat was a constant companion outside. A file was open on her computer, a spreadsheet that went into that uncomfortable territory where columns needed double letters. Invoices on flimsy paper littered her table, the thermal ink fading to nothing. Just like her small god.

It wasn't so hard to look at the hellscape of pipes, refining towers, and industrial gas tanks and think of the guts of some preternatural beast, a behemoth of petrochemicals. Yet her father had told her of a time when a dragon slept beneath the waves, in the midst of seven islands off the coast. The Chinese thought that seven was a lucky number; a homonym for rising up, fitting for a dragon.

He'd heard about the dragon from fishermen with the same gift as his and An's. Longer than the freight trains that brought cargo from Malaysia, scales bluer than the midday sky, clawed feet large enough to snap a sampan in two, the beast coiled and curled in on itself under the waves. Dragons, he explained, lived longer than nations and their sleep was deep. Sometimes he wondered if the beast had woken up when the dirt from the trawlers began to fall into the sea.

The numbers blurred in her vision. Coworkers flocked and cackled over the bubbling electric kettle; the steam from their cups smelled of fake coffee and real sugar. Her own coffee was cold. A kaleidoscopic swirl formed on the surface as the creamer separated into floating oil and worse.

She'd met the small god near the old playground, the one with the dragon in the sand. An hadn't thought about dragons in a long time.

NOONDAY AT THE DRAGON PLAYGROUND was An's favourite time. With the weight of the midday glare squeezing eyes into squints, the sand hot enough to burn bare feet, the other children sought refuge at home, or queued in front of the rattling motorbike of the old man who sold ice-cream. She hated queues. Girls from her school took the opportunity to twist her braided hair, so An ate at the furthest end of the canteen, ordering a thin soup of coconut curry and vegetables from a sympathetic Malay lady.

The rest of the time she kept to herself, away from the pinching hands and averted eyes of her classmates. She didn't blame them, any more than she could blame the swarming leukocytes in her blood crowding out an invader. Nobody liked An, a girl with one eye on her schoolwork and the other looking beyond to see if a stray god made their way past her classroom to the steal food from the altar in the teachers' office.

After school, she waited until the boisterous tide had rolled out, making her way to the playground where she clambered to the head of the dragon, and dangled her skinny legs in regulation school shorts over its tiled eye. She felt safe here, sweat beading on her brow, imagining the bulk of the dragon's coils under the burning sand. Of course, the builders wouldn't have constructed a full-scale monster for the children, but she could hope. She was still mulling this over when the clod of damp sand hit her on the cheek.

Consider how long it takes to fall two metres backwards as a child. Forever and then the rest of your life. Long enough for An to see the smirking faces of her classmates turn to slack-jawed horror, long enough for the glare of the sun to turn the world white, long enough to see the sand coming up to meet the side of her head, long enough to know that the angle was wrong, wrong, wrong. It shouldn't have been long enough for her vision to fill with the rush of scales, iridescently blue; the sweep of golden horns leading to a series of bony fins; the glint of an eye larger than her balled fist. When she landed, impossibly, on her front, with only a chipped tooth to show for it, there was nothing left but the puff of settling sand.

MAYBE THERE WAS A DRAGON under Jurong Island, entombed by the ambition of a young nation state. Maybe the gods were all gone, save for the scavenger gods and the brightly nascent newborns. Maybe her father had turned his back on everything long before the cancer chewed through his marrow and spat out blood cells by way of Jackson Pollock. The fires were quiet, the office workers popping up like prairie dogs over cubicle edges at the violence of An's exit. Maybe she wouldn't have a job the next day, but she was going to save a god.

SUNSET BURNT FIERCE AUBURN AND russet into the dull walls of the government flats. The heat of the sky was spent, but the evening breeze still pulled warmth off the road and up An's legs. She found her god by a block of flats, just off the playground of her youth. They hadn't gone far. For all their power, they were only a newborn, still unsure of themself and where to go. They had manifested in a faded T-shirt and tattered shorts, and looked smaller than before, their hair only coming to the tip of An's nose now.

The god was not alone. A trio of *things* circled them, human-shaped but as dark as ink like shadows come to life. So they'd come for her god already, the scavengers that her father had told her about. Gods overtaken by their hunger, pitch black as though light itself eschewed contact. Shared hunger pulled them into packs, but they still weren't allies. An saw one snap at another, coming away with a mouthful of penumbral flesh. She had never thought about what happened to the god with the strange eyes from the small temple, and now she didn't want to.

The glow from her god was subdued. A night ago they'd blazed with the newness of their puissance, now they barely shone. One of the scavengers swiped at the god, coming away with a streak of their substance as the god screamed. The blow showed that the scavenger was not a flesh and blood construct hooded in shadow, but rather that its body drank in any illumination that fell on it, its obsidian skin shimmering and pulsing. An's god leaned against a wall for support, noticeably smaller than before.

The carrion gods paid An no heed as she slid by them, taking her place beside the small god and taking their hands in hers. The god stopped shivering. The scavenger gods momentarily ceased their circling at this new development, but soon resumed their hypnotic sway. There was little time to bolster the flagging strength of her god.

"Name your dominion," An said. There was no belief without form, her father had told her; definition was its own power.

"You would know, An. You were the one who called me up." The small god's words were high and clear, a glass bell of a voice. "I am set over small chances. My celebrants are the gamblers and all others who hope."

One of the carrion gods brushed An, the touch exploratory but insistent. Its fingers sank knuckle deep into her flesh, precipitating a wave of neuralgia that rode all the way up her arm. An gasped, pulling away in pain. The gap between her and her god widened, and the scavengers tensed.

An swung her body around, shielding the god with her back and arms. "Chance is as good a name as any. I need you to trust me." An hadn't done this before, not in all her years of watching her father from the shadows of the temples of her childhood. But she knew, with a bone-deep knowledge, how to hide a god: you hide a god in your heart. She wrapped her arms around Chance and pressed them in towards her own chest.

She felt, in that space between heartbeats, a moment of transcendence. She was not a god, they were not a human, but together they were both and more. Where the carrion gods took and consumed, her god gave and gave until it seemed that An's veins would burst.

With the small god inside her, the playground and the predators fell away, and so did time. Gods did not experience time as people did; to them there was only the now, an infinitude of moments branching out. An saw her life, possibilities arrayed and stretching out into lives that might have been, futures radiating out from pasts, branching out into snowflake fractals. She moved back in her own timeline, watching that last afternoon before the screech of brakes ended her mother's life, and seeing again how her father slowly shut himself away from temple work — from everything — until the hungry cells emerged.

An gulped cool air into her burning lungs, her tongue dry and her eyes smarting as Chance slid from her body and she returned to the present. Emptied of the god, the air felt a little blander, the colours of the world more muted. An knew, from decades of watching her father over-season his soup, that there was a cost for touching divinity, a debt that accrued forever. This was her life now. An's knees hit the ground hard. The two of them were alone. The scavengers had fled, frightened off by the burst of power from the pair of them.

"They'll be back," Chance said, dark eyes staring into the distance, helping An to her feet. "They'll gather in numbers." Chance seemed a little taller — fuller — after the experience.

"All the things I saw, can I go back?" An asked.

"You could. Many people have lost themselves to the past."

"Like my father," An mumbled. "He walked away from everything after my mother left us."

"He would have spent a lifetime looking in through the windows of a house he could not enter. Your mother was already dead. It was not for the small gods to bring her back."

"And my father? What chance do you offer him?"

Chance turned up their sharp chin and looked An in the eyes. "Five percent to two years, one percent to five. You know these numbers."

"They're not fair."

The god of small chances put their fingertips on An's cheek, they were cool and unyielding. "Every small chance is fair."

An wanted to pull away, but Chance's gentle fingers held her chin like a vise.

"It's not fair to me," she managed.

"Nothing is fair on the scale of one. Pull back. There is a rhythm to the race of electrons, to the ebb and flow of disease through the populations, to the aching groans of the plates under Mount Fuji, to the whimsical blinks of the quasars in deep space. There is a dance, and I keep the beat for all the small chances."

"That doesn't help me."

"No, it doesn't. You can reach out to him, you know."

An could have. Should have. But time had been curtailed. Anything she did with her father could be the last time they did something together, and it wouldn't be perfect. So she precisely, perfectly, nothing.

"He left the temples, he left the gods... He left me," An said at last, words scraping up a dry throat and spat out through parched lips.

"You know why that is," answered Chance, their piping voice steady.

Even now the call of the comfortable past pulled at her: hot, clear soup at dinner, thickened with pork bones and sweetened with dried dates, never the same when her father made it; the smell of her mother's hair, clean and rich, as An was hugged to sleep. So it must have been with her father. "Yes."

"But you live as though your father's death is already in the past," Chance said. An had no answer.

Chance watched the horizon, their lower lip dimpling under their teeth. An recognized the habit; things flowed both ways, it seemed. "More of them are coming back. Too many for the same trick to work twice," Chance said.

"Maybe you should have run," An said.

"I know my chances. I prefer it to be sooner rather than later. In any case, I am happy that we got to speak. So many gods miss the ones that call them up."

An pulled the small god along. She was done running away.

THE GOVERNMENT HAD BUILT FIVE dragon playgrounds, of which only the one from An's childhood still stood. The state hadn't been shy about dragging the carcasses of dead ideas all over the country, so it had always puzzled An that they stopped at five. A country that hated gods and entombed a dragon may have had other plans. She ran her tongue over the jagged edge of her chipped tooth. Maybe not all the dragons were gone.

"They want me. If you go now, you can get away," Chance said as An led them to the mosaic dragon.

An gritted her teeth. "I won't leave you."

The scavengers came, keeping their distance at the rim of the playground and daring each other to strike first. An counted twelve, but there may have been more. She took Chance's hand again. It was only the second time, but maybe it was the last, and that was the most unfair thing of all.

One carrion god darted in behind An and struck Chance, taking a chunk out of their side. An screamed as though it was her own rib that had been smashed, her own flesh torn from her body instead of the shimmering stuff that gods are made of. Chance had a raw animal look on their face. Maybe they knew when the next big asteroid would hit or why the double-slit experiment worked, but their eyes showed whites all around and when they whimpered it was no different from the sound of a child.

An waited, watching the scavengers with her back to the head of the dragon, because she only had a single shot at this. Chance would probably tell her that the odds of her plan succeeding were minuscule, and that it was alright — that all the small gods died or became scavengers themselves.

Nothing was fair on the scale of one.

When the carrion gods, with their inky skins like the wings of dark moths, decided to attack, they did so en masse—scavengers, the lot of them, and unused to the civility of queuing. Before they reached them, An took both of Chance's arms in hers and pressed the god into her.

The afternoon sun shone down on a girl with a face full of sand. The fall wouldn't have killed an average child, but the angle was wrong. This branch of the snowflake of possibilities was dark all around. All outcomes were the same, save the one where the dragon woke from beneath the ground and uncoiled its undulating length across the sandpit, breaking An's fall and blasting grit into the faces of her bullies. Only that one. Only that small chance.

The evening wind caressed the god and the woman, defiant in a circle of skulking figures. Like before, their union generated a burst of energy, but the carrion gods had already learned to keep their distance. An saw the constellations of outcomes swirl before her, each one different, each one an ending.

Chance broke away first; the scavenger gods chased them down. They were ripped apart before the last one even touched them.

That wasn't right. An tried another forking branch.

An held the god close to her. The shadowy figures didn't interact well with human flesh, but interact they did. The two died with their arms around each other.

So many paths, all going dark. All were the same to Chance, the curse of being a god. Sometime between a heat-blasted midday and the death of the sun itself, the dragon would likely wake again. But not in all possibilities. In some branches it died in its sleep, its nightmares and death throes setting off earthquakes in Indonesia. In others it woke too late, distraught over the deaths of its kin under the sea and buried beneath the other playgrounds. Its tears brought rain that flooded half of Singapore for a day.

But it could wake at just the right time, like it had before, twisting and lashing out with the length of its body, serpentine and terrible in its raw power. An wasn't a god. She could choose.

The dragon woke.

When the wind died down and the grains of sand dropped back to the ground, there was nothing to show of the scavenger gods but flopping scraps of dark matter, melting into the ground. Nothing was left of the playground but shattered masonry. The dragon had already taken flight, cutting through the air with the fluid grace of a sea serpent. It was young yet, as dragons counted their ages by the passing of empires. The winds that held it aloft were strong enough to whip the drying clothes from the bamboo poles sticking out from the windows of nearby flats. It met An's gaze from the seventh floor, before speeding up to the clouds.

And then there were no dragons left in Singapore. Maybe elsewhere in the world, because the oceans were deep and there were still valleys hidden by fog in the hinterlands of China. An didn't think to enquire about the chances.

NOBODY SAW THE GOD OF small chances at An's side, but everybody believed in them. There would be other days, other battles, but they'd already won once and that was a step forward. Chance could have worn any form they desired, but they still favoured faded T-shirts and cut-off shorts. Their clothes matched the weather, though they didn't feel heat or humidity. On a whim, they sported studs down their left ear in the colours of the spectrum.

Chinatown bustled: people queued to pray at the hollow temples, others cast their faith towards races or the lottery. An had more tea for her father. There would be other scavengers maybe worse, but the air was thick with incense and hope today. Maybe hope for the small chance of a cure, but there was more than one thing that could be cured in her father, and she didn't need hope for that.

CHOKECHAIN

◄ Andrew Joseph White ►

WHEN I COME HOME FOR winter break, halfway through my sophomore year of college, there's a dead girl sitting with my dad on the living room couch.

She has my face.

I stop halfway through the door, trapped there like I'm staring down a ten-story drop and not some teenage girl in pajama pants. Well — not just any girl. A not-me. A corpse, a blackout-in-progress, a dead thing with my face. And I probably look like an idiot, just staring at her, with snow in my hair and mouth half open. *The dead fish look,* Mom would call it.

But that's not it. Not really. I call it the precious few seconds where you collect yourself before going for the throat like a junkyard dog.

Guess I didn't bury this bitch well enough.

"Hey, welcome home." Dad lowers his newspaper to give me maybe the ghost of a smile. "Traffic wasn't too bad?"

I point at the dead girl. "What the fuck is that?"

"Excuse me!" Dad snaps the newspaper shut like a belt in his hand. Dad is the lily-white ex-hippie kind of father, though — he wouldn't dare beat my ass. But when the dead girl stands? Shit. I step back. Bare my teeth. Swallow down the sick taste in my throat.

"Hi!" She sticks out a hand for me to shake. "Mom told me all about you. She was right, you do kind of look like me. Weird."

The junkyard dog snarls and so do I. *"Who said that?"*

She stammers uselessly.

"Mom?" she says. "Our mom? She — "

177

And then Dad is between us, pushing the dead girl behind him, taking my suitcase and shoving it into my hands. A wheel hits my ribs and I cough.

"No," he says. "I'm not dealing with this. It can wait until Mom gets home." He points at me. "You? Your room. Now."

"What, we're not gonna talk about this?" This dead thing, this dead girl *with my face*. "I'm not just going to — "

"*Now.*"

The dog is on the tip of my tongue, inches away from tearing out a jugular to delight in the arterial spray, but I just yank out the suitcase handle instead. There's a copper taste in my mouth somewhere between blood and stale pennies.

Fine. I'd rather go to my room than deal with this.

"It's okay, honey," Dad murmurs behind me, smoothing the dead girl's hair. I stop halfway up the stairs to watch. She's nodding, eyes shiny with tears, hands pressed together like she's trying to keep from shaking. A delicate thing, almost, if not for the removable panel etched into her throat. It's unmistakably there, the lines so faint you'd think they were drawn there with pen. But I know better. I know *exactly* what the dead girl is. "It's okay. We'll talk this over and it'll all be okay, I promise."

Not a girl. Not a she. Not a person at all.

An android.

It.

I turn away again.

"I'm — " the android says to my back. Its voice trembling but hopeful. "I'm your new sister. Natalie."

It says that name and I just about lose my mind.

I had peeled that name out of my skin with a razor blade and here my parents are, picking scraps of flesh out of the trash to sew onto this *thing*. I slam my bedroom door.

You know, in a way, I'm almost impressed. My parents have never dirtied their hands reaching into the garbage before. I'm the one with filth crusted under his nails.

So what now? What next? The junkyard dog is straining at his lead and I can feel him in my chest. There's a chain rattling in my ribs and a growl somewhere in my sternum.

You'd think they'd know better than to fuck with a rabid dog.

DINNER IS AN UNDER-SEASONED CHICKEN casserole because, you know, white people. Mom texts me to come downstairs and I do, huddled in an oversized hoodie and sweatpants as if smothering myself in old clothes will make me more palatable. Not that I *want* to be palatable. But I do want to get through dinner.

Mom is lurking just inside the kitchen, an ambush predator in chunky businesswoman heels.

"Dad told me about what happened when you got home," she says.

"Did he." The casserole looks like shit and I consider blowing all this off and going to Taco Bell like the antisocial asshole I am. It doesn't help that Dad and the android are talking in the dining room. Probably about me. Dad watches me through the doorway, the unwavering stare of a squirrel keeping too close an eye on a hawk. "Huh."

"I think we need to have a talk about how rude you were."

I open the fridge and pull out milk and a bottle of chocolate syrup. The fridge dings as it realizes there's only half a gallon left and automatically adds it to the grocery list. We have one of those *smart* refrigerators.

"Sorry," I say, grabbing a glass. "Can't talk."

"Why not?"

I mix my drink and take a big swallow, pointing at the glass.

"Drinking chocolate milk. Mouth's a little busy."

There's a defeated sort of silence in the kitchen. And I think I put a little too much syrup in here.

"Right now," Mom says, "I just need you to be civil."

We all get our food and sit. The dining table can technically fit six, but we've only ever needed three of the chairs before, so now there's this awkward shuffling where we try to figure out where we're going to sit and all of us are acutely aware of the fact that where we sit will be our assigned seating for the entirety of winter break. I don't get to keep my old spot, either. Figures. It's the android's now. Cool, this is fine. This is — this is fine.

"You can have chocolate milk with dinner?" the android asks, eying my glass.

"Chocolate milk is a dessert, sweetheart," Mom tells it. "Your sis — br — " She clears her throat. "Is being rude."

I cough and cover my mouth with a napkin to keep milk from

spilling down my chin.

Holy shit.

She can't even say it.

The android looks disappointed. "Oh."

Dad points at his food with more force than necessary. "This casserole is *great,* dear."

Yeah, no, I'm not going to be able to eat. Not tonight. I'm staring at the android across the table, fork resting limply in my hand, watching this mockery of a human pick through the food like it's still getting the hang of eating.

The android is almost pretty, in a plain sort of way. There's nothing distinct about it: just the frizzy brown hair I shaved off, the simple white blouse I tried to throw away. Maybe the makeup I used to force myself to wear.

But it has my face. It has my fucking *face,* I can't eat with this thing at the table with me, it's wearing my old clothes, I want to tear out hair I don't have anymore, I'm going to reach across the table and snap its fingers just to feel something *break* in my hands.

"So," I say, tapping my fork against my plate. A tic. The dog rattling his chain. "How much did it cost?"

"What was that?" Mom says through grit teeth. What she doesn't say comes through loud and clear: *Civil, you ungrateful shit.* Dad takes a drink to stay out of the conversation. The android just blinks, a forkful of gross casserole halfway to its mouth.

"How much did it cost?" I jerk my thumb at it. "How many paychecks did you save for this? Did you take out a loan? And the amount of customization, Jesus Christ." Mom's face goes red. "It's even got the same crooked tooth I do, yeah? Right there on the bottom jaw? A little to the left?"

The android whispers, "I don't understand."

"Stop it." Mom leans across the table. "Look what you're doing, you're scaring her."

Dad almost steps in but I don't let him say a goddamn thing. I get up and slam in my chair so hard it bangs against the table.

"I'm not hungry," I say.

"You are not going to just get up and leave," Mom says. "Absolutely not."

But I do anyway, and I take my chocolate milk with me.

The junkyard dog follows me up the stairs, chain dragging in his mouth. *Bark bark, puppy,* he says. I put a hand over my throat just to feel him speak. *Is that all you got?*

WHEN I TOLD MOM I was transgender, she broke down into sobs, body-heaving sobs, and threw herself on the bed like a fainting couch. *Do you know how hard this is going to be on us? How much you're asking from us? People are going to think differently of us, you know. Of me.* Of me. Of me.

When I told Dad, he pestered me with so many questions I could barely breathe: *are you sure? Maybe you're just a masculine woman. How do you know? What is a man to you? What does it mean to be a man? I just want to make sure you're sure.* And when I stopped answering, it was like we had never spoken at all.

(The junkyard dog fed on the guts I spilled choking it down, tearing myself apart in anger, bleeding at the gums to play innocent, fake it, pretend I didn't want to snap. See, drawing blood gets you put down.)

(Rabid dogs get shot.)

WHEN I SAY *RABID,* THIS is what I mean:

The first time I drew my own blood, I was the same age as everyone else when they scraped their knee on the playground and stared as the little red beads swelled in clusters like eggs on the back of a mother spider. The first time I drew someone else's blood, though, I watched in mild fascination as it dribbled from a shattered nose speckled with glass, twinkling in the dim light of streetlamps. The junkyard dog had crept out of the dark, laughing, dragging his chain behind him. *You want to be a real man?* he'd said. *You know what men do. So do it.*

I was arrested and charged with one count of destruction of property and one count of criminal battery. The guy deserved it, though, so it was fine.

Juvenile court is surreal, you know, when you plead guilty and you're not sorry for what you did. I was sixteen, hair pinned back and curled the way cheerleaders wore it back then, wearing a dress Mom picked out for my court date like it was an *actual* date, the kind with boys and milkshakes. My parents' lawyer was cute, I guess, for thirty-something. I pretended I was dressing up for him.

I told the junkyard dog, "I didn't mean to hit him. I just wanted to break the window. I didn't know he was there."

He said, *You don't really believe that, do you?*

"I do."

You're glad you hurt him.

I shook my head. "I'm not."

You want to be a real man, don't you? Don't you? Because right now, in that dress, you're not convincing anyone.

I eventually learned that being a man doesn't mean you have to be callous and cruel — something certain boys-born-boys never learn. But I also learned that's just the kind of man I am, and I'll take what I can get.

So, yeah. I'm already foaming at the mouth.

WELCOME TO TRANSHEARTBEAT.COM FORUMS! We offer a safe, inclusive space for trans people and their families to speak their minds. Please be respectful!

Forum: Family and Relationships

New thread —

Mom bought a Robo & Co android. Looks just like me, except, you know. Not trans. (Rant)

I posted this yesterday. It's practically a small essay and only makes sense about fifty percent of the time, but it already has seventy comments and there's at least three fights in the ensuing threads. I'm laid out on the couch while the parents are at work, scrolling through the replies on my phone. Most of them are pretty sympathetic — you're not supposed to give advice in a Rant thread, anyway.

"Fuck that SUCKS. Honestly that's super gross. How would THEY feel with replicas of themselves walking around? the fuck"

"I mean cis people are The Worst what did u expect"

There's one or two replies from cisgender people — they're here for the "friends/family of trans people" forums — who tell me to calmly talk it over with my parents as if that's going to help. Yeah, right.

But then: *"Are android replicas of living people even legal?"*

I stop scrolling.

Right now, the android is upstairs. It has its own room, the guest room across the hall that has suddenly become *not* a guest room, and I spent the morning Googling if androids actually sleep or not. Apparently, they're programmed to, but all they can do is lie there with their eyes closed. They're still "on" the same way a smart device is always "on" so it can hear when you yell, "iOven! Preheat to 350!"

I reply, *"?? Elaborate."*

"There was a supreme court case about this shit a while back. Check out this link: https://supremecase.org/martinez-v-robo.html but the gist is, this lady's ex commissioned a full replica of her as an android and she took the company to court for allowing it. She was scared it was going to be used in revenge porn or as a sex doll or something. After all the shit that went down about revenge porn back in 2024, the court wasn't about to fuck up on that again and she won."

"Oh! Good morning."

I hold my phone against my chest as the android picks its way from one stair to the next, holding onto the banister, watching its feet carefully as it goes. It's wearing my old Hello Kitty pajama bottoms.

"I was actually kind of hoping you'd still be home," it says.

It leans against the couch, watching me warily. I glare. Other than the panel on the throat, it looks so realistic. I pick apart its appearance, trying to find something else that would clock it as not human, but come up with nothing. There's even a shine to its lips and a warm glisten to its eyes. I want to grab it by the throat, pull the panel off and reach inside, tear out the wire and peel off the skin, just to see if it bleeds. Just to see if its eyes bulge as it chokes.

"Were you," is all I reply.

"Yeah. I wanted to ask a question." It twists a curl of hair around its finger. Less flirty, more nervous. Pretty sure this thing doesn't know how to be flirty. Nobody wants to program *that* into a robot. "Do you and Mom get along?"

The dog snarls. I wonder how the two of us must look to him, some terrible approximation of identical twins, half-identical, or maybe a quarter — one of us a man, the other made out of lab-grown flesh. That doesn't leave much to have in common.

"We used to," I say.

"Can I ask what happened?"

I shrug. "Who knows. Shaved my head. Stopped wearing dresses." I go back to my phone. "Don't do that and you'll be golden."

"…oh." Its voice is so quiet. Barely there at all. Just a little *oh*.

"You should be fine."

"Okay. Okay."

As soon as it turns away to do God knows what, I go back to the forum.

"*Hopefully your parents aren't planning to turn you into a sex doll,*" the commenter continues, "*but creating an exact replica of a person now requires that person's signed consent. The problem is, considering the fact you're a dude now, the company probably considers you two separate people. It's some bullshit, I know, but it's not an* exact *replica so I don't know what to tell you.*"

There's already another response underneath: "*so what ur saying is that if i wanted to get an android of a genderbent betty white that'd be totally legal*"

"*That's a very specific kink,*" says the commenter, "*but technically yes?*"

I open the link and scan the webpage.

Huh. Ms. Martinez really fucked that robot up.

I WOULD SAY THERE'S AN art to staying sane in a household like this, but it's not much of an art and I'm not much of an artist. So here's the basics: all you have to do is obsessively hold onto the good times until you can get the hell out of there.

Believe it or not, there actually were good times once. I have remnants of them in my room, tucked away where they can't be mistaken for anything more than the survival mechanisms they are. Photos, newspaper scraps, flash drives loaded with memories. Little things, little bits of warmth and not much else.

The only item I let out of containment is an old concert shirt — Metallica, *Master of Puppets*, a hand-me-down from Dad. It's so old the collar's gone wooly and the print is faded. It's just red and white and gold now, black peeking through like cracks in a sidewalk.

And now I can't find it, which is some bullshit, and also how I end up in the android's room.

See, Mom does this thing where she takes all my dirty laundry before I can get around to doing it and returns it with a piece of the android's clothing mixed in. Yesterday, it was a flowy blouse I wore to freshman year picture day. What kind of shit is she trying to pull, honestly? It's not like she can trick me into wearing it by slipping it underneath my jeans.

So either Mom finally threw it away, or —

"Do you have my shirt?"

The android meets my eyes in the mirror. An eyeshadow pallet clatters against the desk. I can see myself in the reflection there, lurking in the doorway, teeth peeking through my lips. The android's room is all peach and gold, pretty enough colors. I look like some terrible thing compared to it all, a land mine in a fine art museum, muddying the room with a boy made of scabs and broken glass.

"No?" it says.

"You don't even know what it looks like." I come in and shut the door behind me. "Let me look."

"Uh — " It backs away as I open the dresser. Fuck. All of these clothes are mine. Not mine *anymore*, sure, but they had been, three drawers full of shit I tried so hard to throw away and now here they are, staring right back at me. I slam one drawer shut and move to another.

I ask, "What are you getting all dressed up for, huh?"

"Class?"

"What class?"

"The, um — orientation classes. I go twice a week."

Hadn't noticed, but alright.

"You need classes to learn how to be a person?"

"I *am* a person," it says. "I'm just bad at it, I guess."

"Are you, though?"

"What?"

"Are you a person?" I close the second drawer. Wasn't there, either. Shit.

"Of course I am."

"Huh." I walk over, slow, a predator's stalk, and come up behind it, hands tightening on its shoulders. It stares hard into the mirror with the stiff posture of a prisoner. "Funny. Never fooled me. All we have to do is take off that panel to prove it, right?"

"Please don't do that," it whispers.

"Why not? Does it hurt? Do robots feel pain?"

"I'm not a robot!"

I tilt my head. My eyes are bright, canine, not mine, not really.

I ask, "Then what the fuck are you?"

The door swings open and Mom comes in, an old dress of mine clenched in her fist.

Her words: "Oh, *hell.*" She doesn't even have to touch me — I scramble back like the bitch is brandishing a red-hot iron. "What has gotten into you! Speaking to your sister like that!"

"I — "

"Come *here.*" Mom grabs me and gets all close and serious like I've done something really, seriously wrong, the kind of thing she did when the police brought me home in cuffs. This time, though, I don't swear. I don't struggle. I just show my teeth. "This is not okay. This kind of behavior? It's not okay at all."

"I was just asking if it'd seen my shirt."

"Not with that language you weren't. Apologize. Now."

"I didn't do anything."

"*Now.*"

The junkyard dog rolls his eyes. *Sounds like your dad,* he says. The android slowly turns, hands clenched in its lap. I make eye contact for just a second.

"Sorry," I mumble.

Mom nods. "See? Was that so hard?"

Then she boots me out of the room. "We're almost late," she hisses. "I don't need you being *difficult.*" And the door slams and I linger there, hand on the molding of the frame, parsing the murmur of their voices as a chain rattles deep in my chest. Ears flat back. Hackles raised.

"Do I have to wear makeup?" the android asks.

"It makes you look cute," Mom says.

"You let my brother dress himself."

"Your — you know, doesn't dress right. I'm just making sure nothing rubs off on you."

"…I don't want to wear that. Can I pick something else?"

"It'll make you look nice. I promise. Now hurry up and put it on, I want to leave soon."

Even it doesn't look good in a dress, the junkyard dog cackles. I tug on the choke chain. The damn thing never knows when to shut the fuck up. *Wait! Wait.*

"What?" I whisper.

Do you still have your old bat?

And then he smiles a toothy smile, all fangs, all the way back into the blackness of his throat.

186

"HEY," DAD SAYS AS I pull kitchen shears from the knife block. "I feel like we should talk."

Never a good sign. *We need to talk* is white middle-class parent speak for *I'm going to tear you a new asshole.* But, like, in a white middle-class parent sort of way. So there's no actual ass-ripping at the end, just a crushing sense of disappointment, uselessness, and the ever-present threat of being disowned.

And, of course, he's engineered the scene like a super-villain, having roped me into helping make dinner so I can't leave without looking like a douche. This pisses off the junkyard dog *so much* and he's snarling at me to leave, *leave, just drop the shears and leave, you don't have to listen to him.* But I don't leave. Funny, the delinquent can't even walk out of a kitchen.

So instead of anything else, I just flash him a half-hearted smile as I snip a raw chicken breast into cubes. The kind of smile I used to give. "Uh oh."

"I just — I just want to apologize for bringing in this new family member so suddenly. It's clearly upset you, and I understand."

I nearly cut off my own pinkie with the kitchen shears.

Is that why he thinks I'm mad?

"But I really do think you two will get along," Dad continues as I fumble with the chicken. "You need to give her a chance. You're a lot alike, you know."

"I wouldn't say that."

Dad shrugs. "I would."

"Alright. I guess."

"Exactly." Dad reaches across me to get a knife from the block and starts cutting up a green pepper. "And you have to cut Mom a little slack, okay? You know, when we got married, all she wanted was a daughter." I choke. "She was *so* happy to get you. And when you cut your hair, when you bought all those clothes from Goodwill, you — you broke her heart. I think this is just how she's processing all of this."

Rattle the chain. "She's been processing it for a long time now."

"It's hard for her. You dropped this on us so suddenly."

"Yeah, well, you've had time to get over it." I grab the raw chicken with my bare hands and pour it into the searing pan. "This isn't about you."

"It may not be *about* us, but it's *affecting* us anyway."

"That's no excuse to treat me like shit in the meantime."

The kitchen goes silent. Well, not entirely silent, because the chicken, unaware of the emotional gravity of the situation, continues to ignorantly sizzle instead of respecting the moment.

"I think you need to give us a little credit," Dad says.

"Say my name, then."

"That isn't the point — "

"Say my name."

A beat. More sizzling.

"We accepted you," he finally decides on. "It just takes time. And it's *rude* and *cruel* to take your feelings out on your new sister. Am I clear?"

Call the android what it is. The dog bares his fangs. *A replacement. A REPLACEMENT. You chicken shit motherfucker.*

The venom on the words burns my throat as I swallow it back down. "I guess."

"Alright. Good." Dad goes back to chopping peppers. "Now, neither of us can take Natalie to her class after dinner tomorrow. Can you drive her?"

I stir the chicken. The oil spits. "Sure."

ACCORDING TO THE ESTIMATES ON Robo & Co's website, the base cost of an android runs around twenty grand — the price of a used car around these parts. When it comes to Mom's android, all the customizations would probably hike it up another ten.

I readjust my bat under the towel so it doesn't look too suspicious, mull over my handiwork for a moment, and go inside to grab the keys.

At thirty thousand dollars, this is a felony. But if Ms. Martinez got away with it, I think my chances are pretty good, too. Not perfect, but good. Good enough.

"You ready?" I holler up the stairs.

It's starting to snow outside, the way it had been when I got home, and it's already getting dark. I huddle next to the radiator, watching fat flakes fall from the sky. The only sound is the truck idling in the driveway. The junkyard dog is pacing, paws hitting the floor in rhythm with my heartbeat. I tug at my scarf like pulling on a choke chain. Just to gag it. Just to tell it to wait.

The android comes down the stairs in my old coat, a black shirt peeking out from the fur collar.

"Why are we leaving so early?" it asks.

"We're gonna make a detour."

"To where?"

"I'll explain in the car. C'mon. I don't want to be late."

It follows me outside, staring at the grey sky, and sticks its tongue out to catch a snowflake. There's some kind of innocence to it. Almost toddler-like, almost sweet. I zip up my coat.

All Robo & Co products comes equipped with a panic system. It's written on the website, plain and clear. *Any extensive damage to the product will immediately alert both Robo & Co and the owner of the product.*

It opens the truck door and gets in, eyes still turned skyward.

The bat rests in the back seat, sleeping under the towel. My nails are digging into my palms. All this isn't *its* fault, sure. But you can't just build a better child out of spare parts when your old one stops being exactly what you want. Is this all I've ever been to my parents? *A daughter?* Not their child, not a human being, but a *daughter?*

Send a message. Bark, bark. *You know what men do, so do it.*

I start the truck and pull out onto the road, turning up the heat.

"So," I say. "I know you haven't seen snow all that much, so I'd figure I'd take you somewhere you can really see it."

"Oh! That sounds nice."

"Yeah. It does, doesn't it. And — consider this an apology. For Wednesday."

"You already apologized, didn't you?"

I shake my head. "I mean it this time."

I set directions on my GPS for an overlook on a secluded mountain drive. It's a nice place. Beautiful, actually. And here I am, about to fuck that up, like I always do.

The android puts a hand over the vent, grimaces, and shuffles out of its coat. "Can you turn the heat down?"

"Sure. I — " I glance over. "Is that my shirt?"

The android looks down. It's my Metallica shirt, all black and red, unmistakably mine down to the frayed bits on the collar. I tear my eyes away to focus on the road.

"I've been looking for that," I say. "I told you I was looking for it. Where did you get it?"

"It was in your things." Its voice is quiet, so distant, I can barely hear

189

it. "I know, I'm sorry, Mom told me I shouldn't take things that aren't mine, but — I don't like the clothes she gave me." I blink dumbly. "I just wanted something else. Sorry."

I shake my head. Clear it like an Etch-A-Sketch. "It's fine, it's fine, it's okay. I just wanted to know. You can wear it."

"Are you sure?"

"Yeah. Yeah, I'm sure."

The android stares at its lap instead of out the window like it had been. "Okay."

Why are you being nice to it? You're just going to kill it.

I tug at my scarf again. Choke. It's not killing. It's property damage. Thirty grand of property damage. A felony. Choke. *Choke.*

Pull on the choke chain until you can't breathe just to shut him up.

THE OVERLOOK IS BEAUTIFUL IN the dark evenings of winter. The truck's engine ticks as it cools — when pretty much every car is electric these days, it makes me wonder if there's a speaker under the hood, click-click-clicking, as if to reassure old-timers who still remember the gasoline crises of yesteryear. Snow gathers on blades of browning grass, tucks itself in the crooks of bare tree branches, and spots the roofs of houses below. Up here, we're alone, and the only other sign of humanity are the gloaming lights dotting the valley like fireflies.

"It's beautiful," the android says. Its feet make little impressions in the snow, small footprints. I swipe them out of existence with my shoe.

"Isn't it?" I say. I open up the back door of the truck and leave it like that to pretend I'm swiping dirt off the rug. The bat is there, hibernating, waiting. "You can go up to the edge and look if you want. There's a railing."

"I'm good here." It wraps my coat around its body, breath coming out in clouds, a yard or two from the edge.

"You won't fall."

"I'm fine."

I wrinkle my nose and step away from the truck, passing it to walk up to the railing and lean over. In the dark, I can barely make out the trees that dot the ten-story drop. My stomach clenches — I hate drops like this. But the junkyard dog is lying in wait, slavering at the ideas swirling in my head. All I have to do is get in one good hit and then I can haul it over the edge. In a forest like this, it'll never be seen again.

"See?" I say. "It's not that scary."

"I don't like heights."

I frown. "Didn't know they programmed in phobias."

"It's not a phobia," it says. "I'm just scared. Aren't you scared of heights?"

"I am," I say, "but I like the fear."

"I don't get it. I'd rather not die is all."

You've got to be *fucking* kidding me.

"That's fair," I whisper.

I watch for a second as it gazes out on the white-dusted landscape, its mouth slightly open as if grasping for what to say, messy chestnut hair whipping around its face in the breeze. It really does look the way I used to. Twins, half-identical, a quarter, exactly alike, standing across from each other in the winter chill.

The junkyard dog snarls. I put a hand around my own throat, fingers on the arteries. Stay quiet. Stay quiet.

"Making a robot scared of death is a pretty shit move," I say.

"You think?"

"It's a really human thing to be scared of. And being human *sucks*. It should be unethical."

"That's the first time I've ever heard that," the android says.

"Figure they never teach that in robot class."

"I guess not," it says with a soft laugh. "Not really. But are you serious? You don't like being a person?"

Stop talking and do it.

"I mean, it's fine most of the time. But most people think I'm a girl and it's really pissing me off and there's not really much I can do about it."

The android cocks its head.

"Is that why Mom doesn't like calling you my brother?" it asks.

"Yeah."

"She never told me your name."

My breath stops.

What is wrong with you? Why are you doing this? Don't hesitate. You chicken shit motherFUCKER.

"Can I ask?" the android says. "What is it?"

"Michael," I whisper. "My name is Michael."

"That's a beautiful name."

"Thank you."

BE A MAN.

"And I like your hair, too." The android reaches over to brush its fingers across my temple, remnants of the buzz cut I've kept since last year. "I asked Mom if I could cut my hair like yours but she said no."

Drawing blood gets you put down.

"Why would you want to cut it like mine?" I ask.

The junkyard dog looks at me in terror.

"I don't know," the android sighs. "I just thought — if you feel better when you look like this, I think I'd feel better, too." My hands start to tremble. It's cold. That's all it is. I'm cold. "But I am kind of annoyed you already picked Michael. I like that name."

I press my thumb against the carotid artery. My head swims. Choke chain.

"I can help you pick a name," I whisper. "If you want."

Rabid dogs get shot.

Choke.

"I think I'd like that," the android says, and he walks up to the railing beside me and smiles.

I smile back, and I can breathe.

SANDALS FULL OF RAINWATER

◄ A.E. Prevost ►

Piscrandiol Deigadis clutched the battered suitcase close, jars rattling inside as the train whined and staggered to a halt. Piscrandiol waited, eyes shut tight, feet and elbows pressing in all around them as passengers rushed for the exit. Over the din of disembarking, the rain made itself insistently known on the steel roof of the car.

The rain had started sixteen miles back, well beyond the border that separated Piscrandiol's native Salphaneyin from Orpanthyre. It had begun as a mist and crested to a deluge, and it had cracked Piscrandiol's life wide open like a miracle. Piscrandiol pressed their palm against the cool glass, heart pounding. Every trickle of water on the other side ghosted a kiss across their skin.

It had not rained in Salphaneyin for so long.

Orpanthyre was a city of rain, a city where no one went thirsty and anyone could find work. The storm battered against the tarred roof of the train station like a thousand shouted promises as Piscrandiol waited for the exodus to subside. Finally, Piscrandiol took a breath, adjusted their skirts, and stepped out onto the platform.

The street outside the station was a noisy jumble: handcarts and chickens and babies, sunken-eyed miners, families struggling not to lose sight of each other in the heaving human tide. Copper roofs covered the downtown sidewalks, patina battered by seasons of rain, which traced elegant green arcs against a backdrop of stone and wood. Piscrandiol let the flow of the crowd lead them away from the station.

Despite the roofs, there was water everywhere: splashed up by carriage wheels and the jostling steps of strangers, pouring out of the rumbling and broken-open sky, rushing down cast iron eavestroughs and churning white in the grate-covered gutters by Piscrandiol's feet. It was an excess, an exuberance of water, enough to fill every well in Salphaneyin. It sloshed through Piscrandiol's sandals and weighed down the hem of their skirts like it had nowhere better to be.

Piscrandiol braced themselves against a stone wall at a crossroads where the crowd thinned out, and forced down a breath, eyes closing for a fluttering moment of reprieve. In just a short while, they'd reunite with their cousin Geluol, who'd left for the city three years ago. There would be a meal, a roof, a bed. All Piscrandiol had to do was keep their feet moving towards Seven Ingot Three Homeshare, and then the ordeal of traveling would be over.

"If it's an umbrella you need, you've certainly come to the right place."

Piscrandiol's knuckles turned white on the handle of their bag. They turned to the source of the voice — tall and ruddy-tan, with elaborate clothes, standing beside a narrow cart hung with dozens of colourful umbrellas.

The stranger graced Piscrandiol with a businesslike smile. "New to the city?"

Piscrandiol nodded, years of Orpan language classes tumbling together and screeching to a halt in their mouth.

"You'll need one of these — get you started right. Salphaney, aren't you? Lots of you coming 'round these days."

Piscrandiol nodded again. They could feel the blush seeping into their cheeks, volunteering all the information their words couldn't provide.

The umbrella-seller smirked. "Look, I've got a nice blue one that matches yunna skirt. Fifteen lam."

Piscrandiol's mind stumbled over the pronoun — first gender, if they remembered right, but was it Piscrandiol they saw that way, or themselves? Piscrandiol had encountered the concept of gender at school, of course, when they'd studied the Orpan language with everyone else, but having it thrown at them in conversation shattered six semesters' worth of confidence.

Piscrandiol shook their head. "I'm sorry," they managed, handing over a few coins before the umbrella seller could say anything else. "I'm sorry." They grabbed the umbrella and hurried back into the crowd.

THE HOMESHARE TURNED OUT TO be a broad, four-storey square of dark tarred wood that flanked an open central quadrangle, with a custodian's office at the front. Rainwater pooled on the floorboards around Piscrandiol's shuffling feet as they tried to take in the fact that they were being turned away.

"Not moun fault we're full up, child," the custodian was saying, round brown eyes watching Piscrandiol like a clock ticking down to the end of their patience. "There's a lot of you, coming into Orpanthyre. Not even just you Salphaney people, either. There's fires in Mollend, flooding downland..." They shook their head, dark coils tumbling about their shoulders. "I don't want to turn yeym out, but there's no room here."

"But...but makes no sense," Piscrandiol said, trembling slightly. "Please, I — I need to see my cousin. Geluol Bibenia?"

The custodian rapped sturdy fingers on the top of their desk. "Bibenia. Wait half a minute, Bibenia. Hiy's the one been called out of town, isn't hiy. Left a message. Wouldn't be for yey, would it?"

Piscrandiol sighed, letting their eyes close briefly. Out of town? "Probably."

"Well, I can't read Tisalpha, but here. I presume this is for yeym then."

The custodian handed Piscrandiol a flat metal container, and they accepted the familiar weight in their hands with some relief. Popping the latches revealed a hastily-imprinted clay tablet, its workmanship unmistakeably Geluol's.

Babyhead, work beckoned & when the work calls I go. Sorry I couldn't be here to welcome you good & proper. We'll catch up when I get back — mining gig's usually 2-3 mo. but then I'll buy you dinner promise. Bunch of dinners. Anyhow if you need anything ask Dolein, they're good people & saving keys to apt. five-four for you. Stay tough. — Dumdum

Piscrandiol couldn't help but smile at the childhood nicknames, but the idea of spending two or three *months* in the city without anyone they knew made the room spin. They closed the case and looked at the custodian. "When?"

"The message? Oh, week ago, maybe. Was it for yeym?"

Piscrandiol nodded, placing their hands on the desk to steady themselves. "Who is Dolein?"

The custodian's patience cracked, a humourless smile carving dimples into their smooth cheeks. "Me."

PISCRANDIOL PUT DOWN THE FIRST month's rent, effectively handing over most of what remained of their savings, and walked into the quadrangle past a busy jumble of sheds and tarps that suggested a vegetable garden and chicken coop. They dragged their suitcase up four steep flights of indoor stairs, legs trembling and aching, and turned the key in the latch of apartment five-four.

Piscrandiol let the weight of their suitcase pull them through the door. The empty rooms echoed the drumbeat of rainfall on the roof immediately above, a hollow sound that trickled into every corner of the space. Piscrandiol wandered to the window and cracked it open, letting the downpour rage against their outstretched hand. They put it to their lips and drank; they splashed rainwater on their face. This was real. This was home.

Well, not quite yet. Piscrandiol carefully opened their suitcase. With all the jostling, they'd feared the worst — but the only casualty of the trip was one aloe leaf, snapped off and oozing. The jars themselves were all intact.

Relieved, Piscrandiol unfolded the trellis against a wall, hanging the hoops straight. The heavier jars went on the bottom, of course — cloudy glass packed with earth and life-giving moisture. Piscrandiol spoke gently over each of the succulents, fingertips soothing leaves and stems, tiny petals, squat bulbs. In the topmost jars, thin, fleshy tendrils of dark blue spread out, banded with luminescent rings that cast a soft fairy-light against the wall — glowweed, Piscrandiol's favourite. *Now* this was home. Whatever came next, just like the plants, Piscrandiol would lay down roots and thrive.

The tendrils' gentle glow wouldn't light the whole apartment, though, and a search through closets and corners came up empty of candles. Piscrandiol steeled themselves in the bathroom mirror before trudging back down the stairs to face Dolein.

THE CUSTODIAN'S OFFICE WAS UNEXPECTEDLY busy. Two road-weary travelers were in heated conversation with Dolein, while a third tended to a small child; a second, older child crouched off to the side, playing with a bit of wire.

"But I'm telling youm we wrote ahead," the tall knife-faced one said, black hair clinging damply to their collar. "Weeks ago."

Dolein pursed their lips. "And *I'm* telling yiym we don't have record of it."

The traveler's barrel-chested companion tugged at their downy beard thoughtfully. "Gislen, if the letter got lost, there's nothing we can do."

"Like hell there isn't. I'm not letting min family rot in the damn rain."

The third adult hoisted up the toddler, offering Piscrandiol a timidly apologetic smile. "I'm sorry, were yey wanting to speak with the building manager?" They eased one long, ink-dark braid away from the child's grabbing hands. "We're in a bit of a situation, I'm afraid."

Piscrandiol shook their head. "I have arrived here today," they said, as if that would explain anything. Classroom sentences snapped apart and melded with others. "I wish to get a candle. For upstairs?"

"Oh, I think we have some," they said, setting the toddler back down. "Outside, though, in the cart. Appi, go play with Tafis, okay?"

The toddler hid their face behind the adult's knee, clinging to the trouser fabric with needy hands. Piscrandiol smiled, lightly, and shook their head. "I can wait."

The tall one, Gislen, walked over to lay a hand on the braided adult's shoulder. "We'll work this out, Annat," they said, voice gentle. Their black eyes took in Piscrandiol. "Hello," they said. "And you are?"

"Hey lives in the building," Gislen's friend said, before Piscrandiol had a chance to embarrass themselves. "Hey're looking for a candle."

"Oh, we have those," Gislen remarked.

Piscrandiol blushed. "I can buy," they insisted.

"Nah, we've got this." Gislen's smile made them blush more. "Refe and Annat can handle the housing muddle; I need some air anyway. Come on."

The tarp was fastened securely to the pull-cart, but Gislen seemed to know the exact location of everything underneath, because it took them mere moments to yank out a fat yellow candle and hand it to Piscrandiol. Piscrandiol thanked them earnestly.

"Not a problem." Gislen rocked on their heels, glancing over at the water spout gushing nearby. "You're from Salphaneyin, right?"

"You can tell?"

"The way you speak," Gislen said, offering Piscrandiol a quick smile. "Nothing wrong with it to mim. Hear you're having quite the drought, right? We're from downcountry, opposite kind of problem. Fields are washed out. Family decided to give it a go in the city."

"Twenty years," Piscrandiol said. "I think. The last time it rained, I was baby."

Gislen frowned, nodding sympathetically. "Rough. Well." They barked a laugh. "Got all the rain you could possibly want here, I guess."

The one with the beard burst through the door. "Listen, shou's being a goddamn hardass— oh hello," they said, noticing Piscrandiol. "Refe Eibas Suu." They shot out a broad hand to shake. "Gislen bothering you?"

Piscrandiol giggled, shaking Refe's hand. "My name is Piscrandiol Deigadis, how do you do. Gislen is very nice."

"Oh, I *see*," Refe grinned pointedly at their companion. "Anyway, not that I wish to interrupt, but— Gis, yi've got to try talking to this person. Shou says they're full up, offers such kind sympathy for the children, of course, but says there's *rules*, Gis, including not renting out an apartment contracted to someone else. If yi've ever heard of such a thing."

Gislen chuckled, shaking their head. "Love, I've spoken all I can to that one. Unless Annat has some tricks up shun sleeve, I think we're at an impasse here."

Something compelled the words out of Piscrandiol's throat. "I—" Both travelers turned to look at them, and they continued, face burning. "I, ah, you can stay with me. Tonight. Your family. I have big space, a-and small things."

Gislen pushed the hair out of their blinking eyes. "We couldn't do that. Put youm out like that."

Piscrandiol shrugged. "The weather is very bad."

"Yeah, it is." Gislen admitted. "I mean... if Annat can't work something out with the building manager... You'd really do that?"

Piscrandiol shrugged again, smiling.

THE CUSTODIAN WOULDN'T COMMIT TO the safety of leaving a pull-cart in the quadrangle, so Gislen and the other four members of the Eibas family, with Piscrandiol's help, lugged everything up to apartment five-four. Appi, the toddler, ran to the plants immediately; only Refe's reflexes saved the trellis from disaster, scooping Appi into their arms, where they squirmed and reached towards the droopy glowweed.

"That's a pretty plant, isn't it, Appi," Refe said. "We don't want to hurt it, right? So don't touch." They turned to Piscrandiol. "Nothing in there that would hurt a child overcome by curiosity, is there?"

Piscrandiol shook their head. "Maybe, if…if Appi decides to fill the belly with rocks and dirt…it could be problem, but the plants? They will not make sick."

"They really are beautiful." Refe grinned. "We're very honoured you invited us into your home tonight, Piscrandiol. We'll pay, of course."

Piscrandiol shook their head. "No, no," they said. "You…your childs — children, they should not be in the rain." They blushed. "Ah, you also should not be in the rain, but…"

Refe laughed, a warm sound that shook their stomach. "I understand. Don't worry about it. We really are thankful."

"Let us provide supper, at the very least," said Annat, carefully putting a metal-cornered crate down on the floor before taking Appi from Refe's shoulder. "We have enough to share."

"That would be nice," Piscrandiol answered, smiling. "Thank you."

The meal was sausages fried on an elaborate stove that Piscrandiol would not have known how to light, along with apples, dry bread, and cheese. Piscrandiol brewed a hot, sweet tea from a bundle of dried herbs, which garnered compliments even from the children. That evening, the Eibas family laid out their mats in the main room and slept in a pile, Tafis and Appi tucked among their three parents. Piscrandiol smiled at the scene of familial comfort, but declined the generous invitation to partake, explaining that they preferred their own mat. They wished the Eibas clan good night and retired to the nearby bedroom.

Piscrandiol laid a thin wool blanket on the floorboards and stretched out on it, listening to the rain. They felt guilty for lying about having a mat, but the companionship in the living room wasn't theirs to enjoy. It should have all been different. It should have been Geluol offering candles and dinner and friendship, not the warm pile of strangers snoring outside of Piscrandiol's door. Geluol, their only family in Orpanthyre; Geluol, who would be gone for months.

Piscrandiol rested their palms against damp eyes, shoulder blades digging into the floor. No one here even spoke Tisalpha; no one knew the same stories or laughed at the same jokes or loved the same food. But going back to the drought and hunger of Salphaneyin…No. Their parents were counting on them to send money home. Their parents were counting on them to thrive.

The grey light of dawn teased Piscrandiol's eyes open from an almost-sleep of fears and memories. They rolled onto their back and let out a soft breath.

Piscrandiol stretched their aching bones by the tall narrow window, watching the world turn slowly golden in the sun. At some point, during the night, the hammering rain had stopped; Piscrandiol rested their forehead on the glass, and watched layer after layer of Orpan architecture reveal itself as the day burned away the lingering mist. It was a beautiful city, really, this foreign place, when there were no people to ruin the view: verdigris domes and wrought iron swirls, tarred wood, green glass, smoke drifting from the factories downwind. A city built of rainy days.

Piscrandiol sighed and headed into the small bathroom, taking a quick wash before changing into clean clothes. They shaved carefully in the plate-sized mirror, taking time not to miss any patches in the corners of their jaw, and brushed the tangles out of their waist-long hair.

"Scrandle?"

Piscrandiol smiled, looking down to the source of the brave attempt at pronouncing their name. "What is it, Appi?"

"Nanat says, Na, Nanat says breakfast is ready." The toddler hopped from one foot to the next. "I need to poop."

Piscrandiol laughed and let the child take over the bathroom, heading out into the living room where Refe was stirring a thick white porridge on the stove. Their sleeves were pushed up, their hairy arms tattooed in bright blues and pinks and greens.

"Just in time," they said, smiling. "It's a sunny day in Orpanthyre. The rarest of miracles."

Piscrandiol glanced out the window. "This is sunny?"

Refe laughed loudly. "I like yunna sense of humour!"

Piscrandiol smiled shyly and busied themselves with making tea. It had been so easy, for a time, to completely forget about the Orpan concept of gender. Of course avoiding pronouns forever would have been too much to hope for.

Studying Orpan at school, they had run up against its dizzying array of pronouns — three genders with three grammatical cases, a system that at least made up in consistency for what it lacked in common sense. Memorizing the words had been work, but not nearly as hard as understanding when to use them. The teacher had tried to explain the concept of gender: a way the Orpan people spoke and presented themselves differently, based on some sort of internal social sense of being. In class, some had gossiped behind chalk-dusted fingers that gender was about what Orpan people had between their legs, but the teacher had overheard and categorically denied it; whatever it was, as far as Piscrandiol was concerned, it was as inscrutable as how bats flew in the dark.

Watching the Eibas family communicate over breakfast, though, with their effortless and ever-shifting palette of pronouns, made Piscrandiol feel clumsy and wrong. For one thing, it didn't even seem like the words people used always stayed the same. Annat said *heym* to refer to Refe, while Gislen said *hem*. Where Gislen called Annat *shum*, Refe said *shumma*. Whatever gender the Eibas clan saw themselves as having, it changed depending on who they were talking to, leaving Piscrandiol scrambling after clues in the context. It all seemed needlessly complicated for something that, as far as Piscrandiol could tell, didn't mean anything at all.

AFTER BREAKFAST, REFE HELPED PISCRANDIOL with tidying up, drying each plate as best they could. "I hate to ask, but the little ones were on their feet all day yesterday, and…Well, is it all right if I stay here with the children while Annat and Gislen go look for somewhere else to stay?" They frowned, a crease puckering their brow. "I'm very sorry to add to the burden we've already placed on you…"

"No, no." Piscrandiol shook their head quickly. "No burden. Please stay." The thought of suddenly being alone in a bare apartment with only the plants for company opened a yawning pit of dread in Piscrandiol's stomach. It wouldn't even be so bad, really, if the Eibas clan stayed a little longer.

Refe was charming and warm, and gestured expansively when they told stories, which happened a lot. The children made a game of exploring the apartment, which allowed Refe and Piscrandiol a quarter hour of storytelling before the toddler was back at the trellis of succulents.

Piscrandiol stood up quickly, but Appi's sibling was already carefully pulling the little one away from the fragile plants. Piscrandiol gave them an appreciative smile.

"Um, Piscrandiol?" Tafis said, squinting at the jars. "Why'd you carry all this stuff with you from Salphaneyin? Gis said you didn't even bring candles."

Piscrandiol looked down, chuckling a little. "Well, ah, hmm. For us, every plant has meaning, has useful. All from my family home in Salphaneyin, but at home," Piscrandiol said, gesturing broadly, "the whole wall. We can stay cool, and — look," they said, pointing to the dip between two fleshy leaves, where moisture was collecting. "We can… ah…A system, it takes water from all leaves and puts together for drink."

Refe walked over. "That's amazing."

"Why don't you just collect rainwater?" Tafis asked, frowning in a sharp way that suddenly brought out the resemblance to Gislen.

"It doesn't rain in Salphaneyin, Tafis," Refe explained.

"Like, at all?"

Refe shook their head. "Right, Piscrandiol?"

Piscrandiol nodded sadly. "Twenty years, almost, no rain."

"Wow," Tafis gawked, looking towards the window. "That must be *amazing*."

Refe laughed and rubbed the child's feathery black hair. "You need rain to make food grow, Taf. And to drink, and clean things, and all that. –Appi, what's that in yenna hand?"

The toddler quickly hid something behind their back, but not before Piscrandiol recognized it.

"It is broken leaf," Piscrandiol said quickly. "I put on window side yesterday. Not dangerous. Good for sunburn."

Refe crouched down in front of the toddler. "Give it to me, honey."

Appi scowled and shook their head.

"I just want to see it, okay? Come on. I'll give it back."

The child hesitated, then grudgingly handed their parent the snapped-off succulent. Refe stood, sighing. "Definitely chewed on."

"Not dangerous," Piscrandiol repeated, reassuringly. "Also…" They indicated a low, moss-like plant with tiny yellow bulbs. "This one, for when you have stomach hurt. Very good, even when small child eats things."

"But this stuff looks really heavy," Tafis said, prodding one of the jars. "Annat said we couldn't bring anything heavy. I had to leave all min best toys."

Piscrandiol's fingertips traced the ridged edge of a leaf. "Heavy, yes," they mused, wondering how in the world they could express in Orpan what the trellis meant to a Salphaney family. "Heavy but...this one," they said, reverently lifting a small jar with sharp, red-tipped leaves, "it is cut from...very old plant. Many generations. And this one, I found in desert. I was about same old as you." They indicated a bubbly little spray of light green. "All here, these are from kitchen of house when I was a child, and — ah! This one," Piscrandiol quirked a smile, showing a coral-blooming cactus, "is ah, how do you say, farewell? Farewell from my first sweetheart." They grinned. "Do you see?"

Refe hoisted Appi into their arms. "Yeah," they said, smiling softly. "I do."

"I don't," said Tafis.

"Some things," Refe said, "you carry around with you no matter what, because... Well, maybe they're heavy, but they lift you up, too, right?"

Tafis tugged on Refe's sleeve. "I don't get it."

Piscrandiol turned to the window, smiling, blinking back tears.

*

Maybe it was the influx of refugees fleeing the devastation of the floods, or Salphaney filling train car after train car, but when Gislen and Annat returned that night, they proclaimed there was not a single available apartment in the city. Piscrandiol grinned from where they sat on the floor, hair twisted into loops by Appi and Tafis, and made the offer they had been thinking about all day.

It was surprisingly easy to agree on the division of rent and chores, easy to accompany Annat to the market to invest in sleeping mats and lanterns, cups and rice and soap, the many necessities of family life. Piscrandiol spared a little for clothing, as well: no one in Orpanthyre wore skirts, since there was always a gutter or a drain for them to get sodden in, so they brought a pair of simple tan trousers, and boots that sealed the water out. Annat taught Piscrandiol how to pull their copper-brown hair into two long braids, flat and skinny down their back; it took hours to get it right, leaving Piscrandiol perplexed by the apparent ease of Annat's deft brown fingers to do the same, but in the end the braids received the Appi tug of approval. Annat laughed with delight.

Annat was also the first to find employment, carding cotton at one of the city's sprawling mills. Things were looking hopeful for Piscrandiol, as well: they were on the mill's waiting list, and would be contacted as soon as a position opened up. Refe, who spent most days out in the city seeking work, told Piscrandiol that if they'd made the list it was best not to continue applying elsewhere, so they ended up shouldering most of the home and childcare duties with Gislen, at least until the family could afford to send Tafis and Appi to school. This suited Piscrandiol just fine.

One morning over a cup of tea, as the children practiced their letters in chalk on the floor by the window, Piscrandiol asked Gislen about Refe's work.

"Heh's a professor, by training," Gislen said, shifting comfortably on the floor cushion. "History. There must be a hundred unemployed professors of history in Orpanthyre, of course, but heh's dead set on finding work in hen field."

Piscrandiol looked up from the dewflowers the two of them had started sketching with a bit of the children's chalk. "It is not good?"

"I mean...Sure, I'd also love to work in my field, but instead, I'm answering every 'help wanted' sign I see. I don't blame Refe, really I don't," they said, running a hand across their forehead with a sigh. "Heh's *good* at hen job. But we can't feed five people — six," they smirked warmly at Piscrandiol, who blushed, "on one person's salary. We'll barely make next month's rent, in this...What." They narrowed their eyes. Piscrandiol was laughing.

"You..." Piscrandiol shifted a bit closer, reaching out to brush the smudge of chalk from Gislen's brow. "This." They raised a chalky fingertip before dotting it playfully on the tip of Gislen's sharp nose.

Gislen laughed and grabbed Piscrandiol's hand, and Piscrandiol's heart rioted in their chest.

Gislen's eyes were black and bright like galaxies, long straight lashes casting flickering shadows over flushed clay-dark cheeks. Gislen's fingers laced with Piscrandiol's tightly, and Gislen's lips...They were soft, hungry, and hot and bitter like tea, and Piscrandiol never wanted the kiss to end.

Appi shrieked something at their sibling, and Gislen and Piscrandiol parted, far too soon. Piscrandiol's heartbeat throbbed against their interlaced fingers. Piscrandiol could barely dare presume — barely had the words to ask — if this was all right, but in the way Gislen held their hand, in Gislen's irrepressible smile, Piscrandiol seemed to understand that the Eibas family would approve. They rested a flushed cheek on Gislen's shoulder and watched the children play.

IT WASN'T MUCH LATER THAT Gislen found work at a butcher shop, and Piscrandiol was left to look after Tafis and Appi alone. Gislen came home every night tired and smelling of blood; Piscrandiol heated water for their bath and regaled them with tales of their day. And when the children slept, there was time enough for the two of them.

"I hate waiting list," Piscrandiol sighed, limbs tangled with Gislen's, blankets kicked to the edge of the mat. "Annat doesn't even need to say anymore. Just comes home and looks sad."

"Something will open up," Gislen said, kissing Piscrandiol's temple. "Refe seems to think so."

Piscrandiol made a quiet noise. "Refe is a good friend. Sometimes, ah, many times, I worry about jealous...About us..."

Gislen smiled. "Very considerate, but you don't need to worry. Refe thinks you're great. You know that, Pisc."

Piscrandiol tucked heir head under Gislen's chin. "I...I don't think I...I'm attracted," they admitted.

"To...Refe?"

Piscrandiol nodded, but looked up sharply when Gislen laughed.

"Oh, that's hardly what I meant. It's not like you're expected to — to be attracted to all of us. Refe never thinks about that stuff, anyway. I mean, it happens sometimes." They grinned. "Or else we wouldn't have Taf and Appi, but..."

Piscrandiol smiled, looking down awkwardly. "Oh, ah, about that, I won't...I mean...When we..."

Gislen nuzzled Piscrandiol's hair. "You're not going to get me pregnant, no. I'm being careful." They stretched happily. "However, I do know that Annat's been thinking about having another baby, so if you're interested..."

Piscrandiol sputtered, and Gislen laughed, muffling it with a pillow. "I'm kidding. Shou *has* been stealing glances at you, though," they said, thin lips drawn into a smirk. "Shou thinks you're adorable but is much too kind to express jealousy."

Piscrandiol tucked their blushing cheek against their lover's arm. "Well, ah, *shou* can, ah, talk to me about it, at some time. I would be happy to know shou better."

Gislen laughed, twining their fingers together. The sound filled up Piscrandiol's heart with light like a balloon.

"All right. That's fine by mim. But…it's not *shou*; for you, it's *shum*."

Piscrandiol squinted, still flushed. "I…Sorry?"

"*Shou* likes *youm*, *you* should talk to *shum*," Gislen said. "Is it okay if I explain?"

Piscrandiol sighed. "You…Orpan has much too many pronouns."

"We don't have that many! Anyway, I haven't wanted to correct you, but you should probably say *yiy* to me instead of *you*, actually."

Piscrandiol grabbed the pillow and smacked Gislen with it. "It is difficult!" They complained. "We have four pronouns; Orpan has forty-five."

Gislen wrestled the pillow from their grasp, grinning. "Fairly certain you have more than four."

Piscrandiol counted irritably on their fingers. "Okay, well, then nine. It is still not forty-five, Gislen."

Gislen smiled, tossing the pillow aside. "I love the way you say min name," they said, and pulled Piscrandiol into a kiss that made them forget about words entirely. It was unreal, finding such brightness in the grey of Orpanthyre's endless storms. Under Gislen's tenderness, their hunger, Piscrandiol unraveled like an abandoned skein.

JUST WHEN IT SEEMED THE rain would go on forever, the season fizzled into something hotter and hazier. The air hung yellow in the evenings; the streets were loud with the buzzing of insects, and blossoms in a riot of colours burst out on the trees. And one heavy, humid day, Refe came home jubilant, arms full of sweets and flowers.

It was a part-time position, Refe was quick to qualify, a teaching assistantship for a single course that was hardly their specialty, but the faculty at Five Rosewater College had seemed happy to take them on, and they would start next week. It was a trek, on the far side of town, but with the additional income they'd finally be able to send the kids to school. Tafis ran around the apartment in glee, and their little sibling followed suit without really knowing why, hands full of candy.

The following week, Piscrandiol walked Tafis and Appi to Ingot City School, and found themselves alone in Orpanthyre for the first time in nearly two months. As they wandered towards the vegetable market, it was hard to ignore that they were the only adult left without a job;

the only member of the household, even, without a place to be. Back at the homeshare, Piscrandiol chopped parsnips and chard and hot green peppers for stew. Two months on the waiting list at the cotton mill. Two *months*. It was impossible nothing had opened up. Unless there wasn't one at all; maybe "waiting list" was just a way to let Salphaney off easy without actually giving them employment.

Piscrandiol slammed the knife into the cutting board.

Geluol hadn't trained as a miner. Their cousin was a poet, a painter, who had woven worlds of beauty onto the best pottery from the family kiln. But Orpanthyre had robbed them of that gift. Orpanthyre had thrown them in a pit full of sweaty, aching bodies and demanded coal. And Geluol was one of the lucky ones; lines stretched along the sidewalk at the day-labour agencies, Salphaney skirts and sandals and unbraided hair, and very few Orpans between them.

Piscrandiol would never get off that waiting list.

They took a deep breath. How could they explain this to Annat, whose eyes held a steadfast shimmer of hope, whose little heart beat so fast in the darkness? How would the Eibas family react, hearing that the city that had welcomed their kin had no mercy for the stranger? The hospitality of their people was tarnished, but rejecting it would paint Piscrandiol as ungrateful.

Pisrandiol's stomach churned with dread. The Eibas clan had been so kind. They could never know.

EVERY DAY PISCRANDIOL VISITED THE vegetable market, and every day they pushed through their awkwardness and asked the merchants if anyone they knew was looking for help. It shouldn't have surprised them that no one ever was. It shouldn't have surprised them that the 'help wanted' signs had all been taken down from the shop windows. It shouldn't have surprised them that by the time they made it to the day-labour lines after market, the jobs for the day were already taken, or that the factories weren't hiring. Every day, Pisrandiol went home filled with grey thoughts, and sought solace in a trellis full of plants that had adjusted far better to Orpanthyre than they had. And every evening, the Eibas clan came home full of stories, and Piscrandiol served them soup and let them talk. No one seemed to notice Piscrandiol's silence and secrets, and Gislen still shared Piscrandiol's sleeping mat, sometimes.

It was so easy to pretend that nothing between them had changed, so tempting. Piscrandiol should have known that Gislen saw through the silence. That they would wait for the middle of a quiet night to bring it up, catching Piscrandiol unwound and vulnerable.

"Is there anything we need to talk about, Pisc?"

It wasn't even a reasonable secret to keep. It was taking up all this space between them and it was pointless — a tangle of shame and worthlessness, a weight of unbelonging. Why couldn't Piscrandiol just let it go?

"Talk to me," Gislen pleaded. Skinny fingers tangled in Piscrandiol's long hair.

"I talk every day," Piscrandiol snapped, pulling away. "I…I talk every day at the market." It was like pruning away what they were too ashamed to share, working to shape a palatable fact. "Every day…every day I speak Orpan until I have no words anymore." The sculpted truth filled Piscrandiol's gut with bitterness.

Gislen sighed. "I'm sorry. I wish I spoke Tisalpha…Maybe you could try teaching the children."

Piscrandiol closed their eyes. "Maybe. I'm so tired. Everything is *shou* this and *yunna* that, and every person knows well how to say it, but I…"

"You'll get there." A hand reached for Piscrandiol's shoulder.

Piscrandiol shrugged off the touch and sat up. "I don't know." They swept their hair off to the side, locks clinging together with cooling sweat. Nothing ever dried in Orpanthyre. "I can't…how am I supposed to *know*."

Gislen sat up beside them. "Your gender? You just do. You don't need to overthink it."

"You — *yiy* just do," Piscrandiol retorted. "Annat just does. Refe just does. Maybe Appi even. I just *don't*."

Gislen sighed. "I'm sure you do, Pisc. Listen — maybe I'm wrong, but you…you're more like Annat than Refe or mim, right? It's not like you can *not have* a gender. Maybe, I don't know, youn culture and min culture present it differently. But — "

"Our culture doesn't present it at *all*, Gislen," Piscrandiol said, glaring at them. "Why is this so hard to understand? We don't think, 'Oh, I am this, that person is an other this'. Some behave this way, some behave that way, but it is not *gender*."

"Pisc, I find it seriously hard to believe that youn entire region doesn't have anyone with gender in it." Gislen rubbed at their forehead.

"Well, I — it doesn't matter what yiy think! I'm sick of — of always being *youn* and *shou* and — I don't want it!"

Gislen tried to take Piscrandiol's hands, but they pulled back.

"All right." Gislen's hands hung in the air. "All right. I can use different words, love, I can...Just tell me what you want."

Piscrandiol ran a hand across their face. They were having an argument, now, and none of it was even the point...Except that it was. Just one more way in which Piscrandiol was an outsider. "It...Yiy're kind, yiy're so kind, Gislen," Piscrandiol murmured, voice dull with exhaustion. "But...It is everywhere. Everywhere I go, I — I can't get away, everyone looks and *assumes*, one thing, another thing..."

"I can't change society, Pisc." Gislen clutched at the blanket. "Even if you don't feel it, you...What can I say? You give people a certain impression. It's just how we work."

Piscrandiol stood and left, naked feet scuffing across the floor to the living room.

"Pisc...?"

Piscrandiol didn't listen. Ignoring the sleeping family, they stood on tip-toes to grab the pruning shears from the top of the trellis before returning. Gislen gasped and took a step back, but Piscrandiol ignored them too, heading for the bathroom.

"What are you doing? Please, I'm sorry — "

Piscrandiol looked straight in the mirror as they lifted the shears. Two feet of stringy red-brown hair fell to the floor like dead leaves, like shed skin. They heard Gislen gasp and stifle a cry, but did not stop until their head felt weightless, untethered. Then they put the shears down on the sink, and looked up.

Gislen was weeping.

Piscrandiol shivered, their shoulder blades catching the chill of the night air. "All it said was lies," they said, feeling like they should cry as well, but finding tears too distant to answer the call. "All these pronouns are lies. So now? Am I different pronouns now?"

"I..." Gislen took a careful step closer, then another, finally pulling Piscrandiol into their arms. "I don't know," they said. "I don't care. I love youm. Yem. None of it, all of it, forget it. Forgive mim. I'm sorry. We'll figure this out. It doesn't matter."

Piscrandiol stood in the resolute affection of Gislen's embrace, until, with time, they stopped shaking.

THE CHILDREN SPENT THE MORNING grabbing handfuls of Piscrandiol's new short hair, getting it to stick up in ways that made them topple over laughing. Piscrandiol knew they should find some way to speak with the adults about what happened, address the rift that was slowly taking form. But the silence stretched out through a day and a night of missed opportunities, and then Tafis came home from school with tiny sprouting peas and asked Piscrandiol for help planting them, and Piscrandiol found it far too easy to focus on that instead.

The quadrangle was crowded with summer-rich gardens, and among them, waterlogged and flecked with moss, Piscrandiol found the patch of soil dedicated to apartment five-four. They spent a morning on their knees in the mud, Tafis eager to help, until the sprouts were nestled in grooves in the fresh-turned earth. Piscrandiol showed the child how to hammer together a frame to help the pea shoots grow tall, and the two of them went out every day to watch the tender green vines reach for the sky, until they grew strong and thick with sweet-smelling flowers.

The garden was a revelation. Little by little, through the days of planting and weeding, Piscrandiol found their spirit returning. Appi surprised them with a shriveled piece of taro that had sprouted long hungry tendrils — a cherished toy, which they'd been hiding somewhere. Piscrandiol and Appi planted it together, reverentially, and it soon spread broad, heart-shaped leaves that thirsted for the sun. Piscrandiol bought seeds from the market to keep it company, traded with neighbours, and even brought down a fat little blockleaf succulent from the trellis upstairs. Soon the garden was flourishing with watercress and climbing spinach, and Tafis' vines had sprouted pods of fat peas that the children scarfed down by the handful. In time everything grew, even hair.

Or, almost. One morning Piscrandiol found the blockleaf sagged and wilted, drowning in the sodden earth. Piscrandiol kneeled at the edge of the plot and dug their trowel into the soil, carefully lifting the plant up. Rot was spreading in its shallow roots; but maybe if they kept it in a pot, with holes in the bottom…

"Cousin!"

It took Piscrandiol a moment before they realized that the deep voice had spoken in Tisalpha. They turned just in time to be swept up in familiar sinewy arms and spun around as if the mud on their knees and the plant clutched in their hand didn't matter. They stared up into a grinning umber face.

Geluol was back.

Piscrandiol's cousin hit it off immediately with the Eibas clan, talking easily about everything and nothing, and also talking about Piscrandiol, which made them want to disappear. Annat insisted they have a special supper, and Refe ran out to get a whole goose already roasted while Annat and Gislen fried vegetables and Tafis tended the rice. Piscrandiol threw together a salad of garden greens and stumbled through their cousin's giddy questions. Had they gotten the tablet; had Dolein helped them out? How had they met the Eibas family and ended up living with them? Did they have a job? Were they seeing anyone? Piscrandiol tumbled through replies in a mother tongue that felt clumsy until it didn't, and suddenly they had their own voice again.

And Geluol...Geluol was perfect at Orpan, too, navigating pronouns like all of it was a breeze, like they'd always known how, like gender was the simplest thing in the world. Watching them all chat over tea in the lamplight, with Appi falling asleep in their lap, Piscrandiol wondered when Geluol had become more of a stranger than the rest of them. Piscrandiol stroked Appi's ink-black curls and stared into the lamp's flickering flame.

THE NEXT MORNING, BEFORE THEY could change their mind, Piscrandiol pulled Gislen aside. "I've been lying to you."

Gislen frowned and cast a glance over their shoulder where Annat was dressing the children. "What?"

Pisc tucked their hair behind their ears. "For a few weeks. I'm sorry."

Gislen glanced away again, then took Piscrandiol's hand. "Let's go outside."

Pisc nodded. Their hand felt cold and clammy inside Gislen's all the way down the stairs.

They stood on the covered walkway outside their door, sheltered from the light rain.

"What's going on, Pisc?"

Piscrandiol watched the rain trickle down the taro leaves. "I've been looking for work."

Gislen turned and looked at them. "Yeah?"

Piscrandiol nodded. Thunder rumbled, but distant.

"And?" Gislen said, encouraging. "Did...did something happen? Did you find something?"

Piscrandiol bit their lip and shook their head.

Gislen took a deep breath. "So...what, uh, what have you been lying about?"

Piscrandiol glanced over. "Annat...Annat believes the waiting list, and Refe said, I mean, Refe said I shouldn't look, and...I don't think the waiting list is real, or, not real for *me*, and..." They took Gislen's hands, looking up into their gaze. "You all work so hard. But no job wants Piscrandiol. So many Salphaney looking for work. So I...I make soup, and I grow vegetables, and every day I look for work, but there is no work. And my parents, I need to send money, and you, your family, I take advantage. You are so generous, but this city, I can't always..."

Gislen gently squeezed their hands. "Oh, love," they murmured, tugging until Piscrandiol was in their arms. "Oh, love."

Pisc closed their eyes, cheek on Gislen's shoulder. Gislen was quiet for a good long time, and Piscrandiol hung on, scared that when they let go, Gislen would say something terrible.

"You're not taking advantage of anyone, Pisc," Gislen said, finally. "I love yem. We *all* love yem. The children think you are the greatest thing they've ever met."

Pisc chuckled, in spite of themselves, and gave Gislen a squeeze.

"Listen," Gislen continued, parting enough to be able to meet Piscrandiol's eyes. "I'm so sorry if we gave yem the impression you...you shouldn't be looking for work because Annat put yem on a waiting list. You can do whatever you want. And we're *happy* having you at home, if that's what you want. I didn't realize we were putting this pressure on yem. I know we didn't mean to."

Piscrandiol smiled weakly. "Yiy're mixing up pronouns," they pointed out. "First and second."

Gislen blushed, grinning. "I'm trying something new. Adapting."

Piscrandiol took Gislen's hand back, threading their fingers together. "Geluol has no trouble with pronouns," they complained.

"So what." Gislen kissed Piscrandiol's head. "Some people behave one way, some people behave another way, and that doesn't mean anything, right? That's what you told me. I believe it."

Piscrandiol leaned their temple against Gislen's shoulder and looked out at the garden. The peas were all but harvested, their vines growing tough, but the season was far from over. It would be time to plant something else soon.

OF WARPS AND WEFTS

◄ Innocent Chizaram Ilo ►

IN HIS OTHER LIFE, MY husband is another woman's wife. This does not perturb me. What sprinkles fear-flakes on my bones is the dark splotches my husband's spouse leaves on his brown skin. She makes it obvious. Her catawampus nails burrow deep into the suppleness of my husband's back, her torrid lips besmirch my husband's nipples, and her tongue drips lava that scalds my husband's navel. Every evening, when my husband walks into our bedroom, I am forced to deal with this awareness of sharing him with another person. I struggle not to touch the portions of my husband's body smeared with dark splotches. The whorls of his navel, the folds of his nape, his nipples, and the curly spread of ginger-colored hair on his chest. I understand they no longer belong to me.

Ikoro, my husband's wife, has sworn to make things arduous for me. She does not give half a hoot about my territoriality. Don't get me wrong, I don't usually have a problem with sharing. I have been sharing all my life. My mother had seven daughters and, until her skull got crushed on one of her many expeditions to hunt albatrosses, she shared her love among us. Each day of the week was reserved for a daughter. As the eldest, Monday was my day and my curfew was extended to 11:00 PM, Ginika was allowed an extra helping of jollof rice and grilled pork on Tuesday, Owanne could go swimming with the mermaids on Wednesday, Chinwe danced with the shirtless boys on Tarkwa Beach every Thursday, Ify could wear miniskirts on Friday, Ujunwa was exempted from house chores on Saturday, and Obiageli went for her singing classes on Sunday. But these days, I have begun to loathe the idea of sharing, especially sharing a husband. Last Friday, I came back from a Town Council meeting to find my husband on the bed, his body livid with dark splotches. This repeated show of possessiveness by my husband's wife nauseates me.

As time slips past, the dark splotches on my husband's skin spread like the seaweeds beside River Bambu. Before this month runs out, my husband's palms and soles will be the only thing left for me to caress unless I swallow my pride and caress those parts taken away from me, claimed by my husband's wife, and the thought of this makes my heart's rhythm turn dull and leaden.

"What is love with just palms and soles?" I ask Mba. Mba droops her shaggy tail: a way of saying *A love that sucks.*

My husband is not like the ones you see around with bulgy muscles, trimmed beards, coarse lips, square shoulders, and sturdy feet. He has exquisitely contoured eyebrows, jasmine-scented lips, a raspy voice, feeble arms, and tender skin. He does not sit with an abandoned masculine ease, legs astride. He sits stiffly on a chair, with a straight back and his knees glued together. My husband does not join the company of men at Quidi Bar who stay up late, downing shots of local gin and bragging about the number of women they've bedded. Instead, he enjoys the tranquility of Ekan Hill, where he spends some evenings watching the setting sun graze the hill's peak.

"Sometimes, I need a man who is wild and untamed, but I am not complaining." My voice thins to a whisper. Mba gnaws at the serrated edge of her wheat cracker: a way of saying *You are complaining.*

Lately, my husband has started allowing me to make all the decisions in the house: the petals for our anniversary decoration, the type of primrose for our garden, the brocade material for sewing the curtains, the mahogany for the banister, and the wool for weaving the new rug. He has stopped whining about the thin mesh of cobwebs strung across the ceiling or when I forget to do the dishes.

"Sometimes it seems like I don't even have a husband." I wipe off the teardrop hanging on my left eyelash. Mba flutters her eyelids: a way of saying *Sometimes or all the time?*

In my world, to marry is to begin living two lives. During the day, I am

216

Chime, a married woman with four children carved out of matchsticks. At night, I am Dime, a man married to Felicity, a pink-haired hippie who does not stay at home much. During the day, my husband is Ping, a dragon-poacher's wife. At night, he becomes Ding — my husband, who insists that I put our children in the matchbox every evening before he comes home because their brown heads make him puke. I don't tell Felicity to put away our children when I am Dime. The last thing I feel like is puking when they hop on my back and make me gallop like a horse around the house. I feel loved. They are cute little things, though soon they'll be too grown up enjoy horse rides on my back.

It's still morning. My husband is lying on our four-poster bed. In his eyes I see a blurry image of him as Ping running around a rice field with Ikoro, who catches up, scoops her up, and starts nuzzling her face. The image is clearer now. Ping is wearing cowrie-strung braids and gold-plated filigree earrings. The sand-brown braids are sharp and defined against her black skin. Wait, is the gap between her front teeth widening? Is that a tattoo or another scar on her ankle? I look away as the dragon-poacher rips the chiffon gown off Ping. Soon, they will be lying among the green rice stalks making wild passionate love.

I unzip Ding's skin. Steam escapes from his ribs. I run my fingers along the sliminess of his diaphragm. He jerks. I rush out of the bedroom to the kitchen to wash my hands.

"Pair of show-offs," I curse in my throat as I scrub my hands clean under the tepid sink-water. Mba giggles: a way of saying *You've got no guts for that.*

Sometimes it is hard to fault Ding's behaviour. Ping just married the dragon-poacher a year ago. They are still new in love, like Ding and I used to be. Not anymore. These days, Ding has stopped staring at my body and rearing up with envy when I go to be with my wife. He is too moony from the languorous days of soaking up ecstasies on a rice field to notice the trivialities in my life.

"This is how these things work out." Mba curls up my left foot: a way of saying *Are you just realizing?*

This evening, after my husband slides into me — before I become Dime and leave — I will let him know the ramblings of my heart. I will tell him how I crave for him to compliment my new cornrows and the embroidery I do for his caftans. I want him to know the children miss calling him Baba because they are stuffed in the matchbox when he is around. I will ask him to recall the last time we took long evening walks on Bridge Gringo or played Catching the Sunset like real lovers.

"What is the worst that will happen? He'll smile, tell me he loves me and everything will return to finery." I roll my eyes at Mba, who strolls out of the kitchen: a way of saying *You know things don't work out this way.* And I know then that I won't say it, because what if he says something else? The worst could be so much worse.

Ikem, my last child, hobbles into the kitchen. A flail is chained to his left ankle. At four, Ikem is always easy prey for his siblings' mischievousness. Two months back they told him to climb the roof if he wanted to pluck stars from the sky. Last week, they told him to light a fire above his head if he wanted to grow taller.

"Momma, look, I am a warrior," Ikem says.

He pulls out a sword and waves it at an invisible enemy. He drags the flail along to the food shelf, where he snatches the last packet of coconut candy and wolfs it down in two gulps. The flail leaves a trail of scars on the kitchen floor which reminds me of the marks the dragon-poacher's fingernails leave on my husband's skin. A slight wooziness shrouds my eyes and my legs begin to melt like lit candles.

"Stop it!" I shriek, unwrapping the flail off Ikem's ankle.

"Now I will never become a warrior. Bad Momma!" Ikem slumps on the kitchen floor and starts writhing like an earthworm muddled in salt.

"Stand up!"

"No. Bad Momma!"

I grab Ikem's arm and drag him out of the kitchen. "Ada, Nedu, and Okwui! Come right out."

"If you scold them, I will never become a warrior."

My other children tiptoe out of the bedroom where, I'm sure, they have been eavesdropping.

"Momma." Ada, the eldest, speaks first. Her bold eyes and pouty mouth would have matched mine years ago. That was before I degenerated into this timorous woman who is scared of talking some sense into a dragon-poacher.

"Whose idea was this?" The corners of my mouth constrict.

"He wanted to be a warrior," Nedu says and bites his lips to suppress his laughter.

"And we made him a warrior," Okwui chips in. Okwui dwells in the shadow of his twin brother, always finishing Nedu's sentences.

"Please don't spank them, Momma," Ikem pleads.

"No, they are going to have a cold bath for upsetting my day."

Children like mine who are carved out of matchsticks dread bathing because it leaves them soaked and exhausted for hours. I fill the bathtub with cold water and make sure Ada, Nedu, and Okwui sponge until their skins crinkle like new paper. They step out of the bathtub and huddle against each other to keep warm. I go back to the parlor, where Ikem is fast asleep on the couch. At least Ikem's sleeping and his siblings' after-bath fever will buy me a few hours of peace.

My heart's rhythm is duller than ever. On days like this it feels like it's barely beating.

Noon.

I throw on a faded blue gown and go over Aunty Ukamaka's shop to collect the laundry. Aunty Ukamaka's shop is just across the street, sandwiched between Iya Bola's Restaurant and Okey's Boutique. A popular town joke says if Iya Bola's oily broth stains your clothes, you can either launder them at Aunty Ukamaka's or buy new ones from Okey's. Aunty Ukamaka has been around since forever. She laundered my mother's, grandmother's, and great-grandmother's clothes. I still go to her, even with the new laundromats scattered around Ogbete Market, because no one takes extra care of necklines and the brown rings around the armpit region of clothes better than Aunty Ukamaka.

Aunty Ukamaka is scrubbing a brown cardigan when I walk into the shop, a light splatter of tiny, white bubbles on her face. She wipes her hands on her blouse and offers me a seat.

"Chime, your lips look chapped. Would you like to drink orange juice?" Aunty Ukamaka asks in a typical customer-is-the-soul-of-business tone. She turns the cardigan inside out and continues scrubbing.

"Of course," I say.

"I ran out of orange juice three months ago." Aunty Ukamaka brushes off a sud on the tip of her nose. "Would you try a cup of soda then?"

"If you insist." I stiffen my face to hide the irritation burning inside my cheeks.

"Eish, there is no soda." Aunty Ukamaka folds the cardigan and dumps into a rinsing-bucket. "How about a glass of water?"

"Yes, please."

"No water. I win!"

The woman claps her hands and does a little tap-tap dance. It is now I realize Aunty Ukamaka was playing a game called *What do you want?* A game she invented herself. The last time Aunty Ukamaka and I played *What do you want?* was when I wanted to get married. She offered me bean-cakes, mashed potatoes, and omelet, all of which I said yes to. According to Aunty Ukamaka, the essence of the game is to teach me how to refuse offers.

"Marriage is like an offer. It compels one to exist in two different worlds. Can you really handle that much trouble?" Aunty Ukamaka said after the game.

That was sixteen years ago.

"And you have still not learnt how to refuse offers," Aunty Ukamaka says now. She is smiling, dimples deepening on her cheeks.

"I was playing along. I wanted you to win."

"Nobody plays along in *What do you want?* You lost straight out."

"Fine, you win. Is my laundry ready?"

"Yes. It's on top of the shelf." Aunty Ukamaka points.

"I win."

"Are we playing a game?" Aunty Ukamaka stares in bemusement while I collect the basket containing my freshly laundered clothes.

"Yes. It is a new game called *Is my laundry ready?*" I say as I close the door behind me.

MY KITCHEN IS ALIVE WITH spices in the evenings: thyme, turmeric, curry, and nutmeg. I open the windows to clear the cloud of smoke and let in fresh air. Shredded greens, chopped onions, and ground tomatoes are strewn on the floor, on the table and in the sink. I pour the mashed liver, marinating in Cameroon pepper sauce, into the saucepan. The onions, tomatoes, and green peppers continue to sizzle in the vegetable oil. I drum my fingers on the chopping board as the mashed liver simmers in the saucepan. After cooking, I soak the used pots, bowls, and spoons in soapy water.

All this is a huge waste of time. Ding barely touches my food. He will always leave it on the porch for the damned bats.

Ada runs into the kitchen, with Mba tagging along, when I'm just done drying my hands. She tears open a sachet of Adole Liver Salts, pours it into a glass, dissolves it with the water from the dispenser, and gulps it down.

"What time is he coming tonight?" Ada's voice reeks of something familiar and strange at the same time.

"Are you alright?" I brush aside Ada's question with another question.

"Cramps," Ada replies brusquely. "Why doesn't he want to see us?"

"Have you taken aspirin?"

"I have. Stop trying to ignore me."

I lean against the wall and look my daughter over. She is sixteen and two years away from the age of glory when she can marry and exist in two divergent worlds. It's just like a nanosecond ago when Ada turned twelve and I helped her place ice on her swelling nipples. Time is a swift-passing shadow.

"You know, Aunty Ukamaka is right. Marriage transforms people into something else." Ada cuts in, interrupting my train of thoughts. "I really don't have the muscle for all that drama."

"Have you been speaking to Aunty Ukamaka?" I struggle not to sound horrified. People who don't marry are seen as outlaws. They have few friends and will die alone and unloved. "Marriage is like...a conglomerate of...a mixed bag..." I try to tell Ada but the words refuse to form in my mouth.

Mba climbs on the kitchen table and tips over the pot of mashed liver sauce, spilling the thick, dark grey liquid on the floor. I grab a rag and a bucket and start cleaning the mess. Mba squeezes herself between Ada's legs. The cat's eyes are lit with a phantasmal glow: a way of saying *I did this on purpose.*

"Let me get you vinegar for the oil stain," Ada offers.

"No. Take your siblings into the matchbox and don't come out until I come back in the morning."

"MY BOWL OF MASHED LIVER sauce is empty," Ding says.

"Maybe the bats have eaten it."

Ding does not reply. He picks up a book from the bedside table and his face remains blank as he sifts through the pages. Deep down, I am grateful that Mba spilled the mashed liver sauce.

I undress and catwalk toward Ding. He stirs — a weak stir but still a stir. His palms are cold when they cup my breasts. This coldness endures as he guides me to the bed and lies on top of me. Our bodies refuse to meld into each other. Ding's scars jab against my skin. The coldness continues. It is only when he thrusts in that I feel a faint warmth. Before my insides can nurture the warmth into fire, he slips out. He exhales, lies on his back, and just like that — Wham! Bam! — drifts off to sleep. His chest rises and falls and this makes me wonder if our children are breathing fine in the matchbox.

"Ding, we need to talk." I nudge his shoulder. He mumbles gibberish and dozes off again. I will have to talk to him later, maybe in the morning. It's already time for me to become Dime.

"WATCH WHERE YOU'RE GOING, DUMB-FUCK!" a rickshaw driver hollers, and I step into the gutter to avoid being rammed.

The gutter is brimful with moldy bread and half-drunk soda cans and used blood bags and pig bladders and every other junk a gutter should contain. I mumble an apology to the rickshaw driver who does not seem to care; he's already moved past, hurling insults as he went.

"Dime, is that you?" a voice inquires as I turn onto the street where my hippie wife lives. It is Shuku. She is sitting on a mat in front of her house. A basin is cradled on her lap. In the evenings, Shuku sells hair extensions woven with bat fur. I walk past her every evening, but I don't know a thing about her spouses or who she is in her other life. Some things are better left unearthed.

"How has it been?" I try as much as possible not to sound too concerned.

"I am catching the evening dew. It gives sweet dreams. You can try it. Just a few drops in your eyes and you'd be dreaming in rainbows."

"I'll pass," I say and walk away.

In eleven years of being married to Felicity, I have succeeded in turning down every attempt Shuku makes for us to become friends. If I have learnt anything from having two lives, it is that you should not be too attached to people in your different lives and to keep acquaintances superficial. That way, the lives will not bleed into each other.

Nime, Filo, and Ujam are playing Lego on the balcony when I get to my house.

"Baba is here!" Nime, Filo, and Ujam squeal as they see me.

They push the plastic Lego blocks aside, run to open the door, and hug me so tightly I fear my back will snap.

"Did you buy kwilikwili for us?" they chorus.

Their mouths sag when I say no. Maybe I could afford treats more often if Felicity didn't spend so much of our money throwing wild parties. Of course, I say this in my head. You do not say such things about your wife in the presence of your children or they will start taking sides.

Felicity is not at home and the house is in utter disarray. Not that it is any better when she is around. The children had stacked all the chairs and tables for their Mountain Game in the parlor. I untie Ujam's wooden doll hanging on the ceiling fan, put back the chairs and tables in their right place, and fold the dirty clothes heaped on the floor. Tonight, my children are not too much trouble except for when Ujam lights a match on the rug. Filo sees it in time and puts it out with water. Nime scolds Ujam who begins to cry and I sling him across my shoulder to make him stop crying.

The night is far spent and Felicity is not yet home, so I take the children to the kitchen to cook dinner. Bean porridge spiced with scent-leaf. I dish out the food and we carry our plates to the dining table. Nime, the eldest, between licking porridge off his fork, talks about a girl he thinks he likes. I chuckle and almost send pepper down the wrong way. Nime frowns.

"No, I wasn't laughing at you. It's just that you are growing up so fast and Baba still can't imagine you are having a crush on someone," I explain. This time, I suppress my laughter.

"Baba, what's a crush?" Ujam asks.

"A kind of food." I blink twice to let the lie settle.

Filo says he met Pa Gragra in the morning to teach him how to read people's minds. I cringe. Having a child who can read minds is better imagined than experienced. I will have to walk around Filo with my thoughts open to him like those steaming pots of rice displayed on the counter at Iya Bola's restaurant.

"Who did you tell before going?"

"Mama said I could go."

Felicity is always carefree with the children as if it will compensate for all her excesses. This makes me giddy and I will have to choose my words so as not to be the bad parent. "Honey, I know you think it's cool to read minds but trust me, it's not. Most people's minds are filled with those grubs that climb up the toilet pipes when it rains."

"Ewww!" Filo squeezes his face and feigns wanting to vomit.

Ujam wants to know when he will be allowed to play softball with his brothers. I tell him, as I have done for the past six months that the boy has been pestering me, that he can play tomorrow. Ujam is naive and a part of me prays he remains this way. I don't know how long it will take before he grows up and starts bothering me about his girl crushes and reading people's minds.

When we are done eating, I tuck the children in bed and wait for Felicity in the parlor. The house is quiet now. My lungs drink up the stillness around me, as much as they can carry. I unknot the tassels of the curtains and glide into the soothing darkness.

Tiptoe. Tiptoe. Spin and spin and spin. Dance to the tune of silence. Get aboard the spaceship of serendipity. Waltz across the room and tilt the hands of time backwards until it touches the past — a place where my life is not twinned, where the world is so much smaller and I can understand every bit of it. The music drumming inside my chest stops. Someone is calling me.

"Baba, stop dancing, Ujam is reaching!"

Reaching is common in little children like Ujam. The stump of their placenta sprouts roots and the roots begin to reach, tearing their innards until their mothers or any woman who has given birth rubs her navel on the stump. My mother told me that Eledumare handed this law himself to our foremothers to keep all of us in check, to fetter our legs close to our homes. A mother whose child dies of reaching is seen as a failed woman.

I dash out of the house. Only a thin slice of the moon illuminates the night outside. To find Felicity now will be to find a strand of chestnut hair in a haystack. She could be passed out on the floor at Quidi Bar, gyrating on a man's crotch at Bolingo Square, sprawled on the bench of a tattoo shop in The Place of Outlaws, or swinging from pole to pole at Dare Ridge. On impulse, I rush to Shuku's house and bang on the door. I don't know if Shuku has a child of her own, but all I can do now is hope.

"Dime, is that you?" Shuku answers the door as if she has been waiting for me to knock.

"My son is reaching and my wife is not at home."

Shuku reties the loose wrapper around her waist. "Atibawgu, the man across the street needs my help. His son is reaching."

"What about his wife?" A sleepy voice inside the house asks.

"She is away."

"Is it not the same man who feels he is too grand to engage in small talk?"

"You can come out here and ask him yourself."

Shuku closes the door behind her and asks me to lead the way. Ujam is screaming when we get back to the house. The roots have pierced through his back and anchored to the bed. Shuku pats Ujam's head before rubbing her navel against his. Ujam stops screaming and the roots retract into his body. The little boy sleeps.

"We are all bodies in transit. The least we can do is to look out for each other because we cannot do it all on our own, no matter how strong we think we are." Shuku cuts me short when I try to thank her and apologize for being too grand to engage in small talk. "Goodnight, Dime."

FELICITY RETURNS HOME AN HOUR later. She rattles as she walks into the bedroom. Rusted coins, bent pins, and tiny copper-plates fall from her overstuffed purse. The brass bangles on her right wrist clang on the wine glass she is holding. She smiles, slumps on the bed, and kicks the air like a child stung by a bee.

"My doting husband is awake," Felicity drawls.

I go over to the bed and help her remove her shoes. She pukes all over my shirt when I try to wring the wine glass out of her hand.

"This," she smacks her fingernails on the wine glass, "is tomato sauce and unicorn pee. Strong stuff."

Her grip on the wine glass slackens. I set it on the floor. "Where did you go this time?"

"To the skies." My wife sways her hands. "You can touch, touch, touch — "

"Ujam reached." Felicity does not say anything, so I continue. "You didn't feed the children. The house was a total mess when I came in."

Felicity sits up. She is a bit sober now. "Get a grip. A drink or two takes me away from this twisted web we are living."

"Don't even play the pity card. We all live twinned lives. I still cook and clean the house before coming here and everyone in town knows you don't lift a finger to help Dinma when you are Naife." My voice wobbles between rage and things I cannot explain.

Dinma is Felicity's wife when she is Naife. I have seen her once, on my way to pick up the laundry from Aunty Ukamaka. She rolled her eyes at me when I greeted her and gave me the cold shoulder. Sometimes cross-spouses see each other as competitors. When your marriages have lasted for many years like mine, though, you begin to realize that your cross-spouses are not the problem. Life is the problem.

"What I do in my other life is none of your business!" Felicity grabs the wine glass and splashes its remaining contents on my face. "This is what you get for poking your ugly nose where it's not wanted. By the way, you are sleeping on the floor tonight."

"You know, it won't kill you to take care of our children."

"Blah, blah, blah. The problem with you is you want everybody to be like you. Sorry, it doesn't work that way." Felicity hurls her shoes at me, missing by a hair's breadth. "You want things to be perfect. You want to tell me how to take care of our children. Then you whine in my ears all night about your uncaring husband. Do you get a cookie each time someone spares you an ounce of pity? Fix your problems yourself."

I shower and then go back to the bedroom to unroll the mat to sleep on. Felicity's words are like needles on my skin the entire time. All night I toss and turn on the mat, and it seems that barely a few minutes have passed before Felicity pulls up the curtains and tells me it's already morning.

The house is shiny and neat when I come out of the bathroom. Breakfast is set and Felicity and the children are sitting quietly at the table.

"Dime, we are waiting for you." Felicity calls from the table.

During breakfast, Felicity and I don't talk about last night. The unspoken words hover above us. We continue to avoid each other's eyes after breakfast. Ujam is still weak from last night so I carry him on my shoulder to cheer him up. He tugs at my hair and begs me to stay longer. I tell him no. Life doesn't allow adults those luxuries. I don't say the second part to Ujam; you don't bother children with such things.

"You're a good husband and, I'm sure as hell, a good wife. Don't let people take advantage of that," Felicity says in the bedroom, while I'm becoming Chime again. Felicity is typically late to become Naife, of course. She helps me pick out something from her wardrobe to wear so that Chime won't have to walk back in Dime's clothes.

"Thank you."

As Chime, I plant a soft kiss on both of Felicity's cheeks and walk out of the bedroom.

DING IS PRIMPING WHEN I get back. It is far into the morning and almost overdue for him to become Ping, at which point he will have to do his eyeliner all over again. I hold myself not to laugh. Ding is always this way every morning, at a loss if he is Ding or Ping.

"You think it's funny?" Ding asks.

I'm shocked because we do not usually talk when he is about to become Ping. "Yes." I let out my laughter. "You're doing it too soon. You're still Ding. And you're using up my eyeliner."

Ding's eyes widen. "Oh. Well, it's just makeup."

Ordinarily I'd grunt and walk away, but Felicity's last words to me are echoing in my head.

"What's weird is you can't tell that you're still *my* husband right now," I say.

"Someone is jealous."

I scoff. "Jealous? We've had our days of young love. I just don't want to be the only one making sacrifices for your new marriage. I want to stop locking my children in that stuffy matchbox when you are around. I want my children to see their father every night. I want to feel the warmth of the man I married sixteen years ago at night when you come home. I want you to eat my food and not leave it on the front porch for the bats. And I am not crazy for asking for these things."

"I know I've been selfish ever since Ikoro came into the picture," Ding admits. "But you should understand how these things work. I can't bear to see our children like this. I need more time to get used to being two people. You know how it was when you married Felicity."

"I never abandoned you," I say. "I made room for you in my new love. I want you to do the same."

The air crackles while I wait for Ding to speak. He chews the corners of his lower lip and paces across the room, before he finally nods in understanding and shakes my hand to seal the deal.

"Yes," he says. "I'm sorry." And halfway through saying it I realize that he became Ping, so the apology is from the both of them. I no longer see dark splotches all over their bodies, and it feels like the lifting of a great weight.

"Thank you," I say. "Tell Ikoro I said good morning."

After Ping leaves, I run straight to the children's bedroom and tear open the matchbox. My children are still asleep. I look at their peaceful faces and, for the first time in a long while, my heart's rhythm rises in joy.

CONTROL

◄ Davian Aw ►

THE LIGHT IN CHRIS' ROOM is red. "It's good for photographs," she once explained in that vague way of hers, though Jan's never known her friend to be into photography, and as her eyes adapt to the transmitted feed, the room looks less like a darkroom and more like a hovel abandoned in the light of a dying sun. The blinds on the windows are closed. Harsh light seeps in around the edges. In the background, Jan hears the quiet rush of air-conditioning, and her own skin aches for its relief.

"Dude, we really need to talk about your ad campaign," Chris says. Her voice resonates in Jan's head as though it were her own, lips moving just out of view, and Jan feels the usual reflexive stab of panic that someone has taken control of her body.

"What's wrong with it?" Jan asks. She never gets used to this—hearing her words with Chris' ears, tinny and distant from a speaker.

"Seriously? Look…"

Jan closes her eyes as Chris stands and the image shifts in a wave of almost-nausea. When she next opens them, it's to see Chris' spam wall, her slim forearm—so foreign yet familiar—moving into the visual field to gesture at the scrolling text, each new arrival pushing the rest down toward the deletion line:

// Does your small measurement threatens your relationships? Special means are needed . . . //

// I am leaving soon, and you will forgive me if I

```
speak bluntly . . . //
    // Woman form queue, when you got as much night
energy as this Don Juan maker! //
    // congratulatons you have won the mircosoft lottery
send detail like name, sex, address, creditcard number,
ect to . . . //
```

"I saw our ad in there," Chris says.

"It's free. Everyone with a netcon gets it."

"Yeah, and no one's going to take it seriously."

"At least you saw it, right?"

Chris brushes her words aside. "We need better demographic targeting. Go look for some taitai who can't be bothered with gym."

"Why don't *you* do it?"

Chris pauses. "I don't want to leave too many tracks. I'm just the tech."

"Fine."

Chris claps her hands together. "Great. Find us someone by tomorrow."

The feed cuts off.

```
+ Chris has ended the conversation > end / new
conversation / upgrade to Premium Chat for just $9.95/
month!
    > end
```

Jan thinks maybe it's a sign the two of them are growing up, or maybe it's just a desire to cling to what little they have left of traditional identity; regardless, on net chats they now go simply by their first names. As a teenager, Chris favoured the display name "I'll Sleep When I Sleep."

"I thought it's supposed to be 'I'll Sleep When I'm Dead'," Jan asked, the first time she saw it.

"When I'm dead I won't be sleeping," Chris pointed out. "I'd be dead. I'll sleep when I sleep."

"So . . . when will you sleep?" Jan asked.

"I don't know. It changes every day. I don't want to limit myself."

It's just "Chris", now.

"WE'RE ALL PRISONERS OF OUR brains," Chris once said in one of her frequent random monologues as they waited at the bus stop in front of their school, other students standing with their heads buried in phones, notes, or mindless chatter, dead to every world but their own. "If someone hacks into my brain and tells it there's a velociraptor in front of me, to me it'll be as real as anything else. Except no one else would see it. They'd all think I'm crazy. But if *their* brains get fed the same thing, then everyone sees it and no one is crazy. Sanity is just . . . aligning yourself with consensual reality."

"Like the one that says we're standing at a bus stop?" Jan asked.

"Yeah. But maybe we're just brains in vats." Chris paused, and then, dropping into sudden, absurd gravity: "And I don't dare to take the red pill."

Then Jan's bus arrived.

THEIR FIRST CLIENT IS A pleasant, forty-something woman named Ms. Lee, who eagerly invites them into her spacious District 10 bungalow and offers them expensive chocolates from her recent trip around Europe. Jan takes a couple and thanks her. Chris politely declines.

"Right!" Ms. Lee says, settling down on the sofa. Behind her, high windows frame a rare glimpse of forest. "So, how does this work?"

"It's simple," Chris says. "Everyone knows that headsets can both get output from your brain and deliver input into it. That's how the POVCam tech works. It gets the audiovisual input from your correspondent's brain and delivers it straight to yours, overriding the signals from your optic and auditory nerves so that instead you see and hear the same things they do. It's the same with the POVTouch, Smell, and Taste.

"And then there are those apps that let you record your movements and play them back. They send those same nerve impulses through your spinal cord, where they override the real-time signals so you do the exact same thing all over again. Which was fun at first, but then you had people stuck dancing while their house burnt down, plus you had all those dodgy recordings that made them jump off buildings or striptease in church and stuff. So they banned them. But it was all open source and the code is still out there. And basically—" Chris takes a breath "—I wrote an app combining everything."

Ms. Lee looks slightly nervous. "So you're going to force—"

"No, no, no. We can't make people pay for that. We do the whole thing. A complete, virtual switch-over. You won't just see and hear and feel and whatever that the other person does, you'll be able to control them as well. Instead of a recording, it's a real-time sync. So you'll get all the sensory input that Jan gets. You'll see what her eyes see, and so on. At the same time you'll be able to provide your own output, right into her brain. So when you try to move your arm, your arm won't move, but hers will. And since you're getting her sensory input, you'll feel her arm move as though it were your own. And vice versa. It feels exactly like a body swap, though it's just a trick of the brain."

"And she'll exercise for me?" Ms. Lee asks.

Chris nods. "That's right. For just three hundred dollars an hour."

"We also have a monthly package for ten thousand that comes with a full nutrition plan," Jan adds. "The workouts are two hours a day, three days a week, and we'll handle all your meals. You'll never feel better."

"Yeah. So you can just relax while Jan works out on your behalf, and I'll swap you two at scheduled mealtimes, so your body eats healthy while you don't have to. You'll never find a better gym deal, promise. You'll just have to cover equipment costs."

"It's completely safe," Jan says. "We've tested it out. The core components have been around for years. And if you ever want to stop the sync, you can just turn off your headset—my headset—and it'll end."

"We just need you to try and keep it secret," Chris says. "I don't really want this to get out there yet. There's too much potential for abuse, and besides . . . this way you'll get to impress all your friends."

Chris smiles.

"WHAT'S CHRIS SHORT FOR?" PEOPLE always asked.

"You know what's weird? IRL it's always, 'Is that Christina or Christine or Christal?' But online, they just assume it's Christopher. Rule Thirty, see. No girls on the Internet. It works on the same principle that makes everyone an overweight neckbeard fedora living in their mum's basement, even if they don't have a mum."

"So, what's Chris short for?"

Chris grinned, not looking at Jan, in what might have been shyness or pride. "That's a secret."

"I'm your friend."

"I doubt there's anything in the Official Human Manual that says you've got to tell your friends what your name stands for."

"The Manual?"

"The Official Human Manual," Chris said wistfully. "It's what I call that book that everyone else seemed to get when they were born. They left me out, but I'm onto you guys. It's got all that useful stuff in it, you know—like the maximum length of time to make eye contact with people if you don't want them to freak out and start calling the cops on you. Or why you get in trouble for not following instructions but still get in trouble even when you do. Or why everyone never even seems to question the rule that says you have to eat and drink or you'll die. I mean, that's sinister stuff, but no one seems to notice, so maybe they have a reason for it that no one told me. I figured maybe they read it in a manual somewhere."

Chris fiddled with a pen, her eyes taking on that far-off gaze that Jan had come to recognise.

"Did you get the Manual?" Chris asked flatly, still looking at the pen in furrowed concentration, her expression tinged with a strange sadness.

"No."

Chris nodded, slowly, and then her mind escaped through the twirling pen into another world, and she didn't seem to hear anything Jan said after that.

Sometimes, Jan feels an intense urge to grab Chris around the neck and scream at her until she breaks out of her stupid little bubble to recognize that there's a world out here, with people in it, living and dying outside of her distant, mildly-baffled observation.

But people aren't supposed to do that to their friends.

SEVEN MORE CLIENTS COME THEIR way, four with the food plan until they stop offering it to new clients and reduce their monthly fee to $7k. Jan could not bear to keep eating the same bland meals over and over again.

Her days blend into a haze of non-stop exercise and travel, trying to salvage as much sleep as she can lest clients complain that her body is always tired. Chris drives her from one home to the next and spends the two hours with Jan's body. Watching it. Keeping it safe.

The money piles up in their accounts. Jan gets a double share, and the growing monthly statements provide comfort in those times when she thinks she might want to quit—despairing at the rapidly deteriorating state of her health, weathering the judgemental stares and snide comments from friends and family, tolerating the whispers, the pitiful head shakes, her doctor's concerns.

"What's going on, Jan?" her doctor asks. "You've always been such a health nut. Is everything all right?"

Jan shrugs. "It's just work," she says truthfully, and leaves it at that.

Yet the face that greets her each morning in the bathroom mirror is increasingly that of a stranger, one of the two young women she's become used to seeing flit in and out of the rooms where she works out, or lazing comfortably in a corner, smiling to see her struggling efforts, unspoken taunts sparkling in those eyes.

It becomes a relief each day to escape herself. Her hard work pays off in the other bodies she inhabits: losing their fat and building their muscles, watching them slowly transform from day to day. She falls in love with their increasingly toned physiques, the healthy ease of their movements, their growing strength and energy, that pervasive sense of wellness and peace. She sees some of those same bodies appear on magazine covers and TV, mingling with the rest of society's elites, gushingly praised for how good they look these days ("What's your secret?" tabloid reporters beg to know), and feels an uncommon pride.

Client 5 requests jogs around the neighbourhood. One day, halfway through a lap, Jan finds herself slowing his body to a breathless stop in the twilight. The street ahead lies straight and empty, flanked by an eternity of white terraced houses steady and calm beneath the greying evening sky. Luxury cars sit parked in broad driveways, bicycles safe behind gates, leaning by koi ponds.

Jan feels the sudden urge to run wildly down that road. Something inside her screams for freedom—for escape—to keep running until she runs out of breath and exhaustion drives red to cloud her vision, to keep running until even the all-reaching grasp of the Internet fails at last and throws her rudely from this burdensome cage of flesh out into the weightless ether; because only then maybe, finally, she will find herself.

Jan raises Client 5's hands to Client 5's eyes. She wonders what it is that makes these hands any less hers than her own.

"OH SHIT," CHRIS SAID.

It was the first time Jan had ever heard her swear. But it was with Jan's voice, and it was her own face that Jan saw lit up in awestruck excitement on the other side of the bedroom, holding her hands before her face and turning them back and forth. "This is it. This is the real deal. Jan!"

It was the 59th test. The last few attempts had failed in many small ways: one-sided transfers, syncs that lagged and disrupted that crucial sense of presence, mis-mapped senses that turned vision into smell and taste into music in synaesthetic incoherence, and that frightening time all her senses winked out and left her in an insensible void panicking and desperately hoping the same hadn't happened to Chris and trapped them both in nothingness. But with this test, the final test, Jan knew they had succeeded the moment the program executed and Chris' body became her own, feeling as natural as though she had been born with it. For the first time, the illusion was flawless.

It should not have felt this normal, seeing her body call her name and bound over with a delighted grin on its face to grab her in a hug. Even Chris had never been that exuberant, but the success and the freedom of another body seemed to have liberated her.

"Great," Jan said with a weak smile, hearing Chris' voice as she spoke. She was unsettled by the sight of her own neck, her waves of long black hair tickling her nose, her strong arms wrapped around her in Chris' smaller body and squeezing her against herself. The shape of her teeth against her tongue was distractedly unfamiliar; everything was unfamiliar, from the short mess of hair on her head to the retro band T-shirt and skinny jeans on her legs. Her disoriented mind fixated on that: she was wearing Chris' clothes, and that didn't make sense because Jan was taller, stronger, bigger, and they would never fit. But here she was.

"We should go somewhere. Hang out for a while. See if the sync holds up," Chris rambled, releasing her abruptly from the hug, that distant gaze looking so wrong on her face. "We need to check for any long-term effects. See if any of our friends thinks we're acting strange. . . We should go before my dad gets back."

Jan barely heard what Chris was saying, staring at her body as it talked, feeling uncomfortably like a stranger to herself. Numbly, she made her way to the other side of the room, every sensation new and strange. In the bedroom mirror, Chris' reflection looked curiously back at her. Her face turned when she did, but her eyes were no more readable than before.

How many times had she wondered what really went on in that head? Now, staring out from behind those eyes, she was just as lost as before.

"WHEN DO WE STOP?" JAN asks Chris one night as they drive back to Jan's apartment from the day's last client.

"When we've earned two million dollars. You'll have most of it, but I'm cool with that. You deserve it so much."

```
+ programs > accessories > calculator
Input: (4 x 10000 + 3 x 7000) x 12
Result: 732000
Input: 2000000 / 732000
Result: 2.732240437
> exit
```

"Three years," Jan says.

"Yeah, about there."

The red lights turn green and Chris guns the accelerator. They pass through tree-lined streets dividing tall rows of HDB apartment blocks shading them from the stars.

"I'm tired," Jan says quietly.

"I thought that last client napped all the way through."

"No, mentally. I don't know how much longer I can do this." Jan stares out the window. "Some days I don't even know who I am anymore."

"Why not?" Chris asks.

"I spend too much time being other people."

"It's just their bodies. You're still you."

Billboards flash at them as they drive. Jan wonders what it would be like to have the bodies in those ads. They look so happy. They are so beautiful. But then, so is she for several hours a day, model-worthy frame clad in designer sportswear, using top-of-the-line equipment, walking through expansive homes, surrounded by all the trappings of the rich and sometimes famous.

"You know, I always assumed we'd be splitting the job. You were so excited that first time the swap worked. What gives?"

Silence.

They turn into the car park and into a parking lot. Chris kills the engine. They sit there quietly, staring out the windshield past their reflections to the night-lit street.

"I'll do it," Chris says eventually. "I'll take half, you take half. Same for the cash. We'll take turns with the car."

Jan nods. "Deal."

Chris unlocks the doors. "I'll take first shift tomorrow. Sleep well."

"Thanks, Chris. You too."

Chris gazes after Jan's receding reflection in the windshield. "I'll sleep when I sleep."

THEY HAVE THE APP DOWNLOADED into each of their headsets and executable at a mental touch of a button. They split up each day to work, taking on six clients each, and rescheduling the four meal plans between them so they'll always know where their bodies are. It's easiest when they're already at the client's house and can have a meal together, though Jan can never quite stave off the jealousy of watching her body stuff itself with junk food while she makes her way through salads and granola bars.

```
+ programs > accessories > calculator
Input: (4 x 10000 + 6 x 7000) x 12
Result: 1056000
Input: 2000000 / 576000
Result: 1.893939394
> close program
```

With both of them working, they'd hit two million in under two years.

```
+ Instant Chat request from Jan > accept / deny
    > accept
    + Jan: Client 3 asks if we'll do exams for her kid.
    + Chris: That's cheating.
    + Jan: $1k for Maths PSLE. Double if we get A*.
    + Chris: Ok can.
    + Jan: Cool.
    + Jan has ended the conversation > end / new
conversation / upgrade to Premium Chat for just $9.95/
month!
    > end
```

JAN GETS THE PHONE CALL two and a half months later.

The long-unheard ring is initially unfamiliar to her. Too much time spent conversing through the headset in various degrees of immersion has rendered analogue telephones half-forgotten mysteries of the past, and there's something foreboding in the measured, repeated shrills that pierce her apartment just before midnight.

She goes into the kitchenette, takes the receiver off the hook on the wall, and puts it to her ear.

"Hello?"

"Jan. It's me."

Chris' voice is unusually quiet.

"You're on a phone," Jan says.

"I killed someone."

JAN FINDS CHRIS SITTING ON the bench at a bus stop outside Newton MRT Station, head bowed and hands clasped together, cutting a lone still figure in the night. Jan pulls up in the bus bay and rolls down the window.

"Chris?"

She raises her head at Jan's voice. The once perpetually-present headset is gone.

Chris hesitates, then gets up and goes to the car. She pulls open the door and crawls onto the backseat.

Jan rolls the window back up and drives off slowly.

"Client 7," Chris says after a while. "He said he had work to do and left me to the job. I went to get water, heard noises. I saw myself naked in his room; I mean, they probably do that all the time now, but . . . well. I'd never had to see it before. And . . . this one had a webcam. So I committed suicide on his behalf. Now he's dead."

They drive on in silence.

IT HADN'T BEEN MUCH OF a surprise. Chris wasn't even sure if she cared. She had, from childhood, developed a safe distance from her body and the world; that's how one stayed safe, stayed sane, no matter what happened. If you stayed apart from the world, it couldn't hurt you, even if it tried. She had learnt that lesson long ago. But too many injustices went neglected in this world.

She saw the look of fearful surprise and guilty anger on her face as she strode over in his body, her gaze fixed on his, and for a disoriented moment she felt completely wrong, a large man bearing down on a scared girl.

"I...I wasn't..." he started, stumbling up and backing into the wall.

"No," Chris said softly. She closed his open laptop, and heard muted cries of disappointment.

```
+ Chris' Files > programs > Control 4.2 > open >
settings > Client7
```

"You didn't see anything," Chris said.

```
+ input > visual > off
```

Client 7 screamed at the sudden blindness, flailing wildly, crashing a stack of books to the ground and screaming again as one hit his foot.

"You didn't feel anything," Chris continued, grabbing him roughly by the shoulder before he fell and further damaged her body.

```
+ input > SELECT somatosensory | vestibular |
interoception | olfactory | gustatory > off
```

Client 7 felt a tremor pass through him, and then there was nothing: no feeling in the darkness, no sense of physical existence, his hands opening and closing in the air, grabbing at his neck, shoulders, chest, terror spreading on his sightless face and emerging in another scream as he tried desperately to feel something, *anything*.

Chris held his hands still. "It's over."

```
+ input > SELECT ALL > off
+ output > SELECT ALL > off
```

The screaming cut out. Client 7 collapsed into her borrowed arms, Chris body limp and deactivated, rogue limbs knocking over a lamp on the nightstand.

Chris took a deep breath and shut her eyes. Five...four...three...two... one. Calm.

The weight of her body was surreally light in Client 7's arms. She laid it gently on his bed. She put its clothes back on with a detached tenderness. She thought about its consciousness, booted out of its physical prison into the horrors of full liberty. Perhaps that was true reality. Existence without manipulation.

Chris considered her options. She could take over Client 7's life and force hers on him, but it would be a matter of time before he reported her.

She could undo the blocks and unswitch them—hope he'd learnt his lesson. But he might come after her. Even if she got away today, he would always be out there, waiting. She might never feel safe again. She had lived too long that way.

She wondered how many people had seen her body.

She felt so tired.

Chris left the bedroom and stood for a moment in Client 7's living room. Everything was so quiet.

She could leave him insensible. But, no, that would be beyond cruel.

And there was one more option.

She found his keys and unlocked the main door. She walked back into the living room and over to the balcony. She pushed its glass door open with his hand, feeling the cool metal of the handles against his palm, and stepped out.

A breeze was blowing. Chris closed his eyes and felt it rush through his hair.

She climbed over the edge of the railing, grasping the metal rails, wondering why she was holding on so tight.

How do you die as someone else? the whispered thought sped through her mind. *The flail of limbs that aren't your own, the desperate instinct to survive, protect strange flesh and alien bone; the pounding heart still forcing blood through veins protesting with each thud, the urgent gulps of speeding air, regret, despair, half-uttered prayer, eyes opened wide, no time to cry, when you're not you, how do you d—*

Chris opened her eyes. She was back on Client 7's bed.

She turned off her headset.

She got off the bed and left the apartment, and went to find a payphone to call Jan.

A low drizzle spatters the windows. Jan activates the windshield wipers.

Silence.

Jan almost pities her. Chris wasn't ready for this. Not Chris. Naïve, innocent, idealistic Chris, who spends all her time in inconceivable worlds carved out of abstract philosophies and hypotheticals and profound discourses on the nature of existence, who can find and exploit loopholes in complex computer programs but fail to account for the realities of human curiosity, to whom the human condition is a surreal, odd thing to be studied, not lived, not survived.

And if the truth were otherwise, Jan wouldn't know. There are some things you don't have to tell your friends.

"We need to call this off," Chris says. "They . . . they might find me if I go online again. Arrest me for homicide. If they investigate they'll find our business transactions in his email. I forgot to erase them before I jumped."

Jan signals a left turn and steers the car down a side road.

"We've got enough cash," Chris continues, her voice growing steadier with planning, that protective shield rebuilding itself on cold logic and reason, letting her escape into a place where there's no vulnerability and no pain. "We can be invisible for a while. Ditch the headsets. That way they might forget we exist. Stay off the radar, rebuild our lives. Reclaim our . . . our identities we lost. The kind that will always stay with us."

Chris falls back into the seat and lapses into silence, watching the wipers sweep the water off the windshield in their regulated rhythm. Back and forth. Back and forth.

One hand on the steering wheel, Jan raises the other and turns her headset off. That subtle sense of global connection dies. It's just her, once again, in the quiet left behind by the device that had given her a window into so many other lives. It's just her, guiding the car through rain-veiled streets with the dark outlines of people shuffling along on unknown paths, strangers living strange lives, strangers that could be turned substitute selves in a moment. What would it be like to be them? Truly be them?

But perhaps some things were best left alone.

"You used to ask me what my name was short for," Chris says quietly, gazing past the water-streaked glass into the midnight street. "It's not short for anything. It's just Chris. Chris K. Tang."

And Jan thinks about asking what the K stands for, but at the next red light when she's free to turn around, she sees Chris' eyes closed shut where she sits: one hand clutching the bottom of the seatbelt, her head resting against the side of the door, lost, at last, in the steady tranquillity of sleep.

Jan drives her home.

GHOSTS

◄ Blue Neustifter ►

THERE'S A GHOST IN YOUR house. There has been since you moved in.
You don't call the house haunted; it isn't scary.

The ghost is quiet and kind. They seem to care about you.

You bought magnets for the fridge, sets of letters, bright and colourful and friendly.

The ghost has started using them to talk to you.

YOU GO DOWNSTAIRS one morning, reach to open the door and pull out some juice.

DONT FORGET YOU HAVE A DOCTOR APPOINTMENT AT 2

say the fridge magnets. Then they wiggle and slide around.

ALSO YOURE ALMOST OUT OF ICE CREAM
YOU SHOULD PICK SOME UP TODAY

NEXT MORNING,

YOU WERE SLEEPING POORLY SO I TURNED DOWN THE TEMPERATURE SOME
AND I STARTED YOUR COFFEE

AT AN AFTERNOON trip to the fridge,
    DONT FORGET TO HAVE SOME WATER TODAY
    AND DONT WORK SO LATE THIS EVENING

AFTER A TINDER date leaves,
    I DONT LIKE HIM HE KEPT INTERRUPTING YOU
    ALSO WHEN YOU WERE OUT OF THE ROOM
    HE MADE A MEAN FACE AT THE CAT

AFTER SEVERAL STRESSFUL days in politics the fridge says,
    PLEASE DELETE TWITTER OFF YOUR PHONE ITS MAKING
YOU SAD
    Then,
    HERE I STARTED A CARTOON AND BROUGHT A FUZZY
BLANKET DOWN

SORRY I SCARED YOU WITH THE LOUD THUMP YESTERDAY
    the ghost apologizes once,
    I WAS TRYING TO ALPHABETIZE YOUR BOOKS AND
DROPPED ONE

ONE MORNING THE fridge just says,
    HEY
    Then the letters move slowly, hesitantly.
    I SAW YOU LOOKING AT DRESSES ONLINE AND CRYING
LAST NIGHT
    Another slow rearrangement.
    I THINK YOU WOULD BE PRETTY IN THE BLUE ONE
    ITS OKAY

WHEN THE DRESS arrives, you panic and leave it in the package for several
days.

Eventually the package is moved to the top of your dresser, still sealed.
THE CAT WAS CHEWING ON IT
says the fridge.
TAKE YOUR TIME

THE NIGHT YOU eventually try it on, you only manage to look in the mirror for maybe 30 seconds before sobbing and pulling the dress off, throwing it deep into a closet. You don't look at the fridge. You go straight to bed.

THE NEXT MORNING the dress is on a hanger in the closet, smoothed out. It isn't prominent, just cared for.
I THOUGHT YOU LOOKED NICE
IM SORRY IT HURTS

A COUPLE DAYS of moping and anxiety later,
I NOTICED YOU HAVENT SEEN YOUR THERAPIST LATELY
MAYBE THAT WOULD HELP?

YOUR THERAPIST BOOKS you for a couple weeks out. You're angry a lot. You throw the fridge magnets in a box. You want to be left alone.

YOU DON'T HEAR from the ghost.

THE THERAPIST APPOINTMENT helps. You don't solve anything, but it gives you a place to cry and be listened to.
You put the magnets up before bed. The next morning they say,
IM SORRY YOURE HURTING
I DIDNT MEAN TO MAKE YOU MAD
You lean against the kitchen counter and quietly say you weren't

mad at them. Just at the world and at yourself.

WHY

Because the world is scary and hard.

WHY YOURSELF

Because you want things that are impossible.

The magnets don't move for a moment.

NO

No?

NOT IMPOSSIBLE

JUST HARD

You start to feel angry again.

You breathe like your therapist reminded you about.

You change the subject. You ask where the ghost went.

YOU SEEMED TO WANT SPACE

You did. Or, you thought you did. But it ended up just making it hurt more.

I WORRIED IT MIGHT BUT DIDNT WANT TO FORCE IT

Thanks, you say. After a moment you ask **where** they went.

I CANT LEAVE THE HOUSE

I WENT TO THE ATTIC

The attic?

YOU DONT GO THERE

I DIDNT WANT TO SPY

What do I do, you ask quietly.

I CANT TELL YOU

What would you do, then?

I DONT KNOW

ITS NOT THE SAME

IM NOT LIKE YOU

Like me how?

ALIVE

But you were once.

I GUESS

I DONT REMEMBER

How long have you been here?

DONT KNOW

TIME WORKS WEIRD LIKE THIS

Why are you here?

RIGHT NOW?

BECAUSE I CARE

I'm scared, you say after a long silence.

OF WHAT?

That if I change things will be hard, you whisper.

The letters hesitate for a moment. Then they slowly slide into place.

IT SEEMS LIKE THINGS ARE ALREADY HARD

You start crying again.

YOU KNOW WHAT MAKES ME SAD

the fridge spells out once you've finished crying.

What? you ask.

I DONT KNOW WHO I AM

I DONT KNOW ANYTHING ABOUT MYSELF

That is sad, you agree.

I FEEL THINGS SOMETIMES BUT IT ISNT THE SAME

The letters start rearranging faster as the ghost keeps needing letters that are already in use.

I DONT WANT THINGS

I DONT HAVE A SENSE OF ME

I DONT KNOW WHAT IS LIKE ME OR NOT LIKE ME

I DONT HAVE A STYLE OR A PERSONALITY OR A STORY TO TELL ABOUT MYSELF

IM NOT

— the letters stop.

…not coherent? you ask quietly.

YEAH

You feel a ball of anxiety in your gut. It's been there for months. It feels like it is pulsing there, like a second heartbeat.

You know the feeling, you say quietly.

ITS NOT A GOOD FEELING

No, it isn't.

A long silence.

I HAVE TO BE THIS WAY

YOU DONT

You don't respond. Tears are threatening again and you can't bring yourself to speak.

Another long silence. You wonder if the ghost has left.

You hear a soft creak upstairs. A few seconds later a white hanger with a blue dress floats into the kitchen, hooking onto the refrigerator door to rest.

The letters rearrange again.

YOU DONT HAVE TO BE A GHOST

IT'S A FEW minutes later. You went into the washroom to change: the ghost told you when it first started speaking to you that it stayed out of those rooms, that they were private.

You're in the kitchen, in the blue dress. You feel tall and misshapen and ridiculous. And the ball inside your stomach hurts just a little bit less.

You ask how you look.

GOOD

Good? You snort. You look like a cried-out, awkward mess.

YOU LOOK ALIVE

IT'S A WEEK later. You just got back from therapy again. The tea kettle has the low rumble that means it will begin whistling any moment. A mug with a bag of something flowery sits ready.

WELCOME HOME

the magnets say.

You're being really nice, you reply.

YOUVE HAD A HARD WEEK

You snort quietly.

DID THERAPY HELP?

Some, you say. They gave you some resources, at least.

IM PROUD OF YOU

Thanks, you say quietly.

The kettle whistles.

IT'S A MONTH later. You left out a list of names you got from baby name websites. Every morning the fridge greets you with a

GOOD MORNING

and one of the names from the list so you can see how it feels.

After about three weeks you came downstairs, saw the fridge, and felt a pang in your chest.

Do that one again, you whispered.

Every morning since then, the name hasn't changed. It feels weird. But good.

LIFE IS SCARIER than it was a few months ago. You still don't know where you're going, or what you're doing. You talk to the ghost late into the night sometimes, fears and hopes and anxieties pouring out of you until you're empty.

They're a good listener.

LIFE CAN BE hard. Not everyone understands as you share your new name, as your wardrobe changes, as your priorities and pronouns shift. Some old friends leave. Some new friends appear.

The ghost doesn't leave.

AS THE MONTHS go on, the hard things feel less hard. They're still difficult, but you find that facing obstacles isn't as scary when you have a sense of who you are. And sometimes you think that it's kind of nice, to know you've done things that are scary and made it through.

YOU AND THE ghost have a routine, now. When you get dressed and prepped for the day, you always stop in the kitchen. You do a slow turn, a complete rotation, arms spread wide.

How do I look? you ask the room.

YOU LOOK ALIVE

the ghost always replies.

Day by day, you realize that you feel it, too.

It's good to be alive.

NUCLEAR DISASSOCIATIONS

◄ Aqdas Aftab ►

Nanu and I wake up at the same time in the middle of the night, wheezing, covered in cold sweat, both recovering from rapid heartbeats. I kick the sheets off and rub the fear out of my eyes. It has been two years since the attack, two years since we found safety underground, but Nanu still has nightmares. I reach over to her silhouette, my hand patting her mat aimlessly to feel some comfort, to rub the familiar fabric of her shawl with my fingertips. After wiping her forehead, Nanu moves her mat closer to mine and offers to hold me. I try to extend my arms, but my gills feel bumpy. I'm still not used to these. I don't want anyone to touch them, even Nanu, so I shake my head. Say no when you don't want something. Nanu's constant reiteration echoes through the residual terror of my ebbing nightmare, but somehow, the effort to utter a no still constricts my muscles, somehow; my tongue sticks and stumbles in my mouth every time I try to reject the offer of touch. Instead, I shake my head vigorously, so Nanu can feel my response even in the opacity of the airless night. "Okay, my jaan, let me just sing the azaan to you then." Nanu's musical rendition of the azaan overtakes my fuzzy mindscape, lulling me back and forth from dream to reality, but keeping me from regressing into nightmare.

Some rituals don't change, even when everything else does. Nanu had sung the azaan to me when I was born 20 years ago, when she wanted god's call to be the first sound that her grandchildren heard when we came out of wombs, wet and weepy and hairy. She believes that sleep is

251

half-death. That we rise from death every time we wake up. That our soul changes with every awakening. That every morning, like every bodily metamorphosis, is re-birth. And every awakening, albeit frightening, is like evading death again. "Just a dream, my jaan. I have them, too. Have faith that Allah will protect us here. He has so far, hasn't he?" She strokes my hair.

"You mean 'she'" I mutter with my eyes closed and take her shawl between my thumb and forefinger, circling the tenderness of the fabric gently. I wonder if I fake this annoyance at her to maintain the relationship we had two years ago, when our world was still made up of rooms and streets and bazaars, when our conversations were laced with the gender politics I was learning from exciting books, when our lives still had sunlight. I wonder if I have nostalgia for that normalcy, even though a part of me is relieved that the life I knew is buried under rubble now.

"Yes, She. Whatever you call her or him. Have faith. Allah hu akbar allah hu akbar, hayyee alul falaah, hayyee alul salaaah" She continues singing the azaan and, as always, gets stuck on the phrase *hayyee alul falaaah*, repeating it over and over again.

Nanu's lullabies and azaans rarely soothe me, and often her off-tune singing of an archaic Arabic phrase in a Punjabi accent irritates me, but this time, I let myself feel her gesture. The stillness of the underground darkness has taught me to need her despite the annoyance, and to share my pain with her without revealing the content of my nightmares, which unlike hers, are seldom about the attack that she and I survived together.

I have learned to embrace love with silence in the past two years of living deep within the caves of granite rocks, away from the nuclear radiation above. There isn't much else to do here anyway except make paltry plans with the neighbors about our eventual escape from the nuclear wasteland above us and watch each others' bodies metamorphose. Wings, seeds, wood, claws, mushrooms, horns, I've seen it all by now. But I am bored and tired of everyone's optimism, of their plans to escape without catching any of the nuclear radiation. They think this fucked up metamorphosis is some heavenly signal from God. They think our bodily communication with other survivors elsewhere will somehow help us all make some grand plan to overthrow the armies that still send creeping machines to kill us, the armies of white bodies that can't even step foot on this land as they try to steal it. Nanu thinks she can plot some grand revolution with the survivors from underground while the world bombs itself into tears above us. I keep telling everyone around me it won't work. That we don't even know if anything exists above ground anymore. That we don't even know the exact location of the safe pockets where we were forced to take refuge. But I guess they believe more in faith than in my textbook knowledge of the intricacies of physics. Nanu has guessed that we are somewhere between Kandahar and Gwadar, but no one knows how we ended up here, so far from our different homes.

I spend most of my time daydreaming or writing or eating or carving shapes into walls. Anything to distract myself from everyone's intent calculations, their conjectures about what the world looks like above, their communal ecstatic prayerful singing. Staying at an appropriate distance from the others, I usually direct my energies into imagining new stories, or making new colors with the dyes I squeeze from flowers, or sometimes, but only during very desperate moments, praying quietly.

This is not one of those times. I am used to nightmares. I have had them since I was an almost-pubescent child, groveling for some safety in the secure urban home where the smell of cardamom and cloves woke me up every morning. I look over at Nanu's wrinkles in the dark as she calms her post-nightmare breathing, whispering the same phrase of the azaan, over and over and over again. She still dreams almost every night about the attack. Many people here do. I wonder if Nanu's nightmares about the attack are worse than mine. If remembrances of a nuclear attack are worse than those of insidious familial attacks. I wonder if it's better to be attacked by the people we love, people we can know and name, or by slithering machines controlled by god knows who, by wires and wheels that don't allow us to place blame on a single person. I wonder if Nanu's heartbeat feels more painful because of her asthma, her aging organs, her crinkling leathery skin. I kiss her forehead before falling back to sleep, still circling the fabric of her shawl between my thumb and finger, over and over and over again.

The next morning, I am excited for the monthly gathering led by an auntie who claims to have spent her life healing others. I've always found those social worker types annoying, but I have grown to like this particular auntie. Her healing circle is the only time I interact fully and wholesomely with our neighbors and make all efforts to stay mentally present as everyone digs deep into their feelings about this new underground life. As always, Nanu refuses to attend. She says she'd rather cook and pray and dance to heal, but I think she's just afraid to talk about things that remind her of the attack, that bring back the helplessness she felt during those days. She's similar to Ma in that way, refusing to talk about things that are hard, refusing to verbally acknowledge the terrible.

The gathering starts with the usual exercise of touch. We all stand in a circle and hold hands with a new partner. This month, my partner is orange-pink, with long black curls and eyes that remind me of the inside of cantaloupes. Full, seedy, juicy. I cup his hands, stare into his eyes for many long minutes, and he asks me to feel the wings growing out of his back. Wings on a fruit; I find this being striking. I touch his wings gently. Soft. Velvety. I ask him if I can run my fingers through them. He says *no*. We are supposed to say *no*. At least once. Healer Auntie thought it would be a good idea to practice this every month. To get comfortable with boundaries, since we have no other form of privacy in this large cave. I keep ogling his eyes, hoping this was his compulsory *no*, the *no* he does not mean, the *no* he says simply to practice a refusal. I hope that he will change his answer, but he doesn't. He stares back into my eyes, perhaps hoping the same, that I will ask him to touch a part of me. The intimacy moves something in me, something that makes my hard scales feel squishy, feel like quivering, but I do not invite any touch as usual. I simply cup his hands in mine, looking into his eyes, so sweet and so seedy.

I am a little disappointed when the introductory exercise is over, and everyone starts sharing their feelings verbally. Not because I have to break my gaze with his fruity, fleshy eyes or move away from his sweet-smelling texture, certainly not, he is certainly not the type I like to gaze or smell, but because the sharing becomes sanguine. Once again.

A bright-eyed young person raves about her new experience. "My body changed again last night. I talked to someone old. Beautiful deep voice. They sang to me. I haven't heard such good music in so long. It was the best experience ever!" I roll my eyes, again. Again, I wait for a window to talk about feelings that have become so numb they are unspeakable, about the people we lost but still haven't grieved fully, about the destruction of the world above us, but like always, I don't know how to intervene, how to change the direction of the gathering. *But that is what this gathering is all about isn't it?* I cajole myself as another familiar face rambles on and on about how magical they felt when they first metamorphosed, as if all the rubble and damage of their life finally led to something meaningful. *This gathering is all about honesty after all. This is what Nanu teaches me. To say no. Even if I have to say no to other people's joy.* I wait for a moment of silence as I adjust my tongue, keeping it from touching the roof of my mouth, holding it still as I get ready to speak without stuttering on my words, without choking on my own breath.

"Maybe you all feel good about it because you never really knew what's at stake in changing one's body."

A long awkward pause. I cough to fill up the silence.

"Can you share more?" The fruity person next to me asks. His eyes are nudging, gentle.

"Well, the first time. It was just hard, you know. Hard to adjust. To all these new bonds. With you all and to strangers who spoke through our bodies. To a new body. I wish we could talk about how hard it was."

"But what was the love like for you? The communication?" His eyes speak more this time. I think I hate them. Fleshy fruits inviting nibbles.

"Fucked up. Like I was going mad. I thought I had lost it. Like I was hallucinating this voice inside my belly, like my intestines were talking to me. Really fucked. I just had no control. And I feel the same way every time I go through it, even though I've metamorphosed only three times." I hate that he asks me this pointed question. I hate that I can't explain my feelings to him.

"How come?" An enthusiastic child asks, "I've changed so many times, I can't even count."

"I guess I caught less of the radiation. Or maybe my body was already too transformed for the radiation to do much. Maybe I was already monster enough!" I laugh to replace the awkwardness pulsating through my limbs, suddenly on display for everyone's probing eyes. I shift my arms. Fold them over my gills. Then unfold them, unsure of what to do with my limbs all of a sudden. I feel my back muscles tense up as my gills close in.

Healer Auntie asks me what that means. That she truly wants to understand my experience. I ignore her. Roll my eyes again. Gestures are so much easier than words. Besides, what would she know about all the meanings and all the baggage that my body holds?

"How does it feel to be connected to others in different parts of the world, our kinfolk we've never met?" His annoying eyes again.

"They are not our *kinfolk*." I look around at people's shock. My voice is louder and shakier than I intend. "Sorry to be a killjoy, but really, we never chose these people. I didn't choose to communicate with these people while my body grows strange organs."

"But have you ever considered what the attack led to!" His eyes are dreamy now, his pupils glazed, as if gazing into another world. "They wanted to break us. Those imperialist men. Those military women. That's what they do. Categorize us. Put us into grids. And instead, we became even more bonded. Tied to people elsewhere. Connected through our bodies. Isn't that beautiful? Shouldn't we thank god for the gift of these connections?" I hate that I find his eyes so pretty. I hate that I can feel my cheeks heat up. I hate that I cannot speak coherently, that my tongue feels stuck to my gums, that my heart is racing faster than the bullets tearing human flesh above ground.

A deeply flustering anger rattles me inside my gills and I laugh loudly to break the cadence of the gathering before leaving the circle. "Fuck off. The only thing I thank any deity for is that I share voices and bodies with these strangers way less than you all. I wouldn't stand changing a body every fucking week."

My pulse refuses to slow down as I walk away. My back feels cold with his concerned juicy gaze perforating me, wetting my spine. I know I will ruminate for days about this, that I will regret this unkindness, but I leave the circle anyway and join Nanu in her silent dance, unbind my chest as I move, teaching myself step by step to breathe through these gills I do not want, these gills that will remain unchanged for the next two years. Perhaps this is better than what I had before. Perhaps I can make peace with these gills, with this new scaly skin. Perhaps I can learn to be comfortable in this body. I did spend the many years of familial betrayal before the attack trying to do the same after all.

"Who are you? How can we talk? Am I going crazy?" the voice in my body wouldn't stop asking questions. Shit, it's happening again, and this time, it sounds like a child.

The flab hanging from my gills flutters when I sigh deeply. How do I describe to a child what is happening to them? How do I tell a child that material waste is probably exuding radiations so vicious that veins are disentangling from bones, that the earth is probably shuddering with fear, but somehow we should be happy because we are safe? How should I explain that the dead around them are simply collateral damage for some imagined greater good?

I think of Nanu. Her teachings. Her stillness, her silence, her love. And decide to calm this child whose frightened voice is radiating whimpers through my abdomen.

"Deep breaths, child. Take deep breaths. It's all okay. I am your friend. We are connected now. Do they know where you are?"

The child is crying now.

"It's going to be okay. If this is happening to you, you are probably safe. I am also safe. We are both safe and connected. But your body will change after this is over okay? You might get my gills and I might get parts of you. And don't worry about it. You'll get used to it."

No response. Just hiccups and moans. And then silence.

Another useless conversation with another nuclear survivor somewhere in the world. Nothing comes out of it, no information, no plan for an escape, but I do feel a deep agonizing tenderness towards the child. Their voice disappears but the sadness of this communication lingers within me. Another shift begins in my body. Fuck! I insert my hands deep within the openings in my chest and finger my insides, feeling the sponginess harden slowly. My back closes into my ribs as a fierce wave rushes through my lungs. I hold onto my chest so tightly my breathing is constricted. But no matter how tenaciously I hold my breath, my gills dissolve through my fingers. I feel the rough ridges of my scales smoothen as a silken skin emerges through the rupturing hardness of my shoulders. Sericin erupts and spreads through my upper body, softening the skin on my chest. Tiny multicolored crochets pepper my legs. I had finally decided to learn to use these gills. I had spent two whole years learning to love them. And now again, I had to transform parts of my body. New skin. New silk. New bones. New forms of dysphoria.

"Sit still, baita" Nanu's shadow bends over my metamorphosizing body as she sings the azaan in my ear. "Allaahu akbar, allaahu akbar, hayyee alul salaaah."

"I never learn anything from the comrades, Nanu, nothing. This time, it was a child. I wish I never had this communication." I try to wriggle free of her warm embrace as she finishes singing the azaan. She makes sure to complete the azaan before saying anything else to me.

"Hold still, this is re-birth, a new awakening, a new life!" she sounds hopeful, joyous.

Not surprisingly, Nanu acts like it is my first time on earth. Like a fresh morning. Nanu is used to these changes, but to me, each new body still feels like imprisonment, not like re-birth, and certainly not like a fresh start. Even when I try to get used to the body. Even when I decide to make changes to my skin on my own terms. But I know what Nanu would say if I complained to her. That this is a small price to pay for our sacred familial communication with the survivors elsewhere. That we have to keep communicating with them in order to forge possibilities of escape from living amidst nuclear waste. "They are not just comrades, my jaan, they are our family now. Family bonds are more important than gaining information for resistance or escape," Nanu says after completing her azaan ritual. Her teachings have become tedious now. "Our communication with our kinfolk doesn't have to lead to anything tangible. It just has to be sincere. It has to form connections so we can get to know our kin. All the survivors are family. We all literally share skin and bone and blood. And what is more important than the bond of blood?"

Like always, I shrug and say nothing. Like always, my heart pounds as images from my nightmares flash before me when she uses the language of family. It has been years since I lost my biological parents and sibling. Years since their flesh was branded with thermal burns. Years since I left their bodies and took refuge inside granite with my Nanu. Every remembrance of that time, however momentary, envelops my heart in contradictions: the grief at losing family, the trauma of seeing them bombed, the relief at breaking contact with their abusive tirades, all coalescing into one painful breath.

Somehow, Nanu's descriptions of family as safe, as important, as loving, still confuse me. Still remind me of that house, of that room, of that bed. Of those years when a body was stolen, piece by piece, touch by touch, finger by finger. A body already stolen, plundered again, like this land we hide under, like this bleeding geography that was already occupied by our own military even before it was bombed by imperialists, before some of us died and some of us metamorphosed. But somehow, we are supposed to remember only the last violence. Somehow, we are supposed to celebrate only the most recent survival. Stupidly, we are supposed to lament only the latest attack. Just the machines that blew up our homes. Just the aftershocks of that particular injury. But this body remembers. This body that I see from within and from afar, this body that I step out of to gawk its changing features, sometimes loathingly, sometimes lovingly. This body wanders through this new detached existence while my mind wonders what will become of others like me, ripped apart from such lost ambling bodies even before the machinic assault pierced through our skins, even before we learned to survive by exchanging bodies with each other, with other creatures, with other life that has been trying to teach us symbiosis since centuries. This body speaks secretly to this land, still grieving the years seemingly forgotten, still angry, still bitter over the long past.

The past is too long and too bruised, even Nanu's, but when Nanu has nightmares, she dreams only of those insidious machines that slapped invisible radiation onto human skin. She seems to remember only the debris of this recent terror. But how can I blame her for forgetting, when I've told her nothing about the violence that my first body went through, about the homely attacks that plodded on and lurked under my purple nightshirt before my home was set aflame? I can't tell Nanu about the sibling abuse. I can't tell her about the parental neglect. I can't tell her *now*, I can't do that to her soft heart. Can't tell her that family has never meant sincerity and love to me. How could I explain to Nanu how much I hate adopting other bodies without telling her about the imprints left on my mind and heart from my first body? I guess Ma was right, that some things are best left unsaid.

Nanu, who metamorphoses frequently despite her old age, loves her communication with other nuclear survivors. She has to recover from the excessive fatigue every time she changes a body part, but she thrives over finding community through bodily connection, through other people's voice resounding through her insides. She asks the survivors for recipe ideas that involve the roots and salt she finds underground, she shares folktales when she communicates with someone younger, she laughs and dreams of leading her clan to meet all the nuclear survivors at the utopian cusp where land meets the sea as her body changes over and over and over again. My heart swells seeing Nanu so fulfilled holding her imagined kin deep in her bosom.

But I also know this life isn't for me. This life of forced bodily changes, of pretending that strangers are my family, of pretending that family is good, of imagining that escape means swimming away from Gwadar, of racing heartbeats, of holding silences and secrets so deep that even my nightmares cannot access them.

ON MY 25TH BIRTHDAY, I decide to give up learning to fly. These feathers have been useless, like another vestigial organ I do not need. Nothing like the wings I dreamt of when I was child.

A whole year with these feathers sprouting out of my head, replacing my lashes, creating an ugly moustache above my lips, and still, nothing. No flight, no sway, not even a slight ability to hover. I step out of my skin and stare at my body closely. I feel nothing. No guilt. No hatred. No disgust. No pride. This numbness is exactly what I need to cease all communication with the survivors. To end this metamorphosing existence. To unhear any sound that screams within my belly. When I tell Nanu I have decided to be passive during the communications, to ignore the voices inside my body, she shakes her head slowly, looking at me long and hard. After seeing the resolve in my eyes, she moves her sleeping mat away from mine. Then, one by one, she moves all her objects away from my mat. Her papers, her dyes, her baskets, her shawls. My feathery fingers miss the texture of her shawls folded neatly, far away from me. Granite loneliness really feels crushing and bleak. Land loneliness doesn't compare. But I have to stop the unwanted bodily changes, I have to slow down my heart. *Finally. I must go on. No steps backwards.* Even if Nanu refuses to hold me anymore.

Since communications happen internally, I'm not sure if I can say *no* to them. I'm not sure if my numbness, my disengagement, my dissociation will keep me from changing. But when the voice of another survivor rises inside my stomach soon after my confession to Nanu, I take the deepest breath my lungs can muster, clutching my stomach, feeling it shrink. I hold my breath. When I hear a voice, I force my mind to step out of my body. I start to think about the time I drew for so long I collapsed. I go over my drawings, slowly, with focus. I know how to control my mind, even if I can't control my body. I fixate on my breathing, on my drawings, on that time, on the sketches I made, on the figures I scratched into the wall — but I hear a giggle. My breath catches in my throat. Another giggle, followed by plea for comfort. Familiar voice. Young. Tender. *But I have to refuse any response.* I watch myself sitting cross-legged, staring at Nanu's mat far away from mine, passive, unresponsive. I think of the drawings, I count each line, each curve I had drawn that day — 1, 2, 3, 4, 5, 6, 7 — but my body has started to change. Again.

I keep sitting, staring at Nanu's wrinkled hands as she crushes black salt, her new night ritual before she can sleep. I watch Nanu as she grinds the salt, holding the pestle with both hands, clasping the mortar between her thighs. Perhaps the physical movements help her insomnia. Perhaps she has figured out her own ways of carrying her body into a restful sleep, free of frightened awakenings. I think about her sleep, even as I try to focus on my previous drawings. I am breathing slowly, my feathered chest rising and falling, my lips moving silently as I count, synchronizing my breath with Nanu's repetitive movements as she works the salt. Defeated, my mind steps back into my body. New tingling nerves. New bones. New strange external organs on my chest. Without Nanu's melodic spiritual awakening in my ear.

Metamorphosis, despite the refusal. Metamorphosis, without the love of the azaan. Reluctantly, I run my fingers over my waist and hips to feel what bodily alienness I am supposed to get used to next. Surprised to feel scales appear over my skin, I look away from Nanu and examine my new chest. My heart is still pounding fast and hard, but I have my old, familiar gills back. Fingering the sponginess inside my gills gently, I whisper to my new chest. *Hayee alul falah, hayee alul falah, hayee alul falah.* I keep whispering the same phrase over and over again until I fall asleep.

AUTHOR BIOGRAPHIES

Aqdas Aftab is a Pakistani queer nonbinary writer, currently getting their PhD in decolonial trans literature at the University of Maryland. Their writing has been published in *Bitch Media, Vulture Bones, Crab Fat Magazine, Yes Poetry,* and *The Rumpus.* These days Aqdas is thinking about the relationship between interior metaphysical worlds and the materiality of public life.

Davian Aw is a Singaporean writer and Rhysling Award nominee whose fiction and poetry have appeared in over 30 publications including *Strange Horizons, Augur, Arsenika, Diabolical Plots, Mysterion* and *LONTAR: The Journal of Southeast Asian Speculative Fiction.* He is a cofounder of TransgenderSG.com, the primary online resource for the trans community in Singapore, and has spoken at events pertaining to Christian faith and sexuality. His first book, *Whatever Commandment There May Be*, was published in 2018 and distributed to all the churches in the country. More of Davian's writing can be found at davianaw. wordpress.com

Kylie Ariel Bemis is a trans woman and two-spirit working at the intersection of statistics and computer science. As a teacher and researcher, she currently resides in Boston, MA, but her heart remains in the New Mexican soil. She is an enrolled member of the Zuni tribe.

L Chan hails from Singapore, where he spends most of his energy wrangling two dogs. His work has appeared in places like *Liminal Stories, Arsenika, Podcastle* and the *Dark.* He tweets occasionally @lchanwrites.

Nino Cipri is a queer and trans/nonbinary writer, editor, and educator. They are a graduate of the Clarion Writers' Workshop and the University of Kansas's MFA program. Nino's fiction and essays have been published by dozens of different venues. Their short story collection *Homesick* won the Dzanc Short Fiction Collection Prize, and their novella *Finna* — about queer heartbreak, working retail, and wormholes — will be published by Tor.com in 2020. Nino has also written plays, screenplays, and radio features; performed as a dancer, actor, and puppeteer; and worked as a stagehand, bookseller, bike mechanic, and labor organizer. One time, an angry person on the internet called Nino a verbal terrorist, which was pretty funny.

Tori Curtis lives in beautiful, scenic upstate New York with his unsinkable wife and their dog. He writes domestic SFF with a focus on LGBT and disability narratives. You can find him @tcurtfish on twitter or at toricurtiswrites.com.

Kathryn DeFazio has been writing fiction of varying quality since she learned how to hold a pencil (incorrectly, as it turned out). She works as a freelance writer and lives in Manhattan with her primary partner and step-parrot. According to her mother, she still holds her pencil wrong. "Assistance" is her first published work.

Innocent Chizaram Ilo – When he is not receiving tonnes of rejections from cat adoption agencies, Innocent finds time to read, write, and tweet. He has works published or forthcoming in *Fireside, Reckoning Press, Strange Horizons, Brittle Paper, Cosmic Roots, SSDA* and elsewhere. Innocent is a 2018 Author of Tomorrow and a 2019 Gerald Kraak Award Finalist. He lives in Nigeria.

José Pablo Iriarte is a non-binary Cuban-American writer, high school math teacher, parent of two, and, as of 2019, Nebula Award finalist. José's fiction can be found in in magazines such as *Lightspeed, Strange Horizons*, and *Fireside Fiction*. Learn more at labyrinthrat.com, or look for José on twitter @labyrinthrat.

Margaret Killjoy is a transfeminine author and editor currently living on a land project in the Appalachian mountains. She is the author of the Danielle Cain series of novellas, published by Tor.com. The first book, *The Lamb Will Slaughter the Lion*, was released in 2017, and its sequel *The Barrow Will Send What it May* came out in April 2018. Her work primarily deals with themes of power and anarchism, as well as gender, social transformation, and people living itinerant or criminal lifestyles. Margaret spends her time making crafts and complaining about authoritarian power structures and she blogs at birdsbeforethestorm.net.

Catherine Kim is a queer trans emigrant from Korea who writes stories about identity, kinship, and desire. Her work has previously been featured in the *Nameless Woman* anthology and the Trans Women Writers booklet series. She studied Women, Gender, & Sexuality at Harvard College.

Matthias Klein keeps the body of nir childhood cat in the freezer in the hope of one day performing mad science on him. Nir partner insists on keeping the other dead things ne collects in the garage. Nir work has appeared at *Strange Horizons, Glittership*, and in the *Brave Boy World* anthology, among others. Find nem probably not being morbid enough on twitter @daystromreject.

Everett Maroon is a memoirist, humorist, political commentator, and fiction writer. He has a B.A. in English from Syracuse University and went through an English literature master's program there. Everett is the author of a memoir, *Bumbling into Body Hair*, and a young adult novel, *The Unintentional Time Traveler,* both published by Lethe Press. He has been published in numerous anthologies and has had work published in *Crossed Genres, SPLIT Quarterly, The Daily Dot,* and *Bitch Magazine*. He is currently working on the second book of this young adult time travel trilogy. Everett lives in Walla Walla, Washington with his family and a puppy.

Blue Neustifter – Blue (she/her) is a Canadian statistician, boardgame designer, writer, and trans community builder. She loves her spouse, her queer family, dogs, games, and the confident, unapologetic beauty of trans people. You can find her on Twitter as @Azure_Husky.

A.E. Prevost loves writing about found families, language, gender, mental health, and good things happening to interesting people. Their work has appeared in *Sword and Sonnet* and the gender diverse pronoun special issue of *Capricious*, among others; their story *Sandals Full of Rainwater* was featured on the 2018 Tiptree Award Honor List. A.E. also writes and directs for *The Ling Space*, an educational YouTube series about linguistics, and co-owns the Argo Bookshop, a lovingly curated independent bookstore. A.E. is agender/nonbinary ('they' or any other pronoun is ok), and can be found as @AePrevost on Twitter or at aeprevost.carrd.co.

H. Pueyo is an Argentine-Brazilian writer of comics and speculative fiction. Her work has been published before in English and Portuguese by magazines such as *Clarkesworld, Samovar* and The *Dark*, among others. Find her online at hachepueyo.com, and @hachepueyo on Twitter.

Nibedita Sen is a queer Bengali writer, editor and gamer from Calcutta. She acquired several English degrees in India before deciding she wanted an MFA too, and that she was going to move halfway across the world for it. A graduate of Clarion West 2015, her work has appeared or is forthcoming in *The Dark, Podcastle, Nightmare* and *Fireside*. These days, she can be found in NYC, where she helps edit Glittership, an LGBTQ SFF podcast, enjoys the company of puns and potatoes, and is nearly always hungry. Hit her up on Twitter at @her_nibsen.

Sonya Taaffe reads dead languages and tells living stories. Her short fiction and poetry have been collected most recently in *Forget the Sleepless Shores* (Lethe Press) and previously in *Singing Innocence and Experience, Postcards from the Province of Hyphens, A Mayse-Bikhl*, and *Ghost Signs*. She lives with her husband and two cats in Somerville, Massachusetts, where she writes about film for Patreon and remains proud of naming a Kuiper belt object.

Izzy Wasserstein is a queer, trans writer of fiction and poetry. She teaches writing and literature at a public university on the Great Plains, and shares a house with a variety of animal companions and the writer Nora E. Derrington. Her most recent poetry collection is When Creation Falls (Meadowlark Books, 2018), and her fiction has recently appeared or is forthcoming from *Clarkesworld, Apex, Fireside Magazine*, and elsewhere. She is a member of the 2017 class of Clarion West, and likes to run long distances slowly. Her website is www.izzywasserstein.com.

Andrew Joseph White is a Creative Writing BFA student best described as both "pocket-sized" and "somewhat feral." He lives in Virginia and should probably be doing homework right now. "Chokechain" is his debut short. When he isn't doting on cats or stressing over his first novel, he can be found on Twitter @AJWhiteAuthor.

ABOUT THE EDITOR

Bogi Takács (e/em/eir/emself or they pronouns) is a Hungarian Jewish agender person and a migrant to the United States. E writes, edits and reviews speculative fiction and poetry, and e is a winner of the Lambda award for Best Transgender Fiction for editing *Transcendent 2*; and a Locus and Hugo award finalist. You can find Bogi online at prezzey. net, read eir book reviews at bogireadstheworld.com, or follow eir QUILTBAG space opera webserial at iwunen.net. Bogi is bogiperson on Twitter, Instagram and Patreon. Bogi also had some trans — and intersex! — stories published in 2018: "Four-Point Affective Calibration" in *Lightspeed*, "On Good Friday the Raven Washes Its Young" in *Fireside*, "Volatile Patterns" in the Gender Diverse Pronouns issue of *Capricious*, "An Errant Holy Spark" in *Mother of Invention*, "The Souls of Those Gone Astray from the Path" in *Dracula: Rise of the Beast,* and multiple chapters of a webserial for Broken Eye Books, *The Song of Spores* (ed. Scott Gable).

ABOUT THE COVER ARTIST

August-Lain Weickert is a student of fine arts at Milwaukee Institute of Art and Design whose work primarily uses sculpture and printmaking techniques. His ongoing exploration of transgender identity has breached many unfamiliar media for him, such as digital and photographic work. Just as his transition, and those of many he loves, has made clear the network of uncomfortable truths connected to being "other" in an othering world, he explores unfamiliar media to create a glorification of that very "otherness". In "Peter, Transcended", Lain places a trans body in a position of exaltation, creating breathing room for viewers to recover and reflect; a redemption of the transgender being.

PUBLICATION CREDITS

"Ad Astra Per Aspera" © 2018 by Nino Cipri, first appeared in *Capricious: Gender Diverse Pronouns* special issue (ed. A.C. Buchanan) / "The Substance of My Lives, the Accidents of Our Births" © 2018 by José Pablo Iriarte, first appeared in *Lightspeed* / "You Inside Me" © 2018 by Tori Curtis, first appeared in *Glittership* / "Sphexa, Start Dinosaur" © 2018 by Nibedita Sen, first appeared in *Robot Dinosaur Fiction* (ed. A. Merc Rustad) / "Apotheosis" © 2018 by Catherine Kim, first appeared in *Collected Stories* / "Assistance" © 2018 by Kathryn DeFazio, first appeared in Escape Pod / "Ports of Perceptions" © 2018 by Izzy Wasserstein, first appeared in *Glittership* / "Therapeutic Memory Reversal" © 2018 by Everett Maroon, first appeared on the author's website / "The Art of Quilting" © 2018 by Matthias Klein, first appeared in *Survivor* (ed. Mary Anne Mohanraj and JJ Pionke, Lethe Press) / "The Sixth World" © 2018 by Kylie Ariel Bemis, first appeared in *Nameless Woman: An Anthology of Fiction by Trans Women of Color* (ed. Ellyn Peña, Jamie Berrout and Venus Selenite) / "What the South Wind Whispers" © 2018 by H. Pueyo, first appeared in *Clarkesworld* / "The Face of the Waters" © 2018 by Sonya Taaffe, first appeared in *Forget the Sleepless Shores* (Lethe Press / "Into the Gray" © 2018 by Margaret Killjoy, first appeared on Tor.com / "The God of Small Chances" by L Chan, first appeared in *Augur Magazine* (ed. Kerrie Seljak-Bryne, Alex De Pompa and Mado Christie) / "Chokechain" © 2018 by Andrew Joseph White, first appeared on Medium / "Sandals Full of Rainwater" © 2018 by A.E. Prevost, first appeared in *Capricious: Gender Diverse Pronouns* special issue (ed. A.C. Buchanan) / "Of Warps and Wefts" © 2018 by Innocent Chizaram Ilo, first appeared in *Strange Horizons* / "Control" © 2018 by Davian Aw, first appeared in *Anathema: Spec from the Margins* (ed. Michael Matheson, Andrew Wilmot and Chinelo Onwualu) / "Ghosts" © 2018 by Blue Neustifter, first appeared on Twitter / "Nuclear Disassociations" © 2018 by Aqdas Aftab, first appeared in *Vulture Bones*.

ACKNOWLEDGMENTS

I WORKED ON THIS ANTHOLOGY in the traditional lands of the Kanza and Osage people, who were forcibly removed from their homes in the late 19th century. Today this land is still a home to people from many Indigenous nations, and I would like to acknowledge their presence and express my gratitude toward them.

I would also like to thank everyone who supported the *Transcendent* series in any way, spread the word, requested library copies, and more. You help the series continue and your effort is invaluable.

Big thanks to Aliette de Bodard, Ádám Dobay, Ash, Debra Fran Baker, Lisa M. Bradley, Vajra Chandrasekera, Nino Cipri, Nora E. Derrington, Nicky Drayden, Via Farkas, D Franklin (thank you for your patience!), Orrin and Tama Grey, J. José Jimenez, Project Enigma, Nóra Selmeczi, Kellan Szpara, Izzy Wasserstein, Angela Wilson, JY Yang, and many more people.

Thank you to all the #DiverseBookBloggers and everyone at the KU Child Language/SPLH Student Equity & Inclusion Workgroup (Tree, I tried your advice and it worked!). You make me feel welcome both online and offline.

I would also like to thank the following people for story recommendations, writer referrals and all manner of kind help in locating work eligible for the anthology: Corey Alexander, Aidan Doyle, Shira Glassman, Mason Hawthorne, Julian Jarboe, R. Lemberg, Charles Payseur, dave ring, A. Merc Rustad, TS Porter, B.R. Sanders, Rivers Solomon, John Elizabeth Stintzi and E. Catherine Tobler.

A special thanks to Karla K. McGregor and Holly Storkel for all their support, and for helping me deal with a very difficult work situation while I was reading for the anthology.

And a very warm thanks to Steve Berman for his continued publishing support, to R. Lemberg and Mati for the Various Family things, and also to my Hungarian relatives!

CONTENT NOTICES

Ad Astra Per Aspera: no particular warnings

The Substance of My Lives, the Accidents of Our Births: mentions of bullying, misgendering, murder, allusions to domestic violence

You Inside Me: major themes of body horror and medical neglect, including surgery without anesthesia and complications from transition-related surgery

Sphexa, Start Dinosaur: no particular warnings

Apotheosis: domestic violence, sexual assault, internalized cissexism, suicide, gun violence, cannibalism

Assistance: alcohol, panic attacks, death, internalized ableism, misgendering; brief mention of medication

Ports of Perceptions: drug use, sex

Therapeutic Memory Reversal: parental emotional abuse

The Art of Quilting: stalking, misgendering, family conflict, trauma

The Sixth World: dysphoria, denial, eschatology

When the South Wind Whispers: misgendering, deadname mention, gaslighting, brief mentions of family abuse

The Face of the Waters: mentions of drinking, social anxiety, the chance of drowning, trying to quit smoking

Into the Gray: (non-graphic) sex and (slightly graphic) violence

The God of Small Chances: illness / hospitalization, violence, self-harm, death of a loved one

Chokechain: family conflict, misgendering, graphic imagery including animals and disease, homicidal/violent ideation; brief mentions of sex, including revenge porn, and injury

Sandals Full of Rainwater: anti-immigrant discrimination, dysphoria

Of Warps and Wefts: body transformation, child abuse, death/dying, needles, scars/scarification, sex, sexism/gender discrimination, shaming, violence/combat, vomit

Control: loss of bodily autonomy, brief non-graphic torture, murder, suicide, ableism, non-explicit sexual violation

Ghosts: Ghosts is written in the second-person ("you" as the protagonist) with a protagonist who is implied to be transfeminine, if that would be dysphoric or upsetting. It contains dysphoria, anxiety, and depression. It has a ghost (but a nice one).

Nuclear Disassociations: sexual abuse, symptoms of PTSD, dysphoria